CAROLINE LINDEN

Blame It on Bath

The Truth About the Duke

AVON

An Imprint of HarperCollinsPublishers

AVON BOOKS
An Imprint of HarperCollins*Publishers*
10 East 53rd Street
New York, New York 10022-5299

Copyright © 2012 by P.F. Belsley
Excerpt from *The Way to a Duke's Heart* copyright © 2012 by P.F. Belsley
ISBN 978-0-06-202533-3
www.avonromance.com

First Avon Books mass market printing: March 2012

Avon Trademark Reg. U.S. Pat. Off. and in Other Countries, Marca Registrada, Hecho en U.S.A.
HarperCollins® is a registered trademark of HarperCollins Publishers.

Printed in the U.S.A.

10 9 8 7 6 5 4 3 2 1

To Karen and Larry,
and many more decades of happily-ever-after

Blame
It on Bath

Chapter 1

Gerard de Lacey did not remember his mother.

His older brothers did. Edward had been eight, and Charlie eleven, when she died. He'd been only five, too young to have fixed memories. Sometimes his brothers would mention something about her—the songs she sang to them, the way she made their father laugh, her passion for the gardens—that made Gerard wild with envy they still had some piece of her, and he had almost nothing. Nothing bright and lovely, at any rate. Nothing that was purely his.

He'd seen the portraits of her, of course; the portrait painted when she was a young woman newly engaged to the Duke of Durham, the formal portraits of her and his father after their marriage, the family portraits of her with her sons. He knew she'd been pretty and slim, dark-haired and blue-eyed; but that didn't help. In one portrait she held him on her lap. They must have sat for hours for the artist like that, but try as he might, he couldn't recall the sound of her voice or the feel of her arms around him even though he had been told she was a warm and affectionate mother, and that he had been the particular favorite of her boys. The very fact he had no real memory of her made him miss her even more, more than either of his brothers did, Gerard was sure.

His only memory of her, in fact, was terrible. He remembered the day she died.

His father came to breakfast that morning in the nursery. That was the first clue something was wrong although Gerard didn't realize it at the time. His father was a larger-than-life figure to his young eyes, and it was always thrilling when Father would come striding up the stairs, his heels ringing loudly on the treads, his deep voice booming off the high-vaulted ceilings of Lastings, their house in Sussex. Gerard remembered being tossed in the air, that exhilarating feeling of flying, then the sickening plunge before being caught safely in his father's arms. In later years he discovered it was quite rare for a man like the Duke of Durham to spend so much time with his children, but at the time it only served to make him idolize his father. Durham was the best rider, the keenest hunter, the most jovial companion, the most forceful personality Gerard ever knew.

But that morning, Durham had been none of that. He came up the stairs grave and quiet, while they were eating their porridge. Charlie and Edward must have known why, for they didn't say a word. Gerard, though, had no inkling until his father sat down at the round table with them as Nurse was bringing their toast.

"I've brought some sad news, my lads," said the duke heavily.

Gerard thought it was about the puppies, just born to the duke's best pointer bitch. Why he remembered the damned dogs and not his mother, he never could fathom.

"It's Mother, isn't it?" Edward said in a small voice.

The duke hesitated, then nodded. Edward put down his spoon.

"What's wrong with Mother?" Gerard asked.

"She was very ill," Father replied. "But now, unfortunately, she's died." Edward said nothing. Charlie put his head down on his arms. "I've written to your aunt, Lady Dowling," Father went on. "I invited her and your cousin Philip to come stay for a few months."

"I don't want Aunt Margaret," said Gerard. "I want Mother."

"She's dead," Edward whispered.

Gerard scowled at him. "She is not!"

"Gerard, son, she is," Father told him. "I wish it weren't so."

His chin wobbled. Gerard knew what dead meant. It meant they took the dog—or person, he supposed, but so far he'd only seen dogs die—and dug a hole behind the stable to put them in. Surely Father would never let them do that to Mother. "I don't believe it."

The duke was quiet for a moment. Gerard never forgot how the morning sun shone on his father's forehead, the skin smooth where his hair had receded. "Would you like to see her?"

Gerard nodded. After a moment, so did Edward.

"Yes, sir," mumbled Charlie. "Please."

The duke nodded once, and all three boys slid off their chairs to follow him, breakfast forgotten. They went down the narrow stairs that led directly into the duchess's sitting room. It was still and quiet in there, which was unusual. Gerard often came running down those stairs to see her and climb into her lap, and the room was always full of people: the housekeeper, the duchess's maid, servants carrying tea trays and stoking the fires and bringing letters. She never minded it, and never told him not to come, or even not to run. Today the room was deserted. The duke opened the door to her bedroom and waved one hand, sending the servants within scurrying for the door. Then Father stepped back and let them come in.

Later, Gerard would wish he hadn't done it. He thought perhaps, without that last, terrible view of her, he might have clung instead to some other, happier, memory of his mother. But as a child he had no idea, and he went into the room to see her lying on the bed, so altered from her normal self he could hardly recognize her. Her dark hair was pulled back from her face, which seemed to have sunk into her head. The covers had been stripped back from the bed, and she wore a stark white nightgown, which only made her skin look gray instead of its normal pink-and-white prettiness. A bundle of cloth was tucked into the crook of her arm. She didn't look like she was sleeping.

Beside him Edward made a gasping, snuffling sound. The duke put his hand on Edward's shoulder. "I'm sorry, lads," he said again, very quietly. "You may go if you like."

"Thank you, sir," choked Charlie, before he turned and ran for the door. Edward sniffled, then dragged his sleeve across his face before he, too, went out without a word.

Gerard inched closer to his father. It looked a little like Mother, there on the bed, but not really. "Is she really dead?" He looked up to see his father's slight nod. "Why did she die, Father?"

For a moment the duke was silent. He wore an odd expression, rather like the one Edward had the time he realized he'd broken his own new compass: distraught and guilty at the same time. Edward had even punched Charlie when Charlie pointed out it was his own fault. "It is God's retribution," said the duke at last, almost inaudibly. "She was too good for me."

Gerard looked back at his mother. He thought she was perfect. He wanted to touch her face, on the chance it might wake her up, but didn't dare. "Are we going to bury her behind the stable?" he asked sadly. "She won't like that, Father."

The duke sighed, then leaned down and scooped up Gerard in his arms. "No, son, we won't put her there," he murmured. "She'll lie in the mausoleum by the chapel, and someday you'll lay me there beside her, to keep her company."

"I don't want you to die. I don't want *her* to die."

"Neither do I," said the duke, his voice bleak and hollow. "Neither do I."

"What is that?" Gerard pointed at the bundle of cloth. He could see the family crest embroidered on it in silver thread.

"Your sister. She was born too early."

"Oh." He stared at the bundle, wide-eyed. "Did she die, too?"

"Yes."

Gerard put his head on his father's shoulder. He

started to put his thumb into his mouth out of habit, then remembered himself and folded his hand into a fist. "Will she stay with Mother?"

The duke's grip on him tightened. "Yes. She'll stay with Mother, and I'll stay with you and your brothers."

"Thank you, Father," Gerard said softly. "I don't want you to go away, too."

"I won't, lad," whispered his father. "I promise."

And Durham kept his word. He never married again, but oversaw his sons' rearing personally, with as much demanding exactitude as he expended on everything else. Gerard recited Latin verbs and history lessons to his father until he knew them perfectly. He stood and confessed his misdeeds to his father, then took his punishment from the duke's own hand. His father sat him on his first horse, and bought him his first commission, as a junior lieutenant of cavalry. A man must deserve responsibility, the duke said, declaring he wouldn't buy a captaincy or a majority for a twenty-year-old boy so he could get himself and others killed. At the time Gerard seethed with impatience, but as he grew more experienced in the military, he acknowledged that his father was right. A lieutenant followed orders, hopefully learning from his superior officers before he, too, had the duty to order men into battle and the responsibility for leading them wisely. Too many majors and colonels, it became clear, had skipped the crucial step of learning, and the burden of command sat uneasily or lightly on them. It was yet another confirmation of Durham's care for his children.

But Gerard's faith in his father took a dreadful

blow when the duke died. With his dying breath Durham begged forgiveness, but only when they were preparing to lay him in the mausoleum beside the long-dead duchess and infant daughter did Gerard and his brothers discover what sin Durham had committed. A clandestine, scandalous marriage, years before he inherited the dukedom . . . or married Gerard's mother. A Fleet marriage that was never annulled or terminated in divorce. A marriage that could cost Gerard and his older brothers everything they'd grown up believing was theirs because it could invalidate Durham's marriage to their mother and render them all illegitimate. And all because Durham, in his boundless arrogance and faith in his own judgment, concealed it from his sons even when threatened with exposure and ruined by a blackmailer.

Gerard was furious with his father for that. The dukedom of Durham was enormous, one of the wealthiest in England, and all their expectations were tied to it. This sin, bursting like grapeshot among them, stripped everything away. Durham had left some specific bequests in his will, of the unentailed property he had bought as duke and of their mother's dowry funds; but compared to what they would have had, it was laughable.

Charlie, who had been raised to become a duke, was left a country house in Lincolnshire that nobody had much used or cared for during Durham's lifetime, and barely enough funds to maintain it. Edward, who had devoted most of his life to running the Durham properties efficiently and prosperously, would see all his work go to benefit another, most likely that preening boor Augustus, their father's distant cousin. And Gerard, the youngest, who had always known he would have to find some other way to distinguish himself, would be forced to give up the army career he had chosen, bled for, and come to value very highly, to be left with nothing. They would all be bastards, cast out of most good society, with only a thousand pounds a year to live on and no property at all.

And his mother . . . Gerard stayed behind after Edward and the rector and the few servants invited had left, when his father's body had been laid to rest in the crypt. Edward gave him a curious glance, but Gerard shook his head. He knew they had much to attend to, and no time to stand around in some pose of mourning. He and Edward agreed they must go to London at once, to tell Charlie about their misfortune since Charlie hadn't managed to make it back to Sussex even for Durham's funeral. They had to decide what must be done to protect their inheritance because none of them was giving it up without a fight. Gerard just needed a moment before rushing off.

So he stood in the family mausoleum, alone with the ghosts of generations, and laid his hand against the cold stone plaque on his mother's bier. ANNE, DUCHESS OF DURHAM, it read, with the dates of her life. Below was a small note about the infant buried with her. She didn't even have a name. Of course, she could be as illegitimate as the rest of them, thanks to their father's carelessness. If everything fell apart, would the next duke—Augustus, curse him—remove Anne and her nameless daughter?

He closed his eyes and said a silent promise to her. He wouldn't let that happen to her—for her sake, for his own sake, for his brothers', even for his father's. One way or another, Gerard intended to save his family from the ruin that loomed before them.

Chapter 2

Gerard and Edward accomplished their first goal quickly since their brother Charlie turned out to be confined to his bed in London with a broken leg. As suspected, Charlie showed little sorrow for their father's death, but shockingly, he evinced little care for the possibility that they might lose everything. Edward was sure Charlie did care, but that didn't even truly matter to Gerard. Of greater interest to him was what they should do to solve the problem, and there was little agreement on that.

Edward favored calling in the best solicitors in London and staking a strong legal claim to Durham before anyone else could. Once the title was awarded to Charlie, it couldn't be taken away, no matter what evidence turned up. Gerard thought this was fine, as a starting point. He hadn't Edward's patience and discipline. Solicitors acted at the pace of half-asleep snails, and if they failed in the end, it would be far too late to do anything else. Charlie, of course, agreed this was a sensible plan, willing as ever to shrug off any responsibility. Charlie would have agreed with whatever was put to him so long as he could continue his self-absorbed ways. As proof, he also agreed with Gerard's proposal that they pursue the blackmailer and deal with him in ways no solicitor could. Ever the peacemaker, Edward declared he would engage the solicitor, and Gerard could do his best to find the blackmailer. It was left unsaid that Charlie would probably do very little of any use.

However, despite Gerard's urging to say nothing of the possible bigamy to anyone, Edward insisted on trusting his fiancée, Lady Louisa Halston. Within two days, the most rabid gossip sheet in town printed their private scandal for all of London to read. It became impossible to walk down a street in town without being gaped at, pointed at, or jokingly asked if he intended to hie off to the Continent with his mother's jewels. Gerard would have been tempted to have it out with his brother for trusting a woman, except that Lady Louisa also took pains to jilt Edward in the most public and humiliating way possible: in the pages of that same gossip sheet.

Edward was better off without her—Louisa was a dull, quiet creature, although pretty enough—but he had cared for the girl. Gerard couldn't rub salt in his brother's wounded pride. There was nothing to be done but double his determination to find that blackmailer and dispose of him and whatever "proof" he might have of Durham's clandestine marriage.

He covered every possibility in London. One of the letters demanded five thousand pounds, in coin, to be left in a London churchyard on a certain gravestone. Gerard visited the church, spent a few hours chatting with the friendly rector, and learned that the grave specified was over a hundred years old and probably hadn't been touched or visited in decades, nor had anyone asked about it. The rector was quite sure no one could have come around at night, either, as he personally locked the gate every evening. It struck Gerard as curious; why seek a ransom if no one ever attempted to collect it? The demand was made in the third letter, and the fourth letter made no mention of money at all.

That only made him more eager to get out of the city. Edward insisted he would deal with the gossip in town although his plan, which turned out to involve a Titian-haired widow with a magnificent bosom and a siren's voice, sounded shaky to Gerard. Not the part about the redhead—that part he understood very well, although his brother insisted it was only business between them. But it was Edward's concern, and if he lost a bit of his reserve under the sensual widow's influence, Gerard thought it would serve him well after Louisa's callous treatment. All the better if Edward actually succeeded in tamping down the gossip as well.

There was one other reason he needed to leave London, one he hadn't felt like sharing with either of his brothers. Whether legitimate or not, Gerard was a third son. Even under the best of circumstances, he would be expected to make his own way. The title, with its properties and wealth and duties, would go to Charlie. Edward would most likely continue to run the estates, as it was highly improbable Charlie would take an interest now or develop the skills needed to take over anytime soon. Gerard had chosen the army and done well there, but it wouldn't sustain him forever. Durham had advised him years ago that he should take notice of pretty young ladies with large dowries, and now this "Durham Dilemma," as the gossips were calling it, only made that more urgent. Gerard meant to find the blackmailer, but he also intended to find himself a wealthy bride before his situation grew any worse. And since every lady in town was whispering of the scandal already, his best chances lay in towns outside London—towns like Bath, where two of the blackmail messages had originated.

He managed to secure extended leave from his regiment, but then his horse needed to be reshod. An old friend from the army turned up and insisted on dining with him one night and drew him into another engagement the next evening. But finally he settled his affairs, bade his brothers farewell, and made his way out of the city, across the river. Traffic was surprisingly heavy on the road, and it was evening by the time he reached The Duck and Dog on the southernmost outskirts of London. Reluctantly he told his man, Bragg, they would stop for the night here. He had wished to be farther along, but he was hungry, and at least tomorrow they could be off at first light.

After a hearty dinner and an excellent bottle of wine, he took out the pernicious letters once more. Two had been sent from Bath and one from London. The fourth postmark was smudged beyond reading, but as it was the first and oldest letter, Gerard set it aside. Why would they be sent from different towns? The blackmailer must travel, fairly often, between London and Bath. The first letter was dated almost a year ago. The second letter, bearing a Bath postmark, was dated eight months ago; the third, mailed from London, almost six months ago; and the fourth, again from Bath, was just over seven weeks old. Did that mean another letter would soon follow? Or would Durham's death change the blackmailer's calculations?

Gerard leaned back in the chair and thought. Properly, the blackmailer would assume his demands should be directed to Charlie, unless the fellow knew anything at all about their family. Charlie might be the heir, but anyone familiar with the de Laceys would know that appealing to Edward would yield swifter and surer results. Naturally in public Edward deferred to Charlie, but in private, Edward was the unquestioned authority behind the Durham name. Perhaps the next letter would ask for money again. Perhaps it would demand something completely new, given the changed circumstances. Gerard pulled off his boots and slouched deeper into the armchair, letting all the mysteries run laps around his brain in search of an answer.

He had just begun to doze off when someone tapped at the door. It was a light, quick knock-knock-knock, almost as if the person were testing the wood rather than requesting admittance. Gerard stayed slumped in his chair, his eyes unwilling to open just yet. Perhaps the intruder would go away, and he could drift back into the pleasant, half-asleep state he'd been in. But the knock sounded again, faster and a little harder. With a sigh, he pushed himself up from the surprisingly comfortable armchair. The blackmail letters he tucked back into his saddle-bag. He'd read them enough to know every word by heart even when he wasn't too tired to see straight.

He stretched his arms and rolled his head, feeling the muscles in his back tighten and twinge. Sleeping in the chair was probably a bad idea. Sleeping in the bed sounded pretty damned good, though.

Snapping his braces back over his shoulders, he padded across the room in stocking feet and pulled open the door. To his surprise, it wasn't the innkeeper nor even a chambermaid, but a woman of moderately advanced age, thin and short, a pinched expression on her weathered face. She wore all black except for the ivory lace cap on her gray head. Someone's hired companion, or the mistress of the local girls' school. Either that, or Newgate had begun hiring female warders. Gerard couldn't think of a single reason for a woman like her to be at his door, particularly since he hadn't told anyone except his brothers where he was going. It put him on guard. "Good evening," he said, keeping a firm grip on the door.

"Good evening, Captain." Her faded green eyes flickered up and down him, clearly unimpressed. "You are Captain Lord Gerard de Lacey, are you not?"

Gerard's gaze darted left, then right, but she was alone in the corridor. "Yes."

She gave a small nod. "My mistress will see you."

His eyebrows went up. "Will she, indeed? And who, pray, is your mistress?"

"A lady."

"What is her name?"

Her lips pursed up as if she were trying to swallow them. "Will you come, or will you not?"

Gerard met her glower with a shrug. "Not. Good night, madam."

"I cannot say her name," hissed the strange woman as he moved to close the door. "But she must see you. I beg of you, sir, *please*."

"Why can't you tell me?" He crossed his arms. "If she wishes to see me, she won't be able to conceal herself for long."

"She does not wish to conceal herself from *you*," muttered the woman with a ferocious scowl. "She is a lady in need. Will you come, as a gentleman, or will you not?"

Gerard smiled faintly at the stress she laid on the word "gentleman." "What's she in need of? Should I bring my pistol?"

Her lips twitched, and her head came up. She gave him another examination. "Not this time," she said, a little more civilly. "She awaits you in the private parlor below."

"Very well," he said, but she had already turned on her heel and walked away. He leaned into the corridor to watch her go, the lace lappets on her cap bobbing sharply with each step. She didn't look back.

He closed the door. How odd. Who was the mystery lady? And how the devil had she fastened on him as her savior? Gerard knew his abiding weakness was curiosity; it had gotten him into more scrapes than he could count, and this time would probably be no different. His visitor had said not to bring a pistol *this* time, as if there would be other times when he should bring one. He sat down and wondered what sort of lady would need him to bring a pistol, then he pulled on his boots again. He slid his knife down inside the left one, no matter what the old woman said.

He went down the stairs, his imagination running

in ten different directions at once. This person knew who he was, so it wasn't just some woman in distress appealing to the most capable-looking man she saw or because of his army coat. Whoever she was, she must have followed him across the river from London. He supposed it was possible he was walking into some sort of trap, but it seemed unlikely. He didn't have anything worth stealing except his horse, and that could have been done without her speaking to him. Besides, this was a reputable inn, well kept and close to the main road. He was perfectly able to defend himself, and looked it. It could be tied to that wretched Durham Dilemma, but that could be as much to his advantage as anyone else's.

At the private parlor he knocked twice, then pushed the door open peremptorily. The old woman who had sought him out earlier gave him another dark look as she hurried forward. She grabbed his sleeve and almost pulled him into the room, whisking the door closed as soon as he was through it. He gave her a piqued glance, but this time she looked less impatient and more tense. Frightened, even. She motioned him on. Gerard said nothing and stepped farther into the room.

It was empty save for the figure standing in the far corner, concealed in a cloak with the hood pulled over her head. The hem of a skirt peeped out beneath the cloak; otherwise there was no clue to the person's sex or identity. He folded his arms and waited.

After a moment the cloaked figure stepped forward. "Good evening, Captain. Thank you for seeing me." Her voice was low, soft and pretty. Definitely a woman.

Gerard made a very slight bow. "How could I refuse such a summons?"

He couldn't see her face but sensed the exchange of a glance between her and the older woman. "I apologize for approaching you this way."

"Not at all," he replied. "I haven't been so intrigued in days."

She didn't move. "Before I explain, I must beg your promise not to speak of my visit."

"Who might be asking?"

She hesitated again. "I will understand if you refuse my request for any reason. I will go away and leave you in peace forever if you wish. I only ask that you not tell anyone I came to see you. Please, sir."

He narrowed his eyes. Her face was still lost in the deep cowl of her hood, but he heard the thread of worry in her voice. "Very well. I won't speak of it."

Her shoulders fell in relief. "Thank you." She raised one gloved hand and pushed back the hood of her cloak.

His first thought was that he'd been right about the old woman's being a schoolmistress; this must be her prize student, the one who would someday take her place. She wasn't pretty at all, with too-prominent cheekbones and a wide mouth. Her hair was dark blond and scraped back from her face as severely as the schoolmistress's. She had fine eyes, dark in the firelight and thickly lashed, but the expression in them was opaque and utterly without warmth. Her lips were pressed into a grim line that gave no hint of their shape. She stared at him, unsmiling, for a moment, as open in her appraisal as he was in his.

Gerard couldn't recall the last time a woman had looked him over so frankly. "Shall we sit down?"

He must have passed inspection. More amused than anything else, he decided to stay and see what she had to ask of him. He took the seat she gestured to, in front of the fire, and she finally came forward to take the opposite chair. The old woman fluttered around the back of the room before bringing two glasses of wine. Gerard waved her off, and she shot him a disapproving look but set the glass on the table beside him. His companion took a small sip of her wine and handed it back to her servant—he couldn't believe the old woman was anything else from the way she hovered so solicitously at the younger lady's elbow—who retired to the back of the room.

"Your maid wouldn't tell me your name, yet she made certain of who I was," Gerard said. "I don't like being toyed with, so let's dispense with the mystery, shall we?"

"My name is Katherine Howe," she said. "I don't expect you to know it."

"Or remember it after tonight, apparently."

She looked at him oddly, almost as if she didn't understand what he said. "I know of your family—I was raised near Lastings in Sussex. Then I was Katherine Hollenbrook. My father was Mr. Edgar Hollenbrook of Henfield. He was a wool merchant."

He tilted his head and studied her more minutely. She had the air of a judge contemplating sentencing him to hard labor, grave and reserved and so very stiff in her chair. "I'm afraid I don't recognize the name. I've not been in Henfield these last five years or more."

"I don't expect you to recognize it. I tell you merely to assure you that I'm familiar with your situation and am not acting capriciously. My family knew of yours—your father in particular. I decided to approach you when I heard the recent rumors in London."

Gerard's temper stirred. "Well, if you've come to stir up trouble in that regard, you'll have to join the queue," he drawled. "And I think that ends our conversation." He started to get to his feet.

"Wait." She held up her hand. "I haven't finished."

"Yes, I think you have." He started walking toward the door.

"I came to make you a proposition," she said in a rush as his hand closed on the doorknob. "One that will suit both our needs."

He turned and flashed a disdainful smirk at her. How dare she come try to take advantage of his family's troubles? "Unless you want to come upstairs and warm my bed for the night, I can't think of anything you could offer me to suit my *needs*."

Her jaw firmed. Her glare was withering. If she'd had a switch, she probably would have blistered his palm with it. "I came to propose a marriage, Captain," she said coldly. "If the rumors are true, you will be disinherited and declared a bastard. You will need money. I have money, but need a protector."

"I don't need money badly enough to marry the first woman who offers herself," he growled.

She raised her chin. "You will."

"I'll let you know when it happens."

"Don't you *dare* leave, Captain!"

Gerard was so astonished by the order, he turned around. She was pale and rigid with fury, on her feet now with hands in fists at her sides. The old woman stood behind her, clutching the wine bottle as if to hurl it at his head if he set foot outside the room. He put his hands on his hips, annoyed with himself as much as with her. Damn his curiosity. He should have ignored the knock on his door and stayed peaceably in his room. "Why not?"

"Please let me explain," she said stiffly. Her throat worked. "I apologize for the abruptness of my manner. I haven't much time before I must be home."

"You came to propose marriage to a man you'd never met, and you can't spare more than a few minutes for it?"

"No," she said bitterly. "I'll be missed if I don't return soon, and if that occurs, this will all have been for naught, whatever you decide." She took a deep breath. "I am in a desperate moment, Captain. Please listen to what I have to say. If you decline, I'll leave, and you'll never hear from me again, you have my word."

Gerard sighed. Damned, *damned* curiosity. "Very well." He stalked back to the chair and dropped into it.

Slowly Katherine Howe sank to her seat as well, watching him as if afraid he would bolt from the room. "I need a husband," she said baldly. "You are—or very soon may be—in want of a wife with money if the rumors about your father are true. I have heard you will be left virtually penniless if your brother cannot inherit the dukedom of Durham."

"Not quite," Gerard said in clipped tones, "but go on."

She clasped her hands in her lap, lacing her fingers together. Her thumbs dug into the backs of her hands so hard, the leather of her gloves creased. "My father left me a large fortune. He made it in trade, but money is money. When I was younger, he arranged an advantageous marriage for me, to Viscount Howe of West Sussex. Lord Howe was older than I, but desperately in need of funds. My parents were pleased with the connection, Howe was pleased with my marriage portion, and it was done. Howe died last year, and his nephew Lucien inherited the viscountcy."

"And you cannot wait to cast off the widow's weeds?" Gerard asked when she fell silent.

"Very much the contrary." Her expression turned stony. "I would gladly wear them for the rest of my life. Instead I'm now being pressured to marry Lucien, whom I cannot abide."

"I presume he wants your money as well."

Again she gave him that queer look. "No. It is worse. Not only did Howe spend my marriage portion, he borrowed a large sum from my father. The expectation, of course, was that my father's wealth would descend to me at his death, then to my children, and there would be no need for repayment. Unfortunately for Lucien, Howe died before my father, without a child. By the terms of my father's will and the loan agreement, I now hold the note against the Howe estate. Not only must Lucien return half my dowry since I had no children, but he owes me the sum of the loan as well."

"Which, naturally, he does not have." Gerard guessed.

She nodded once. "My husband did not spend wisely. Even if Lucien wished to, it's unlikely he could borrow enough to repay me, given the state of the Howe finances. He could pursue an heiress, but most would be unhappy to hear that the bulk of their fortune must be paid out immediately to me."

Gerard studied her. In the firelight she looked almost bloodless, cold and hard like alabaster. "You needn't call in the loan—ever, let alone at once."

"But I could," was her answer. "And Lucien will never forget it."

He leaned back in his chair and stretched out his feet toward the fire. "So the new Lord Howe finds it easier to wed you than bestir himself to honor his uncle's debts in some other way. Sounds a bit lazy to me."

"Yes."

"And you would rather marry a complete stranger than simply take your own house and hire a solicitor."

She sighed and spoke with slow deliberation. "Lucien has all my property still under his control. He will not let me leave at will. Mrs. Dennis is the only person in the whole household I can trust." The old lady sharpened her minatory eye on Gerard. "And I would rather *die* than marry Lucien. I am sure my death would suit him just as well as a wedding— perhaps even more so—which is why I will take any other option open to me. And at the moment, those options are limited to you."

Gerard picked up the glass of wine the older woman had poured for him earlier. He held it up as if studying the hue of the burgundy, then took a long sip. He hated being treated like an idiot, particularly by a woman who claimed to be in desperate need of his help. She was going to have to work for it if she truly wanted him to marry her. Because, curse it all, she was absolutely right about his needing money, from her or some other heiress. "And why have I been so fortunate to be preferred over both Lucien and death?"

"My father respected your father. He called him an honorable man."

He raised one eyebrow skeptically. "You chose me because of my father?"

"You're a military man of some acclaim. I've read about you in the papers."

"You must have an extraordinary memory to remember a passing mention here and there. And I don't think war heroes make the best husbands in any event."

She gave him a quelling look, as if he were a naughty schoolboy for contradicting her. "If you wish to hear my explanation, perhaps you could keep silent long enough for me to give it."

Gerard grinned, perversely amused at her prissy manner. "Of course. Go on, my dear."

A flicker of discomfort crossed her face at the endearment. Interesting, he thought, but she didn't say anything about it. "As I was saying," she continued acidly, "I believe you to be an honorable man. I did not choose you at random but based on your family and your personal merit. Whatever else you might think of my request, please don't think it hasty or ill considered."

"As you wish." He sipped some more wine. "You've set forth a persuasive case for you to marry me, illustrious, dashing fellow that I am. Now tell me why *I* should marry *you*."

Mrs. Dennis stirred, her face pinched up in disapproval. "No!" Katherine Howe turned her head sharply toward her servant. "It is a fair question." She faced Gerard again, and took a deep breath. "Rumor holds that you are about to lose your entire inheritance. If you are stripped of your birthright and pronounced a bastard, as whispers in London indicate, you won't be an eligible husband for any young lady, let alone one of good family and fortune. You hold a captaincy, but you're ambitious; it will be expensive to rise to higher rank. In addition, I imagine it would be quite difficult to adjust to life without a fortune when you've been raised as a son of immense wealth and privilege. In your place, any clever man would look around at once for an heiress to marry, while the scandalous rumors are still just rumor and not known fact. If the rumors are disproved, you would still be a third son, who no doubt would have wanted an heiress anyway. If the rumors stand . . ." She shrugged, a very slight movement. "Your chances of finding a wealthy wife are at their best right now."

"Hmm." Right in every particular, to Gerard's disgust. She might look as plain as boiled pudding, but there was nothing lacking in her brain. "But why you in particular?"

"My fortune is over one hundred thousand pounds, including the loan Lucien still owes."

Indeed. That was far more than he had expected,

and Gerard had to work hard to keep his astonishment from showing. He could tell from her face that the sum was her trump card, that she expected him to be bowled over by the amount and fall to his knees, stammering acceptance. And damn it all, it was a near call. Many men would have, even those not caught in the coils of his present situation. Gerard hated to admit it, but part of him wanted to do it. He'd wanted to find a wealthy bride, and here was one presenting herself to him without any effort on his part—yet—and with a larger fortune than he'd even hoped for. All he had to say was yes.

But the other, more cynical, part of him wasn't about to be bought that easily. Marriage was forever, as his father had demonstrated all too well, and the only thing worse than not being able to find a wife was having one he would give anything to be rid of. Gerard had seen men who had sold themselves for a fortune and spent the rest of their lives repenting the poor bargain. Katherine Howe didn't look intimidating, but he'd seen enough steel in her to know she wasn't going to be a quiet, biddable wife who never troubled him. Not even for a hundred thousand pounds would Gerard let himself be tied to her apron strings or kept under her thumb, and she might as well realize that now.

"Impressive," he said carelessly. "What else? There's more to marriage than money."

For the first time a spot of color came into her cheeks. "I won't be a demanding wife, Captain, but I will be a loyal one. I shall do my utmost not to impose on you. I know I'm not a beauty, and I am old, past the usual age for bearing children. But in every other respect I shall give you no reason to regret wedding me."

"Then you don't intend this to be a sterile marriage of convenience?"

The color in her face grew brighter. "I would be satisfied with one. But if you insist on more, I will agree."

And then she would lie there like a wooden doll, he thought. It must be a sign of what lengths she would go to in order to persuade him. She obviously wasn't keen on the prospect, given her stiff, prickly attitude and obvious disinterest in lovemaking. He didn't see the need to force a wife to accommodate him when he could easily find someone else who would actually enjoy the experience. Still, he didn't want to tie himself for life to a cold, untouchable woman. Who knew—perhaps with a little coaxing, Katherine Howe would thaw and soften. Some men might see it as a challenge to warm her up. Gerard, unfortunately, tended to be one of those men.

"Very well," he replied opaquely, neither confirming nor denying her implied question. "But—you'll pardon my wariness—your proposal comes with some significant shadows about it. You've done your research; I hope you'll allow me to do mine as I ponder your proposal."

"Of course." She put one hand into her pocket and drew out a sealed letter. "You may speak to my father's solicitor in the City, who knows all the particulars. This letter will assure him he may speak to you in confidence. I hope that will be sufficient."

Gerard took the packet and tapped it against his knee. "It should be." Along with some other discreet probing of his own, of course. "How shall I inform you of my decision? Where is your home?"

"You cannot come to the house," she said quickly. "Whatever your answer is. I—I shall return here. How long do you need?"

"I hadn't planned to stay that long," Gerard said, watching her from beneath lowered eyelids. "I have pressing concerns elsewhere and expected to quit London in the morning."

She didn't move. "Should I take that as refusal?"

"No." He turned her letter over, gingerly, as one might handle any dangerous object. Was this the solution to his quandary or an invitation to further disaster? "Not yet."

"I also would appreciate an answer as soon as possible," she said.

He glanced at her. "So you can find another candidate if I say no."

"Yes." She spat the word out.

"Very well." Gerard sat forward in his chair. "Two days? Three?"

She flinched backward at his movement, but nodded. "Yes. I can return in three nights."

"I suppose I can't offer to escort you home."

"No, that isn't necessary." She got to her feet, and Gerard did the same. Although not a tiny thing, she still only came to his shoulder. Watching her intently in the firelight, Gerard caught the flicker of unease in her face as she sized him up from so close. He wondered if her husband had beaten her; she had the defiant but skittish posture of someone who'd been abused. "Thank you," she said stiffly, raising her gaze to his.

He bowed, never looking away from her face. "It appears I should thank you. I shall expect you in three nights."

She just nodded, and he turned to go. At the door he paused and looked back at her. He held up the letter, which had his name written on the front in a neat, small hand. "Were you that certain I would say yes?"

"No." She was pulling her cloak around her again but met his eyes steadily. "But I was that certain you would consider it."

Chapter 3

The second the door closed behind Captain de Lacey, Katherine whirled to Mrs. Dennis. "What do you think, Birdie?" she whispered as she retied her cloak. "What is your impression of him?"

Birdie snorted, reaching for her own cloak. "Determined. Suspicious. Not used to being thwarted. That one'll work out every secret you have."

"But big," Katherine said softly, casting another glance at the door. "And strong." Gerard de Lacey was tall and broad and all man. Not fat in the slightest, and he looked strong enough to break her in two. When he'd reached out to take the letter from her, just the size of his hands had taken her aback. She remembered him as a tall stripling of a fellow, his boyish face alight with laughter. That had been over a decade ago, but she hadn't been able to alter the image in her mind. The Gerard she remembered was kind and patient, even to a plain, awkward girl too shy to speak properly to him. She knew she hadn't improved in looks, but at least she'd become bolder.

Of course he barely resembled that boy in her memory, from the several stone of muscle he'd put on to the way his face had filled out and grown sharply attractive. When he stepped into the room, her first thought was that Birdie must have knocked on the wrong door and summoned the wrong man, a powerful, dangerous man with a cynical intelligence glinting in his eyes. Not until she took a step forward and got a better look at his face was she assured it really was Gerard de Lacey, the charming boy grown into a man. It was clear he didn't remember her at all—she hadn't really expected him to although some stupid corner of her heart harbored hope that he might, just a little. Once she saw him, though, it was almost a relief he did not. If she'd known before their meeting how much he had changed . . .

But she hadn't. Katherine tried not to think about those changes except as they related to her immediate need, and not how much they appealed to more frivolous feelings like attraction. She needed a husband who would stand between her and Lucien Howe's demands. Gerard de Lacey needed a wife with money. Whether he was strong and broad-shouldered, or skinny and balding, all that mattered was his willingness to help her. She had chosen him mainly for his family connections and his need of her, not his physical appeal. She would do well to keep that thought firmly in mind, and all others out.

She finished tying her cloak and pulled the hood far down over her face until she could only see the floor in front of her. Birdie went to the door and peered cautiously out, then whispered for her to come. Without a word Katherine followed. Her heart had barely calmed down from the shock of Captain de Lacey's appearance and the stress of their interview; now it thumped hard and fast inside her chest as they hurried quietly down the back corridor of the inn and out the door to the stand of trees near the road where they had told the hired hackney to wait. If she got caught sneaking out of London this way, it wouldn't matter what the captain decided; she'd never be able to get out of the house again to hear his answer.

The driver had drifted off to sleep on his box but roused when Birdie poked his foot. Katherine climbed into the carriage without looking his way. A moment later Birdie joined her, and the cab lurched forward.

"I offered him an extra half crown if he gets us back before the hour," Birdie said.

"Very good." Katherine undid the bundle of clothing left on the floor of the carriage. She knew they were cutting it very fine with this expedition and hadn't a moment to waste. She shook out her nightdress and handed it to Birdie with her slippers.

"You spoke longer than anticipated with him." Birdie took the cloak from her when Katherine pulled it off. "Was he not what you expected?"

"Partially." Katherine stripped off her gloves and began unbuttoning her dress. "Not quite as I remembered him, but he'll do."

Birdie sniffed. She had fretted over this from the moment Katherine told her of it, but like the dutiful abigail she was, she hadn't argued. Katherine still felt Birdie's worry, for it scraped at the edges of her own mind. She had turned this plan over in her mind for some time, but choosing the captain in particular was the act of an impulse. She saw his name—or rather, his father's name—in the scandal papers, and the idea came to her like a bolt of lightning. She had been straining to think of a gentleman who might suit her purpose and be amenable to her suggestion, and here was one she knew, however slightly, and even admired, however secretly, in dire need of someone just like her. It seemed a sign of divine providence.

It had taken her two days to learn where to find him without arousing suspicion, and then she had almost missed him entirely, for he was about to leave town. Birdie paid a large percentage of Katherine's dwindling pin money to a groom at Durham House to find out where he was headed. By a stroke of good fortune, Lucien was out that night at one of his meetings, and Katherine was able to plead a headache to her mother, then sneak out with Birdie after dinner. Then they traveled all the way across London, over the river to this inn on the main road away from town. It took quite some time, but Katherine was immensely grateful it was even possible. Just one more day of delay would have meant disaster, for the captain would have been too far out of town for her to catch.

Not that she was safe yet, though. She wriggled out of the dress and petticoat, and Birdie bundled them into a ball. It took some doing to unlace her stays and get them off in the dark, narrow carriage, even with Birdie's help, but she finally slipped her nightdress over her head. She took off her shoes and put on her slippers over her woolen stockings. The chill night air raised gooseflesh on her limbs, and she shivered as she pulled the cloak gratefully back around herself.

"You'll catch your death of cold," muttered Birdie. "Such foolishness this was."

"It would have been more foolish to do nothing," Katherine replied.

"Hard to say yet."

"I say so."

Birdie's mouth twisted, but she said nothing more. She motioned with one hand. "Turn, so I can take down your hair."

Katherine obediently twisted on the seat. She clenched her teeth as Birdie tugged and pulled, fishing out the handful of pins that secured her hair in a tight knot at her neck. She wished she'd been able to meet the captain looking well dressed and groomed instead of like a runaway from the workhouse, but it was vital she not be seen or recognized. Her mother had assured Lucien that Katherine would surely accept his proposal, so he grudgingly allowed her some freedom. If he came to suspect she was scheming to wed someone else and deprive him of her money, he would put an end to it at once. And to be honest, Katherine admitted that even at her best, her looks weren't likely to sway the captain one way or another. Perhaps it was better that he saw her first at her most drab; then she could only improve on further acquaintance.

Birdie was just plaiting her hair into a long braid when the carriage slowed to a stop. Again the abigail stepped down first, waving behind her back for Katherine when it was safe. Head down, she slipped from the cab and walked quickly away, whisking into the darkest shadows in an alley nearby. After Birdie paid the driver and the cab rattled away over the cobbles,

Katherine peeked around the corner. The square was dark and quiet. The house across the street was also rather dark, which was a good sign; Lucien probably wasn't home yet.

Birdie hustled up and Katherine handed her the bundle of clothes. Together they hurried silently across the street, circling the square until they reached the mews near the house. Again Birdie went in first. Katherine huddled in her cloak, waiting, sure the pounding of her heart would be audible to each and every neighbor. She listened to Birdie talk with the housekeeper for a moment, then with a male servant. The minutes ticked by, and her feet grew numb in her slippers. She could hear an occasional carriage rattle past on the street in front of the house but kept her eyes resolutely fixed on the door.

Finally Birdie opened it and beckoned to her. Instantly Katherine slipped into the house, shedding her cloak in one quick motion into Birdie's waiting arm. Her abigail pressed a candle into her hand and pushed her toward the stairs. "He's home," she whispered, putting her cheek almost against Katherine's as she draped a shawl around her shoulders. "Go quietly."

Katherine nodded. Her nerves were gone now, for the most part. She was back in the house, dressed for bed, with no proof she'd been away. She mounted the stairs quietly but no longer afraid of being caught.

Which, of course, she was, by Lucien himself, in the corridor outside her room. "There you are," he said in his vaguely reproving way. "You weren't in your room."

Of course he looked in her room. He considered

every inch of the house his, open to his inspection at any moment. Katherine walked past him and opened her door, no longer wasting her breath in protesting it. "I wanted a cup of tea and went to fetch Birdie."

"She should answer the bell," he said, following her into the room but leaving the door open. "I've half a mind to sack such a lazy servant."

"She is my abigail, and I would be lost without her. I gave her leave to go out this evening since I was indisposed." Katherine hated to subject Birdie to Lucien's censure, but everyone knew Birdie had left the house. There was nothing to gain by trying to hide it. At least claiming she had given Birdie permission to go meant Lucien couldn't direct his full ire on the abigail. Katherine set her candle down on the mantel. The room looked as she had left it, a fire burning low and a lamp glowing on the table by the armchair near the hearth. "Why were you looking for me?"

He glanced pointedly at the bed, cloaked in shadows in the corner but clearly untouched. "I wished to see that you were well, but obviously you are. Your headache, I presume, is better?"

"Some. I couldn't sleep," she said evenly. "I was reading." She gestured toward the chair.

He walked over and picked up the book she had left on the table. "*Tillotson's Sermons*." He glanced at her, pleasure lighting his face for the first time. "I'm pleased to see you reading it."

"Every night." Lucien had given her the book and urged her to read it, so she did. Every night she read another sentence or two, just to prove it. She might have had more respect for Lucien's devout faith if he hadn't used it as a cudgel against her, berating her for any sign of independence or gaiety, which he termed willfulness and indecency. Katherine never thought of herself as a frivolous person, but her heart and soul strained against the dour, obedient cage into which Lucien wanted to shut her. Even her late husband Lord Howe enjoyed the theater, and he'd certainly had no objection to drink and fine clothing.

Lucien turned the book over, seeing where she had marked her place. "I see you haven't progressed far."

"I have tried to give it the thought and consideration you requested."

He shot her a keen look, but Katherine knew her face was placid and serene. She had become quite expert at masking any sign of impatience or disgust, happiness or eagerness, any emotion at all, really. Howe had liked his wife to be ever calm and undemanding; vigorous emotion wasn't healthy for women, he claimed. Lucien only enlarged upon that desire, wanting her to be subservient and biddable, subjecting herself to his judgment at all times. Katherine sometimes wasn't sure if she still knew how to smile or laugh, although she was pretty certain she could still lose her temper, given enough privacy and space to do so. Even now, when the chill of her evening's daring escapade still clung to her skin and Lucien watched her with sharp, critical eyes, she could feel the heat of fury licking at the edges of her mind. She couldn't give in to it, but she could still feel it.

"I hope it will show you enlightenment on what you must do," Lucien said. His moment of approval had faded already, and he fixed a stern eye on her. "You cannot put it off forever, Katherine."

"I hardly think it has been forever," she replied. "Not even a year yet of mourning for your uncle."

He pressed his lips together in irritation and glared at her, but he was caught by his own words there. Lucien had never been subtle about his belief that a woman should obey every dictate of propriety, and at first he praised her circumspection. Then he learned how badly indebted his inherited estate was to her, however, and his views on mourning periods underwent a marked change. Katherine had used that mourning like a shield as she tried to find a way out, but she had a feeling Lucien would soon declare her mourning—and his patience—at an end. Katherine pictured tall, strong, handsome Gerard de Lacey facing down Lucien, whisking her away from the grim, ascetic life Lucien planned, and said a silent prayer he would agree to her proposal.

"Nevertheless," Lucien said in a cool voice, "we cannot delay forever, my dear. Your respect for my late uncle's memory does you great credit, but we must secure the estate. I am sure no one could fault you for shortening your mourning when the circumstances are so pressing. You know we came to town only to settle your affairs and make arrangements for the wedding. I expect us to be married by the end of this month at the very latest."

She felt a bit light-headed at the sudden demand. "That is very soon," Katherine protested.

"I cannot afford to wait," he exclaimed. "The *estate* cannot afford it. The Howes have been a vital part of Sussex for centuries, and now, because of your obstinacy, we may have to withdraw that support. Why do you refuse to do what is best for everyone?"

Katherine had already thought of how her resistance would affect the people on the estate, the tenants and servants and merchants who benefited from the Howe family. She didn't want to hurt them at all, and this mess was none of their making. But mostly her acquiescence would benefit Lucien, not to mention put an end to any hope she had of private happiness, and she just couldn't do it. Even if it made her selfish and cruel to all the Howe dependents, she couldn't marry Lucien.

Lucien's eyes darkened at her stubborn silence. He stepped closer, and she barely stopped herself from edging backward. He put one finger under her chin and tipped up her face until she met his eyes. "My dear," he said almost kindly, "you must acclimate your mind to this. You know full well there are too many reasons for it and none at all against it."

Katherine stayed mute, knowing he didn't really care how many reasons she could think of against it.

"Our marriage will remove all of the drain on the family coffers," he went on. "I have need of a wife, and you are alone, without a husband or father to guide you. If you do not marry me, we are both ruined—I by the terms of that unfortunate note between my uncle and your father, and you because . . . well, my dear, I don't mean to be cruel, but it's not likely you'll receive another offer. You are more than thirty years old now."

He didn't say the rest, although she'd overheard him say it before: who would want a plain, mulish, likely barren widow of advanced age, even if she was rich? That had been before he realized how much her money was keeping him afloat, but she remembered. Even if it was true, she felt the sting. She turned her head, out of his touch. "I know how old I am."

"You know there's no way around it," he said, still in the gently urging tone. Lucien could be very smooth when it suited him. "I'll procure a license tomorrow. Tell your mother she must conclude your purchases in a week's time. We shall return to Sussex directly after the wedding."

She said nothing, and Lucien smiled. He laid the book of sermons back on the table and left, closing the door behind him. Katherine's heart hurt with each beat. Would Gerard de Lacey accept her offer? Without him, she didn't know how she would escape Lucien. He wasn't a cruel man, that she had seen, but neither was he a tenderhearted or even an amiable sort. He had already persuaded her mother, who'd been urging Katherine for some time now to say yes. From a distance, Katherine could even admit it appeared a good match; she was a plain, drab widow well past her prime, and Lucien had a viscountcy and a handsome face. Even his religious fervor wouldn't be seen by many as an obstacle.

His badly indebted estate would be one, though. As long as he held her funds, Lucien could maintain the facade that he was well-off, but the moment that money was withdrawn, he would be all but ruined. He would have to disclose as much to any potential bride's parents, and Katherine knew his pride forbade that. Even if it meant he had to marry her, a woman he tolerated with mild impatience and condescension, Lucien was adamant that no one should know his heritage was supported almost entirely by a merchant's money. For all that he spoke so piously of God's will, he cared a great deal for the opinion of other men.

She sank into the chair and tucked her shawl more securely around her. The fire snapped quietly in the hearth, but she barely felt the heat of it. Her feet were still numb. Katherine rested her cheek against the threadbare wing of the chair and closed her eyes. It was a mad, incredible thing she had done tonight; part of her could hardly believe she'd gone through with it. Chasing across London after a complete stranger and begging him to marry her! Anyone who knew her would be amazed that placid, quiet Katherine Howe would even think of such a thing, let alone carry it off. Anyone who knew her would expect her to acknowledge the practical soundness of Lucien's arguments and quietly accept his proposal. Surely after Lord Howe, who had been more than twenty years her senior, a husband like Lucien would be a delight. He was young, handsome, and respectable. Marriage to him would allow her to stay in her home of the last ten years, retain her status, and perhaps even have children. It would please her mother, who'd grown used to life as a relation of the Viscount Howe and thought Katherine was being a silly ninny. "Who else would have you, darling?" she asked in all innocent earnestness, the last time she visited. Katherine hadn't had an answer because, of course, probably no one much better than Lucien would have her.

But . . . Captain de Lacey was considering it. Something warm and giddy fluttered inside her stomach. Not just any man other than Lucien, but Gerard de Lacey, who could have any woman in England if he set his mind to it. Even though she knew his acceptance, *if* he accepted, would be because of her money and not because of her person, Katherine couldn't completely snuff out the lingering girlish thrill at the thought of having him for her husband. She knew it was stupid; she really had no acquaintance with him, and her memory of him had already proven worthless. It might have been a terrible mistake, choosing him, but her mind refused to accept that. It wasn't as though she'd had so many men to choose from, after all.

There was a faint scratch at the door. Birdie, most likely, come to check on her. Katherine raised her head, and called, "Come in."

Birdie slipped into the room, a steaming cup of tea in her hand. She closed the door, then hurried over to set the cup down on the table beside Katherine. "Are you ill?" she murmured in concern. "I knew you'd catch a chill . . ."

"No, I'm just cold." Katherine sat up with a sigh and reached for the tea. The warmth of the cup against her hands burned for a moment, then felt unbearably good. She was thoroughly chilled, not just from her secret excursion but from Lucien's promise: within a week. So it was imperative that she sneak out of the house again in three days to hear the captain's answer. Lucien regularly went to philosophical meetings on that night, but it was possible his impatience for the wedding would throw him off. Perhaps she should pretend a serious illness sooner, to keep him from the room. He had come looking for her tonight, when she had claimed a terrible headache. A catarrh, perhaps, or an ague. It would have to be serious enough to keep her mother from visiting but not serious enough to make her want to install a physician in the room. Her escape must be carefully planned, and quickly. She cradled the cup in both hands and raised it to her face, inhaling deeply. "Thank you, Birdie."

The older woman gave her a meaningful look over the rim of the teacup as Katherine sipped the scalding tea. She knew the thanks were for more than just tea. "Regrets?"

"None." There was no hesitation in her answer. Lucien had driven away any trace of regret.

Birdie sighed, lines of tension appearing across her forehead. "I hope this proceeds as you wish, madam."

Katherine thought of the captain again, from his long, confident stride to the charming way his mouth curled at the corners when he was amused. She felt again the force of Lucien's stare as he told her to accept the inevitable. The captain didn't love her, or even know her; but unlike Lucien, someday he might. And Katherine knew that if he did come to like her, perhaps even care for her a little, she could love him back. She was already halfway there, when he barely knew her name. She would have to guard herself carefully around him in case his feelings never progressed past gratitude and gentlemanly consideration, but that little kernel of hope, of possibility, was enough. "So do I, Birdie," she whispered. "So do I."

Chapter 4

Gerard set off toward London early the next morning. Late into the night he had been torn between laughing off Katherine Howe's odd proposal and going on his way in search of the blackmailer, and taking advantage of her desperation to snatch up a rich wife while she still wanted him. It appeared to be a circular problem: as long as the blackmailer was still free and able to cause trouble, Gerard was in desperate need of everything Katherine Howe offered . . . but haring off to catch the villain might cost him his best chance at financial security if he failed. It was unlikely other heiresses in possession of a hundred thousand pounds could be found at will. Finally he admitted he would have to verify just how real her proposal was, the sooner the better. If she had lied to him or misrepresented her situation, he could be on his way at once. He almost hoped for that outcome as he crossed the Thames, heading toward Holborn, where her solicitor had his offices. If everything she said was true . . . He had to make very certain of it before he decided, but he also had to do it quickly.

Mr. Tyrell had plain but comfortable premises

near Cary Street, not far from Lincoln's Inn Fields. Gerard hadn't had occasion to visit many solicitors, but he judged Mr. Tyrell to be a successful man. He sent in Lady Howe's letter with his card by way of introduction and was shown in soon after. Tyrell greeted him very affably, looking rather genial and placid; but Gerard didn't miss the shrewdness of his gaze.

"How may I help you, sir?" Tyrell leaned back in his chair, the sunlight glinting off his round spectacles.

"I require information about Lady Howe," Gerard said. "As her letter indicated."

"Yes, indeed. Lady Howe instructed me to answer all your questions with perfect candor."

Gerard smiled. Tyrell didn't look like he would say a word that wasn't in direct response to a question, but he expected that. *Damned lawyers.* "How long have you known and been employed by the lady?"

"I was employed by her father originally," said Tyrell readily. "When he died, she asked me to stay on. I first met her when she was a child."

"What sort of man was her father?" Gerard couldn't forget what she had said the night before, that her father had respected his, and that was what had led her to propose marriage to him.

"Driven. Demanding. Ambitious and intelligent. I never saw anyone get the better of him in business."

Those attributes could explain why Hollenbrook admired Durham, who had been all of those things. Gerard wondered if the daughter was cut from the same cloth. "What was his background?"

"Common." Tyrell lifted one shoulder, not displaying a whiff of surprise at Gerard's inquiries. "I've no idea who his parents were—Lady Howe would be better able to tell you that—but I believe he started as a young man in the mill he later came to own. Within twenty years he built up a considerable trade in dry goods and made a fortune supplying the army."

"Indeed," muttered Gerard. He had his own opinion of the people who supplied the army, and much of it wasn't flattering. "How large a fortune?" he asked abruptly.

Tyrell's glasses glittered as the attorney tilted his head. "Almost one hundred thirty thousand pounds, at his death."

Christ. Had Lady Howe understated things?

"Thirty thousand pounds was left for his widow," Tyrell went on. "The remainder to his daughter and her heirs."

No, she'd been exactly right. "Outright? Not to her husband?" Gerard knew very well a married woman's property belonged to her husband. Katherine Howe might think it was hers, might desire it to be hers, but the law might not agree.

"Outright," said Tyrell with a slight smile. "Lord Howe died three weeks before Mr. Hollenbrook. I believe Mr. Hollenbrook changed his will before His Lordship was cold in the grave."

Then the money was really hers. A widow was almost as independent, legally, as a man. Why couldn't she simply refuse this nephew's entreaty to marry him? She said she didn't want to marry again, but *must*.

"Forgive me," Gerard said, trying to sound somewhat confused and apologetic. "I understood Lady

Howe to be in a tight circumstance. It sounds to me as though she's a widow in possession of a large fortune, hardly desperate."

"I'm sure the lady knows her circumstances well enough to give a good report of them."

Gerard realized he was drumming his fingers on his boot, resting on his knee. Tyrell was as slippery as he'd expected him to be. He didn't have time for this nonsense. He sat forward and propped one elbow on the solicitor's desk. "Mr. Tyrell, I am here at Lady Howe's instigation, as you well know from her letter. I am contemplating marrying the lady, and would like a full and accurate picture of her situation. I haven't time to query you for hours in search of what I need to know, and I must make my decision soon."

"Very good, Captain," replied Tyrell, unruffled. "But Lady Howe is a very wealthy woman, with little experience of managing her own affairs. You must understand, in my position as her solicitor and as executor of her father's estate, I wish to protect her interests as much as possible—including, of course, from fortune hunters."

"Didn't she mention it?" Gerard asked in a silky voice. His patience was all but gone. "She proposed marriage to *me*. If anyone is in danger of being deceived, I suspect it is I."

Finally a moment of surprise flickered over Tyrell's face. "Ah."

"Indeed. As she herself explicitly acknowledged, her fortune is a factor in my decision, but far from the only one. And as far as the fortune itself . . ." He lifted one shoulder. "I have every expectation of a substantial inheritance of my own."

"So I understand," said the solicitor, proving himself acquainted with London gossip.

Gerard pushed his family's problem from his mind to focus on the question at hand. "So the money is hers, but there is a problem—over a loan, I believe."

"Yes." Tyrell's eyes narrowed on Gerard. He was quiet for a moment, glancing down at something on his desk. Lady Howe's letter, most likely. When he looked up, the easy but opaque expression was gone from his face. He looked at Gerard with frank appraisal in his gaze. "Very well," he murmured, then said in a normal voice, "Before the late Lord Howe's death, he borrowed a large sum from his father-in-law. Mr. Hollenbrook was reluctant to lend the money; he did not have a high regard for the viscount's economy, but for his daughter's sake, he made the loan. My client wasn't a foolish man, however, and he demanded security. Lord Howe was quite desperate, for he agreed to stake a prime, unentailed, piece of his land as security. The note was written so that if Mr. Hollenbrook died before it was repaid, the balance would be forgiven as part of Lady Howe's inheritance. No doubt this is what Lord Howe anticipated, as Mr. Hollenbrook was in declining health by then. If Lord Howe predeceased Mr. Hollenbrook, however, the note endured, and the security could be seized at any time if payment was not made. This is indeed what happened, and thus Lady Howe became the holder of the note against her late husband's estate."

"A curious agreement between a man and his son-in-law."

Mr. Tyrell's smile was flat. "Mr. Hollenbrook had

come to regret his daughter's marriage. Mrs. Hollenbrook, I believe, was the force behind it. She comes from a higher society than her husband and was quite keen for her daughter to marry well. Howe held an old and respectable title, with a very pretty estate in Sussex. He was also in dire need of money. Miss Hollenbrook brought him twenty thousand pounds as dowry, and within five years every shilling of it was gone. Hollenbrook confided to me that he no longer trusted Lord Howe, which was why he insisted on such terms in the note."

Gerard nodded. That also agreed with what Katherine Howe told him. Her proposal was sounding more and more ideal for his needs. "How much is the note for?"

"Ten thousand pounds. In addition, half of Lady Howe's dowry must be returned, since she was left a widow with no children. Mr. Hollenbrook crafted a very exact marriage settlement. I highly doubt the new Lord Howe has the funds to pay it, even in increments. There is a mortgage upon his estate, and if he loses the land held in security, he'll probably not be able to pay his mortgage."

And there was the reason Lucien Howe wanted to marry her. Not only to gain the balance of Lady Howe's money but to keep his estate solvent and intact. From what she said, the man hadn't been very clever or tender in making his offer. Of course, she'd been neither of those things when she made her shocking proposal to him, either, but Gerard was coming to understand that better.

"What sort of man is Lucien Howe?" he asked.

"Young," said Tyrell. "Arrogant. Greatly annoyed

to discover just how indebted he is to Lady Howe. He called upon me soon after his uncle's death, claiming to be Lady Howe's guardian and demanding I relinquish control of her funds to him."

"I doubt Lady Howe agreed to that."

Tyrell dipped his head in acknowledgment. "The new Viscount Howe left my offices disappointed."

"So twenty thousand is tied up in this loan," said Gerard slowly. "The balance—some eighty thousand pounds—is hers already. How is it invested?"

"Safely," replied Mr. Tyrell.

He grinned. "Excellent. Thank you for your time, sir."

He left the solicitor's offices and headed across town. Tyrell had answered his first question about Katherine Howe's money, but that alone wasn't enough. Her family was beginning to sound as shrewd as his. Howe must have been a slippery fellow for Hollenbrook to demand so much of him, and his heir sounded little better. Gerard wasn't afraid of bold actions, but he tried to avoid stupid ones if at all possible. What sort of man, precisely, would he be facing in Lucien Howe if he married Katherine? Gerard certainly didn't intend to just turn his back on twenty thousand pounds. He headed up Oxford Street, on his way to Cavendish Square, where he rapped the knocker of the Earl of Dowling's home.

As expected, he was admitted at once, despite the early hour. The butler showed him directly to the countess's bedchamber, where the lady was still in her dressing gown. "Gerard, you naughty boy," she cried, holding out her hands to him. "You've been in town several days and not come to see me!"

He laughed, kissing her cheek. "But here I am now—and surely sooner than Edward or Charlie."

She made a face and waved one hand. "Edward will call in due time. I expect he has a list of tasks to accomplish, and somewhere on that list is written 'Visit elderly aunt.' Come, sit, we must have tea—and breakfast, if you are hungry."

Gerard pulled out a chair for her. "Then you may wait a while. Edward always attends to business before pleasure, and visiting you brings nothing but pleasure."

She laughed and settled into the chair he held for her. Without asking, Gerard plucked up a fluffy shawl from a nearby chaise and draped it over his aunt's shoulders. She gave him an exasperated glance but left it around her. At her gesture, he took the chair opposite her.

"Now, what do you want to know?" she asked, when her servants finished laying out breakfast and bowed out of the room. "I know you and your brother never have time for an old lady unless you need something."

"I've always time for the most beautiful lady in London," he protested. "More likely you haven't got time for me, with all your beaux around here. I don't know how Dowling stands it."

Margaret smiled. Even at seventy she was still very handsome. Her hair had faded from golden blond to pure silver, and her face had settled into a webbing of fine lines, but she was as slim and erect as in her bridal portrait, painted some forty years ago. It was hard to believe she had almost been a spinster, unwed until she was thirty, when her older brother Francis,

Gerard's father, unexpectedly inherited the dukedom of Durham. Overnight Margaret became one of the most eligible ladies in England, with a generous dowry from her brother, and snapped up the Earl of Dowling in a matter of weeks. "Beaux! Those are my grandchildren, you scamp."

Gerard laughed. His cousin Philip, Margaret's only child, had four sons, all under the age of twelve. "I daresay those aren't the only ones who call."

"Your brother Charles is the only handsome fellow who is not my son or grandson who calls on me regularly," she said, pouring a cup of tea and setting it in front of him. "And even he comes only to share the gossip."

"Charlie?" He was honestly astonished that his indolent brother found time to call on their aunt—but then again, Gerard had decided sometime ago that anyone who tried to decipher Charlie's actions and motives was asking for madness. "He forgot to mention he'd seen you."

"Every other Tuesday he comes, always with a lovely bouquet of flowers." She fixed a glance on Gerard's empty hands, which he instinctively put in his lap beneath the table. Margaret laughed. "Don't be silly. I'm delighted to see you, with or without flowers. But I know you, young man; Charles comes because he has nothing better to do with himself. You, on the other hand, always have something to do and can hardly wait to do it. So I ask again, what do you want?"

"I think I came to apologize for taking you for granted," he said, humbled again by his aunt's sharp perception. "But I did hope you might be able to help me, yes."

"Of course I will, if I am able." She raised her eyebrows. "What is it you need to know?"

"Do you know anything about Viscount Howe of Sussex? The title recently changed hands from uncle to nephew."

"Is it the uncle or the nephew you want to know about?"

"The nephew, Lucien Howe," said Gerard. "Although anything you can tell me about the uncle or his widow would also be welcome."

Margaret dipped a spoon into her poached egg and took a delicate nibble. "The uncle, Thomas Howe, was a wastrel. I believe his particular vice was horses, but I'm not certain. Philip once had a near run with him over a horse race, and Howe came to the house breathing fire over being owed money. Dowling sent him off with a flea in his ear about taking advantage of lads not in charge of their fortune yet—Philip was barely eighteen and wrongly thought he was too old to be thrashed."

"And Philip was always held up to us as such a good example!" Gerard shook his head in mock sorrow.

She wagged her finger at him. "Philip's a very good man. Marriage settled him so admirably. You ought to consider it yourself."

"I *am* thinking of it." He grinned at his aunt's astonished expression. "Which is why I need to know about Lady Howe, as she's the bride under consideration."

Slowly Margaret put down her spoon. "Really, Gerard?"

"Yes, Aunt, really."

"Well, I must say she's about the last woman I would have expected you to choose," she murmured, still studying him in surprise. "Lady Howe . . . Much younger than her husband, I believe. A merchant's daughter? Or perhaps a tradesman's? Howe married her for the money, of course, but I can't say I ever met her. She certainly never figured much in London society." She turned a full frown on him. "But if you want to marry the lady, Gerard, you had better know more about her than I."

"Don't fret, Aunt. I'm trying to learn."

Margaret sighed and leaned back in her chair. "You're marrying her for the money as well, aren't you?"

Gerard loved his aunt and had enormous respect for her, but his temper roused at her tone. "Not entirely," he said tightly. "I would be a fool not to take her fortune into account, though, particularly given my new circumstances."

Her expression changed. "Oh yes," she said with a lilt of embarrassment. "I'd almost forgotten that."

He should be so fortunate. His father's scandalous bequest had never been far from Gerard's mind since the moment the solicitor reluctantly revealed it to him and Edward. His father had begged their forgiveness with his last breath but he hadn't had the courage to confess the sin himself. Durham left it to his solicitor to tell his sons they might be disinherited bastards, shorn of the Durham name and estate and all that went with them. "Yes," he muttered. "If only we *all* could forget it. But failing that, I must consider Lady Howe."

"Of course," she said at once. "Of course you must. I don't know what your father was thinking . . ." She shook her head. "When I heard the rumors, I tried to recall anything I might have heard, but I was young then. It was so long ago."

Gerard fiddled with his teacup. Margaret, of course, had been there sixty years ago when his father allegedly married an actress named Dorothy Cope. She was his sister. Durham might have told her something, anything, which could explain what he did. "Did you never have any idea he'd married?"

"None at all—but then, I was a child. Francis went off to London when I was nine years old, perhaps ten. We none of us heard much about him, although it was no secret he was hotheaded and somewhat wild when he was a young man." She sighed, then rallied a bittersweet smile. "I was a good sister. I knew nothing of what he did and asked no impertinent questions. No doubt the answers would have scalded my ears in any event."

"They've certainly burned us." He ran one hand over his face, fighting down his simmering fury at his father.

"He was extremely hesitant to marry, though," Margaret went on, more slowly. "When the title came to him, I remember teasing him he would have no choice but to take a wife, and he was quite adamant he would not. I thought he had suffered a broken heart in his youth—men can be so hurt by those, no matter what they say to the contrary—but when he met your mother . . ." A faint smile lit her face. "He was a different man with her. It was clear to see he loved her deeply, and she him. The years he had with her were the happiest I ever saw him."

Gerard bowed his head, struck again by someone else's memory of his mother. It quite hamstrung his anger at his father. Still, it didn't change his situation now. "Edward's hired a solicitor to try to straighten the mess."

"I shouldn't think it will take much!" She drew a deep breath and gave a decisive nod. "Who was the woman, anyway? Nobody. What court would invalidate your mother's marriage—and offend all her family—to name you illegitimate? This will all be settled as it should be, in favor of you three. Anything else is simply inconceivable."

"Not really, if Cousin Augustus shows up and makes a strong case."

Margaret shuddered. "Heaven help Durham if Augustus gets his filthy fingers on it. Such a terrible young man he was. That entire branch of the family was rotten, through and through."

Gerard privately thought his own suffering would be just as bad as the dukedom's, if not worse, should Augustus succeed to the title. "I share your hopes, Aunt, but cannot share your confidence. So about Lady Howe . . ."

"Oh! Yes," she murmured, her gaze growing distant. "Howe died last year, I believe—I can't recall of what, or precisely when. The new viscount is a handsome fellow, young and serious. Old Howe was a bit of a devil, and his heir is rather the opposite, I gather." She looked at him, a pleased smile breaking over her face. "But of course: you should ask

Clarissa! She knows everything about everyone and loves nothing more than sharing it. She usually calls in the mornings; why don't you wait and ask her?"

The very last thing on earth Gerard wanted to do was sit and chat with his aunt's bosom friend, Lady Clarissa Eccleston. Lady Eccleston was an inveterate spy who always managed to know far more about other people's lives than any disinterested person had a right to know. There was no possibility she wouldn't be brimming with curiosity about his father's scandal, but perhaps she would rein it in out of respect for Lady Dowling, if nothing else. Otherwise, he hated to admit, she was practically ideal for his purposes. If anyone could tell him about Lady Howe, it would be Lady Eccleston. "Very well," he said, with a distinct lack of enthusiasm.

His aunt merely smiled and shooed him out the door. "Trust me," she called to him as he headed for the stairs. "Clarissa will know."

Chapter 5

Gerard went to the drawing room to await Lady Eccleston while his aunt dressed. The butler brought him some coffee, steaming hot and very strong, and he took it to the window to sip while he reviewed the morning so far.

First, and most importantly, Lady Howe was as wealthy as she'd promised. That really was her main attraction, even allowing for the unpleasantness of the unpaid twenty thousand pounds. Gerard thought he could manage well enough on six or seven thousand a year, which would be the income from her inheritance combined with the share of his mother's dowry left to him. He could pursue his army career unhindered, and most likely his wife would prefer it as well. There was obviously no affection binding them together, and the lady gave no sign she hoped that would change. Katherine Howe looked as if she didn't want to be touched, which had the unfortunate effect of making him want to try it, just to see. She'd worn her cloak through their entire interview, so he had no idea of her figure. Wouldn't it be a fine joke on him if he married a plain-faced woman for her money, and she turned out to have a bewitching body that left him tied in knots of lust?

But that was neither here nor there. She had the money he needed; what else would she bring him? A secure, uneventful life, or endless headaches over that damned loan? What sort of woman was she— snappish and controlling, pious and delicate, meek and quiet? Gerard admitted he didn't have a lot of choice, but he wanted at least to know what he was getting into before he bound himself to her.

Lady Eccleston arrived just as Margaret came down to join him. She was very much as Gerard remembered her, as plump as Margaret was slim and twice as talkative. Her eyes lit up when she saw him, and he endured several minutes of her fussing as she asked after his health, his brothers, his spirits since his father's death, even his commanding officer's compassion in the wake of the Durham uproar. As if army men routinely retired into seclusion to mourn anyone's passing. They'd granted him leave, but only once Gerard explained the knotty circumstances and how they would oblige him to sell out if he couldn't settle the matter. There was a war going on, after all.

"Gerard has condescended to sit with us today because he needs you, Clarissa," said Margaret, with a smiling glance at him.

Her mouth formed a perfect O of delight. "Indeed! How so?" Gerard opened his mouth, but she wasn't done. "Is it anything related to that dreadful business with your father? Such a dreadful shock it was to your dear aunt, to hear such things about him. She was quite undone, young man, quite undone! I do hope you and your brothers have taken steps to banish such talk from London. It's not good for dear Margaret's health!"

Gerard glanced at his aunt in wary alarm, and she waved one hand with a sigh. "Pish, Clarissa," she said. "My health is fine. And please don't speak of . . . all that disgraceful gossip. He wants to know about a lady."

"A lady!" Clarissa Eccleston breathed. Her false sympathy brightened back into delight. "Which one, dear?"

"Now, Lady Eccleston, you mustn't say a word of this to anyone," warned Gerard. "I really must insist."

"Of course, of course," she cried. "I wouldn't dream of it!"

He feared she did dream of just such things and wouldn't be able to stop herself from telling everyone in London he was after Lady Howe. "I do want to know about a lady," he said with a flash of inspiration, "but if she should reject me . . . As you know, my father's troubles—" He stopped short, affecting a burst of emotion.

"Oh!" she breathed, her eyes rounding. "I quite understand. Of course I won't say a word."

He didn't have much choice. Gerard shot a suffering look at his aunt, who had gotten him into this, and said a prayer she would be able to impress some discretion on her friend. "Thank you, Lady Eccleston. It's such a relief to know I may rely on your understanding."

"Well! Let's hear it, then. What do you want to know? Who is the fortunate girl?" She wriggled in her seat, her nose practically quivering, as she sat at attention like an eager retriever pup.

"Lady Katherine Howe," said Gerard, trying to banish the thought of Lady Eccleston as a dog. "Anything and everything."

"Howe, Howe," murmured Lady Eccleston, her face fierce with concentration. "I do know that name . . ."

"You remember, Clarissa," said Margaret. "The young zealot."

"Oh—Lucien Howe!" Her eyes gleamed in victory, and she beamed at Gerard. "Of course I remember. What about him?"

"Really it was Lady Howe I wished to know about," he replied, "but what of Lucien Howe?"

"A Puritan," she said at once. "He really ought to have been born a century or two ago. He's with the Calvinists, or the Methodists, or whichever group it is that doesn't want dancing or singing or ribbons on ladies' bonnets. Such a pity, really, for he's a handsome fellow and far too young to be such a dried-up stick about life."

"So he's not a fribble."

"No, no, no, not at all." Lady Eccleston held out her cup for more tea, which Margaret poured, and reached for another biscuit. "Quite the opposite, in fact. I hear he's utterly devoted to his new title and responsibilities. Bit of a shame, really, for a handsome young viscount to be so dull. What's gotten into young people these days?" She clucked her tongue and shook her head, setting her faded red ringlets bobbing. "In my day, a handsome young gentleman of means would no more have spent his evenings at devotional meetings than he would have taken to plowing his own fields. It weakens the spleen, my father would have said, to sit and ponder sermons all day. But then, my father was a Whig, and you know they never did run much to religion."

"It's a prosperous estate, then?" He sensed the conversation could very easily spiral out of control, and he would be trapped for hours by good manners if he didn't make efforts to keep things in line.

"Hmm." Lady Eccleston's round little chin jerked rapidly up and down as she chewed her biscuit. "I think so—no one's talking about ruination, and as you know, the only thing more exciting than a new fortune is imminent ruin."

"Yes," said Gerard dryly. "So I have learned. But what of Lady Howe?"

Lady Eccleston popped the last of the biscuit into her mouth. Her eyes grew faraway with thought. "I don't know very much," she said at last, sounding surprised and disappointed by her own failing. "I don't think she's been much in London. Howe was here every Season, of course, but if he ever brought his wife, I can't recall it. He certainly gave everyone the impression she was delicate, or painfully shy, or some such thing. There were rumors she was deformed or disfigured, but I doubt that; Howe was much too proud to marry a gargoyle, even one with a large fortune. But I've never met her. I know of her mother—Mary Hollenbrook. Would you like to hear about her?"

Gerard hesitated, then nodded. Every little bit was important, given his complete lack of knowledge.

Lady Eccleston flashed him a bright smile and took a deep breath. "*She* was quite a beauty! No money in her family, of course, but her father was a baron, which made her proud. Well, not too proud, for she married a tradesman of some sort, although he was rich when she married him, then grew exceedingly richer. I must say, those marriages rarely work out; it's much better when the bride brings money into a noble family, then everyone is happy. If she marries down just because he's rich, why, what's the result? They might have connections because of her, but really the result is the same, merely more tradesmen."

"Which is precisely what Lady Howe did," Gerard interrupted. "And I gather it wasn't terribly happy."

She shrugged it off. "Oh, well, at least it was the proper order of things! One can never account for happiness in marriage anyway, it's too unpredictable—anything with men always is. But Mrs. Hollenbrook—I think she must have been disappointed in her daughter. All the beauties are when their daughters are plain. No doubt that's why she was in favor of the Howe marriage. Howe was a handsome man in his youth, but by the time he married he was forty or more." She paused for breath.

"Poor young lady," said Margaret. "How terrible to be an heiress, then wed to a man old enough to be your father."

"Perhaps he was the only one who'd have her."

"Clarissa, you know very well she could have horns on her head and still be a sought-after girl, given a large enough dowry."

Lady Eccleston giggled like a girl. "Why, that is very true! And I do believe she must have had an enormous one, for Howe couldn't keep two farthings if someone sewed them to his glove."

"Then she's a respectable lady?" Gerard asked in one last desperate attempt to get anything useful from this. "I know she's not a great beauty. I know she has a fortune. I want to know something of her character as well as her situation."

Lady Eccleston thought so hard, her face turned pink. Gerard could almost see the wheels frantically spinning inside her brain as she searched for any scrap of information about Katherine Howe. "I just don't know," she admitted at last. "She's not out in society much, or if she is, she's so quiet and withdrawn, no one speaks of her."

"But she's in London now," Gerard murmured, half to himself. "I wonder why . . . ?"

"Is she?" Lady Eccleston perked up. "A wealthy widow, come to town? I must hear more of this!"

"Clarissa, Gerard is considering marrying her," Margaret reminded her friend. "And you promised not to say a word."

She pursed her lips in affront. "Of course, Margaret," she exclaimed. "But whatever I hear, I would be sure to tell dear Gerard right away!"

The solicitor. Of course, Gerard realized; she was in town because it was her money now. She must have wanted to see Mr. Tyrell herself, or needed to, in order to sign papers. Lucien Howe must be hoping to draw up marriage contracts as well. Tyrell mentioned Howe had been to see him.

"I beg pardon, Lady Eccleston," he said, interrupting the good-natured bickering between his aunt and her friend. "Do you happen to know where the Howes are lodging?"

"Portman Square," she said promptly. "Number ten."

He didn't even want to know how she knew that. The catalog of information about other people contained inside her head must be simply astounding. Gerard got to his feet and bowed. "Ladies, it has been an absolute pleasure. I beg you will excuse me, though."

"Of course, dear." Aunt Margaret rose and lifted her cheek for his kiss. "Do be sure to write now and then, Gerard, if you have no more patience for visiting. I shall be desperate to know how you decide."

He smiled. "So shall I, Aunt." He bowed crisply to Lady Eccleston. "Thank you, ma'am, for all of your assistance."

"Of course! Anything for a handsome man in a scarlet coat!" she tittered.

After he left the ladies, Gerard paused on the pavement outside Dowling House. That had been helpful, he supposed, even if it hadn't taught him much about the woman herself. He would have preferred to know *something* about her, but if Lady Eccleston must be his source, perhaps he was better off not hearing anything. For a moment he considered returning home to Durham House in Berkeley Square, but discarded the idea. He'd already said farewell to his brothers. It was highly unlikely Edward would know anything about Lady Howe or her family since he was in London society even less than Gerard himself was. Charlie might know something about the Howes, but he wouldn't give up the information without learning why Gerard wanted to know. And he had no intention of telling his brothers about Katherine Howe until—or if—he must.

He turned his horse toward Portman Square. Riding past her house wouldn't tell him anything, but he had to do something while he considered his next move. She said she couldn't return to hear his answer for three days, and she didn't want him to call on her, which would have been far easier. Of course it wasn't generally acceptable for a lady to call on a man unrelated to her late at night, and although it was rare for a woman to approach a man about marriage, Gerard was sure stranger things had happened. But for her to have chosen him, whom she didn't know at all . . . He sensed there was more to her decision than simple admiration for his father. He completely dismissed her mention of his military career; he was only a captain, hardly ever offered the chance to perform acts of daring and bravery. Perhaps she saw a chance to connect herself to one of the finest families in England by taking advantage of the scandal over his father's first marriage. Gerard found that hard to believe as well. There were plenty of men from the finest families who would be glad to entertain her offer and her fortune. Besides, in his case, it might turn out to be a spectacularly bad gamble if things went badly for them in the courts, and he was declared illegitimate.

So what had brought Lady Howe to his door? She must have been quite desperate to do it and probably had a great fear of the consequences if she were discovered. She preferred death to marrying her late husband's nephew, she'd said, and somehow Gerard believed her. She was a widow, though, with no father or brothers. That was as free and independent as a woman could be. Moreover, she wasn't poor, which certainly gave her liberty many other widows wouldn't have. Why couldn't she simply refuse to marry again and use her fortune to buy herself a house? She wasn't spineless, as evidenced by her bold proposition to him.

He thought back over Lady Eccleston's remarks. A beautiful, vain mother, disappointed in her plain daughter who nonetheless managed to make a brilliant marriage, at least in status. If Lucien Howe persuaded the mother, perhaps Katherine Howe had no ally inside her own home except the servant who accompanied her. A zealot, Lady Eccleston called Lucien Howe. Zealots weren't known for their tolerant, forgiving natures, even when financial ruin wasn't nipping at their heels. If Lord Howe were truly set on marrying Katherine to save his estate, he would surely be furious at her for arranging a different marriage on her own. Gerard had a feeling he'd have to deal with Lord Howe more than once if he ended up marrying Katherine Howe.

That really wasn't what he wanted. His hope had been to marry an heiress to make his life easier, not harder. On the other hand, Lady Howe had far more money than he'd anticipated, even if Lucien Howe never repaid a farthing of what he owed her. Was a hundred thousand pounds worth dealing with an irate, possibly incensed, viscount? Or at worst, if the damned loan was forgiven, eighty thousand pounds?

Gerard was pretty confident the answer would turn out to be, for better or for worse, yes.

Chapter 6

On the third day after Lady Howe had made her proposition, Gerard went down and told the landlord he needed the private parlor for the evening and was expecting guests. The man gave him a knowing look, as if Gerard would be entertaining a bevy of courtesans or similar creatures, and promised to make the arrangements. When he showed Gerard to the room after dinner, there was a bottle of wine waiting with a pair of glasses, a crackling fire, and the drapes drawn. Gerard thanked him, poured a glass of wine, and sat down to wait.

Hour after hour crept by. The fire burned down, and the wine disappeared. By the time the faint sound of a church bell chiming ten filtered into the room, he had almost decided she wasn't coming. Combined with the wine, this put Gerard in a grim temper. She had thrown down her gauntlet with its tempting prize at the end, begged him to consider it for three days, then not even sent word she wasn't coming back. The landlord brought another bottle of wine, and Gerard filled his glass again. If she didn't arrive by eleven, he was going to bed, and at first light he would be on his way, focused once more on the rather pressing business he'd put aside at her instigation.

Of course, it might not be her fault. Perhaps she was being kept under lock and key, strictly watched, and had no chance to come to him. That was fairly melodramatic, even for a miserly, stiff-necked chap like Lucien Howe apparently was. Perhaps the solicitor reported back to her, unflatteringly, about Gerard and his prospects. Perhaps she changed her mind about her proposal to marry a man she didn't know—or a man on the verge of scandal and disgrace. Or a man who visited her solicitor for an exact accounting of her fortune before deciding whether or not to take her as his wife. Reflection, aided by the wine, mellowed his mood somewhat. There were so many reasons why she shouldn't return, Gerard was mildly startled when the door opened at last, and her frumpy servant peeked in. She scowled when she saw him but stepped back out of the doorway, so Lady Howe could come in.

As before, she was hidden in a plain dark cloak, the hood enveloping her face. She stopped short when she saw him lounging in the armchair, one boot on the fender, his coat and waistcoat unbuttoned.

"I was beginning to worry," he drawled, when the silence grew taut and uncomfortable. "I thought you'd changed your mind."

She pushed back the hood. "Why would you think that?"

He shrugged. "You were the one who insisted I delay for three days. That's plenty of time for a lady to change her mind. Of course, since I agreed to consider your proposition, it would be only polite to return, even if merely to tell me personally that your offer was no longer good."

She stared at him, her mouth flattened in a tense line. "Please, Captain, do not waste my time or yours. Have you an answer for me?"

Gerard pushed off the fender and stood up. The bottle of wine humming through his veins magnified the urge to unsettle her, to exert some control over the situation. To let her know just what she was getting in him while she still had the right to slap his face and walk away. He glanced at the older woman, hovering in the shadows behind her mistress. "You may go."

The servant woman puffed up like an angry hen. Lady Howe blanched. "I would like Mrs. Dennis to stay."

"And I would like some privacy," he said in a silky voice. "If she doesn't go, I will."

Her eyes darted from side to side, but she nodded at her servant. "Wait outside, please, Birdie."

With one more black look at Gerard, the woman left, pulling the door to behind her. He ambled across the room and pushed it shut the rest of the way with a bang. He ignored the startled exclamation from outside the door and turned to his future bride. She raised her chin and held her ground. Anger sparkled in her eyes, but she said nothing. For several minutes they just took each other's measure.

"Please, take off your cloak," he said.

Her shoulders hunched, even though he'd spoken politely, without a drop of implicit threat. "I don't see the need. We both know my person isn't a factor in your decision."

"Do we both know that?" Gerard cocked his head.

"It shouldn't be," she said stiffly.

"Ah." He walked back to the table where the wine sat with his glass and the unused one, her glass. He picked up the bottle and began pouring. "Of course we aren't acquainted at all, so forgive me for presuming. But you might as well know right now I don't view marriage as just a business transaction. I'm not for sale any more than I expect you to be. Before I can give you my answer, I have to know—for myself—if we suit at all."

"What do you mean, *suit*?" Her suspicion was almost palpable.

"Marriage, my dear, is for life. Trust me on this. How much worse would both our predicaments be if we were to wed in intemperate haste, only to discover in a month or a year that we actively detest each other?"

Two thin lines creased her brow. "You're a romantic?"

Gerard laughed. "Not even close! I never said love must figure into it."

"Then . . . You want children?"

He smiled cynically at the shock in her tone. "Why yes, my dear. What a shame, to have so much money and no one to leave it to."

"I'm too old to bear a child," she protested. "I'm already thirty!"

"Not too old at all," he countered at once. "My aunt was two-and-thirty when she bore my cousin."

Katherine Howe swallowed. "What if I am unable?"

He shrugged. "Then my disappointment would lie

with God, not with you. We cannot know unless we try."

"And you wish to try," she repeated as if she couldn't believe her ears. "With me."

"If you're to be my wife . . ." He dipped his head in a slow nod. "Yes."

For a moment she was so still, only the shallow rise and fall of her bosom betrayed her vitality. Then she reached up and untied her cloak. With a sharp twist of her shoulders she shed the garment, dropping it into Gerard's extended hand. He tossed it over the chair behind him, taking full advantage of the chance to study her. Her dress was a shade of light brown with lace all around the high neck, certainly not seductive or even very stylish. She was slim, almost thin; he could see her collarbones clearly. But he also could see the swells of her breasts, and she must have hips under that awful dress.

"Do you like that gown?" he asked. She wasn't a beauty, but surely there were more flattering dresses she could have chosen.

She inhaled a shaky breath. "It is my best. We had guests for dinner tonight, and I had no time to change."

"That's not what I asked." He was standing very close to her, and it clearly unnerved her. Her eyelashes fluttered ceaselessly as her gaze moved about the room even though she never met his gaze.

"No," she said. "I'm not particularly fond of it, but everyone said it suits me."

Gerard knew enough about women to sense that being told an unappealing dress suited her wouldn't make any female happy. "Your mother says so?" he hazarded a guess.

She blinked, finally darting a wary glance at him. "Do—do you know my mother, sir?"

"No, but I've heard of her in the last three days. It seems there's more to hear of her than of you." He raised an eyebrow at her frozen expression. "Did you think I wouldn't ask about you?"

"No." Her lips barely moved. "What is your answer, Captain?"

She wasn't ugly. A bit plain, perhaps, although she'd undoubtedly look better in a different gown. She could use more flesh on her bones, but that was a small matter. Her hair was styled more attractively than before, comparatively speaking; less like a governess's and more like a spinster's. Why did women think tight little ringlets above the ears were attractive? It made them look like spaniels. But the candlelight glinted brass-bright off her hair, deeper than blond though not brunette. He reached up and touched one spiral curl, and found it stiff with pomade. What would it look like taken down?

She wasn't stupid or meek. In fact, she had quite a bit of backbone to propose marriage to him, and with such clearheaded forethought. That boded well. Gerard didn't like women who were led by impulse, swinging from whim to whim as their humors changed. At least a reasonable woman could be dealt with rationally. If anything, she'd seemed too cool and logical so far, almost bloodless in her approach; but he sensed there was temper and spirit inside her. He was probably a damned fool, but he found that hidden passion lurking beneath her drab, frosty exterior to be immensely tantalizing. If she'd been an empty-headed heiress, throwing herself at him with drama and tears, he doubted he would have been intrigued enough to entertain her proposal at all.

Katherine Howe, however, was giving every impression of wishing herself miles away right now. He edged deliberately closer, noting how she tensed up at his approach.

"Are you frightened of me?" he asked softly.

The pulse throbbed frantically under her skin, but her voice was even. "Not at all."

One corner of Gerard's mouth lifted. This woman had bottom. "Then look at me."

She inhaled deeply and lifted her eyes to meet his. They weren't black, he realized, but deep, deep blue.

"If you marry me," he said quietly, "I expect you to be my wife in every way. I expect your loyalty to be unwavering—question my actions in private if you will, but never turn on me in public. You are already aware of the potential problem in my family, with my inheritance, and if it ends badly, I never want to hear a remonstrance about our lost social standing or anything related to it. Do you agree to this?"

Her eyes narrowed. She gave a barely perceptible jerk of her chin, *yes*.

Gerard tilted his head in acknowledgment. "In return, I will regard you above other women and protect you with my life. I will expect to dine with you regularly, take you to the theater or other amusements when it pleases us, share your bed at least some nights. I will consider your thoughts and opinions on our shared life and be as decent and honorable a husband as I can be. I don't expect us to share a deep love, but I would like affection, if possible, and most certainly respect."

"Will you keep a mistress?" she asked.

"I don't have one now, but if we find we don't suit in bed, I certainly wouldn't deny us both the freedom to find pleasure elsewhere." He waited, but she said nothing, just stared at him with dark, shadowed eyes. She was so grave and somber, despite the flush in her cheeks and the pounding pulse at the base of her throat. Again the devil inside him itched to make her laugh, or lose her temper, or scream in passion. "Do you still agree?" he prompted her.

For a moment she didn't move or speak. "If that is your way of accepting my proposal," she said, "then I agree."

He grinned in spite of himself. "Then *I*, Lady Howe, do gladly consent to become your husband." He cupped one hand behind her neck and kissed her.

Katherine's knees went weak with relief when she realized he was going to agree, and it put her at a significant disadvantage when he unexpectedly laced his long fingers around the nape of her neck and pressed his mouth to hers. She swayed and almost fell, but his free arm went around her, pulling her up onto her toes and flush against him. She grappled for balance, closing her hands on his upper arms. His biceps flexed under her grip, he adjusted his hold on her, and somehow her body fit smoothly into place against his. She dimly registered the size and strength of him, but by far the greater portion of her thoughts was completely scattered away by his kiss.

It was gentle but somehow compelling. Despite the slight scratch of stubble his lips were soft and smooth.

They moved lightly over hers, teasing, tugging, exploring. Katherine was shocked; she'd been kissed before, but usually on the cheek or a quick, impersonal press of her husband's mouth against hers. It never lasted this long, or felt this delicious. It was as disorienting as it was wonderful. For a moment she simply fell into the pleasure of being held this way by this man. Her tense fingers eased on his arms, and she let out a tiny sigh.

His hand shifted, sliding from the back of her neck to her jaw. His thumb stroked lightly under her chin, and she flinched in surprise. He angled his head more and traced the seam between her lips with the tip of his tongue. Katherine hesitantly parted her lips when he did it again, and he growled low in his throat, the sound redolent with satisfaction, as his tongue swept into her mouth. Automatically she tried to retreat, but he gathered her closer without any apparent effort, tipping up her chin a little farther as he tasted her mouth leisurely and sensuously. She felt overwhelmed by him—his size, his strength as he held her, the warm taste of burgundy wine on his tongue, the way he made her heart pound so hard she thought she might faint. She didn't know what to do—what he expected or wanted her to do—so she could only stand there and let him kiss her. And the sole thought her brain could form was one of thanks that he had said yes before he kissed her this way.

After an eternity, much too soon, he raised his head and looked down at her for a moment in silence, his expression somehow hot and fierce in the firelight. "Yes, that will do," he murmured as he released her. "For now."

Her cheeks burned. Reason flooded back through her. "You should have asked," she said tightly.

That naughty, sensual grin bent her new fiancé's wicked mouth. "*You* asked *me*." Katherine just glared at him, scrabbling for her lost dignity. Her breasts still tingled from being pressed so intimately against his chest, and from the way his eyes glinted as they slid over her, he knew it. "Or did you not know what a husband's duty included?"

Duty. Of course. She flattened her hands against her skirt and reined in her body's reaction, aided considerably by his choice of words. "Of course I do," she said, making her voice carefully free of emotion. "You merely startled me."

"Good," he said, sounding suspiciously amused. "We can be married tomorrow."

Katherine's mouth fell open. "Tomorrow? What do you mean?"

He produced a paper from his pocket and handed it to her. She unfolded it and read the special license, giving the bearer permission to marry at any time without banns. He couldn't have shocked her more thoroughly if he'd produced a vicar from the cupboard. She looked up at him, speechless.

He cocked his head when she just gaped at him. "Have you changed your mind? It's not too late."

"No! I— I—" She looked away from him, away from his intense gaze, down at the paper in her hand. Not only was he willing to have her, he kissed her. He wanted to make love to her. He was going to marry her *tomorrow*. This was not at all what she had expected. A thrill of excitement twined with the panic unfurling in her stomach. "You surprise me," she said, trying to hide both emotions. "I didn't anticipate such haste."

"Unfortunately, my dear, I don't have time to spare. You knew I was on my way out of town three days ago." He crossed the room to the table and came back with a glass in one hand.

Her mind leaped from one topic to another without pausing long enough to make any decisions. Somehow she'd completely lost control of what should have been a very controlled situation. He took the license from her and handed her the glass, the wine he had poured earlier. "Where are you going?" was all she managed to ask.

He just smiled, a watchful, wry expression on his face as he tucked the license back into his pocket. "Where my search takes me. I assume you will come with me. That is, after all, why I procured the license. I also thought you wouldn't want to return to Lucien Howe's home, given how far you've gone to avoid wedding him. No doubt he won't be the most gracious of hosts after tomorrow."

Yes, that was true. She dipped her head in acknowledgment.

The captain nodded. "I thought as much. You and your maid should remain here tonight. Tomorrow we can be married at the church, then collect your things. You can pack in an hour or two, can you not?"

"Remain here?" Katherine was appalled all over again. She'd be discovered missing for certain . . . except, that wouldn't matter much now, would it?

Lucien couldn't do anything to her with the captain standing beside her as her husband. In fact, the greater danger probably lay in returning to Portman Square tonight. If she had been missed, Lucien would be furious, and heaven only knew what he would do to prevent her from leaving again. Perhaps it was best to grasp this chance to put herself out of his reach entirely. After all, Lucien had probably gotten a special license as well since he expected to marry her in a few days' time himself. And what purpose would waiting serve? She certainly didn't expect the captain to go through some charade of courting her.

"The inn's not full. I can secure a room for you and your maid." Gerard de Lacey gave her a sinful glance from under his eyelashes. "Unless you'd rather have your wedding night early."

Katherine felt the heat pool in her cheeks, and in her belly, at that glance, and for a moment the word *yes* almost leaped off her tongue. It was even more than she'd hoped for, or dreamed of . . . But she mustn't give in to that. It shocked her he might want her that way, but of course it wouldn't last. He was making a good show, out of gratitude most likely. She would be a fool to think it was real. "You may take another room," she said. "Birdie will stay with me." He nodded, and she held up one hand. "I meant for the foreseeable future, Captain. I will go with you, but my maid is coming with me."

"Of course," he said, unperturbed. "I never expected less." He raised his glass in salute and drained it with a twist of his wrist.

She nodded. "Then we understand each other."

"Not yet," he said with a chuckle. "But we will." He strode to the door and opened it. "You may go to her," she heard him tell Birdie, and the sound of his boots echoed in the corridor as he walked away.

Birdie rushed into the room, closing the door behind her. "What did he do to you?" she demanded. "I vow, my heart was going so fast, I thought sure we'd be caught!"

"He said yes," Katherine murmured.

"And now—oh dear, it's quite late, we'll have to hurry, hurry back to town!" Still shaking her head, Birdie snatched up Katherine's cloak and held it up. "Come, m'lady, we really must make haste!"

"No." Katherine took a sip of the wine the captain had given her. Gerard. Her soon-to-be-husband. She took another sip to hide the shiver that rippled through her at the thought. "We're to stay here tonight. The captain and I will be married in the morning."

Birdie stared at her, mouth gaping, the cloak dragging on the floor. "Tomorrow?"

Katherine nodded, drinking more wine. It would go to her head, but she felt half-drunk already, off-balance and unable to keep her thoughts in order. The wine tasted like him—of course, because he had been drinking it before he kissed her. The memory made her lift the glass again. "It makes perfect sense, really. The only way things can go awry is if Lucien somehow discovers what I've done before I'm married to the captain. Returning home now only affords him a chance to interfere." Birdie's expression remained fearful. Katherine reached for her hand. "Don't worry, Birdie. It may seem sudden and rash, but this *is* what I wanted. Why would I back out now?"

The maid's lip quivered before she bit it. "I know, madam. I cannot help but worry."

"Well, some worries must be put aside and not indulged," said Katherine quietly. "I made my choice." Birdie closed her eyes and nodded. "We're leaving tomorrow on the captain's business. I hope you will come with me."

Birdie's eyes popped open, snapping with outrage. "Of course I'm coming with you," she said in indignation. "Where else would I go?"

Katherine just shook her head, mutely relieved Birdie was still supporting her. Birdie had been hired years ago as her nurse, slowly becoming her governess, then her abigail. She'd been a poor widow, grieving after the deaths of her husband and only child, when she first came to care for Katherine, a plain, serious girl born to vex a vivacious, pretty mother. Birdie understood Katherine's quiet stubbornness and subtle humor far more than Mrs. Hollenbrook ever did.

Katherine's father grasped how vital Birdie was to Katherine, and at her marriage to Lord Howe, he quietly settled a good sum of money on Birdie so she would be independent of Howe's whims. It hadn't mattered—Howe turned out not to mind too much what his wife did or what servant she preferred— but it sealed Birdie's loyalty to Katherine and her father.

By the time the captain came back with the inn-keeper, Katherine had regained her composure. She was able to return the look he gave her with one of cool civility, not faltering even when he made no effort to hide his grin. It didn't matter if she amused him. It didn't matter if he kissed her. Theirs was a marriage of convenience, whether he ended up coming to her bed or not. She knew before asking him to marry her that he was brash and a bit quick-tempered, bold and daring. Of course his manly pride would have to exert itself after the blunt way she usurped the typically male role. She mustn't be surprised if he insisted on claiming his husbandly rights, just to establish who was the master in their marriage, no matter whose money supported them.

But he was saving her from Lucien. Katherine realized how thoroughly as the innkeeper showed her and Birdie to a large, clean room. The captain might have asked her to stay here tonight for his own purposes as well—he wouldn't want his wealthy bride to change her mind overnight and refuse to wed him after all—but at least he had the courtesy to present it in a light beneficial to her. Now there was no way Lucien could thwart her plans since they would be accomplished before he even knew what they were.

The men left them at the door, the captain with a polite kiss on her hand and a gleaming look that almost made her blush again. "Good night, sir," she told him primly, closing the door in his face, listening to his muted laugh as he walked away. *Convenience,* she reminded herself.

"Oh, madam," said Birdie on a sigh. "I do hope you know what you've gotten into."

Not anymore, whispered a nervous voice in her head. "Don't worry, Birdie," she replied. "Everything will be fine."

Chapter 7

The next morning, Katherine rose early. She dressed again in her fawn dress, the silk sadly crumpled despite Birdie's efforts to lay it flat on the table. The innkeeper sent up a tray with breakfast, and on it were a brush and comb along with some orange water. Birdie dampened her hair and combed out all the curls Katherine's mother insisted she wear, but then there was nothing they could do except pin it up in a plain chignon. Her hair, though shiny and thick, was absolutely, hopelessly, plain and straight. Katherine dabbed the orange water behind her ears, grateful she would smell nice if nothing else, and went down to meet her bridegroom.

He looked fresh and handsome, dazzlingly masculine in his scarlet coat and tall, polished boots. He was signing the register as she came downstairs and glanced up at her from beneath a rumpled wave of dark hair falling over his brow. His blue eyes gleamed as he flashed her a quick smile. It was all Katherine could do to nod in reply. Good gracious; she was taken off guard by how very attractive he was in the full light of day, freshly shaved and washed, wearing his spotless uniform. It was almost impossible to credit that this man, this dashing, virile son of one of the oldest and noblest families in England, was going to marry *her*. He must be absolutely desperate for the money, she told herself, waiting as he paid the innkeeper and crossed the room to where she stood with Birdie.

"Good morning, my dear," he said, bowing.

"Good morning, sir." She bobbed a curtsey. "I trust you haven't lost your nerve."

"It would take a bit more than you to make me lose my nerve," he said. "Have you eaten?"

She nodded. A cup of tea had been more than enough.

He tugged on his gloves and set his hat on his head, tilted rakishly, then offered his arm without another word. Telling herself not to be a goose, Katherine placed her hand on his wrist and followed him out. In the courtyard, a driver jumped down from the box of his carriage as they approached. "Good day, ma'am," he said, sweeping off his cap as he held the door open for her. The captain handed her inside, then Birdie, and climbed in himself.

Birdie wedged herself next to Katherine in the seat and sat watching the captain opposite them with thin-lipped suspicion. Katherine would have to remind her later to be more respectful, but today she was so on edge herself, she let it go. For his part, the captain merely smiled at them. "I hope you slept well."

"Yes," said Katherine.

"Tolerably," sniffed Birdie.

"If I'd had any way to contact you, I would have suggested such a course earlier, so you could prepare."

"You explained it with perfect logic last night," Katherine replied. "I should have thought of it myself."

He wore that faint, irritating, little smile again. "But you couldn't know which way my decision would go. How awkward it would have been had you arrived with luggage, and I declined."

"You've got the right of that," said Birdie under her breath. Katherine could tell it wasn't anger but anxiety making Birdie so testy. He wasn't helping with his air of general good humor and witty comments. Katherine had never been good at that sort of thing; it made her feel sluggish and stupid, and instinctively she tried to cut him off.

"If you want me to fall at your feet in gratitude, Captain, you shall wait in vain," she told him with frosty calm. "I don't think this arrangement serves you very ill."

"No, it benefits me greatly."

"It benefits us both," she said sharply. He met her eyes for a moment, then smiled again. He had a way of looking at her that made her think of Birdie's words the other night, that he would work out all her secrets. Katherine felt like the most appalling dunce when he looked at her that way. She was an oddity, a curiosity to him, and she hated it. Unfortunately she had no idea how to change it. She turned to look out the window just as the carriage slowed and halted.

"We've already arrived?" she exclaimed. "Why, we could have walked so short a distance!"

"My aunt would blister my ears if I made my bride walk to the church on her wedding day," her soon-to-be-husband replied. He opened the door and got out before helping down Birdie, then her. When she stood beside him, he kept hold of her hand until she looked up at him. "Last chance, love," he murmured. "Are you ready? 'Til death do us part, after this."

The future loomed before her, blindingly, frighteningly, blank. It could be lovely, or horrible, but at least it was her own choice. She pulled her hand from his. "Yes." Holding her cloak around her, she started up the steps of the small church, the captain following. The vicar was waiting for them, smiling broadly, and they all went into the church, Katherine feeling anxious and somehow excited, Birdie looking grim, and the captain far too calm and relaxed.

The ceremony was over quickly, with but two surprises. The first came at the beginning, when the vicar's wife came out to serve as witness and handed Katherine a lovely bouquet of pink rosebuds, barely open and still so fresh, they had a few drops of dew clinging to the petals. When Katherine stammered an astonished thanks, the woman pressed her hand and leaned forward to whisper that of course it was her bridegroom who sent them early that morning. Katherine looked at him from beneath her eyelashes, wondering what he meant by it, but he paid her no mind as he conversed quietly with the vicar.

The second surprise came near the end of the ceremony. When the vicar asked the captain to put the ring on her finger, Katherine expected a plain narrow band, or even none at all. Instead he placed a beautifully shaped gold ring on her finger. She barely had time to look at it before the vicar was pronouncing them man and wife. Her new husband looked down at her with his wicked grin, and for a moment she thought he was going to kiss her again as he had last night, right there in front of Birdie and the vicar and his wife. She braced herself, but he had already turned away to shake the vicar's hand. Katherine let out her breath slowly, both disappointed and relieved.

Birdie bustled up and kissed her on the cheek. "I wish you great joy," she said in a trembling voice. "Truly I do, my dear."

"Thank you, Birdie." Katherine squeezed her hand. "I owe you a great debt for helping me do this."

Her abigail cast a speculative glance at the captain. "I hope it brings you the peace and contentment you desire, and not . . ." She stopped and shook her head. "At least he brought a proper ring."

"And flowers." Katherine held them up. "I didn't expect that." She turned her hand from side to side, studying the ring. It was delicately curved in the shape of a curling vine, etched with flowers and leaves. She stole another look at the man who had put it on her finger. He was tall and handsome, nobly connected—for now—and even thoughtful. Perhaps they would come to know each other well enough to share affection, even love. Perhaps in time theirs would blossom from a marriage of convenience, forged out of mutual need for what the other had, to something better. Perhaps . . .

The vicar escorted them to the vestry to sign the register. The captain signed his name with a flourish and handed her the pen. Katherine peeked at his name—Gerard Philip Francis de Lacey—before signing her own. Next to his vibrant scrawl, hers looked small and insignificant. Just like everything else about the pair of us, she thought with a sigh.

He was watching her, and when she laid down the pen, he pulled her a little apart from the others. Birdie started to follow, but he gave her such a look, she stopped in her tracks. Birdie glanced to Katherine in appeal, but she shook her head. He was her husband now, and he had the right to talk to her. And she had better get used to it just as much as Birdie.

"We'll go to Portman Square next," he told her. "You need to pack your things and make arrangements for what cannot be taken with us. It will have to be sent along later. However, we don't have much time. I had intended to be gone already."

She nodded. "I understand. It won't take long to pack."

"Do you expect Lord Howe to cause a scene?"

She swallowed hard. "I don't know. He may. If my mother is there, you may depend on her causing one." She glanced up at him. "I am sorry—"

He laughed. "Don't worry, love. I have no objection to scenes—I'm perfectly capable of causing one myself. I just wanted to know what to expect. We'll be all right, hmm?" Still smiling, he tipped up her chin and kissed her on the mouth. The kiss was soft and light, but bowled her over just as much as the one last night had done. When he lifted his head a moment later, she almost toppled right into him. He caught her against him very naturally, but Katherine wiggled away, flustered by her uncharacteristic lack of composure.

"Your marriage lines, my lord, my lady," said the vicar behind her. She turned and managed a smile for him. The man beamed back at her, as he had done all morning. The captain must have told him some nonsense about their marriage, or else the man was a grinning fool.

Her husband reached out and took the two pieces of paper from the vicar, handing one to Katherine. "Should Lord Howe require proof," he murmured as he stuffed his copy, unread, into his coat.

Katherine scanned the marriage certificate. Katherine Howe, widow, aged 30 . . . Gerard de Lacey, bachelor, aged 28 . . . Oh heavens. Her face heated as she quickly folded the paper and slipped it into her cloak pocket. She was two years older than he!

"Are you ready, Lady Gerard?" her husband asked. He extended his hand and winked at her.

She was Lady Gerard de Lacey now, no longer Viscountess Howe. Her first husband never winked at her, and even though Katherine reminded herself this marriage was no more founded on love than her first had been, a hesitant smile crept over her face all the same. He looked just as boyish as she remembered him when he winked. She put her hand in his. "Yes, Captain."

He pulled her close again and leaned down. "Gerard," he breathed in her ear. "Unless you plan to follow my every order, like a cavalryman."

"That's really not necessary," she whispered back.

His fingers tightened on hers. "Today it is."

She took a deep breath. It seemed he was determined to continue this farce of intimacy. "Very well. Gerard." Just his name tasted sweet and dangerous on her tongue, much like his kiss. She looked up into his laughing blue eyes and wondered if she hadn't made a terrible mistake after all.

Chapter 8

Gerard thought his bride was tensed up so tightly she might snap under the strain as the carriage rolled toward Portman Square. Her fingers were knotted in her lap, her mouth was one thin line, and he didn't think she'd moved except to breathe since they left the church. Her maid had assumed the air of a warrior girding for battle, which sat rather oddly on her plump, dowdy form. He wondered what sort of confrontation they were dreading, then decided he didn't much care. Gerard's pocket crinkled with the legal, binding proof of his marriage, and if Lord Howe had any dispute with it, he would be happy to unleash Edward's expensive solicitors on the viscount.

The thought of his brother made him pause. He really ought to take Katherine around to Durham House and introduce her to Edward, and possibly even let Charlie meet her. Aunt Margaret would be very irked at him for not bringing Katherine to tea with her, as the only female relation in his family. Of course, visiting family would consume the rest of the day at the very least, and probably more—he would surely face an inquisition from Edward about his sudden and unexpected choice of wife—so Gerard brushed the idea away. He had more pressing things to deal with and could always write to his brothers and let them know.

He looked at his new bride again and felt a hard, smooth pulse of satisfaction. He'd wanted a wealthy wife, and now he had one. It freed him entirely from worries about his private finances and allowed him to devote himself wholly to preserving his family's place. Whatever else happened, he had secured his own career and home. He still meant to find the villain who had blackmailed his father and threatened him and his brothers, but Gerard was positively roaring with triumph inside his own head. Her family came from trade, but he didn't give a damn since her fortune more than compensated for it. She wasn't a beauty, but she was clever and quick, and no shrinking violet. Outwardly she appeared prim and somber, but there'd been a moment, when he kissed her last night, when Gerard thought to himself that it might be a pleasure to melt away her chilly shell. That there was passion and heat in her, deeply hidden and suppressed or perhaps merely left fallow. It didn't sound as though Howe had been a devoted husband, years older and interested mainly in her money. Gerard had married her for the money as well, but he intended to find more in his marriage—if possible, his wife's unplumbed sensuality.

He was quite distracted by the thought of teaching her all manner of erotic skills—if she knew absolutely nothing about pleasing a man, he could teach her exactly what he liked best—when he realized the carriage was stopping. Neither of the women said anything. They both looked as grim and nervous as raw soldiers facing their first battle, and Gerard wondered what sort of monster they were facing in Lucien Howe.

Or rather, what sort of monster *he* was facing. This was his part, after all, the reason why Katherine had come to him and made her blunt proposal. He was her knight, Sir Gawain to Lord Howe's dragon. Accordingly he stepped down from the carriage and straightened his jacket, cocked his hat at the proper angle, and held out a hand for his bride. "Shall we, my dear?" he asked with a confident smile.

Her hand felt cold and stiff in his. She tried to pull loose the second her feet were on the pavement, but Gerard maintained his grip. He lowered his head, and said softly, "Don't show your apprehension. You were perfectly entitled to wed whomever you chose. He can't do anything to you."

She flashed him a doubtful look but nodded and tucked her hand more securely around his arm. Together they went up the few steps to the house, from which Gerard could already hear the sounds of tumult.

He had to knock three times before anyone came to the door. The flustered servant who finally yanked it open barely looked at them. "Yes, sir?" he said breathlessly. Then his eyes landed on Katherine, and he froze like a startled deer.

"Is Lord Howe in, Hardy?" she asked. Gerard was silently impressed by how calm she sounded.

His mouth sagged open. "Y-yes, my lady." He collected himself and stepped back, so they could enter.

Gerard handed over his hat and took the cloak from her shoulders, listening to the sounds of a house being searched.

The servant didn't seem to know what to do; he hesitated, looking at Katherine, then up the stairs. "We will wait in the drawing room," she told him, and made a tiny motion with one hand. "Tell Lord Howe."

"Yes, madam," said the footman in relief. He bounded away, and Gerard followed his wife into a simple but elegant drawing room. It paled next to Durham House, Gerard's family's town house, but he could see the expense that had gone into it. Howe had made good use of Katherine's money.

"He's bound to be angry," Katherine said, very softly.

Gerard shrugged. "I thought we were past caring what he thought."

Some color came back into her cheeks, and she nodded. He could tell she was still uneasy, though. He slipped his arm around her waist and drew her near. She came reluctantly, as if she were uncomfortable being held, but when he raised her chin to look at him, her eyes were all but pleading. He smiled. "Don't worry," he whispered. "All will be well."

"I hope so." None of the tension faded from her face, which irked him. She must have thought him up to this task. It was a little annoying that she couldn't show her faith by at least breathing normally.

The door was thrown open then, and a man strode into the room, only to stop short. "Katherine!"

She tried to jump back, but Gerard tightened his arm around her. There was no reason Lucien Howe shouldn't know from the beginning she belonged to him now.

Howe's expression of blank shock transformed in an instant into icy, furious comprehension. "Katherine," he said again, his voice brittle. "How good of you to come home, after frightening us all out of our wits by going missing. Your mother has been frantic with worry."

"I must take the blame for that, sir," said Gerard, before she could speak. "I refused to let her return home—I feared if I let her go, she might change her mind and never see me again."

Howe looked between the two of them. He clearly understood what was happening. "Indeed."

Katherine stirred in his arm, and this time Gerard let her step away. "I'm sorry to have caused worry here, Lucien," she said. "But I have some news." She hesitated, glancing at Gerard from the corner of her eye. "Very happy news. May I present to you Captain Lord Gerard de Lacey . . . my husband."

A muscle twitched in Howe's jaw as he glared at her. He was a handsome fellow, with wavy blond hair brushed back from his high forehead and piercing blue eyes. His clothing was austere in style though very high in quality. But there was nothing of joviality about him, and he looked as kind and warm as a fireplace poker. For once Lady Eccleston had been unerring in her assessment. Howe was exactly the sort of starched, pompous arse Gerard hated, and instinctively he warmed to the battle.

"You are married?" It sounded as though Howe was biting off each word.

Gerard smiled broadly. "This very morning! Naturally we should have taken a bit more time, had a bit more of a celebration, but I insisted until Kate finally agreed with me." He caught her hand half-way through this declaration, so felt her start at the nickname. He winked at her and pressed her knuckles to his lips. "I'm rather impatient where she's concerned."

"Gerard," she said in the same quiet, placid voice as before, "do let me introduce you. This is Lord Lucien Howe, my late husband's nephew."

"A pleasure, sir." Gerard bowed. Howe barely returned it.

"I've come to pack my things," Katherine went on. "My husband has business out of town, and we must be on our way soon. I'm sorry to be so abrupt."

"Yes," said Howe tightly. "I imagine you are."

"I would like to see Mama before we go," she said. "Is she here?"

Howe jerked his head in a nod. Katherine released Gerard's hand; he wondered if she realized that she'd been clinging to him more than he'd been clinging to her. But her regal manner hadn't betrayed any sign of it. "Let me fetch her," she said to him. "I would like to introduce you to her."

"Of course, my dear. I cannot wait to meet your mother."

She nodded and left. Howe silently stepped out of her way and closed the door when she was gone. He walked back across the room toward Gerard, arms folded over his chest. "I should sue you for damages."

"Damages?" Gerard affected surprise. "For what?"

"A hasty marriage, without word to the bride's family . . . How dare you swindle us this way?"

"She's not your daughter. I wonder what claim you could lay to her at all, as a widow of legal age and no blood relation to you. And what, pray, are your losses?"

Howe's gaze narrowed. "De Lacey . . . Yes . . . I've heard of you: the Durham Dilemma."

Gerard cursed inside his head but kept the careful smile fixed on his face. He flicked one hand. "I see you read the gossip rags. Very amusing, isn't it, what people come up with?"

"Everyone's speaking of it." Howe came slowly nearer, studying Gerard with shrewd eyes. "So that's why you married her," he murmured. "Very clever, de Lacey."

"You've no idea why I married her, nor would you understand if I told you," Gerard replied. He found himself wanting to punch Howe, right in his perfectly shaped nose. He propped a fist on his hip. "But I do assure you, it's done. What God hath joined together, and all that."

"You're just as badly in want of money as I am." Howe smirked, but it was bitter and vicious. "Everyone knows you'll be declared a bastard by the end of the Season."

Gerard bared his teeth smiling back. "Care to make a wager to that effect?"

Howe just looked superior—smug. Infuriatingly so.

"That does remind me," Gerard went on. He hadn't planned to twist the knife in Howe, but he had no qualm about doing it. "Naturally I'm reviewing my wife's property, and her solicitor mentioned there is a promissory note against your estate. I gather you've not read the terms of that note?" The viscount's glare turned murderous. "No? Well, there's plenty of time. Tyrell implied no payments had been made thus far, which I'm sure you'll rectify at once. I believe the security is a fair piece of your property, which will become mine in default." He smiled again. "I should hate to wreck such an old and respectable estate."

"This is intolerable," Howe seethed, his face as dark as a thundercloud. "You know very well what you've done to me!"

There were times Gerard particularly enjoyed being taller than average. He folded his arms and looked down at the other man. "Of all the people you might blame for your situation, I should be low on the list, and Katherine even lower. One hates to speak ill of the dead, but your uncle really did you no favors."

"Katherine had a duty," spat out Howe, "one she has clearly chosen to ignore."

"What duty did she have to you?" Gerard lost his smile. "Now her duty is to me, and mine to her. I trust everyone will keep that in mind."

Whatever Howe would have said was lost. Katherine opened the door and came in, followed closely by a very beautiful woman. Even with Lady Eccleston's advance warning, Gerard was taken aback by the delicacy of her features. He barely restrained himself from looking at her daughter, his wife, in disbelief. They looked absolutely nothing alike—and yet were mother and daughter.

"Mama, may I present to you my husband, Captain Lord Gerard de Lacey," Katherine murmured. "Sir, this is my mother, Mrs. Hollenbrook."

Gerard bowed deeply to his mother-in-law. Up

close one could see the lines at Mrs. Hollenbrook's mouth and the corners of her eyes, but that was the only sign she was old enough to have a grown daughter. Her hair was pure gold, arranged in glossy ringlets after the latest fashion. Her skin was as unblemished and pale as new porcelain. Her eyes were crystal-clear blue, thickly lashed; it was perhaps the only feature her daughter shared, Gerard thought, although Kate's eyes were darker. Mrs. Hollenbrook's figure was superb, and she had all the grasp of flattering fashion her daughter lacked.

Mrs. Hollenbrook's eyes widened even more as she took him in. "Oh, my," she said in a light, silvery voice. "What a surprise—and a pleasure—to make your acquaintance, sir."

"And I yours, madam."

"It would have been proper to have this introduction sooner," she said with a reproving glance at her daughter. "I understand you are already married."

"Happily so, Mrs. Hollenbrook, despite our lack of propriety." He flashed a warm look at Katherine, who regarded him steadily without a trace of smile. She looked so somber and grave, one would think she wasn't happy with the marriage even though she had initiated it and pursued it. "Come, Kate, don't be so severe on me," he added, trying for a penitent expression when he really wanted to throw up his hands in exasperation. Couldn't she at least pretend? "I've taken all the blame for the importunate speed of our union. Can you not forgive me, dearest?"

Her mother turned to her in surprise. "Good heavens, Katherine. He *wanted* to marry you?"

"Of course he did," said Howe coldly. "He's one of the Durham sons, ma'am."

"Ah!" Her face lit with delight. "The Duke of Durham's sons! Three of the most eligible bachelors in England!"

"Not any longer," muttered Lucien Howe.

"And one wanted my Katherine!" Mrs. Hollenbrook beamed at Gerard, ignoring Howe's remark. "Well, I might have hoped for the eldest, but you're quite a handsome fellow."

Gerard ignored the shaded compliment to himself, caught up in watching Kate. He already liked that nickname very much; she should try being Kate instead of Katherine. She stood in silence as her mother expressed amazement that anyone wanted her, let alone one of the Durham family. There was an air of remoteness about her, as if she was accustomed to this and had managed to distance herself from it. He frowned slightly. Surely a mother would think more of her child.

"Thank you, Mrs. Hollenbrook, but as long as my wife prefers me to my brothers, I shall be content," he said. "I am the tallest, you know."

She laughed. "And devilishly charming, I see. Well! This is all quite a shock, but you are very welcome to our family. We all thought Katherine would marry dear Lucien, so you must forgive some upset on his part."

Gerard smiled. "Of course. In his place I should feel devastated to have lost her. Rest assured I shall appreciate my good fortune all the rest of my days."

"Mama, I must pack," said Katherine quietly.

"The captain has business out of town, and we are leaving today."

"Oh, no!" Her mother's eyes rounded. "Leaving? Of course you may not go! We must have a wedding breakfast—Katherine, whatever *are* you wearing? And your hair is simply frightful. Lucien, dear, send for tea, so we may get to know my new son-in-law better. Katherine, do go up and change into something more flattering."

"This is my best dress, Mama," Katherine said. Her mother blinked at the dress as if she'd never seen it before. "And I will change, but into my traveling clothes."

Mrs. Hollenbrook's eyes welled up. She put one hand to her lips. "You cannot go," she said plaintively. "Can a mother not celebrate her daughter's wedding? You must stay the night at the very least. We must send word to the newspapers—my daughter, married to a Durham! You'll need wedding clothes, Katherine, and really, my dear, you must call on at least a few people—imagine, a Durham! Everyone will want to meet him, dearest. We'll be invited to dine everywhere, and it would be very bad of us not to accept. No, you simply cannot leave before the end of the week."

"No, Mama," Katherine tried to say.

A tear leaked from her mother's eye, then another. It looked natural, but Gerard had a feeling Mrs. Hollenbrook could weep on a moment's notice. "Katherine, dear, how can you be so cruel to your mother? And at such a happy time. Lucien, you must help me persuade her."

"Clearly I am not good at persuading her," replied

Howe, still glowering at Katherine. Gerard wondered again that she could stand this torrent of pressure and pleas. Perhaps this was why she chose to sneak off in the dark of night to propose her bargain to him.

"As much as it pains me, dear madam," he said, stepping into the breach once more, "we must be off. My affairs require it. However, I feel certain there will be a great ball at Durham House later this Season to celebrate; my brothers will want to welcome my wife to our family just as warmly as you have added me to yours, and my aunt, the Countess of Dowling, will be over the moon at having another female in the family at last. I feel certain there will be celebration in excess, in due time. But for today, to my sorrow"—he lifted her hand to his lips—"we must say farewell." He turned to his wife. "Kate, darling, we must be on our way."

"I—yes," she said. "I shall go make sure Birdie packs everything."

He beamed at her. "Excellent. I'll come with you." And he walked out of the room, taking her with him despite the open astonishment on Mrs. Hollenbrook's face and the thunderous scowl on Lord Howe's.

"Wait!" she exclaimed, as he hurried her up the stairs. "You don't have to come with me!"

"We'll never get out of here if your mother has her way," he muttered. "This room?"

She nodded, and he turned into the open door near the stairs. It was a modest room, with all the severity of the drawing room below and little of the elegance. Mrs. Dennis was already digging in the bureau drawers, and she looked up in shock at his appearance in the room. "We're traveling lightly," he informed both women. "Whatever you can't fit in one valise must stay behind. The rest will have to be sent on later."

"My lady needs a trunk at least," protested Mrs. Dennis.

Gerard cocked an eyebrow. "One valise," he repeated. "And we leave within the hour."

His wife stared at him, dazed. "Birdie, you'd better go pack your own things," she said at last. "I shall manage."

"Excellent thought," Gerard said. "One valise, Mrs. Dennis." She glared at him but whisked out the door. He turned to his wife. "What do you need?"

She hesitated, then went to the bureau. "Unmentionables."

He grinned at her rigid back. "Very well." He scooped up her hairbrush and comb from the dressing table and put them in the valise. There was very little in the room. "Are you taking this?" He picked up the book from the table by the chair. *Tillotson's Sermons.* He tried not to make a face. God help him if he had to watch her read this every night.

She took it from him and dropped it back on the table with a thump. "No."

"Good."

She glanced guardedly at him but continued packing. A stack of white linen went into the bag— unmentionables, of course—two pairs of plain sturdy shoes, and some dresses, all in plain, dark colors. "Do you not like bright colors?" he couldn't help asking. Gerard didn't think of himself as a dandy, but he felt like a peacock in his scarlet coat and white breeches, compared to his wife in her brown dress.

"They don't suit me." She put a thick shawl into the valise. Gray, of course.

"That wasn't what I asked." He looked at her critically. "I think red would suit you."

Her head whipped up. "Red!"

"Yes. Perhaps blue as well. To match your eyes."

"I have a blue dress." She touched one dress, a blue so deep it was almost black.

"I meant something pretty," he said bluntly.

For a moment she said nothing, just stood staring into her valise. "You don't have to try to make me prettier, Captain. It's hopeless."

He crossed the room and lifted her chin, inspecting her features. "You're not a beauty like your mother; is that what you're trying to tell me? Well, don't bother. I can see for myself very well how you look. If you prefer brown, I shan't strip it from you. But for myself, I find a bit of color very beneficial to the spirits. You can't have missed how dashing and magnificent I look in my red coat." He purposely puffed out his chest, and a faint bit of pink came into her cheeks. He leaned down until their faces were very close. "You might try it, eh? Just one red dress, to humor me."

"Perhaps," she murmured.

He grinned. "Excellent. And my name is Gerard." Then he kissed her. He meant it to be light and chaste since they really did need to be on their way soon. But this time she opened her mouth at once, and he couldn't help tasting her. And there it was again, that flickering spark of passion. She didn't precisely kiss him back, but she wasn't a limp doll, either. Almost without thought, his arm went around her, and he drew her into him, deepening the kiss. He felt the tension in her shoulders and unconsciously spread his hand on her back, circling his fingers. The taut muscles under his fingertips softened, and then she all but melted into him. Her fingers curled into the folds of his sleeves, and she rose up against him.

That was enough for Gerard. He slid his hand around the curve of her skull to hold her just so, and took ownership of her mouth. Aside from the soft bursts of her breath coming faster and faster against his skin, she didn't flinch as he delved deep into her mouth, languorously sliding his tongue across hers. He shifted his grip to brush his thumb over her jaw. She had lovely, soft skin, and for the first time he felt a genuine urgency to explore the rest of her. She was a challenge, and by God he loved a challenge, but now she was also his wife—his to kiss, his to hold, his to bed, and his to bring to the pinnacle of pleasure . . .

He lifted his head and looked down at her. Her eyelashes fluttered open, and for a moment her eyes were as deep and clear as the summer sky at twilight, not cold or reserved at all.

"You always look so surprised when I kiss you," he murmured. "Do you not like it?"

She flinched as if she'd just been accused of some terrible crime. "I—I don't know."

Gerard smiled a little. He couldn't help it. "Don't worry, love. You will." He turned away to collect more for her valise, and in the mirror caught sight of her reflection. She stood very still, then raised one hand and hesitantly touched her lips. His eyes narrowed; what the devil was she thinking? But then she looked up and met his gaze in her mirror. Her hand fell, and she turned away.

He stole a bemused glance at her over his shoulder. No man with any sense in his head made the mistake of thinking he understood women, but he was utterly mystified by this one. She had asked him to marry her but didn't expect him to touch her. When he did, she responded with alacrity—shy and inexperienced she might be, but there was a thread of yearning in her kiss. The instant he released her, though, she acted as violated as a nun.

Well. They had years to sort that out between them. Today he intended to finally escape London and begin his pursuit of the blackmailer before the scoundrel did any more damage to his family's name. Personal pleasures would have to wait a while.

Chapter 9

Not until they were bundled into the hired coach did Katherine have time to really think about what had happened. Birdie kept yawning behind her hand until she finally dropped off to sleep two miles or so out of London. That left her in peace, finally alone to contemplate the consequences of her actions. The captain was riding his horse, and she could see him if she sat forward and craned her neck out the window. She'd already done it twice and refused to do it again. There was little reason to. He was stuck with her now, and she with him.

She had never seen anyone manage her mother quite as well as he did. When the captain told her they planned to leave within an hour of arriving in Portman Square, Mama laid out every excuse Katherine expected. Normally people, particularly men, were so moved by Mama's pleas that they gave in at once, or certainly once she began weeping so beautifully and so sadly. Somehow Captain de Lacey made Mama smile instead—mentioning a grand ball at Durham House was a master stroke—and got them out the door in exactly an hour. The same carriage they had ridden in to the church had evidently been hired to take them wherever he was going. After a detour through Holborn, where Mr. Tyrell wished them happy and duly recorded their marriage, the carriage turned west, driving past Hyde Park Corner and out of London. Katherine was sure she'd left behind a hundred things she would need, and Birdie seemed permanently outraged by his peremptory behavior; but somehow Katherine felt more relief than anything else. As expected, Lucien was no match for the tall and confident captain. Her new husband was like a force of nature. And just like that, she was being whisked away from her old constrained and quiet life to a new life, one of which she had absolutely no conception.

It was a little unnerving, she supposed. Part of her was increasingly worried she'd gotten herself married to someone so different from herself that they would never understand each other. But she couldn't deny that part of her was breathless with hope. He smiled at her, and kissed her, even when he didn't need to for appearances' sake. He called her Kate. He could be everything she hoped for . . .

No sooner than this thought crossed her mind, Katherine reminded herself not to presume. Above all, theirs was a practical marriage. Their real future wouldn't become apparent for weeks and months, when the novelty and first rush of gratitude had worn off on both sides. Lord Howe had been a kind husband in the beginning as well, no doubt from being so flush with cash again. She would do well to remind herself how he'd been after a few years of marriage, when he couldn't wait to be off to London without her and looked bored and impatient every time she opened her mouth.

The miles rolled on. It was just after noon when they started, and the captain didn't show much interest in pausing to rest. They only stopped to change horses after a few hours, which gave Katherine and Birdie a welcome chance to stretch their legs and attend to other needs.

"How much longer do you suppose we're to ride?" Birdie asked, as they took a turn around the coaching yard. She looked a little pale and drawn, but at least she had ceased muttering indignantly.

"I don't know." They were on the Bristol Road, but otherwise Katherine had no idea where they were headed. He hadn't said, and she hadn't asked.

Birdie sighed, wincing as she walked. "Goodness, m'lady, I know he's what you wanted, but he certainly is a man of action!"

"I know," Katherine replied, "and so far it's worked out rather well for us. I never thought Lucien would just let us walk away like that."

"We've not heard the last from him, mark my words." Birdie pressed her hands to her lower back and groaned. Katherine rolled her shoulders, trying to stretch discreetly. The captain had disappeared into the coaching inn when they arrived. She walked toward the door and spied him laughing with some other men in the taproom, a mug of ale in his hand. She wondered how he could do that, be so jovial with complete strangers. He was the son of a duke yet was talking so freely with coach drivers and farmers, one would never guess his origins. She knew people thought she was cold and aloof, but part of her longed to be able to laugh so freely, like he did. Perhaps she could learn the trick from him and not find herself always on the outer edge of every social gathering. She hoped she could puzzle it out before she gave her new husband a complete disgust of her, as she had done to her first husband.

As she watched, a serving maid brought out a basket, batting her eyelashes and swishing her skirts as she handed it to the captain. Katherine felt her stomach clench as she watched for his reaction, but he merely smiled at the girl and drained his tankard before heading out the door, right toward where his bride stood spying on him. Katherine scurried back to Birdie's side as he emerged into the late-afternoon sunlight and joined them.

"Got some feeling back in your feet?" He grinned at her. "I apologize for the haste, but it can't be helped."

"Where are we going?" asked Katherine, conscious of Birdie's aching back.

"Bath," he said. "I need to find someone there."

"Bath is still seventy miles away!"

"We'll stop for the night in a few hours." He walked them back to the carriage, newly harnessed to a fresh team of horses, and helped them both inside. He handed Katherine the covered basket. "My apologies we can't stop for proper tea." He winked at her and closed the door. A few moments later he was back on his own horse, directing the driver. With a jerk the carriage started forward again.

"Well." Birdie was digging in the basket. "At least he has some consideration." She held up rolls, a wedge of cheese, some sliced cold tongue wrapped in a napkin, pears, and a corked jug that turned out to contain cider, tart and cool.

"He has more than *some* consideration, Birdie." Katherine's eyes fell on the bouquet of pink roses, tucked in the seat corner. She'd kept them from the church. They weren't even drooping yet. Where had he gotten roses on such short notice?

"I know, madam," Birdie said in a softer tone. "I pray he has far more of it than we've seen so far, even."

Katherine went still as she grasped Birdie's meaning. Tonight was her wedding night. To a man she hardly knew. Her lips tingled as she recalled his kiss, how gentle and yet how masterful. And he said he planned to make love to her . . . tonight? In an inn on the side of the road? Would it be like his kiss, seductive and sweet, or would he do it just to get it over with? And what should she do? "That's enough, Birdie," she said coolly. Chastened, the abigail said nothing more of it.

By the time they turned into another coaching inn, twilight was falling. When Katherine stepped down from the carriage, her knees almost buckled and gave out. The captain, holding her hand, caught her before she could fall and put his arm around her as he escorted her into the inn. He said a few words to the innkeeper, and soon they were being shown to a large room, plain but tidy, with a fire already laid in the hearth. Her husband helped her to the armchair near the fireplace.

"Feeling a bit sore?" She nodded, and he flashed her a sympathetic look. "I'm very sorry for it. I have to see to my horse, but I can send for a bath if you'd like."

As tempting as it sounded, Katherine thought of his walking in on her as she bathed and shook her head. The servants had brought his luggage and hers into the room; naturally, since they were husband and wife now. "Thank you, no. I shall wash up as usual."

"Very good. I'll arrange for dinner." He left, and she heard his voice in the corridor outside, telling the innkeeper to send warm water for her to wash in and a large dinner with good wine. Birdie tapped at the door when his footsteps died away and slipped into the room at Katherine's summons.

"It's about time we stopped," she muttered. "Will you bathe, madam?"

"Not tonight. We shall have another long day on the roads tomorrow." Katherine caught Birdie's wince. "Just help me undress, then you may go to bed, Birdie. I'll arrange for a dinner tray for you."

"His Lordship already did so," her servant said. "Just now, outside the door. I credit him this, madam, he's taking proper care of you."

Katherine smiled thinly as she pushed herself back onto her stiff legs. "I take it you're growing fonder of him, then."

Birdie sniffed. "I'd take a stick to him if he didn't see to your comfort after the jolting he put us through today."

"You won't take a stick to anyone, any more than you would have done to Lord Howe," Katherine said sharply. She knew Birdie meant nothing by her words and would never dare carry them out, but if the captain overheard her, it could go very badly for Birdie. Lucien would have sacked her for far less. "Don't say such nonsense."

Birdie pressed her lips together, but she came and started unlacing Katherine's traveling dress. "He's not the same sort as Lord Howe."

"Of course he's not. That doesn't mean you should forget yourself, even when he's not around." She pulled her arms out of the sleeves, and Birdie helped her wiggle out of the dress. She put on her nightdress and bundled up in her dressing gown. Servants came with wash water and got the fire going, which made the room cozy and warm in no time, and brought a large tray with dinner. Once she had washed up and Birdie had combed out her hair for the night, Katherine sent her abigail off to bed. With a worried but grateful look, Birdie left.

She sat down at the small table and peeked under the covers of the dishes. She was hungry, and it smelled good. The captain had been gone a long time, and she didn't know if he would expect her to wait for him. She held back as long as she could, but gradually the growling of her belly became too much to bear. It had been well over an hour since he left. Surely he would understand if she ate just a little. She lifted one cover again and sniffed.

The door burst open, and Katherine jerked backward in her chair. The captain strode in, his saddlebags over one shoulder and his hat in his hand. He closed the door and dropped the saddlebags on the floor near the hearth. "You've not eaten?" he asked, spying the still-covered dishes.

She shook her head. He was unbuttoning his coat. A moment later the bright scarlet jacket was hanging on the back of the spare chair, and he was working on his waistcoat. Katherine curled her toes under her feet. *Wedding night, wedding night, wedding night,* seemed to echo in her heartbeat.

"There was no need to wait," he said as he stripped off yet another layer of clothing. "You must be half-starved, and tired to boot." The waistcoat joined the coat. He untied his cravat and began unwinding it. Katherine watched from under her eyelashes as he moved about the room, utterly at ease, removing his watch from a pocket and rummaging in his saddle-bags. He looked so very big and male, even larger and more intimidating than when clothed, for now she could see the muscles in his throat and arms. Lord Howe had been a slender, elegant man. She didn't think she'd ever seen stubble on his face, unlike the dark bristles that shadowed Gerard de Lacey's jaw and throat, and she'd never watched Lord Howe undress.

He caught her watching him. "Aren't you hungry?" he asked in surprise. "I expected you to be starved after such a long day. You're as thin as a reed, Kate."

She cleared her throat. "Why do you call me that?"

He grinned. "Do you like it? I do."

"No one's ever called me Kate." Her father had called her Katie when she was a child, but her mother fretted over the low-class sound of it. By the time she was twelve, he never said it anymore.

"Unless you have a strenuous objection, I should like to call you that." He pulled loose the button at his shirt's neck and slipped the braces from his shoulders. He leaned over the basin and splashed a great quantity of water over his face and head, coming away dripping wet halfway down his chest. Katherine tried not to stare as he dried off.

"Do you?" he asked. The white linen of his shirt clung wetly to his shoulders. The vigorous toweling made his hair stand up in a riot of damp waves.

"Do I what?" she whispered. Somehow those curls in his hair appealed to her. She barely let herself look at his shoulders and arms, where muscles and sinew were perfectly outlined by the wet fabric.

"Have an objection to being called Kate." He dropped into the seat opposite her and began removing covers from the dishes. "I hope not. Are you hungry?"

Mutely she nodded. He looked pleased and heaped a plate for her, and an even larger one for himself. He poured the wine and set the tray aside. "May I call you Kate?" he asked again, and she realized he had asked twice already.

She drew a quick breath. "Of course."

"Very good," he murmured. "Kate."

Then they ate in near silence. She supposed she should say something, but between the fatigue of the journey, the stress of the last few days, and the nervous anticipation of the evening ahead, her tongue wouldn't move. She ate mechanically, consumed by what might come next. But although he ate with perfect manners, her husband seemed just as tired and quiet as she felt. Aside from refilling her wineglass, he left her alone.

When the meal was done, he rang for the servants to come take away the dishes. She ran her hands over her knees as they cleared the table and left. The door closed, and she was alone with him. The air felt thin. The fire seemed to blaze hotter than ever, and the room suddenly grew small. *Wedding night, wedding night.*

The captain appeared unaffected by similar nerves. He pulled off his boots and slumped in his chair, stretching out his feet toward the fire. His head fell back, and he sighed wearily.

She must have made some small noise, for he glanced at her. "Yes?"

Katherine wet her lips. She had to say something other than what she was thinking about, how very undressed he was becoming. "There is a hole in your stocking."

He raised his foot. The tip of his toe peeked through a small hole. "Ah. So there is. Bragg must have missed it."

"Your man?" she asked cautiously. "I did not realize . . ."

"I sent him on ahead," he said, when she fell silent. "My batman. A master of organization and efficiency." He wiggled his toes. "Except, obviously, for the mending."

"I could darn it for you," she offered.

"Thank you." He twisted in his chair to regard her with mild surprise. That rumpled wave of hair fell over his brow again. "We shall have to get to know each other, Kate. You're always so nervous when I look at you."

"I'm sorry." Unconsciously she straightened, smoothing her expression.

He sighed. "There's no need for that. Don't shy away from me."

Katherine didn't know what to do. "I'm not afraid of you," she insisted. "Do you think I would have proposed what I did if I feared you? No, I told you I esteem you very highly—"

"There's a vast gulf between esteem and affection." He rose from his chair and came to stand in front of her, hand extended. "Come here."

Slowly she put her hand in his and let him pull her to her feet. Heart thumping, muscles frozen, she waited as he brushed her hair back from her forehead, his large hands gentle. "You have nothing to fear," he whispered. "I'm here to protect you."

"Thank you." She cringed as she said it.

He tipped up her chin until she looked at him. His blue eyes were thoughtful. "I don't know what sort of chap Lord Howe was, but I gather he wasn't much like me. Rest assured I shan't beat you for disagreeing with me, or punish you for speaking your mind. And for God's sake stop thanking me. You've brought something of unquestionable value to this marriage, while time will only tell if you received as much in return." A corner of his mouth crooked up, and his eyes sparkled with mirth. "How are you to know if I'm preferable to Lucien?"

The very fact that you could ask the question, she thought. "I have no doubts, Captain."

He released her. "Gerard. You said it this morning."

She hesitated. "Gerard," she said softly.

"Much better." He yawned and stretched his arms overhead. The ceiling wasn't terribly low, but he could have pressed his palms against it. "Shall we go to bed? Tomorrow will be another long journey."

Her muscles knotted up even worse than before. Somehow she nodded. Katherine took off her dressing gown and laid it across the chair. She climbed into the bed, keeping self-consciously to one side, and stared at the ceiling as he moved about the room, tossing another log on the fire and shedding his breeches and stockings before blowing out the lamps. The whole mattress dipped as he slid in beside her.

"Good night, Kate," he murmured, leaning over her. His lips brushed hers, too lightly. "Sleep well."

"Good night," she whispered back.

He turned onto his back and after a moment of shifting was still. Within minutes his breathing deepened into the slow cadence of sleep. Katherine wished she could do the same. It was her wedding night, and even though she told herself it was a relief he hadn't tried to make love to her, part of her was irrationally let down. He had said he wanted to make love to her, and now that it was time, he went to sleep. She was sore and tired from the coach ride, but her mind refused to rest, not when he was lying beside her so close she could feel the warmth of his body. She lay listening to the sound of his breathing for some time, until she was certain he slept deeply, then slipped from the bed.

The room was dark, but the moon was near full. She pulled back the sturdy curtains at the window, letting a slice of pale moonlight fall across the bed, onto Gerard's face. She crept back across the room and settled herself in bed again, lying on her side facing him. For the first time she felt at liberty to look at him as much as she wanted, and she did so, as greedy as a hungry child left unattended with a whole pudding.

He had changed a great deal, but she would never forget her first sight of him more than a decade ago. She had walked into town by herself that day in search of the latest Gothic novel. Her mother had told her to go in the carriage, but Katherine wanted to be free to take her time, to dawdle along, to read a chapter or two if the novel proved engrossing. The rain put an end to that idea, of course; she'd had the book tucked tightly under her arms and cloak before she was halfway home. She was pretty well soaked to the skin, bonnet drooping hopelessly, when a horse pulled up beside her, its prancing hoofs splashing mud onto her skirt.

"Whoa, there!" The young man controlled his horse with ease. "It's rather a dreadful day for a walk, miss."

She remembered looking up in astonishment, shocked both that someone stopped to speak to her and at the manner of that address. Even on that rainy day, his blue eyes seemed dazzling. He was smiling at her, with an air of exuberant merriment about him quite at odds with the wretched weather. Somehow she gave a hesitant nod and mumbled something inane. He leaned down and extended his hand, sending a cascade of water from the brim of his hat. "May I take you up, miss?" he asked. "It's dashed cold in this rain."

The words would be forever branded on her memory. He had offered so gallantly, as if she were the town beauty instead of the plain, awkward daughter of an upstart merchant, as another young buck had once referred to her. And he was no ordinary young man being polite; Katherine knew exactly who he was once she got a good look at his face. The Duke of Durham's sons were famously regarded as the three most eligible gentlemen in Sussex. Katherine had seen all three in Henfield from time to time

but never spoken to any of them. The gentleman on
the horse was the youngest, a tall, lanky young man
with too-long dark hair falling over his brow in a
very dashing way—or as dashing as one could be,
dripping wet. He waggled his gloved fingers as she
continued to gaze dumbly at him. "Come," he added
in a cajoling tone. "Let me see you home."

Rain sluiced down the back of her neck, her boots
were ankle deep in mud, and she still had two miles
to go—and Katherine didn't know what to say. Who
would have guessed that a handsome gentleman,
the son of a duke, would ask to see her home when
she looked as though she'd been dragged through a
pond? "I don't mind the walk," she said stupidly.
His greatcoat was securely buttoned up to his chin,
and with his hat pulled low, he was about as dry as
anyone could be in the downpour. She had a sudden
fear that she would only prove herself a complete
idiot if she accepted his offer, and surely that would
be even worse than looking like one.

He laughed. "I would, in your place. You don't
want to take a chill; I would never forgive myself if
you did."

"It's not far," she protested weakly, even as her
hand rose toward his of its own volition.

"Then it will be no trouble at all. Come; put your
foot on mine—there—step up—and here you are."
With almost effortless ease he pulled her up onto
the saddle in front of him. Katherine balanced awkwardly, not sure what to cling to. He shifted behind
her, then folded the fronts of his coat around her, settling her securely against him. Underneath the greatcoat he was warm and dry, and the feel of his chest

at her back almost made her lungs stop working. She glanced down at the ground as he nudged the horse into motion. Far below, a veritable stream ran down the middle of the muddy, rutted lane where she had stood just moments ago.

Good heavens. This must be a dream, or perhaps a fit of delusion. She was riding in front of Lord Gerard de Lacey, wrapped in his greatcoat with his arm snug around her waist to hold her steady. Things like this did not happen to her. Any moment now, she would startle herself awake and be standing in the mud again.

"I hope you completed whatever errand brought you out into this gale." His voice rumbled in his chest, and his breath was warm on her cheek. Her heart seemed to be doing a dizzying dance inside her breast.

"I only wanted a book." She shifted it clumsily under her wet cloak. Why couldn't she think of something entertaining to say? "It was silly to go out just for that . . ."

"Nonsense," he said with another laugh. "Some things require urgent action."

She smiled in uneasy gratitude. "Thank you for taking me home."

"What sort of gentleman would leave a lady to walk in this?" A gust of wind threw a sheet of rain straight at them, and Katherine reflexively ducked into the shelter of his coat as the horse shied and snorted. His arms tightened around her as he brought the horse back under control, and for a moment she could almost pretend it was an embrace. She pressed her cheek against his lapel, inhaling the warm scent of his cravat, and a little piece of her heart fluttered helplessly.

The next two miles passed in the blink of an eye. He made a few jokes and good-natured curses about the weather, and she managed to smile and even laugh. This was unreal. She no longer felt the rain or the cold; instead she felt like a princess, safe in the arms of a handsome prince—she, who had never been sought out by any young man. When the gates of her home appeared, she was somewhat dismayed it was over.

"There is my gate," she said, turning her head to tell him.

"This one?" His blue eyes flashed, so very close to hers. "Shall I turn in?"

She shook her head. "Let me down at the gate, please."

Perhaps he understood that she preferred no one see her riding with him; he surely couldn't know why, but he merely nodded and halted the horse. He dismounted and lifted her down. "Safe and sound, I hope," he said with a grin. Before she could register his intent, he had caught her hand and brushed a soft kiss on her knuckles. "Take care to get warm and dry right away."

She nodded as he swung back into the saddle. "Thank you," she whispered.

He leaned down toward her and touched the brim of his hat. "It was my pleasure," he whispered back, and winked at her. Then he clucked to his horse and rode off at a brisk trot.

She stood at the gate for several minutes until he vanished into the gloomy rain without a backward glance. Her pulse hadn't recovered by the time she reached the house, nor even through the hot bath her mother insisted she take. She told no one about her rescuer; who would believe her if she did? In the days that followed, she nursed a number of secret fantasies wherein he returned to find her—to see that she hadn't taken a chill, to ask to take her riding again, to declare that he'd been unable to forget her. He never did, of course. She told herself not to be silly, but her heart proved itself very silly indeed where he was concerned.

Gerard de Lacey had lived in her memory since that rainy day as someone just shy of perfect. Katherine knew, of course, that she was quite below the notice of such a man. Even when Papa made his modest fortune into a large one, and Mama expressed a wish that Katherine were more of a beauty so she might have a chance of snaring one of the Durham sons, she knew it was ridiculous. It didn't stop her from watching for him every time she went into town, but Katherine was too practical to hold out foolish hopes. An older, widowed gentleman like Viscount Howe was a tremendous catch for someone like her, as Mama repeatedly told her. She did as her parents wished and married Lord Howe. Gerard de Lacey went off to fight Napoleon, his name appearing from time to time in the newspaper reports. Katherine prayed for his safety every night, for it hurt to think of that kind, charming young man dying on a distant battlefield. Her prayers were answered, for he returned whole and hearty to England, only to land in the newspapers again—but this time as a man about to be stripped of his illustrious inheritance and cast out of the social class he had been born to.

And now he was lying next to her in bed, her husband before God and man. With trembling fingers she reached out and touched a lock of his hair where it lay on the pillow. The carved gold ring on her finger shone in the moonlight. His ring.

In her heart of hearts, Katherine admitted that she had acted as she did—proposing marriage to a man she didn't really know—because it was Gerard and not merely because she was horrified at the thought of wedding Lucien. The other Durham sons were in the exact same circumstance as Gerard, and she hadn't even thought of making her bold offer to either of them.

Seeing him should have smacked some sense into her. He was no longer the carefree boy she'd met so long ago but a war-hardened soldier, grown broad and strong and far more serious, even if he did seem to be laughing at her much of the time. This Gerard was even more attractive than the younger man, although of a darker, more seductive appeal. It made her shiver with pleasure, that he was hers, and quake with fear, that this man could never be happy with the likes of her, not for long. She had no idea how to talk to men, how to flirt and entrance and seduce. She didn't know how to please a man in bed; Howe had been satisfied for her to lie still and leave him to his business. Katherine wished mightily that she did know, or could learn, because now that Gerard was in her bed, she wanted to keep him there.

For now he slept on, unaware of her wistful desires and fierce hopes. She studied every feature of his face, from the dark wavy hair that still tumbled over his forehead and curled damply at his neck, to his defined cheekbones and sensual mouth, to his firm, square jaw. Her knight, her hero, the ideal man she had kept in her heart for a dozen years. The man she had dreamed of, then seized her chance to get when he landed in dire circumstances. Her husband, who had whisked her out of Lucien's grasp and taken pains to secure access to her funds before leaving London but who also kissed her and slept beside her even after she assured him it wasn't necessary. And with each passing hour, it became clearer that she knew absolutely nothing about him.

Chapter 10

Gerard woke in a very agreeable position, stretched out in a warm, comfortable bed with one arm around a woman's waist and one leg nestled between hers. For a while he floated in barely awake bliss, aware only of the soft feminine shape against him, the warmth of her skin through the thin fabric of her nightdress, the curve of her arse against his groin, the way her slim legs closed around his thigh. God, it was good to be back in England, sleeping in a proper bed again with an armful of woman. He'd spent too many nights in an army camp cot, freezing cold and so bone-tired he didn't even notice he was alone.

But this . . . This was very nice to wake up to. She smelled delicious, faintly like the oranges that grew everywhere in Spain. He gathered her closer, inhaling the fragrance that clung to her hair. His hand fell very naturally around her breast. It was small but plump, with a pert nipple that rose under his fingers. Languidly he thumbed it, making an aroused growl deep in his throat as it swelled to erectness. His own erection grew taut and heavy, and he flexed his spine, pressing against her bottom. It had been too long since he made love to a woman in the first blush of day, and now he had a wife to make love to whenever he liked.

Ah, yes. His wife. Soft and pliant when in his arms, stiff and formal when not. The challenge he'd been unable to resist.

He pressed his lips to the back of her neck, inhaling deeply of tart citrus. "Good morning, my dear."

"Good morning," she murmured. Now that he was more awake, Gerard could feel her heartbeat under his palm, pounding away as he toyed with her breast.

"I hope you slept well." Was this frightening her? She held so incredibly still, but she wasn't stiff. Gerard decided he wanted her to become accustomed to this sort of thing, and besides, it felt damned good, so he kept on as he was without pushing matters forward.

"Very well, thank you."

He laughed. For some reason this brought a fine tension to the muscles in her back. "So formal, Kate! We're in bed together."

"Yes, Captain. Gerard," she corrected herself quickly.

"Much better," he told her. "Someday you'll say that name first, I hope." He stretched, deliberately rubbing against her. He'd thought she was a bit thin, but right now her shape felt just right. Soon—though not soon enough—he would explore it at leisure. He was a married man now and needn't live like a monk. Certainly not when all he had to do was tug up her nightdress to enjoy the pleasures, even rights, of marriage so close at hand . . .

The neigh of a horse pierced the quiet of the morning. Gerard reluctantly remembered where they were and why. There would be plenty of time to make love to his new wife when they reached Bath, but until then there was a journey of almost sixty miles to make. He stretched again, reluctantly releasing her to roll over. "As delightful as it would be to stay here for the next hour, we must be on our way."

"Of course." She didn't move. Gerard propped himself up on one elbow and turned her onto her back so he could see her face. She gazed up at him, unsmiling, her dark eyes as serious as ever.

"Someday," he said, "I'm going to pierce that hauteur of yours."

Her expression froze. "I'm not haughty."

"No?" He twirled a lock of her hair around his fingers. In the glowing morning light it was deep gold, like polished brass. "And yet you look so distant, as if part of you is miles away, and the rest, the part here with me, is simply enduring."

All the color drained from her face. "I am sorry to appear so. I do not mean to."

He paused. She was honestly stricken. "Then smile," he whispered, tracing a fingertip along her lower lip. "It lifts my spirits." Slowly her mouth curved into a shy smile although her eyes remained wary. It did improve her looks tremendously. He wondered why she did it so rarely. Again he considered if Howe might have abused her in some way or merely quashed her spirit by virtue of being so much older. He didn't think he'd ever met a woman as somber as Katherine. Or rather, Kate. His Kate.

"Now I feel able to face the day," he said with a

grin, pressing a quick kiss on her nose. "Up with you, my lady!" He tossed back the covers and got out of bed. He pretended not to notice the blush that stained her cheeks as she leaped from the bed and scrambled for her dressing gown. It was cool, not cold, in the room, but Gerard made a point of stirring up the banked fire, giving her a few minutes of privacy. When he glanced over his shoulder, she had retreated behind the dressing screen in the corner.

By the time he dressed and tended to an abbreviated toilette, there was a knock on the door. "Good morning, Mrs. Dennis," he said as he opened it.

The older lady looked him up and down. An upbraiding was on the tip of her tongue, he could see, but she merely nodded once and replied in kind. Then she hurried to the screen and disappeared behind it, whence began a furious rumble of whispers. He finished tying his cravat, watching the screen with some irritation, before shrugging it off. No doubt to a lady as reserved as Kate, he seemed very forward and impertinent, but Gerard refused to change who he was for her. If she'd wanted another sort of man, she should have thought of that before begging him to marry her. He still didn't know why she'd picked him, but in time he'd find out; Gerard knew he could be a persistent devil, and when he wanted to know something, he rarely gave up without success. He pulled on his coat and tossed the last of his things back into the valise before heaving his saddlebags over his shoulder again.

"I'm going down now," he announced to the room. The whispers hushed. "We leave in an hour. I'll make certain breakfast is sent up."

For a moment all was silence, then Kate stepped from behind the screen, still muffled in her dressing gown. "Thank you, sir. We will be ready to leave on time."

He finally figured out what bothered him about her way of speaking. It was lofty and cool, not with disdain so much as an air of forcing herself to do it, as if she'd rather not have to say anything at all. The only time she spoke naturally was when he shocked her, it seemed; he remembered how she had reacted to his announcements that they would marry the next day and that he wanted to have children. He filed the thought away for future contemplation, although it seemed very likely he would shock his bride frequently if those were the statements that unsettled her.

For now he just nodded and let himself out of the room. They had over fifty miles to cover today, and he wanted to get a quick start. He ordered breakfast for himself and asked for a tray to be sent up to the room, then paid the bill. A message was waiting for him as well from Bragg, who had gone on ahead to secure a house. Initially Gerard had planned to set up at an inn, but the question of marriage changed all that. Once he decided to accept Katherine's proposal, Bragg went on ahead to make arrangements. One couldn't expect a newlywed bride to live at an inn for weeks, after all. Some men probably wouldn't have asked her to come along at all, given the journey and the task that lay ahead of him.

But he was confident taking Kate with him was the right choice. The alternative would be to leave her in London, either alone in a hastily rented house or at

Durham House, foisted on his brother Edward's hospitality. Edward would be very hospitable to her, of course, but he barely considered the idea. He didn't want to return to London in a month or two to find his brother knew his wife better than he did, and he absolutely refused to leave her anywhere Lucien Howe could try to manipulate her and her money. Before they left London, Gerard drew a hundred pounds from her funds, just to prove he could, and to establish his control of them. No formal claim had been filed against his and his brothers' legitimacy, so Edward still controlled the Durham accounts, and none of them lacked money, but Gerard wasn't taking any chances. He thought he'd spend the hundred pounds on new clothes for Kate in Bath because he didn't want to see that brown dress ever again.

He hoped she would be able to amuse herself in Bath. He'd been in the town a few years ago when on liberty from the army and thought it a fine place. There was plenty of shopping, which ought to make any woman happy, and generally good society. Kate had proven herself resilient and accommodating up till now. He wouldn't be able to squire her around much and trusted she would accept that as she accepted all his other decisions because he would not be persuaded out of it.

The last blackmail letter had been postmarked in Bath. It reached Durham's hand when the duke was dying, and Gerard could only imagine the alarm it must have caused his father. All of them could only imagine, because Durham, arrogant fool that he was, said nothing of the letters even to Edward, who lived under the same roof and managed all the estate affairs. The only explanation they had was a summary from their father, delivered after his death by the apologetic solicitor, along with the duke's materials related to the disaster: four short, devastating letters from the blackmailer, and reams of reports from the investigators hired to track him down.

Despite the failure of his father's agents in finding the blackmailer, Gerard was sure he could do it. First, he had a driving personal interest in the affair that went beyond any dedication or loyalty to an employer. His name and his place in life hung in the balance—although thanks to Kate, his fortune no longer did. Secondly, it was his mother who would suffer the insult of being named a bigamous wife, and Gerard, who had lost everything else of her, was determined not to let that happen to her memory. And lastly, he had a few advantages his father's hired men had not had; everyone already knew of the scandal, probably even in Bath, so there was no need to operate in perfect stealth. As one of the sons caught in the so-called Durham Dilemma, everyone would be keen to talk to him about it and share his thoughts and opinions on the matter. And, without flattering himself too much, he knew he had a knack for getting people to talk to him. Everyone but his wife, anyway.

Gerard ate quickly and went out to see that the carriage was ready, with a new impatience to be off. Once he solved the mystery of the blackmail, he could get on to unlocking the mystery of his bride.

Birdie was sure Katherine was lying when she said she was fine. She fussed and worried until Katherine finally said the captain hadn't made love to her, nor been anything but polite and decent.

"No?" Birdie's face sagged in relief. "Thank God. I know he's your husband, madam, and that you chose this, but—goodness, he's such a big fellow! And you a widow these many months!"

"None of that is your concern," Katherine said as she splashed water on her face. Perhaps she had been wrong to confide in Birdie that she expected this to be a marriage of convenience. Perhaps she had been wrong to think it would be. The captain was certainly ready and able to consummate it that morning.

"I can't help but worry." Birdie shook out her traveling dress and held it up as Katherine dried off. "Soldiers, madam, are often rough sorts, and he's a young man, apt to be driven by his baser passions. He might overwhelm you, and no one could stop him."

He did overwhelm her, but not quite as Birdie thought. Katherine half wished he would be overwhelmed by passion for her; but the prospect was so foreign, so unnerving, she was generally glad he wasn't. Passions faded, after all. It would be much better to build a mutual respect between them and have a relationship based on that instead of some wild, ungovernable lust—as if she could inspire wild, ungovernable lust in the first place. And the longer she could delay any lovemaking between them, the more time she had to learn what to do when the moment arrived. Her hope was to become friends before he felt obliged to take her to bed. That would hopefully temper any disappointment or disgust he might feel about her wifely performance.

"He's a gentleman," was all she told Birdie. "And he has behaved as one. You mind your tongue, even when he's not around," she added, seeing Birdie draw breath and guessing at her response. "Just because we spoke frankly of Lord Howe doesn't mean we shall be harsh on the captain."

"Hmph." Birdie closed her mouth, but her expression said it all as she pulled Katherine's traveling dress into place.

"Birdie, I want to be happy," she said softly. "I hope to be. You must stop thinking of yourself as my protector, at least against him. In truth, he's been everything I asked him to be."

Her abigail didn't look convinced but said no more about it. She packed while Katherine ate breakfast and rang for a servant to fetch the luggage when they were ready to go.

Downstairs the innkeeper met them with a smile and assured them their carriage was almost ready, gesturing through the open door. Just there, in the courtyard, was His Lordship, checking the last of the preparations. Katherine peeped out and watched him tending to his horse.

Today he wore regular clothing, no longer his sharp military uniform, but it made him no less imposing. Or perhaps that was due to the memory, branded on her skin, of his big body pressed so intimately against hers, his hand cupped about her breast, his male organ rigid and hot against her backside. She had thought, as he lay so relaxed, touching her so leisurely and familiarly, that he would put her on her back and have her, daylight or not. But he didn't. He kissed her, very lightly, then threw back the blankets and got out of bed as if the thought had never entered his mind.

Perhaps it hadn't. Perhaps he dreamed of another woman and lost interest as soon as he realized whom he held in reality.

In the yard, he finished tightening the girth of his saddle and started toward the door where they waited. Katherine nodded her thanks to the inn-keeper and pushed open the door. It was still early, with the chill of morning in the air, and she wrapped her cloak snugly around herself as she crossed the courtyard. Her husband met her with a keen look.

"My humble apologies in advance, my dear, for another hard day of travel."

Birdie let out an almost soundless sigh. Katherine didn't relish getting back in the carriage, either, but that didn't matter. "There's no need to apologize," she said. "At least it is to be the last, for a little while, I trust?"

He grinned. "Indeed. And Bragg should have the house all set to rights by the time we arrive, down to a hot bath waiting."

She smiled back at him, hesitantly. "That will be most welcome."

His eyes lit up, and his grin grew wider. "I would be a very poor husband to drag you across England this way and not have a luxurious bath waiting at the end."

Katherine's heart leaped that she pleased him. She kept smiling but unfortunately couldn't think what to say. Disagree, and protest that he had been an ideal husband thus far? Agree, and seem to reprove him for his demands? She had made him smile and didn't want to stop; but how to do that? Of course, the longer she stood there smiling like a fool, he probably thought her more stupid than anything else. He gave her a quizzical look, his grin still lingering, then put out his hand to help her into the carriage. Once she and Birdie settled inside, he closed the door himself.

"Captain," she said on impulse. He paused, his piercing blue eyes fixed on her, and she almost forgot how to speak under the intensity of his attention. "Thank you," she said lamely.

He leaned his shoulder against the carriage door, setting his face very near hers. "Someday," he murmured, "I shall do something truly worthy of thanks, and will collect your gratitude then. For now, I count myself lucky you aren't cursing my name."

"I would never do such a thing."

He chuckled. "If you can say the same tonight, I may believe you." He slapped the side of the carriage and called out to the driver, who set them in motion at once. A moment later he trotted past on his horse, tipping his hat to her as he did.

She craned her neck and watched him ride up in front of the horses. If she had thought his attractiveness was due to his officer's clothing, she was proven wrong. Gerard de Lacey was just as handsome, if not more so, in a plain blue coat and buckskin breeches. It made her heart hurt to look at him and dream of the future that might be. If only she had any sort of feminine wiles to practice on him. If only she weren't such a dunce when he spoke to her. She did so want him to like her.

That day, although they traveled farther than the day before, felt shorter, no doubt because there was no rushed wedding and confrontation with Lucien. Katherine rested her head against the window frame and watched the countryside undulate past them. The only breaks in the monotony of it were tollgates and the quick stops to change horses. A large hamper of food was already in the carriage when they left that morning, so they barely stopped to eat. The sun was setting when they crested the last hill and could see Bath gleaming in the dying light below them.

Katherine looked out the window with interest as they drove through the town. Lord Howe had traveled only to London, and most times he'd left her at home in Sussex; it would have been too taxing for her to go with him, he always told her. She thought it would have merely been too taxing on his patience for her to join him during the elegant, sparkling Season, where plain, quiet women had no place. Her new husband hadn't even suggested she remain behind. Either he thought her sturdier than Howe did, or he wanted her by him. She hoped it was both, really.

They stopped on a square in front of a tall town house, not unlike Portman Square except for the complete uniformity between the house and its neighbors. Katherine stepped down from the carriage and looked around. The green at the heart of the square was surrounded by a wrought-iron railing, and in the center was an obelisk. The street was wide and well kept. An auspicious beginning, she told herself.

Inside, the house was equally agreeable. The rooms were wide and gracious although the furnishings were heavy and old-fashioned. The tall windows at the front of the house would let in plenty of light. Katherine took off her cloak and tried to examine the rooms without any uncouth curiosity as the footman flitted in and out of the hall, carrying in the luggage.

The captain, however, seemed less pleased. His expression was distinctly unimpressed as he, too, looked around their new abode. "It will do, I suppose," he muttered. "Bragg!"

A wiry, bowlegged man who had the captain's valise in one hand hurried over. "Welcome to Bath, sir," he said in a gravelly voice. "And my lady." He bowed, displaying a round bald spot at his crown amid the cropped red waves of hair.

"This is Bragg, my batman," the captain told her. "If ever you need anything, set Bragg on it at once."

"Thank you," she replied, "but I think Mrs. Dennis will be able to do for me." She felt an instinctive urge to keep Birdie closer than ever, realizing for the first time how alone she was with her new husband. Even if they each knew no one in town, she had no doubt he would soon have a wide circle of acquaintances, while she . . . She hoped she would feel more at ease in Bath society than she had in London society.

He gave her a curious look. "As you wish. See to a hot bath for my lady, Bragg."

"The water's already warming," said the batman.

"Good man. Show me the upstairs. I really thought you'd find someplace bigger . . ." Without waiting for her, the captain headed toward the stairs, his man a half step behind. Katherine followed silently; there would be time to explore the rest of the house tomorrow.

The bedroom was large and warm, thanks to the fire already crackling in the grate. She walked to the window and pulled the drape aside to peek out at the square. The last rays of sunlight just brushed the top of the houses across from them, and the sky above the chimneys was a deep, velvety blue. A carriage rolled up the street across the square, its lamps winking brightly in the twilight. Bath was beautiful, she thought, and said a quick prayer it would be happy as well.

"Is it a fine view?" The captain had come up behind her. She started at his voice, so close to her shoulder, but managed not to flinch away.

"Yes." She pulled back the drape so he could see.

Her husband leaned forward, over her shoulder. His face was right next to hers. She could see the dust of the road settled in the folds of his cravat and smell his shaving soap mixed with the odors of sweat and horse. "I hope you find the house satisfactory," he said, still peering through the window.

"Very much so." It was hard not to stare at his profile.

He tilted his head and glanced at her. "I trust you'll be at home in Bath. It's a fine place—or was, the last time I was here. Unfortunately business may keep me occupied a great deal."

She longed to know what it was. He'd said he had to find someone here; who? Someone who could help disprove the scandalous rumors about his father? Someone else? But if he wanted her to know, he would tell her. "Of course," she murmured. "I shall manage."

"Good girl." He gave her a quick smile, then turned away and strode across the room. "Bragg, where's my dinner?" he called into the hallway, laughing a moment later at the muffled reply. "I'll leave you to your toilette," he said to Katherine, who still stood at the window. "I did promise you a nice, hot bath, did I not?"

"Yes. How kind of you to remember," she said, but he had already left the room. Katherine sighed as Birdie bustled in.

It didn't take Birdie long to unpack her few things. She thought of all her belongings in London. Now that they had arrived and the captain made clear he expected her to amuse herself in Bath, she felt a bit annoyed that he hadn't allowed her time to pack more. Surely an extra day wouldn't have made so very great a difference. She had left behind almost everything she valued, and now she was to be alone in a strange town.

After two long days of jolting about in the coach, the hot bath felt delicious. Birdie had kept the bottle of orange water, and put a few drops in the steaming tub. Katherine soaked for a scandalously long time, feeling at leisure to do so for the first time in months. She gathered from something Birdie muttered that her husband had left not just her room but the whole house, which meant she could do as she pleased. Hadn't he told her to be at home here? She felt at home lolling in the water, and only got out when it cooled enough to make her shiver as Birdie poured buckets of water over her head.

She sent Birdie off to her own bath and bed soon after that, when the captain's man, Bragg, brought a tray with dinner. Warm, clean, fed, and tired, Katherine curled up in a comfortable chair near the window. Would the captain be home soon? Would he expect her to be waiting for him? Howe never had, but Lucien made a habit of knocking at her door every night. At first she had thought it merely over-solicitous, but later decided it was more watchful.

She wished she knew more about her husband. He seemed nothing like Lucien—although it must be noted the captain now possessed what Lucien had wanted, her fortune. Perhaps Lucien, too, would have left her alone after he got the money. Katherine repressed a shudder; it still made her skin crawl to think of marrying Lucien, even now that she was safe from that fate.

Gerard de Lacey, though . . . Gerard did not make her skin crawl. He made her nerves jangle and her stomach tighten, but not in a bad way. Everything she thought about him might turn out to be wrong, but somewhere deep inside him, she was sure, he was still, in some small way, that kind and gallant young man who had helped her once.

Out in the night, a bell chimed the hour. It wasn't very late, but Katherine felt as though she hadn't really slept in weeks, ever since Lucien told her he expected them to marry. Even last night, removed from Lucien's reach, she'd been too aware of the man sleeping beside her to get much rest. Tonight she felt truly exhausted, wrung out in mind and body, but also finally at some peace. When she startled herself awake for the second time, she decided to go to bed. She set the screen in front of the fire and was just moving to blow out the lamps when she felt a breath of cool air at her back. Slowly she turned, and loung-ing in the doorway was her husband, watching her.

"Good evening, my lady," he said, his voice a silky rumble.

Katherine froze. Her stomach took a giant leap, then plummeted to her knees. He looked tousled and vital and utterly focused on her.

"I trust you've had your bath, and a good dinner," he added.

Mutely she nodded.

"Very good." He stepped into the room and closed the door. "Then let's go to bed."

Chapter 11

Gerard hadn't been in Bath half a day, and already he was displeased with the place.

First there was the house. He had told Bragg to take a fashionable place across the river near Sydney Gardens, for the sake of his privacy and also for Kate's. She had spent most of her time in the country, and he'd never heard her express any sadness at that. She was a quiet woman, and if she wanted to spend her time in solitary walks through the countryside, he wanted to make it easier for her to do so. Gerard remembered the gardens across the River Avon as lush and beautiful, almost idyllic. Instead of all that, however, Bragg had only managed to find a house in Queen Square, right in the fusty middle of Bath. No doubt their neighbors would be gossiping old ladies who would peck at Kate and him the entire time. Bragg threw up his hands and declared everything in Sydney Gardens was taken, and this was the best he could find. Gerard sighed and waved it off because Bragg was usually right; but he wasn't happy to be installed so awkwardly and uncomfortably in the town.

He left Kate to her bathing, thinking she deserved some peace after the last two days, but the urge to get out and do something still roiled under his skin. There was very little he could do at that hour, but Gerard remembered where the taverns were, so he put on his coat again and went out, striding along the pavements that gradually narrowed as he left the better part of town. The stench of the river grew worse, rank with horses and offal and other smells he didn't care to investigate. He stepped around a pair of whores loitering on the pavement and ducked into a tavern. It was smoky and loud, just the sort of carousing place he was used to in the army. He ordered a pint of ale and found a seat at a table by the door.

The simplest approach, and therefore probably the best, was the most direct. Gerard had one principal clue to the blackmailer's identity: the letters themselves. With luck, the post office in Bath, where two of the letters had originated, would be able to shed some light on the sender. There were receiving houses all over town, but he planned to start with the main post office. Once he had a name, or a description, the real hunt could begin.

He finished his ale and left the pub, walking until the night sky was a canopy of black speckled with stars. The exercise did much to settle his mind, and he finally returned to Queen Square, where Bragg had a cold dinner and a full report waiting for him. His man had a habit of reporting back to him as if they were still on campaign, and tonight was no different. Bragg was a keen observer, so Gerard ate and listened in silence as he divulged what he knew of the neighbors—not much as yet, although there were, as expected, several curious older ladies on the Square anxious to meet the new tenants—and the house and servants. The upstairs maid was inclined to sloth, but the cook was good, and the footman had been put on notice that the new master expected military precision.

"M'lady's maid will probably frighten them more than you or I do, though," Bragg added.

Gerard grinned. "Mrs. Dennis is more formidable than half the English Army."

Bragg shuddered. "Right you are, Cap'n. Already she's scolded me about the house, the bath for her ladyship, and then her own accommodations. How was I to know the lady's maid would want the ironing in her room?"

"Give her whatever she wants, at least for the first few days. I carried Her Ladyship out of London without more than a few hours' notice, and Mrs. Dennis got her feathers thoroughly ruffled."

"Aye, sir." Bragg cleared away the dishes from dinner and brought out a bottle of port. "Her Ladyship seems the very model of a lady."

He paused in the act of pouring the wine. "She is. That's all you need to say about her, Bragg."

"Aye, sir." Bragg knew an order when he heard one. He carried out the tray.

Gerard brooded over his port. He didn't want to worry about how his wife would get on in Bath. He was a fairly self-sufficient sort of fellow and had little patience for people who needed to be amused or coddled. In Sydney Gardens, they would have had privacy and space. She'd have to make the best of Queen Square. He swallowed the last of the wine and got to his feet. Perhaps he'd better go see how Kate was settling in.

And then he could take her to bed. Gerard's pulse jumped as that thought crossed his mind. Yes, that sounded damned good right now. A good tupping would dissipate the last of the tension that had dogged him all day. He could still feel the shape of her in his arms, warm and soft, and he was suddenly exceedingly keen to fulfill his marital duties.

He opened the bedroom door and paused. Kate was sitting in the chair by the fireplace, her feet tucked up under her. Her face was turned away from him, but there was something very sweet and relaxed about her pose. As he watched, she started, rubbing one hand over her face before she rose from the chair and stretched rather sensuously. The firelight illuminated her figure through the night rail she wore. Gerard's eyes slid over nicely rounded hips and a trim waist. His skin prickled in anticipation.

Kate adjusted the fire screen and turned to blow out the lamp before she realized he was there. He could tell the exact moment she became aware of his presence. Her back stiffened, her head came up, and her shoulders hunched forward, all before she even glanced his way. When she faced him, her expression was blank, her eyes watchful. She looked nervous— not that Gerard could think of any reason he might have given for it. Someday soon he was going to find out what set her on edge because he hated to think his wife was uneasy around him. Hopefully it was merely the awkwardness of unfamiliarity, which he was confident could be remedied by time . . . time, and some persistent seduction.

"Good evening, my lady," he said. "I trust you've had your bath and a good dinner." He could see she had; her hair gleamed like polished brass in the muted lamplight, the ends still curling damply. She gave a tiny nod. He pushed away from the doorway and closed the door. He could see the curve of her breasts through the nightgown. He very much hoped he and Kate were compatible in bed, for he was finding her more intriguing by the hour. "Very good. Then let's go to bed."

She didn't move. Her color faded, and Gerard knew she took his meaning. He shrugged off his coat and tossed it on a chair. "Are you nervous?"

"No," she said. "I'm not a virgin."

He grinned. "You're fond of lovemaking, then?"

She opened her mouth, then closed it.

"I thought so." He shed his waistcoat and began unknotting his cravat. "I beg you will remember I am not Lord Howe."

"I would never confuse you with him," she said, her voice a little strained.

Gerard unwound the cravat and let the linen fall to the floor. He crossed the room and laid his hands gently on her shoulders. He felt the small shiver that went through her. "You should enjoy it. I mean for you to enjoy it, with me."

Her pulse beat like a hummingbird's wing. "I'm sure it will be quite pleasant."

His mouth curled. Somehow, whether she intended it or not, Kate knew just how to provoke him and taunt him and push him to make good on his words—better, even. "We'll have to see, won't we?"

She swallowed.

His blood humming now, Gerard took off his boots,
then his stockings. Kate watched without a word, her
hands clutching fistfuls of her nightdress. When he
began pulling off his shirt, she inhaled deeply. "I'll
put out the lamps," she blurted, and rushed to blow
out the nearest one. He said nothing. She was nervous, and if darkness reassured her, so be it.

He stepped out of his trousers and drawers as she
put out the last lamp. The room was plunged into
darkness, the fire having died down to coals. Her
white nightdress stood out as his eyes adjusted, and
Gerard caught her when she would have hurried past
him to the bed. "Don't be afraid," he murmured. He
slipped one arm around her waist and threaded the
fingers of his free hand into her hair. "Trust me."
And he kissed her.

Katherine's heart nearly burst. He was naked—
naked!—and holding her against him as he kissed
her. She felt light-headed, shaky on her feet, but
there was nothing to steady herself on except Gerard,
and he was naked—completely, shockingly, utterly
naked. Her hand brushed against his bare thigh, and
she quickly raised her hands to his arms. That seemed
safer, until he made a rough noise of satisfaction in
his throat and gathered her even closer. His skin was
hot, so much warmer than hers. She could feel the
heat of him through her nightdress, especially his
male organ, which pressed against her belly, growing harder by the minute. It gave her a thrill of both
panic and delight. He was aroused—by her. She still
desperately feared being a disappointment, but for
now, perhaps, there was hope.

Gradually she relaxed into his kiss. It was just as lovely as the others had been. When he nipped at her lower lip, she let him in, his tongue sweeping sensuously over hers. Hesitantly she tried to reply in kind, and he growled again. The muscles of his arms grew taut under her palms, and without breaking the kiss, he somehow managed to lift her in his arms and carry her to the bed. He set her down on her feet, and Katherine swayed and almost fell. If he kept kissing her like that all night, he could do anything he liked to her.

"Shh," her husband murmured in his low, rumbling voice. Somehow he undid all the buttons down the front of her nightdress in the blink of an eye and tugged it down. Katherine clapped her hands to her bosom in alarm as the fabric slid over her shoulders, but he calmly brushed them away, slipping the garment down until it dropped into a puddle at her feet.

For a moment he just stood there, his head bent as he looked at her—or so she thought. The fire had almost burned to ash, and she could barely make out his form in front of her. Without physical contact, both her head and her skin cooled rapidly. Her hands balled into fists as a chill rippled over her. What was wrong? Had he changed his mind?

She jumped when his fingertips brushed her hipbone. He stepped closer, making that quiet shushing sound under his breath as both his hands wandered over her. He stroked the curve of her waist. He drew his hands up her ribs to cup the slight swells of her breasts. Like the touch of a hot iron, it recalled the easy way he had fondled her that morning, and her nipples tightened at the memory. He seemed to like it;

he circled his thumbs over the hard buds, his breathing gone deep and harsh. She was trembling. He was making her stomach flutter, and she shifted her feet, squeezing her legs together as something seemed to melt there.

"Touch me," he breathed, abandoning her breasts to run his fingertips up her spine. Katherine's back arched involuntarily. She could almost hear him smiling his slow, wicked grin as he did it again, then again, until she made a gasping squeak of pleasure. "Touch me," he whispered. "I want to feel your hands, Kate . . ."

She grabbed his arms, and his hands flattened on her lower back, urging her against him. Katherine collided with a wall of solid male flesh that seemed to sizzle where it touched hers. It was shocking and wonderful at the same time. She rested her cheek against his chest, marveling at the muffled thump of his heart and the tickle of hair against her temple. He was still just running his hands up and down her back, as if he were as content to hold her as she was to be held. This wasn't frightening or demanding. It was wonderful, really, and she let her fingers wander over the solid bulge of his biceps.

His hold tightened, and he lifted her onto the bed, bearing her down onto her back without breaking contact between them. She took a deep breath, thinking of what was to come, and he cupped her cheek to kiss her. By the time she realized what he was doing, he had settled his weight between her legs, and she could feel the head of his organ brushing against her. "Shh," he crooned again. "Don't worry—let me make it better . . ."

Katherine nodded, although whether he could see in the darkness, she didn't know. She hoped he would kiss her again, for she forgot everything but the drowning pleasure of that when he did, but instead his lips whispered over her brow before moving down the side of her neck. The slight scrape of stubble against that sensitive skin made her shiver. He murmured wordlessly, his lips traced over her collarbone and shoulder. His other hand began stroking in long, sure sweeps up her arm, then down, then raising her arm above her head and draping it over the pillow. His knee nudged her thigh, and she obediently shifted her leg out of the way. He hummed a deep note of approval and slid down until his head was level with her breasts.

He explored them gently. He nuzzled the underside of one while palming the other with his large, warm hand. Katherine dimly thought she should be mortified—she knew gentlemen liked large breasts on a woman, and hers were so small Howe had merely sighed in pity over them—but *goodness,* what Gerard was doing felt wonderful. His tongue traced delicate loops and whorls across her ribs, his thumb mirroring those actions on the opposite side. When he scraped his teeth lightly across one nipple, she gasped, and when he sucked it into his mouth, she shook like a leaf in a breeze. Her flesh seemed to burn under the touch of his mouth and his fingers until she was sure her skin was glowing. Both her arms were over her head now, clutching at the pillows to keep her body from floating off the mattress in sheer bliss.

When he touched her lower, his palm cupping over the nest of curls between her legs, she arched off the bed—not in fright, as he evidently thought from the way he soothed her again, but from shock at the sensation. Howe had touched her there, but it never felt like this. Gerard's fingers were gentle but insistent; he didn't poke them inside her at once, but danced around, stroking, circling, working his way through the folds of flesh until he reached one spot so sensitive, she made a strangled noise of alarm. It wasn't right—she'd felt that to the tips of her fingers and the soles of her feet.

"Shh," he whispered even as he made the torment worse. "Trust me, Kate."

Hadn't she already? Trusted that he was honorable enough to marry, bound herself to him, handed over her fortune to him, left London with him, and now surrendered her body to him? He could have anything he wanted of her if he only asked. She wanted to please him in bed. With a big breath, she nodded, and let him do as he wished.

Sometime later he moved, the hair on his legs tickling her inner thighs, and he adjusted himself against her. Katherine told herself to stay relaxed and let him, but it had been a long time since a man had made love to her. She tensed, which only made his entry harder. Gerard had teased her into a quivering tangle of sensation, and now he seemed so large, so thick, her nerves screamed as he pressed into her body. He was a much bigger man than Howe had been, in all ways. It didn't hurt and pinch as it often had before, but she felt invaded and stretched. She spread her legs wider apart, hoping to make it easier.

Gerard paused, sucking in a deep breath as she moved. "God, Kate," he growled. "My *God*. Like that, yes." He caught her knee and hooked it over his hip, sliding deeper in the process. She arched her back, truthfully trying to wiggle away from him for a moment, but he took hold of her other knee and urged it around him, too. He pushed until she thought she would faint at the fullness inside her.

Finally he stopped. Katherine realized she was trembling again and breathing just as hard as her husband, who seemed to be trying to master himself. One hand was braced beside her, and he smoothed back her hair with the other. His fingers shook a little. "Katherine," he said thickly, "put your arms around my waist. I'll do better next time, I swear it."

He never called her Katherine. Uncertainly she did as he said. The muscles of his back were like iron. At her touch he ducked his head and kissed her, a deep, ravishing kiss that left her head spinning.

She felt the flex and strain of his muscles as he began to move in long, hard thrusts. She felt every inch of penetration as if it were the first time when his hips drove forward, although the discomfort faded quickly. He pushed himself up and took hold of the headboard; dimly she could hear it creak. The motion forced her hands down his back, until she was nearly cupping his bottom in her hands. He gripped her hip, holding her in place. Every surge of his body into hers rocked her whole form, curled as she was around him. It was overwhelming. The sensation was too much. She squeezed her eyes shut and clung to him, feeling as if she would burst from the pressure, the unbearable heat in her belly that grew harder and hotter with every stroke of his hips.

It broke like a shower of sparks against her skin,

like nothing she had ever felt before. She clutched at him, her cry muffled against his chest. He thrust hard into her, then stayed there as she shook and convulsed around him. Dimly she heard him groan. Her head fell to the pillow, her neck too weak to hold it up. All her muscles felt soft and shaky, in fact.

"Kate." Her name was a ragged breath against her temple as he kissed her. As her mind cleared, she realized she was clinging to him tightly, keeping him deep inside her. She would have to let go of him . . . in just a moment. That had been blissful. Wonderful. Everything she'd ever dreamed it might be, between a man and woman. She scrunched her eyes closed and listened to the pounding of his heart against her cheek.

"*That's* what it should be like, my dear," he said softly.

Chapter 12

∽∾∾

Gerard woke in a fine mood. The sun was rising, light streaming through the gaps in the drapes when he slipped from the bed. Kate still slept, her hair a wild tangle across her bare shoulders and breasts, her face soft and young in sleep. He contemplated his bride for a moment. Howe must have been an idiot. Kate wasn't a beauty, and her figure wasn't lush, but she was exquisitely responsive, and her body . . . His blood surged at the memory of how tightly and wetly she sheathed him. And how pliantly she opened herself to him. His intention to be slow and gentle vanished, blown away by the single soft moan that slipped from her lips as he entered her, then he'd been lost to the driving need to bury himself in her again and again. And despite his lack of finesse, she still reached climax. His Kate was a more sensual being than expected. Yes, he was going to like being married.

Which only freed him up even more to pursue that bloody blackmailer. By day he could set himself on the hunt for his father's tormenter, and by night he could lose himself in the pleasures of seducing his wife.

Bragg, already accustomed to Gerard's army hours, had coffee waiting when he stepped into the dressing room. "What shall I do today, sir?"

"See that Lady Gerard is settled. Show her the house, and . . . anything else she wants." He honestly had no idea what his wife would want to do. What did ladies do all day? "Find out where the library is. If she wants to attend the theater, take a box. A good one this time, Bragg."

"Aye, sir."

"And see to a carriage, or a chair." Gerard slathered shaving soap over his chin. "She'll want to go shopping and visiting, no doubt."

When he was ready to go out, he peeked into the bedroom. Kate was still in bed, but awake, staring at the ceiling and twisting a lock of hair around her fingers. She looked so pensive, he paused. Had he been too rough last night? He opened the door. "Good morning, my dear."

She lurched upright at his voice, then turned bright red as she jerked the covers up to her chin. Gerard, who rather appreciated the glimpse of her pale, pert breasts, grinned. "No need to hide." He came to sit on the side of the bed. "I trust you're well this morning."

Her eyes were deep pools of blue in the morning light. "Yes, Captain," she whispered. "Gerard."

"You never said anything last night." He traced his finger over her arm, feeling how her muscles tensed as she clutched the bedclothes to her like a shield. "Was it . . . uncomfortable?"

"It didn't hurt," she murmured. "Thank you."

"Well, that is high praise," he said dryly. "I shall

do better. I want you to enjoy it when I make love to you."

She looked nervous. "I will try." Gerard cocked his head, wondering why she said it that way. "Did you enjoy it?" she asked, glancing sideways at him like a skittish horse. "Was I . . . pleasing?"

"Yes," he reassured her, and some of the tension went out of her arms. "Don't be afraid of me, Kate."

She was quiet for a moment. "I'm not afraid of you. We aren't very well acquainted, though, and I do wish to be a good wife."

"Men are simple creatures, darling," he said with a laugh. "We want to be well fed, amused, and loved. A good meal, a quality horse race, and a woman waiting in his bed are all it takes to make a man happy. You'll be a splendid wife." He leaned forward and kissed her lightly. "I'll be out most of the day. Bragg has his instructions. Do let him know if you need anything as you settle in."

"Thank you," she said. Gerard, already halfway to the door, paused to smile at her before he left. Kate would be fine. He was fortunate she had such a calm and steady disposition.

He skipped his morning ride. The horse needed a rest after two long days of travel. Instead he walked the streets of Bath, reacquainting himself with the town in daylight. Up and down the hills he strode, past the gleaming stone that glowed in the morning sun and along the verdant banks of the rushing Avon. It was still a beautiful town, and he filled his lungs with fresh air, appreciating it all the more for having been in London.

When the post office opened, he made his way

there. The postmaster, Mr. Watson, was a business-like fellow, and once Gerard put the problem to him the right way, he was eager to help. Of the blackmail letter sent eight months ago, there seemed little hope; but the one posted a mere seven weeks before had far more potential. The clerks were summoned and shown the letters, which Gerard had brought with him. One man did indeed remember them. Both were addressed to His Grace the Duke of Durham, which was unusual, and the postage had also been prepaid, a significant enough sum to have attracted notice. Given the combination, the clerk was certain he remembered the man who posted the letter.

"I would know him again if I saw him," he vowed.

"Have you seen him since?" Gerard asked.

"No, sir. He's not a regular patron, at least not to this post office."

"Can you describe him?"

The clerk did, although a hundred men might have answered to the same description. Medium tall and spare, in his prime years, brown hair, spectacles, dressed well enough for a lawyer or a shopkeeper but not better.

"And he had a mark on his cheek," added the clerk, pointing out the location on his own face. "A scar of some sort."

Gerard produced the older letter again. "Are you quite certain you never saw him before? I wonder if someone else posted this letter. It's most certainly from the same person, mailed six months earlier, with the same direction."

The clerk peered at both letters, but finally shook his head. "They do look very similar, but I couldn't recall so far back. Another clerk might have served him."

"May I see them?" Mr. Watson asked. The clerk handed them to the postmaster, who held the two letters side by side. "The writing appears to be the same," he said, studying them. "In fact . . ." He squinted at one, then the other. "I would almost say they were written at the same time."

"Oh?" Gerard sat up straighter. He'd scrutinized both letters, and the writing was identical. Of course, he paid more attention to the postmarks and other clues, but if he had missed anything, he was anxious to hear it.

"It rather looks as though the author misspelled the town, then corrected it, on both letters." He gave them back to Gerard, who spent a good few minutes looking.

"Notice the stroke of the pen from the 't' to the 'y,'" said the postmaster. "The 'e' has been written over it, not as part of the original stroke."

"It's very cramped writing." Gerard bent over the letters. "How can you see such a thing?"

Mr. Watson rummaged in his desk and produced a magnifying lens. "Does this help?" As Gerard turned the lens on the letter, the postmaster added, a touch grandly, "I once served in the Dead Letter Office, sir. We're trained to spot any such clue that might identify a letter."

"How fortunate I am to have encountered you, then," Gerard replied. "I think you're correct. The writer originally wrote 'Styning,' and then added the 'e' later. It's clear on this one—he wasn't very artful, and his pen strayed across the 'y'—but on this one I should never have believed it without the lens. Well spotted, Mr. Watson."

"Thank you, sir."

Of course, what good did that information do him? Did the same error mean the letters had been written at the same time, or just that the sender repeated his mistakes? Gerard mustered a smile and turned to the clerk, still perched attentively on his chair. "If the man who sent these should return, I would be very glad to have a word with him. Here is my card." He scribbled the Queen Square house number on the back.

"Very good, sir." Mr. Watson took the card and cleared his throat. "Of course I can only notify him of your interest, unless you are alleging some illegal activity has taken place in connection with these letters . . . ?"

It bloody well should be illegal to blackmail a duke, but Gerard was aware he had little to stand on. He was not the Duke of Durham, and he wasn't about to make any more scandal over this blasted Durham Dilemma. He'd brought the letters to the post office sealed, and not opened them. Mr. Watson and his clerk didn't need to know what message was inside them. All together, that meant he really couldn't cry foul too loudly.

He made himself flick one hand in response to Mr. Watson's muted question. "No, no. I doubt he is any danger to anyone. The letters were obviously unsigned, but I have a great interest in speaking to the author on my brother's behalf. If the fellow should come in again, I would be very glad to know of it. Give him my card and express my eagerness to see him. I would be"—he paused delicately—"most grateful for any assistance."

The clerk bobbed his head. Mr. Watson smiled and got to his feet, hand extended. "Of course, sir. Brynfield here will keep an eye out, you may depend on it."

Gerard shook the postmaster's hand. "Excellent. A good day to you both."

He left the post office and resumed walking the streets, although this time without purpose or direction. He thought more clearly when he was active, and this was a moment for thinking. The two letters from Bath were sent six months apart; why would they have been written at the same time? Or perhaps that was wrong, and the sender had a persistent inability to spell and always had to correct his work. And yet, why bother to correct a misspelling on a blackmail letter? If Gerard intended to blackmail someone, he would use the worst spelling and handwriting possible. In fact, he would probably hire someone to write the notes, another person to address them, and a third to send them, so no one could trace them back to him.

His steps slowed. Perhaps that was an idea. If the letters were all written at one time, as Mr. Watson suggested, it might have been done to hand them off to a third party who would post them. If the actual blackmailer didn't know when they would be sent, that could explain why no one ever inquired after the ransom that was demanded. Perhaps he didn't know the letter *had* been sent.

Then he shook his head. What sort of idiot would blackmail the Duke of Durham for five thousand pounds and not even keep track of the letters, let alone the ransom demand? Where was the point in that? This villain had already proven himself crafty enough to avoid Durham's investigators and escape detection. His evil letters hadn't gained him anything yet, but he clearly wanted something out of it. Gerard just hadn't figured out what that was yet.

Sunk deep in thought, he wandered up to Milsom Street, where a number of fine shops were located. Perhaps he should buy something for Kate, sweets or a book or something. He remembered how earnestly she'd told him she wanted to be a good wife and felt a twinge of regret he had to spend the first few weeks of his marriage on this blasted blackmailing problem instead of introducing his bride to his family and setting her up in a proper home. She'd been so agreeable about everything—particularly last night, to Gerard's deep satisfaction—he owed her some small token.

Half an hour later he was ready to admit defeat. A book seemed a fine idea; what did she like to read? He didn't know. Perhaps a shawl, or a new bonnet; what sort would she admire? He didn't know. Gloves? Music? A fan? Perhaps jewels, although he had intended only a small trinket. He'd never seen so much as a simple locket around her neck. Perhaps she didn't care for jewels . . . unlike every other woman of his acquaintance. He was scowling at the jeweler's window when the sound of his name roused him.

"Imagine meeting you here!" cried the man advancing on him. "I thought you were still in camp with the rest of the regiment."

"I was." Gerard shook hands with Daniel Carter, an officer in his regiment and a good friend. Carter had been shot in the leg a few months ago and still leaned heavily on a cane. "My father died," Gerard explained. "I was given some leave to tidy up his affairs."

"Ah. So sorry," murmured Carter.

Gerard nodded in acknowledgment. "What brings you to Bath?"

"As you can see, I'm no good to the army yet." Carter grimaced as he shifted his weight. "Another month, perhaps."

"We shall return at the same time then, I hope."

"Very good!" Carter's face brightened. "Have you any time for pleasure in Bath? My sister's been looking out for me, but I'm a dashed dull fellow, with this leg. She's very good-natured about it, but I'm sure she'd be glad of a more jovial fellow's arm from time to time. Ah—there she is now. Cora," he called to a woman just leaving a shop behind him. "Come say hello to a most excellent friend of mine."

She joined them and was introduced. Cora Fitzwilliam was a tall, slender woman with a dazzling smile and a warm, open manner. After a few pleasantries about the weather, Mrs. Fitzwilliam turned to him. "Captain, do you attend the theater? Much to my delight, they're presenting a comedy this week."

"Cora loves a farce," said her brother. "And a good laugh is always welcome. De Lacey, you must join us."

"I'd be delighted. I intended to take a box, in fact." Gerard laughed, shamefaced, as a thought struck him. "For my wife."

"Wife!" exclaimed Carter. "The most dashing bachelor in the army, wed? Have I been away that long?"

Gerard shook his head, still smiling. "No, not at all. It was a bit of a whirlwind courtship, and now I've made her come all the way to Bath. I was just contemplating a small token of apology when you saw me." He cocked his head at the window.

"No one is better at choosing jewelry than Cora," said Carter with amusement. "I daresay she could offer you a word of advice if you like."

"I would be very glad of a woman's opinion," Gerard said in relief. "I've little experience of jewels."

"Of course," cried Mrs. Fitzwilliam. "And Danny shall be so pleased he doesn't have to offer his opinion at all!"

"Ecstatic," confirmed Carter, and they all laughed. "Then if you don't mind, I shall walk up the street to the coffee shop and wait for you there," he said to his sister. "A pleasure to see you again." He bowed his head at Gerard and limped up the street.

"I hope I haven't inconvenienced you." He turned to watch his friend go. "He's doing quite well." Carter's leg had been perilously close to amputation. Gerard remembered him swearing viciously at the surgeons when they were arguing over whether to dig out the bullet or take the whole leg off at the thigh. Only when Carter appealed to the regiment's colonel did the doctors agree to leave it on. "I was told he would never walk again."

"Yes, he's doing very well," she answered softly, also watching Carter, her face shadowed with concern. "And I do believe seeing a friendly face will help even more. He'd much rather be on campaign than trapped in Bath amusing his sister. How very fortunate we ran into you." She mustered a smile and put her hand on Gerard's arm. "But enough of Danny. Let us find something lovely for your wife."

Katherine spent her first day in Bath exploring the house. Bragg hovered at her elbow every step of the way, clearly under orders to wait on her no matter how much she assured him she was quite satisfied to inspect the rooms alone. Her first impression was confirmed—nice rooms, dull furnishings—and she resolved to open the drapes as wide as possible since the house was a little dark.

She was in the narrow dining room when the front door knocker banged, the sound echoing through the hall. Katherine looked up, startled. Who could it be? She knew no one, and wasn't dressed for visitors at all. She'd been officially still in mourning for Lord Howe when she went to London, and so only had dark, somber clothes to pack when Gerard insisted they must be off in an hour's time. Until Lucien sent the rest of her things as she asked him to do, her wardrobe was tightly constrained. "I'm not in," she said quickly when Bragg glanced at her. "Not today."

He nodded and went off to answer the door. Katherine rushed across the room to hover behind the door, wildly curious to know who was calling. Someone to see the captain? He said he'd been to Bath before and had important business here again. Ought she to receive the visitor, in case it was something of importance to him?

"Lady Darby and Mrs. Woodforde extend their compliments to the lady of the house," announced a regal male voice, "and welcome her to Queen Square. When it is convenient, they shall call on her and invite her to tea, as a gesture of neighborly goodwill."

"I'm sure she'll be very gratified," said Bragg's gravelly voice. "Captain and Lady Gerard de Lacey send their compliments to the ladies."

The door closed. Bragg came back into the dining room with the small salver bearing two cards, which he offered to Katherine. "Lady Darby lives next door, ma'am," he said. "I believe Mrs. Woodforde is her sister, who lives across the Square."

"Oh." Katherine fingered the cards. They were for her. "Thank you, Bragg."

She went upstairs to review her wardrobe once more. Clearly it was time to cast off mourning, but she had no pretty clothes. Her mother, who possessed an unquestionable flair for fashion, always sighed over Katherine's coloring and figure and declared her beyond hope. She urged dark colors and simple gowns on Katherine, saying vivid colors and elaborate styles would overwhelm her. Howe had agreed, as did Lucien, and among the three of them, she had little freedom to dress more gaily. Katherine remembered Gerard's distaste at the sight of her clothing and felt a spark of rebellion. She would order a red dress, and a bright blue one. And if they looked hideous on her, then . . . well, at least he couldn't scold her for doing what he urged.

But even if she ordered the dresses that afternoon, they wouldn't be ready for days. She looked at herself in the mirror, studying the simple dark blue frock she wore. There was a bit of ivory trim on the bodice, but certainly nothing that might be termed beautiful or stylish. She would have to order more. If only something could be found to flatter her.

She deliberated a moment, then rang the bell. "Do you know where I might find a dressmaker's shop?" she asked Bragg when he came.

"Most likely in Milsom Street, my lady," he answered. "Plenty of shops in Milsom Street and Bond Street; one of them's bound to be a dressmaker. I could send a boy to see."

"No, thank you, I shall see for myself. Is Milsom Street close by?"

"Aye, madam; 'tis just up the hill a bit. Shall I call a chair?"

"No," she said again, beginning to smile. "I shall walk."

A while later she set out with Birdie, who clutched a rough street map sketched by Bragg. She was glad to be out of doors and took the opportunity to look around at everything. Bath seemed to be constructed entirely of pale stone that glowed in the sunlight, with bursts of greenery everywhere. It also seemed to be located on the side of a mountain. Birdie was puffing by the time they reached Milsom Street.

"I see why they have chairmen," she said between gasps.

Katherine smiled. "We'll become used to it. I see no need to be carried about."

"Wait until you must walk down that hill," Birdie grumbled.

Without any fixed destination, they walked slowly, stopping to look in the shop windows at bonnets, prints, bolts of silk, leather-bound books, and every other sort of thing a person could buy. Katherine was amazed and delighted. Bragg was right; there were plenty of shops, including two dressmakers. She was about to enter one, a lovely little shop with the most beautiful fashion dolls in the window, when Birdie made a sharp, shocked sound behind her.

"What is it?" Katherine turned, worried the hills might have been too much for her abigail.

Birdie had her mouth pursed in disapproval. "Nothing at all, madam. Let's go in."

But she saw him. Her husband had just come out of a shop across the street, and was now strolling along with a woman on his arm. They had their heads close together in conversation. They were near enough for Katherine to see that the lady was very beautiful, with dark curls pinned up beneath her fashionable straw hat and a generous bosom under her stylish pelisse. Whatever they were discussing engrossed them; neither looked away from the other until Gerard opened the door of a coffee shop and ushered his companion inside.

"Shall you order a blue dress or a green one?" asked Birdie. "I vow, that color in the window would look very well on you."

Katherine said nothing. She waited until a few carriages passed, then crossed the street. Gerard and the woman had come from a jeweler's shop. For a moment she stood looking at the bracelets tastefully displayed in the window. Howe had had mistresses. Discovering the first one shocked her; she'd gone to her mother in tears when she realized her husband was visiting, and lavishing jewelry on, a handsome widow in the next town barely three months after wedding her. Her mother chided her for being silly about it. Men like Howe were supposed to have mistresses, she explained. It was the way of their class.

Katherine had better not kick up a fuss or Howe might punish her by withholding her pin money. After that Katherine didn't say a word. To her knowledge, Howe had visited at least three other women during their marriage, and after the first shock wore off, she realized she hadn't minded very much.

But Gerard said he wouldn't take a mistress unless they didn't suit each other in bed. Perhaps he had lied that morning when he said he was pleased. Perhaps she had been so disappointing last night, he couldn't wait to find another woman. Perhaps the woman had been waiting for him, and she was the reason they had come to Bath. And he rushed right out to see her and buy her jewels.

Katherine heaved a silent sigh. Perhaps it was none of that. Perhaps it was just that her husband preferred livelier company, or more fashionable women, or felt compelled to offer his arm to an unescorted lady. She didn't know him well enough to guess why he was strolling leisurely about town with another woman after telling his wife he would be consumed with business every day, and she must amuse herself. She had tried to tell herself their marriage would be like this, but she didn't realize until now just how much she'd hoped it would not.

"Madam." Birdie broke into her thoughts. "Let's order some dresses, my lady," she said gently. "It's time to shed these drab clothes."

All her anticipation of that had faded, but she refused to be put off. She had endured it before, and she could endure it now. "Yes," she said, turning her back on the jewelry shop. "Let's order a dozen dresses."

Chapter 13

Gerard returned home with much on his mind. Visiting the post office had yielded more questions than answers, it seemed. He had a description of the man who mailed the letters but nothing else of real value. He didn't know what to make of the idea that all the letters were written at one time, and the first thing he did on reaching Queen Square was retrieve the other two letters, posted from London and an unknown town, and compare the writing under a strong light with a lens. Only on one letter had the town been spelled correctly the first time, and the correction on the first letter was identical to the correction on one of the Bath letters. It clearly looked like the work of someone who wrote the same thing three times incorrectly, amended them with increasing exasperation, then got it right the fourth time.

And what that said about the blackmailer, he had no idea.

He got out the reports from his father's investigators and read them all again. They appeared to have spent more time looking for Dorothy Cope herself, and to a lesser extent the so-called minister who had married her to Gerard's father, a man called Ogilvie, than for the actual blackmailer. That must have been at Durham's direction; Durham would have preferred to cut off the blackmailer's ability to harm with one ruthless stroke, then laugh at the villain's threats. Gerard, on the other hand, didn't give a damn if he found Dorothy Cope or the Reverend Mr. Ogilvie if he could instead find the man who knew about them and relieve him of any damaging evidence. If Ogilvie or Mrs. Cope still lived, they would be elderly. As long as neither one of them had sent those bloody letters, Gerard had no interest in disturbing their lives. He just wouldn't allow them to disrupt his.

Bragg tapped at the door. "Dinner is ready, Captain."

"Thank you. Is Her Ladyship waiting?"

"Yes, sir, in the drawing room."

Gerard nodded and waved him off. He pulled on his jacket and patted the pocket; the necklace he'd bought for Kate was still within. He left the tiny study and went into the drawing room, where she was sitting very still and erect on the hideous sofa. Even with all the lamps lit, the room was oppressively dark, with a brown rug on the floor, heavy green draperies at the windows, and muddy green silk on the walls. The furniture was of dark, heavy wood, upholstered in the same sickly green as the walls. It depressed his spirits just to walk into the room. "Shall we dine?" he asked Kate abruptly, not wanting to spend another minute in there. "I apologize for keeping you waiting."

She rose without a word and laid her hand on his arm. Not until they were seated in the dining room—

little better than the drawing room, although the mustard yellow color of the walls was a trifle brighter—did Gerard realize she was avoiding his gaze. Her expression was smooth and placid, and she was polite to the servants, but she never looked his way. When dinner had been served, he snapped his fingers and waved at Bragg and the footman, who silently left the room and closed the doors.

Gerard didn't know what might have irked her, so he waited. In his experience, an angry woman was rarely a silent woman. But Kate picked up her fork and began eating without so much as a word. He gave a mental shrug and turned to his own dinner, but eventually he had to know. "What did you do today, my dear?"

"I looked over the house," she answered. "Birdie and I went for a stroll."

"Excellent." Gerard could practically see frost on her breath when she spoke, but he couldn't imagine why. They'd been on rather good terms when they parted this morning—or so he'd thought. "I trust you found everything in order."

"Yes."

"Did Bragg make himself useful?"

"Yes."

"Did you like the town?"

She took a sip of wine. "Bath is lovely."

He leaned back in his chair. "What's wrong, Kate?"

Her jaw twitched. "Nothing. Why do you ask?"

"You seem quiet."

Her gaze flashed his way for a second. "What is there to say?"

"You haven't anything at all to say to your husband?"

"I answered all your questions."

That she had. Gerard poured more wine. Perhaps he should let it go . . . If only he were able. "I met an old friend today," he said, switching tactics. "He invited us to attend the theater with him the evening after next."

She put down her fork. "I'd rather not."

"Do you not enjoy the theater? We could attend the Assembly Rooms instead. They often have very fine entertainments there, balls and concerts."

Faint color bloomed in her cheeks, but she still didn't look at him. "I have nothing against the theater. I simply don't wish to go out yet."

He frowned. "Not at all? Bath is a capital place. I hate to think you want to sit at home alone."

She hesitated. "I haven't anything proper to wear to the theater."

"Is that all?" Gerard exclaimed. "Order some gowns."

"I did." She raised her eyes to his at last. "Several. In Milsom Street."

Of course—a woman needed clothing, and he'd made her leave London with only a single valise. "I hope at least one is red," he said with a grin and a wink. "We shall wait until your new wardrobe is ready and go to the theater then. I'll take a box and invite my friends to sit with us. You'll like them, I know. Lieutenant Carter is with my own regiment; a tremendous fellow, recovering from a leg wound. And his sister will be with him, a very charming widowed lady. I should like to have them around to dinner as well."

Kate sat in silence, her hands in her lap. "Perhaps. Was she the lady you were walking with on Milsom Street today?"

"Hmm? Yes, Mrs. Fitzwilliam. She's been caring for Carter, and if we can persuade him to go out more, I think she would be very grateful."

"I see," his wife murmured.

Belatedly it dawned on Gerard what she was really asking. Kate sat stiffly in her chair, shoulders a little hunched, eyes shadowed. There was a fierce, troubled expression on her face. For a moment he felt affronted. Already she doubted him? But perhaps he should have expected it. Most likely this was another of Lord Howe's legacies. He pushed back his chair and tossed aside his napkin. "Come here."

She started. "What?"

"Come here." He reached out one hand. Slowly she got out of her chair and gave him her hand. Gerard pulled, tumbling her into his lap. "Put your hand in my pocket."

She quit struggling to right herself, and her eyes rounded in shock. "*What?*"

"My left pocket," he repeated. "Take out what's in there." Gingerly she put her hand into his pocket and drew out the jeweler's box. "Open it," he told her. He couldn't help noticing her fingers trembled as she did so.

For a moment she just stared at the necklace. It wasn't the most elaborate piece, but he thought it suited her. Mrs. Fitzwilliam had steered him away from lockets and chokers toward this simple but striking pendant. The oval amethyst stone was surrounded by two dozen small pearls and hung on a long gold chain. As soon as he saw it, he pictured it nestled between Kate's bare breasts, the deep violet of the stone reflecting the hidden lights in her eyes.

"Do you like it?"

"Yes," she whispered. "It's beautiful."

He took the box from her and removed the necklace. "I met Mrs. Fitzwilliam this afternoon for the first time," he said, unhooking the clasp. "I asked her advice because I know little of jewels." That was always Charlie's domain; Gerard still recalled his father's snarling over the bills from London jewelers for Charlie's mistress of the moment. Never buy jewels for a woman unless you are assured of equal value in return, Durham had advised him and Edward. "And I am not having an affair with her," he added, fastening the chain at the nape of her neck.

"I didn't think . . ." Her voice died away as she fingered the pendant.

"Yes, you did." He leaned back. "Aren't you going to thank me?"

"Thank you," she said at once. "Very much."

"Not like that."

She blushed again, but leaned forward and pressed her lips to his. This time he let her control the kiss. After a moment she touched her tongue to his lip, and obediently he opened his mouth. Her tongue was gentle, a bit shy, but Gerard found himself being rapidly carried away by her earnestness. Four days ago she'd let him kiss her; today she cupped her hands around his jaw and kissed him. By the time she lifted her head, his heart was thumping, and his trousers were growing tight.

"Was that what you meant?" she whispered. When

Kate had been well kissed her voice took on a husky, sensual timbre. He liked it.

"A fair start," he murmured. "I feel slightly gratified."

"Slightly!"

"A little." He smiled at her. "What else can you think of?"

She gazed back at him, her eyes dilated but steady. "Do you want to go upstairs?"

He rather liked this; sitting on his lap, she had to hold tight to him, and her breasts, with the amethyst pendant nestled between them, were right at eye level. "There's no need for that. Lift your skirt."

She jumped as he tickled the inside of her ankle. "We are in the dining room!" she whispered in horror.

"Bragg won't come in." Gerard nuzzled the underside of her jaw. "You smell delicious . . ."

"Someone else might!" She ducked away from his kiss. "To clear the dishes!"

Gerard sighed and lifted her off him. He strode across the room, catching up a chair as he went, and wedged the chair under the doorknob of the door into the hall. He went to the sideboard and shoved it until the corner of it blocked the other door. He turned back to Kate, who was watching with her mouth open and bright spots of pink in her cheeks, and took off his jacket and tossed it aside. "Now, lift your skirt."

Katherine was speechless—and, to her intense shock, aroused. He wanted to have her here, in the dining room, where dinner still sat on the table, growing cold. The pendant he had given her brushed against her breasts every time she moved, sending ripples of gooseflesh over her skin that seemed to course straight between her legs. He wasn't having an affair with that lady in Milsom Street. That mattered a great deal to her. She grasped her skirt and pulled it upward a few inches.

"Good," he murmured, unbuttoning his waistcoat as he watched her. "Further, please."

Her face was hot as she complied. Her knees shook as she exposed them.

He dropped into a chair and crooked one finger at her. "Come here."

Slowly she did, still clutching handfuls of her skirt. Gerard sat forward and skimmed his palm over her leg when she stopped in front of him. "You have lovely legs." His eyes were as bright as blue flames. His hand stroked higher, up her thigh. "Lift your skirt higher," he said softly. "All the way, Kate."

"This is indecent," she whispered.

"And the shift." A wild, sinful grin touched his mouth. "There's nothing indecent about a wife pleasing her husband."

"This really pleases you?" But it was obvious it did. Katherine took a deep breath and inched her skirt higher.

"If you ever have doubts about how to please me, I shall be glad to tell you just . . . exactly . . . what to do." With a deft turn of his wrist, he flipped up the hem of her dress and petticoat, completely exposing her. Katherine flinched, but he held tight to her clothing and kept her in place. "I told you this morning," he murmured, tracing his fingertips down her belly into the curls between her thighs, "men are simple

creatures. Let me touch you like this . . ." His fingers
drifted lower, and Katherine quivered. "Kiss me as
you did a few moments ago . . ." He tucked the folds
of fabric into her fist, then slid his free hand around
her hip to grasp her bottom and draw her nearer.
"And I shall be a happy man."

She had to brace one hand against his shoulder
as his wicked fingers teased her. Of their own volition her hips began to move, rocking into the deliri-
ous sensation he caused. "I shall"—he slid one long
finger inside her, and Katherine almost fell over—"I
shall try," she gasped. It was torture to stand here
and let him caress her like that.

"And if you respond to me as you did last night . . ."
He laughed quietly, and pushed another finger inside,
sliding high and then withdrawing. "As your body is
doing now—Good Lord, Kate, I can't wait . . ." He
tore open the buttons on his trousers, then hauled her
forward. "Spread your legs to either side of me," he
rasped. "Now sink down—there—*Yes*—like that—"
He threw back his head and groaned as she eased her
weight down, onto his organ. It was awkward and
strange, with her legs draped over his and his fingers
still stroking her as he slid into her.

Perhaps because of the different position, it didn't
feel as intrusive this time. She pressed her slippers
into the carpet and tried to balance. He grabbed her
waist and held her as he slid lower in the chair. "You
are in command," he said tightly. "Do as you wish."

She didn't move. "Tell me what to do."

His eyes flew open, and he looked at her. For a
moment the silence stretched taut, Katherine balanced on the balls of her feet, Gerard breathing hard

beneath her, the junction of their bodies hidden under the billows of her skirt. "Hold on to my shoulders," he said at last. "Push with your feet to rise up, then fall." She tried it. When she sank down, he flexed his hips to surge upward into her, and she gasped. "Do it again," he commanded. "And again."

She caught the rhythm. Katherine bowed her head and closed her eyes, concentrating on every feeling. She took him into her body, then pulled away. Unlike last night, where she had allowed him in, this time it seemed she was taking from him. It made her feel powerful, in a way; rather than lying tamely on her back, she was on top, moving as slowly or as quickly as she desired. She tried it both ways, privately reveling in how her actions seemed to affect her husband. He was watching her with feverishly bright eyes, his jaw tensed. She paused once to adjust her footing and unthinkingly squeezed her thighs together. Gerard's whole body spasmed, and he sucked in a loud breath, so she did it again, just to marvel that she could cause that.

His hands slid beneath her skirt, and as she moved on him, he began to touch her. Now her body jerked and swayed involuntarily as his fingers circled and stroked that hidden little spot she had never known existed. Gerard whispered terse instructions from time to time, telling her to lean backward and not to stop moving. But she couldn't, not when there was such a rushing in her ears and her muscles were all drawn taut and she could barely hold herself upright. Gerard made a harsh sound and tossed his head to one side, but he kept teasing her, kept stroking her, kept tormenting her until Katherine gasped and broke, release flooding through her in a hot, liquid wave. His hands clamped down on her hips, holding them tightly to his as she shivered and sobbed in relief.

He gathered her to his chest, one hand still curved around her bottom so she wouldn't fall. Of course, she was also still impaled on him, and felt as though she couldn't separate herself from him if she wished. Not that she wished to at all. A vaguely silly smile curled her lips at the image, and she rubbed her cheek against his chest. What a ninny she'd been. "Thank you for the necklace," she murmured.

Gerard chuckled. "I'm delighted you like it. If it doesn't match any of your new gowns, you'll have to wear it, and nothing else, for me."

"That's indecent." But she smiled anyway. His heartbeat was a strong steady thump beneath her temple.

"By God, I hope so."

She lifted her head to look at him. "You're not much concerned with propriety."

He regarded her from under lowered eyelids, his eyes still gleaming. "*Some* propriety. But at home, when we are alone . . ." One corner of his mouth curled wickedly. "I hope to tempt you into ever greater indecency."

"In the library, I suppose?"

His smile grew broader. "A capital idea, Lady Gerard."

Her heart soared at the way he looked at her. Perhaps this was the way to win his love. Once she'd gotten over the initial shock, she realized it was rather exciting to make love in the dining room. Until now, she'd forgotten where they were anyway. And it was tremendously thrilling to know he wanted her at all.

But it happened because she'd made a gross error in judgment about him. He'd been exasperated with her when he pulled her into his lap. She should apologize before he had time to think on it. "I'm sorry I leaped to conclusions earlier," she said hesitantly. "I had no grounds to do so."

He sighed. "How many mistresses did Howe have?"

She didn't move. "Four I knew of."

"Ah. Once again"—he tapped her nose—"I am not Howe. Don't presume I'm anything like him."

Never. She had never felt so much breathless hope for her future with Lord Howe, never felt suffocated by joy when Howe touched her, and certainly never lifted her skirts for Howe in the dining room. Every time she saw some sign that Gerard wasn't interested in her affections, he managed to do something else that completely overwhelmed her reserve and put her in ever-deeper danger of falling madly in love with him. She smiled, trying to keep her expression serene instead of glowing with incipient adoration. "I won't. Ever again."

Chapter 14

L ady Darby and her sister, Mrs. Woodforde,
might have been two halves of the same person.

They spoke in the same quick, lilting voice, and
regularly finished each other's sentences. Their brains
seemed to run along exactly the same lines and at the
same tempo. Even their gestures were the same. And
to cap it all off, they looked virtually identical. Lady
Darby was a little plumper, and Mrs. Woodforde a
little taller, but otherwise, Katherine thought, their
own mother might mistake one for the other.

Together, they were two of the most entertaining
people she had ever encountered. From the moment
they called, she was caught up in the rapid swirl of
their conversation, sent in one direction, then another, flooded with information about other residents
of Bath and the peculiarities of Queen Square one
moment and barraged with polite questions about
herself the next. All of it was done in such a deft and
friendly way, though, she found herself smiling and
answering freely.

"We are just so delighted to have such a pretty
new neighbor, *delighted*!" declared Mrs. Woodforde,

beaming. "Barbara, isn't she the loveliest girl you've ever seen?"

Lady Darby nodded vigorously. "Indeed! What I wouldn't give for such fine skin and eyes."

"You flatter me," Katherine said with a blush of discomfort.

"Stuff and nonsense. Barbara was considered a pretty girl in her youth, but she never had a good complexion." Mrs. Woodforde leaned forward and whispered loudly, "Cow pox, you know."

"Hush, Alice!" cried Lady Darby. "It is two trifling scars!"

"I think she must have been a great beauty," said Katherine, not certain how to react.

"Well, perhaps," allowed Mrs. Woodforde as her sister smiled in delight at Katherine. "We are twins, you know."

"I am the younger," put in Lady Darby.

"I am the prettier," added Mrs. Woodforde with a triumphant air. Katherine bit back a smile, only to let it out when both older ladies burst into laughter at each other.

"You must forgive us, Lady Gerard. We have only each other most of the time, and sometimes forget ourselves." Mrs. Woodforde dabbed at her eyes, still chuckling.

"Yes, no daughters to pass on our great beauty to," said Lady Darby, sending her sister into another gale of laughter. "And our sons all gone off here and there! Mrs. Woodforde's eldest is at sea, like his father was, and my boy has taken up the law, in London. So you've done a great service to us all, bringing your tall, handsome husband to ornament our Square."

Lady Darby winked at her. "Shall we see you at the Assembly Rooms soon?"

"Er . . . Possibly." Katherine smiled to cover the fact that she didn't know if her husband liked to dance or play cards. "The captain has taken a box at the theater."

"Excellent! We attend the theater every week, twice if the weather is poor. Good weather, as you must know, Lady Gerard, leads to a great many entertainments in Bath. And in the autumn, there are festive activities, which you will no doubt enjoy—you *do* plan to remain in Bath through the end of the year?"

"I—well . . ."

"Hush, Alice," Lady Darby scolded her sister. "Bath is miserable in winter, and you know it. You fly for the coast at the first frost."

" 'Tis not miserable," Mrs. Woodforde cried. "We go to Portishead for the admiral's health." Her husband was a retired Admiral of the White, as she had mentioned three times already.

Lady Darby sniffed. "By health, you mean his desire to be solitary."

"He enjoys better health out of society," her sister retorted.

"I am sure his absence does society no harm, either." Both ladies went off in another fit of laughter. Making sport of each other's husbands appeared to be a habit of theirs. "Quite unlike your husband, Lady Gerard. We do so hope to see a good deal of both of you."

"They're newly married, Barbara!" Mrs. Woodforde fanned herself. "We shall be lucky to see them at all!"

"Pish." Lady Darby made a face. "Newly married was the only time Sir Philip would escort me about. We are hardly ever together now."

"And I don't see why you are complaining about it!" More laughter. "But really, Lady Gerard, you must have him wound around your little finger by now! He's a very fortunate fellow in our opinion, surely you can persuade him."

"Of course she can," declared Lady Darby. "I implore you, Lady Gerard. We are so very delighted to have new neighbors. Queen Square shall be ever so much livelier now you are here. You *must* dine with us."

"I should like that very much." Katherine smiled a little nervously. She had gathered from Bragg that gossipy old ladies were not the company Gerard enjoyed best, but one must be neighborly. And it was so lovely to be invited anywhere, and to be free to accept as she wished, she decided she would go alone if she must. The two ladies were so warm and amusing, surely one dinner would do no harm.

By the time her callers left, after much more amusement over husbands and unstinting encouragement to fling herself headlong into the social whirl of Bath, Katherine felt a bit battered. She was glad they called, but goodness, they could talk a deaf man into madness. She hoped her husband wouldn't be displeased that she'd accepted an invitation to dine with them at some point. She resolved to tell him about the ladies that night at dinner.

As usual, he was out all day, doing she knew not what, and returned home looking somber and a touch impatient. They had been in Bath several days now, and every day was the same. Gerard left early in the morning and didn't return until dinner. They dined together, talked of trifling matters or nothing at all, then went to bed. That last part was invariably wonderful. However much Katherine despaired of the gulf between them emotionally, she was continually astonished and thrilled by the physical pleasures of her marriage. Far from being put off by her lack of knowledge or ability, Gerard was happy to teach her. After the night he seduced her into lifting her skirt in the dining room, when she confessed she didn't know what to do, he didn't hesitate to tell her, in explicit and naughty detail, how best to please them both. It made her blush to think of the things she had done at his instruction—blush, and grow a bit aroused. In bed, her marriage was a hundred times better than anything she ever dreamed it might be.

But out of bed, they were still strangers. She still had no idea why they'd come to Bath, although it clearly had something to do with the scandal that was breaking when they left London. She still only knew the main details of that story since it hadn't reached the Bath papers, and Gerard didn't order the London papers. She had gleaned some knowledge of his personal habits and likes, but of his private thoughts and feelings, she knew almost nothing. As much as she told herself it was still early, she felt a bit of despair creeping in. Being close to him, intimately so at nights, was making her want more. Her belief that she could be content with a gradual growth of friendship and affection was suffering severely. Every rapture he wrung from her body, every pleasure he introduced her to, only made her feel more keenly the lack of everything else. His lovemaking had stripped away her stiff and proper hide, leaving her heart defenseless and exposed.

This night she cast about for a way to catch his interest. Perhaps it was her fault he didn't share himself with her; she knew she was a rather dull person, with simple, quiet tastes. She must make a greater effort. "Our neighbors came to call today," she said as he sliced the beef.

"Oh? Are they entertaining?"

She thought of the two ladies making each other laugh so hard their faces were pink. "Yes. They invited us to dine with them."

"Excellent," he murmured, pouring gravy over his plate. "By all means. Who are they?"

"Lady Woodforde, from across the Square, and Lady Darby, from next door."

His eyes flashed to hers. Slowly he put down his fork. "Elderly ladies?"

Katherine cleared her throat. "They aren't so very old. And they were very amiable."

"Hmm." Gerard stabbed at his potatoes, his piercing gaze never wavering from her. "I refuse to be a source of interest and information to the gossips."

"I don't think you are, except for being a tall, handsome army officer who is totally unknown to them and new to their street."

He grunted. "So far."

She cast about for another topic as he began eating, since this one was clearly not promising. "Did you make progress today?"

He looked at her, narrow-eyed. "Progress?"

"On whatever you came to Bath to do."

After a moment he shrugged. "Not enough. Don't speak of it to the ladies who called."

Katherine picked at her food in silence. Gerard ate heartily, as if the discussion were at an end. "I don't want to cause trouble," she said at last, after Bragg had cleared away the dishes, and they were alone again. "But I don't know how to avoid it if I don't know what it is."

"You're not causing trouble." He sighed and leaned back in his chair, tipping his glass of wine to his lips. "But any sort of attention or gossip could complicate things. I need stealth at the moment. Even better would be anonymity, but that's clearly out of the question."

"Why?" she asked. "What are you trying to do?"

He shook his head. "Nothing you need to worry about, Kate."

She clasped her hands in her lap. "I see."

"Do you?" He drank more wine and refilled his glass. "It's a ruddy Gordian knot, and I can't seem to unravel it."

"Perhaps you need to take a sword to it."

He laughed. "Perhaps I do! If only I knew where to make the cut."

Katherine glanced at him. He looked tired but on edge. "Perhaps I can help," she offered.

"Oh?" One corner of his mouth still curled. "I'm sure you can. Come here, m'lady."

"No, truly." She stayed in her chair even when he put out one hand to her. "If you tell me what you're trying to do, I might be able to help in some small way."

He dropped his hand. "I don't think you can."

She bit her lower lip in frustration. He was growing annoyed, when she was only trying to understand and help. "I don't want to pry. Different people see things different ways. I feel unable to offer even sympathy and support since I don't know what you're trying to do."

"Does it matter?" He cocked his head. "Does one need to know all before offering sympathy and support?"

"It would be nice if you talked to me!" she exclaimed. "You have my sympathy, you have my support, and I have nothing from you!"

His eyebrows shot up at this outburst. Katherine felt her face flush deep, burning red as she realized how much she'd lost her temper. "Nothing?" he asked in a dangerous voice.

She looked at his expression, and the flush spread across the rest of her body. "Well, not—not *nothing*," she stammered. "But . . . we don't talk of anything. Lady Darby asked me if we would go to the Assembly Rooms, and I couldn't answer because I don't know if you like to dance."

"Yes, I like to dance. And play cards and hear concerts. We shall attend the Assembly Rooms tonight if you wish."

Her new wardrobe still hadn't been completed. She had no gowns fit for society, and he clearly hadn't noticed; she was still wearing the plain dark blue dress she'd worn every night for dinner. She sighed. "Thank you. I don't wish to go tonight."

He scrubbed his hands over his face. "Kate, I haven't the patience for puzzles now. What do you want?"

I want you to take an interest in me, she thought.

How could one ask for that? "I want to be a good wife," she said softly.

"Excellent. Come upstairs and show me."

What a grand joke on her. She had hoped he would warm to her physically once they were acquainted and familiar with each other. Instead he took her to bed and made sweet, wicked love to her without appearing to care to be acquainted at all. She didn't know how to respond to that. On one level she was deliriously happy with her marriage, but on another, she felt more and more distressed.

"Kate?" he prompted, when she said nothing. He leaned toward her, a seductive smile touching his lips. "Come upstairs, love," he murmured. "Let me atone for my ill temper."

She stared at him with a sinking heart. Just the timbre of his voice made her body start to melt. She had to clench her hands together in her lap to keep from taking his hand and letting him do whatever he wished with her body. She had to clench her thighs together to quell the urge to follow whatever wicked instructions he planned to give tonight. He was so devilishly handsome, so virile, so charming. She had to protect herself somehow. "Not tonight," she said, dredging up all the calm coolness she had once relied on so heavily. It felt heavy and confining, but also safe. "I feel a headache."

"I'll be gentle." He stroked his fingertips along her forearm. All her nerves sang in joy. All her muscles knotted with the effort of resistance.

"No," she said, turning away from the sight of his beautiful face, dark and focused with passion, before she wavered.

"Oh, Kate." A bit of laughter lurked in his voice. "Let me apologize. Do you want to attend the Assembly Rooms tomorrow?"

She took a deep breath, steeling her nerve, and glanced at him. "Do you wish to go?"

"Absolutely." He smiled in sensual promise. "Now come upstairs."

"It won't interfere with your business in Bath?" She was weakening in spite of her resolution. Perhaps it would be a start. Dancing with each other, they would have to talk of something. And they would have to speak to other people as well, which might establish more openness between them. Perhaps she could bribe the dressmaker to deliver one decent dress by tomorrow evening, and if she looked presentable enough, he would take new notice of her.

But at the mention of his private affairs, Gerard's mouth firmed, and he flicked his fingers. "Don't worry about that. It's a dull and dry story, and I would rather do something far more interesting with you."

She had been patronized too often by Lord Howe and Lucien not to recognize it now. With great effort Katherine clamped down on the craving of her body for the physical pleasure Gerard offered. It wasn't enough that her silly, feckless heart had thrown itself into his hands; her body cried out for his touch. Only her mind was left to sound a warning, that she was in danger of enslaving herself to a man who gave little of himself in return. Howe had had the use of her body, but he never tempted her heart or engaged her mind. It was no difficulty to view their marriage as a business arrangement that required certain tasks of her, much the way Birdie did the ironing as part of her duties as abigail. But with Gerard she had hoped for something else, something more. She had hoped for some small measure of the companionship she had yearned for her entire life and was taken off guard by how much it hurt to find he didn't want any at all.

Stiffly she shook her head. "I'm very sorry, sir." Her words sounded distant. "I feel exceedingly unwell tonight."

His brow creased. "It came on very suddenly."

She kept her face still and expressionless. It had once been so easy to do that; now it felt like her skin might crack. "Yes. If you will excuse me, I shall retire for the night."

"Shall I send for Mrs. Dennis?" He sounded confused.

"Yes, thank you. Good night." She gripped the folds of her skirt as she rose and went to the door. Her hands shook with the urge to cover her face. Head held high, she walked sedately from the room, up the stairs, and into her dressing room. Then she sat down on the chaise and let the tears fall.

Gerard watched his wife leave, confounded by the entire conversation. What had he done wrong? It must have been something egregious, for she'd turned back into an ice maiden before his eyes. Her expression fell away, her eyes grew distant, and her voice . . . He frowned. He hated that emotionless tone, as if every word had to be wrung from her lips, and none of it meant anything to her.

He rang for Bragg to finish clearing the table. "I'm going for a walk," he told his man, before striding into the hall and jamming his hat on his head. He let himself out and paused on the steps for a moment, drawing in a deep breath of night air while he tugged on his gloves. A glance upward showed light glowing in the bedchamber window. He was tempted to go upstairs and coax her out of her temper. There was never a misunderstanding between them in bed, and Gerard was growing addicted to the nightly lessons in pleasure. Even though he was ostensibly the teacher, he was often caught by surprise at how erotic her response to his direction was. It was the best part of his days, in fact, an oasis of pure pleasure amid the grim, and so far thankless, duty of hunting the man who was trying to destroy his family. He'd been all over Bath and the surrounding area, searching for any hint of the man who had sent those letters, and found nothing. It was a relief to come home every evening and lose himself in making love to her. Why would she want to know the tedious details of his day when they could be so much more pleasantly occupied?

He set off at a brisk pace, irked that he had to take his exercise alone and outside instead of in bed with Kate. But if she wanted to deny them both, so be it. He knew she reached climax when he made love to her—he made sure of it—and he knew her body well enough by now to know she'd been aroused at the dinner table. He wouldn't be the only one going to bed frustrated tonight. Not that it made him feel any better. Why the devil would she plead a headache when they both wanted a good tupping?

A stiff breeze coming off the river helped cool his blood. He paced along the banks until a passing carriage caught his eye. It trundled up the hill in the general direction of the Assembly Rooms, lamps aglow. With a sigh, he turned his steps in that direction. Perhaps Kate cared more than she let on about social outings. He remembered that she didn't have any suitable gowns when they arrived and wondered if her new wardrobe was still on order. He turned up Milsom Street and located the dressmaker's shop, its bow window dark. Tomorrow he would see she had a proper gown and take her to the Assembly. He thought of holding her in his arms as they danced, of her smiling up at him, of the amethyst pendant gleaming at her bosom. And then he would take her home and peel the dress off her, and make love to her while she wore his necklace and nothing else. Yes, that was a fine idea.

He strolled on. Having a plan made him feel much better. He could invite Carter and his sister to join them. It would be good to have friends to converse with, especially if any whispers started circulating about the damned Durham Dilemma.

Suddenly it occurred to him that Kate would suffer from those whispers, too. She was part of the family now, part of Durham. He knew she was aware of the rumors; she'd known before asking him to marry her. Given how little success he'd had in finding the blackmailer, though, they might well both be considered outcasts before the end of the month. Again he wondered what moved her to bind herself to him when his prospects were so uncertain. Somehow he'd have to tease that explanation from her.

But until then . . . He swore out loud, and a couple walking past recoiled in affront. He tipped his hat and murmured an apology as he hurried away. He should assure Kate that he was trying to address the problem. That was surely what was behind her questions tonight, perhaps even her refusal of his offer to go out. He had unconsciously been treating her like one of his men in the regiment, giving orders and not explaining himself because he was the commanding officer and his word was to be obeyed without question. A wife was not a soldier. A woman rarely liked to be ordered about. Damn. He'd convinced himself he was sparing her the tedium of his task when really he appeared to be letting ruin overtake them both. No wonder she was annoyed at him.

Gerard turned his steps toward Queen Square. As he approached his own house, he glanced at the other lighted windows glowing along the street, wondering if perhaps the gossipy old ladies who called today had said something. He imagined someone like Lady Eccleston getting her claws into Kate and pouring a river of lies and innuendos into her ear. Some of the rumors about his father's activities were reprehensible. They reached his ears no matter how hard he tried to avoid them. And if the old crows tried to pry more information out of Kate . . . He jogged up the steps and let himself in, glancing up to see if she'd put out the lamp yet. The bedroom window was dark.

In the hall he handed his coat and hat to Bragg. "Did you overhear any mention of that damned dilemma when my lady had visitors today?" he asked quietly.

"No, sir." Bragg took his gloves as Gerard pulled them off. "There was much laughing and chattering.

Milady was smiling when they left, and everyone seemed quite cordial."

"Good." That was some relief, at least. For now.

He went upstairs and prepared for bed, slipping quietly into the bedchamber. Kate lay on her side with her back to him, curled up on the far edge of the bed. He set the lamp on the table and eased under the covers, sliding up close to her. She didn't move or speak, but her eyes were open. "Kate." He stroked her shoulder, disappointingly clad in a voluminous nightdress. "Do you really want to know why I came to Bath?"

For a moment she didn't answer. "Yes," she whispered.

He exhaled and settled a little more comfortably against her. "I intend to find the man who's trying to destroy my family name. The one who threatens to expose my father's shameful past and strip me and my brothers of our inheritance."

She turned her head a little. "How shall you find him?"

"By dogged determination. It's nothing exciting. In fact, it's rather lowering to talk about. I fear it would put you to sleep if I listed all the persons I've asked for help, all the rogues I've tried to bribe for information, all the pointless trips I've made."

"I wouldn't go to sleep." She rolled to face him. "What will you do when you find him?"

Kill him, quickly and quietly. Or as close to that as he could manage. "I'll determine that when I find him," he replied. "And I will find him. One way or another, all this nonsense about my father's scandal will be dealt with and settled. I don't want you worried about it. But the gossip could grow ugly, and I wish I could shield you from it."

"I knew it might." She smiled at him, her honest, true smile. It was a little bit shy, but it brightened her eyes and softened her face remarkably. She was almost pretty when she smiled this way. "I made my vows honestly."

He grinned in relief that the disagreement was over. Just as he'd thought, all was well between them in bed. "As did I." He gathered her close, reaching for the buttons on her nightdress. "As did I."

Chapter 15

⚬⚬

The next day, the dressmaker herself delivered three new gowns, apologizing profusely for the delay. Katherine thanked her in bemusement; she hadn't expected the dresses already, let alone a personal visit from the modiste.

"His Lordship said you would be wanting more as well," added Mrs. Goddard. "I promise next time to be more prompt."

"I see," said Katherine slowly. Gerard had done this? He'd been gone when she woke this morning. "And did His Lordship say anything else?"

"He mentioned he'd like to see a red gown next time." The woman's sharp gaze swept Katherine from head to foot. "It would have to be the proper shade of red, but you've got the complexion for it."

"Er . . . yes. I shall consider it."

Mrs. Goddard's smile was relieved. "Very good, madam. Now, shall we check the fit?"

While Katherine stood on the stool and let Mrs. Goddard make fine adjustments to the gowns, she studied herself in the mirror. Did she have the coloring for a red gown? Her mother had always said no, muted colors were best for her. She'd never had a bright dress with a low décolletage and a narrow skirt that skimmed her hips. The one she wore now was rich, vibrant blue, cut in the latest style and trimmed with seed pearls on the bodice and around the sleeves. It was a much lovelier dress than she'd ever owned before, and not just because it was a beautiful color. It suited her, she realized with amazement, better than any other dress ever had. The new petticoat was lighter and less full than her old ones, and the gown floated softly over it in slim lines. She looked taller, almost willowy. Her bosom even looked fuller.

"I look lovely," she murmured, turning slightly to see different angles.

"Very lovely," declared Mrs. Goddard. "Such a fine, slim figure! You've no need for those ruffles and trimmings. The cut must suit the figure, and the color the woman."

Katherine continued to stare at herself. "I've always thought colors didn't suit me."

"Every woman has her colors."

"Yes," she whispered, beginning to smile. "Even I."

What a difference a dress made. Mrs. Goddard delivered one evening gown and two day dresses, which meant Katherine finally had decent clothes to wear. After the dressmaker left, she laid out all her old dresses and surveyed them. Next to the new day dress of cream and gold stripes she wore now, her old clothing looked grim and tired. Even the dark blue dress looked like the garb of a woman twice her age. "Get rid of them all," she told Birdie. "I don't want to see them again."

"And about time, too," declared her abigail. "His

Lordship knows what he's about, ordering you to wear colors."

Katherine glanced at her. "That almost sounded like praise."

Birdie sniffed as she gathered up the dreary dresses. "I must say, he's been very decent since we reached Bath. His man Bragg is a bit rough, but accommodating enough. At least he's used to following orders and doing as he's told. All in all, 'tis a great deal better than life under Lord Howe."

She had to smile. "I expected nothing less." And it was, even with her uncertainties. When Gerard had left the house after dinner the night before, Katherine had felt a moment of alarm. When she peeked out the window to see him striding away, her heart nearly stopped. The last thing she wanted to do was drive him away. Her determination to keep some protective distance between them, to shield her too-vulnerable heart, only lasted until she thought of his turning away from her altogether. She had suffered real fear that he would spend the night elsewhere, in the arms of another woman. If he decided he would rather make love to someone else, Katherine worried she would have no use at all to him anymore. Her fortune was his, whether he ever spoke to her again or not. She had to adjust her thinking; if they got along best in bed, perhaps she should try to spend more time there with him. It would hardly be punishing.

But then he came home and confided in her. Not a great unburdening of his soul, but he told her why they were in Bath and why he went out all day. It didn't surprise her at all that he wanted to hunt down the man responsible for the scandal threatening his family, and she could understand why he'd been so secretive about it. It warmed her heart that he had decided to tell her after all. And then he turned her over and made love to her until she could barely breathe, let alone ask more questions. It made up her mind. She had hoped to win her husband's affection before attempting to stoke his desire for her, but there was no reason it couldn't work in the other direction. The flattering new dress only made it seem more possible.

That evening she had Birdie dress her hair for an evening out. She put on the luminous blue gown and dabbed orange water behind her ears before fastening the amethyst pendant around her neck.

"You look beautiful, Miss Katherine," whispered Birdie, one hand pressed to her throat. "Your father would be so proud."

"Thank you, Birdie." She squeezed the older woman's hand. As she regarded herself in the mirror, she thought it might even be true.

Gerard's reaction was even more gratifying. He stopped cold when she came down the stairs, and a slow smile spread over his face. "Good evening," he said, taking her hand as she reached the bottom step. "Mrs. Goddard earned every penny."

Katherine blushed with pleasure. "Thank you for prompting her to deliver a gown early."

He waved it aside. "I wanted to enjoy the sight of you wearing a decent gown for once." He lowered his head to murmur in her ear, "I already enjoy the sight of you wearing nothing at all."

Her blush grew hotter, but she was becoming used to his wicked ways. "That would be highly shocking at the Assembly Rooms."

He laughed as he offered his arm. "And a bit improper, even for me."

By the time they arrived at the New Assembly Rooms, Katherine felt like she was floating on air. She never imagined how much a mere dress could change everything. As they walked through the corridor toward the ballroom, women paused to watch them and whisper behind their fans. They were probably noticing Gerard more than her, as he was dazzling in his scarlet coat again; but for the first time in her life Katherine didn't feel insignificant and invisible. She kept her head high and smiled whenever they stopped to greet someone. It came as no surprise to her that Gerard already seemed to know half the town, while she only saw a familiar face when Lady Darby waved cheerily to her from across the room.

"There's Carter and his sister," said Gerard to her. "I've wanted to introduce you for some time."

She was glad he had waited. Up close, Cora Fitzwilliam was even more beautiful than she was from across Milsom Street. At least tonight Katherine felt at only a modest disadvantage next to the lady; in her dowdy old blue dress, she would have felt hopelessly plain. To her relief, though, Mrs. Fitzwilliam was perfectly warm and charming, and her brother, Lieutenant Carter, was just as cordial.

"I've so looked forward to meeting you," said Mrs. Fitzwilliam, drawing her a bit apart from the gentlemen. "I cannot tell you how pleased Danny was to meet Captain de Lacey in town. He's been so low, and the captain has given him purpose and determination again by asking his help. Merely having a reason to leave the house has given his spirits a tremendous lift."

"Oh," said Katherine in surprise. "I didn't know he'd seen Lieutenant Carter much."

Mrs. Fitzwilliam laughed. "Well, only a few times—but I understand the captain's business is very delicate. Danny strictly warned me not to say a word to anyone. I only mention it to you because it would embarrass my brother if I said anything to Captain de Lacey."

"Yes," Katherine murmured. "Of course." So Gerard had confided in someone—just not her. But perhaps Lieutenant Carter had skills and talents that were useful in the search, while she did not. "I understand I have you to thank as well," she said to Mrs. Fitzwilliam, touching her pendant. "The captain told me you advised him at the jeweler's."

Mrs. Fitzwilliam smiled and pressed her hand. "It was my pleasure! It does look splendid on you, as he said it would."

"He did?" Katherine smiled tentatively.

"He did." The other woman leaned closer, her dark eyes warm. "I understand he had never before bought jewels for a woman."

Katherine touched the pendant again. "He did very well."

She couldn't recall a happier evening. Lady Darby came to exclaim over her gown and pronounced her the prettiest girl in the room. The Woodfordes, she said, wouldn't attend because the admiral was feeling ill. She also took to Mrs. Fitzwilliam as if they were kindred spirits, and Katherine was soon caught up in smiling and laughing as the two of them chattered like old friends. No one who knew her from before would recognize her, she thought at one point, not even herself.

Gerard led her out to dance a country set that admitted little chance of talking, but that was best. For the first time in her life, Katherine felt the scrutiny of everyone in the room upon her. Every time Gerard took her hand or met her eyes with a sinful little smile playing about his lips, her heart nearly tripped. It was all she could do to follow the steps and not embarrass either of them. After that, other gentlemen asked her to dance, and Katherine was so shocked by the attention she said yes to everyone until she suddenly found herself engaged for every dance. That had never happened to her before. In the back of her mind, she knew it was due to her marriage and her companions and perhaps her new dress, not to any sudden improvement in her looks or manner, but for tonight, she was happy to revel in her new, unexpected, fashionability.

She finally begged off a dance after two hours. Her feet ached, and she felt almost light-headed from the heat and press of the crowd and the unfamiliar exercise and the two glasses of champagne she'd consumed. A little unsteadily, she made her way back to Mrs. Fitzwilliam, who had refused all partners and remained with her brother. He leaned on a cane—Gerard told her he'd been shot in the leg and sent home to recuperate—and thus couldn't dance. They were arguing over it when Katherine joined them.

"I'm not martyring myself," Mrs. Fitzwilliam was insisting. "If you want to get away from me, ask someone to dance."

"No lady would risk her toes getting mashed by my cane, Cora," he snapped. "But you should be having a good time."

"I am," she said serenely. "See? Lady Gerard has returned to save me from your bad manners."

Lieutenant Carter's face fell. For a moment he looked wretched, but he mustered a smile. "Then allow me to redeem myself and fetch some wine for you, ladies."

"Lemonade, please, sir," said Katherine, fanning herself. "Thank you."

He bowed and set off through the crowd. His sister watched him go, her expression tinged with worry. "I hope I'm not intruding, Mrs. Fitzwilliam," Katherine murmured.

Mrs. Fitzwilliam shook herself and smiled. "Not at all, Lady Gerard. If you stay and talk with me, Danny won't be able to scold me for not dancing."

Katherine was silent for a moment. Was she not dancing because she refused to leave her brother or because she didn't want to? "I'm not used to dancing so much. I may have to sit out a long while."

Her companion's eyes flashed with gratitude. "You must call me Cora. I feel we're to be real friends."

Katherine slowly smiled. "Only if you will call me Katherine."

"I would be honored." Cora tilted her head. "I always envied the name Katherine. I should have liked to be called Kate."

"My husband is the only one who calls me that."

Cora laughed, with a conspiratorial wrinkling of her nose. "How endearing!"

"Yes." Katherine thought about it. It was endear-

ing that he gave her a nickname. At first it sounded
odd and overly familiar, but now she liked the sound
of it. It drew a bright line between somber, retiring
Lady Howe and this new Lady Gerard, who had arrived on the arm of the handsomest man in town and
had a partner for every dance. Tonight she felt much
more like Kate than prim Katherine. On impulse she
turned to Cora. "Perhaps you will call me Kate as
well."

Cora blinked, then smiled anew. "With pleasure."

Yes. She took a deep breath and said the name to
herself, testing it. Not Katherine, but Kate. It sounded
warmer, happier, simple but lovely. From now on,
she resolved to be that new person she had somehow
become tonight, and name herself accordingly.

Chapter 16

Bringing Kate out for the evening was half-brilliant, half-idiotic.

On the positive side, his wife had never looked better. No one would call her a beauty, but tonight . . . well, tonight she was quite fetching, to tell the truth. He'd been right that a decent dress would make a world of difference, but he'd had no idea how much. The dull brown dress she once called her best made her look pale and skinny. Even Gerard, who knew every curve of her body, was astonished at how the new blue gown made the most of her slim figure. He was sure he wasn't the only man entranced by her newly displayed bosom, perfectly set off by the amethyst pendant. Certainly the number of gentlemen who appeared to solicit an invitation and a dance did nothing to diminish that belief. He felt the fierce satisfaction of a speculator who'd bought a piece of land for its rich soil, only to discover a large vein of coal ran through it as well. He would have been satisfied with the marriage if it only brought him a fortune and a wife who didn't trouble him much; instead he had the fortune, a surprisingly pleasing marital bed, and now a rather handsome wife as well.

Unfortunately that wasn't the only result of the evening's expedition. Within half an hour of walking through the doors, that cursed phrase caught his ear: the Durham Dilemma. At first he tried to ignore it and concentrate on his wife's obvious delight in the evening, but it stuck in his mind like a bramble. He tried to talk to Carter, who'd been helping him make a few discreet inquiries about town, but the murmurs seemed to circle around him like smoke from a fetid fire, subtly poisoning the air.

Gerard hadn't ordered the newspapers on purpose. He hadn't gone out in society, also on purpose. He had done his best to be unremarkable and uninteresting in Bath, some hundred miles from London, and still his father's sordid secret plagued him. He'd known that was probably inevitable, but damn it all, he would have preferred not to have it spoil this night.

His temper built at a slow burn until he couldn't take it anymore. If he caught one more man staring at him with avid curiosity and delighted shock in his gaze, he'd put his fist through something—or someone. He scanned the room, and saw Kate dancing with yet another fellow, smiling happily as they stepped through the quadrille. At least she seemed spared the tarnish of the scandal so far. He muttered a word to Carter and left the ballroom, hoping a bit of fresh air would cool the fury boiling inside him.

It was deserted under the shelter of the portico. A cool, misty rain had begun falling and steamed down the sides of the building, trailing into the gutters. The drops were so fine, they made only a muted whisper.

A passing horse splashed by, its hooves clattering on the wet streets. He took a deep breath and let it out, wishing he weren't so powerless. He had left London determined to do something to solve the problem and only found himself following one blind lead after another. What a fine joke it would be on him if he spent weeks chasing phantoms, and his brother Edward's legal strategy tidied up the problem without any need to find the blackmailer. He ran one hand over his head and bit back a frustrated curse. He was simply incapable of waiting patiently for that to happen, but so far his efforts all seemed impotent and wasted.

Behind him the door opened and closed. Another man stepped out. Gerard caught the sharp aroma of a Spanish cigar, something he'd not smelled since he returned to England. He moved a few steps away, not much in the mood to talk.

"Beastly weather," said the other man after a few minutes of silence. "Bloody Bath."

"I like it," Gerard replied. "It reminds me I'm in England."

A quiet chuckle was the only answer. A distant roll of thunder sounded, as slow and undulating as if the gods barely had the will to send it.

"De Lacey, am I right?" The other man came toward him. He blew out another puff of smoke.

Gerard watched it evaporate in the misty rain. "Yes."

His companion smiled. He was a good decade or more older than Gerard, a distinguished-looking man with streaks of silver in his dark hair. He was impeccably dressed, and a gold signet flashed on his left hand as he removed the cigar from his mouth. "Condolences on your father's passing," he said.

"Thank you," murmured Gerard, inclining his head a degree. Apparently solitude was too much to ask tonight. "Forgive me, I haven't the honor . . ."

"I'm Worley." The man returned Gerard's slight bow. "Of Uppercombe."

That meant nothing to him. "A pleasure, sir."

Worley still wore his small smile. "You're the one who married Howe's widow."

"Yes." That was no secret, and he'd rather be known for that than for the damned Durham Dilemma. There was really nothing exceptional about Worley but that annoying smile, as if he laughed at some private jest. Gerard wished he would go away.

Worley peered out into the rain. "Well done, young man. Quite a purse on that lady. I always knew you were the most resourceful of Durham's boys."

Something resonated deep inside his breast at those words—not in preening satisfaction, but in alert to some undercurrent in Worley's words. Who the hell was Worley, and why had he come out in the rain to speak to him? Because, Gerard was instinctively certain, it was not mere chance. "My brother Edward would be ill pleased to hear such a slur upon his character," he said, almost carelessly.

Worley puffed on his cigar, blowing out a long stream of smoke. Gerard shoved his hands into his pockets and leaned back against the wall, away from the plume and into a better position to see Worley. He didn't think he'd ever heard the man's name before, but Worley clearly knew something about his family. "Ah, yes. Edward the diligent one. Rather too bound by rules and tradition, don't you think?" Worley tilted his head to look at Gerard. "Of course you do.

Otherwise you'd still be in London, waiting for the lawyers to do their worst." He tapped ash from his cigar. "Not out here in the wilds of Bath, with no apparent purpose."

"My wedding trip." Gerard lifted one shoulder. "An escape from the suffocation of London."

Worley's sly smile widened. "Of course."

"You seem well acquainted with my family, sir. You must forgive me—I've been out of the country a great deal—but were you a friend of my father?"

"Friend." Worley considered. "I shouldn't say friends," he replied thoughtfully. "We had business together from time to time. I had a great respect for your father." He heaved a sigh. "Such a shock, the rumors that have abounded since his death."

All Gerard's instincts sat up at attention. Everyone in London, and apparently in Bath as well, wanted to talk about his personal scandal, true; but something was different about Worley's curiosity. His sigh managed to imply glee rather than sorrow. Gerard made a bored face even though Worley had his complete concentration now. "Oh. *That.* I expect that to blow over before we return to the city. People will find something new and scandalous to talk about before the end of the month."

"Yes, of course," murmured Worley. "Your brothers, I hope, are bearing up as well as you?"

"I suppose Edward wishes he could escape London as I did, but he's tied up with the attorneys over Father's will. He is, as you said, the most diligent of us three. And Gresham—or I should call him Durham now . . ." Gerard shrugged. "I daresay he hardly noticed. He's accustomed to being talked about."

As fleeting as a flash of lightning, a frown touched Worley's brow. If Gerard hadn't been watching closely, he would have missed it entirely. "Quite right," Worley said easily, no trace of displeasure in his voice. He took a long draw on his cigar, and the end glowed vivid orange as it turned to ash. "One mustn't allow the gossips any sort of triumph."

"No," Gerard agreed. "Durham would have thrashed us all if we gave any credence to lies and defamation."

Worley flicked the butt of his cigar into the gutter. "Of course. It's been a pleasure, de Lacey. Good evening."

"Sir." Gerard bowed his head courteously, watching from under his eyelashes as Worley strode back into the building. What was behind that strange conversation, he wondered. Perhaps it was just spiteful enjoyment of another's trouble. Perhaps Worley had borne some grudge against Durham, or one of Gerard's brothers. Perhaps Worley, like his brother Edward's onetime fiancée, sold gossipy tidbits to the local papers to supplement his income. Perhaps. But Gerard felt Lord Worley would bear a little watching, just the same.

Chapter 17

The next morning Kate woke earlier than usual, but she was still surprised to find Gerard in bed beside her. Normally he was gone as soon as the sun rose, and she often didn't see him until dinner. But this morning he lay in bed, staring up at the ceiling with a grim set to his face. She murmured good morning to him, and he replied in kind, but with a distracted manner. With a sinking heart she slipped out of bed and went to the dressing room.

She wondered what had happened at the ball. Most of the evening had been lovely, with making Cora's acquaintance and her own unexpected popularity, to say nothing of the pleasure of dancing with Gerard, even just once. He had disappeared for most of the ball, and she presumed he'd gone to play cards or do other things gentlemen generally preferred to dancing, but when he returned to take her home, she knew something was wrong. The carriage ride home had been almost silent, and she didn't have the courage to ask if he, too, had heard the whispers about the Durham Dilemma, or if something else angered him. His dark mood cast a pall over the evening that had been so wonderful, and then he vanished into his study when they reached home, leaving her to go to bed alone for the first night in their marriage.

When she was finished with her morning needs, she tried to steady her nerve. He had come home and confided in her a bit the other night. She wouldn't nag but merely offer a sympathetic ear. Perhaps she should confess what she heard of the Durham Dilemma—which was mainly what she had read in the gossip papers in London, but he must hate every word of it. She fidgeted with the sleeve of her dressing gown as she weighed the risks. Perhaps she should say nothing of that and tell him instead how much she enjoyed the previous evening and hoped he had, too. If he wished to tell her more, surely that was invitation enough. She drew a deep breath and went back into the bedroom.

He had flung back the covers but was still lying in bed, arms folded under his head and one knee propped up. Her throat closed up. He slept as naked as a newborn babe, she knew that; but this was the first time she'd gotten a good look at him in full light. He was magnificent, from the top of his dark, tousled head, over a broad chest dusted with dark hair, a lean belly and hips, and long powerful limbs, to the bottom of his big feet. It struck her anew that she had to be the most fortunate woman in England to have such a creature for her husband, in her bed, regarding her with knowing eyes from under his long eyelashes.

"You like to look at me, don't you?"

She whipped around, mortified. "I didn't mean to stare—"

"Yes, you did, and thank God for it." He snagged her wrist and pulled until she reluctantly sat on the edge of the bed. "You should like to look at me—not at other men, naturally, but it warms my heart to know you find me pleasing."

Pleasing. Her mouth was dry, and she could feel the wet heat between her legs. She dared to look again. Gerard was as pleasing as a man could be, to her eyes, whether clothed or bare. It shocked her that he lolled in bed naked and didn't mind if she admired his body, but it gave her a burst of bravado. "I've only really seen you," she said. "Do other men look the same?"

"Not half as fine," he scoffed. "How fortunate you are to have me, eh?"

"I have never denied it." Her gaze caught on one part of him, which was growing larger and harder as she watched.

He noticed. "You like me here, in particular?" He stroked one hand over his organ.

Kate blushed and looked away. "Yes. That part is also pleasing."

He chuckled softly. "Merely pleasing?"

She stole another glance at it. Even wrapped in his big hand, it looked large. She remembered how it felt when he thrust inside her and squirmed a little. "Not 'merely,' no," she managed to say. "*Very* pleasing."

He lifted his hand away. "Touch me, then."

She darted a shocked look at him. He was serious, despite the wicked smile that lingered on his lips. She reached out and gently touched him. "More," he said, his voice deepening. She jumped, but lightly ran her palm down his length. "Harder," he murmured.

She hesitated, then gave him a firm stroke. To her surprise Gerard sucked in his breath and put back his head. "Again," he growled when she paused. "Do that again, Kate."

She did, growing more confident with each stroke. He was satiny smooth, incredibly hot, and pulsing with life against her hand. "What do you call . . . this?" she asked.

"A hundred different things," he said, now breathing deeply and unevenly.

"Like what?" She ran her thumb lightly over the swollen head, and his whole body jerked.

"What do *you* call it?"

She paused. "I don't know. A man's part, or organ."

He laughed. "Prim words! Prick. Tool. Cock."

"Prick?" She gave a small laugh in spite of herself. "Like a needle?"

"Neither so sharp, nor so slender."

"I don't like 'tool,' either."

"Darling, if you keep stroking it as you're doing, you may call it anything you like."

"Cock sounds like an animal," she said, and audaciously wrapped her fingers around him as he had done himself. "It doesn't look like an animal at all."

In the blink of an eye Gerard rose, caught her around the waist, and flipped her onto her back. She looked breathlessly up into his face, dark and taut. "But it is a beast," he whispered, swooping down to kiss her as he shoved aside the dressing gown she wore. "Wild, untamed, and voraciously hungry." His hand was between her legs, his fingers exploring the dampness hidden in the dark blond curls there. "If you taunt it, madam, it may devour you . . . although I see you are a willing sacrifice." He fitted himself against her and nudged.

Kate arched beneath him, wantonly begging to be devoured. "What do you call that?" she asked, blushing anew. "That part of me you wish to—to devour."

"This?" He paused to touch her again, his thumb teasing lightly over the tiny bit of flesh that made her gasp and tremble. "The French call it *le chat*—the pussy. The Welsh named it quim. The crude English call it by its purpose: cock lane. But I . . ." He thrust forward, deeply into her. "I call it paradise."

"Blasphemy," she managed to say.

"Gospel," he said, harsh and low. He pushed into her again, harder and deeper. Kate mewed, half in desire, half in alarm. "Shh," he whispered, sliding one hand under her hip and tilting her to a better angle. "I'm doing penance."

"For—for what sin?" She clutched at his arms, trying to right herself under the onslaught of his desire.

"Arrogance." One by one he caught her hands and held them fast, spreading her arms to pin her to the bed. "Greed." His hips flexed, and he thrust so deep, she thought he would split her in half. His lips brushed hers as he settled his weight over her, holding her down, open and helpless under him. "But my greatest sin . . . Ah, that would be lust," he whispered against her mouth.

" 'Tis not a sin"—she gulped back a moan as he thrust again—"to desire your own wife."

"But to devour her?" He was moving again, nudging her thighs wider apart so he could drive himself into her even farther. Kate felt tears gather behind her eyelids as her insides clenched and shivered at the raw power of his possession. He had never taken her like this before, as if he couldn't get enough and couldn't restrain himself from taking it. He was right, though; she was a willing sacrifice to that desire, whatever he meant by penance.

"Surely . . . Surely it was part of the vows . . ."

His grin was savage. "If the curate said anything about this, I didn't hear it." He ducked his head and sucked at the tender skin below her ear. Kate bared the side of her throat and made a high, gasping sound as his teeth nipped her neck. He laughed, wickedly and quietly, surging into her even harder.

This wasn't love. She knew it wasn't. But it was more than she'd ever hoped for, and for this moment, it felt like love.

She writhed beneath him, her legs tangling with his before she hitched them up securely around his hips. He rode her hard, pulling her arms above her head at one point so he could hold her wrists with one hand, freeing the other arm to curl around her shoulders for greater leverage. His blue eyes glowed like lightning under his half-closed eyelids. His skin against hers was slick and hot. He flooded her every sense, breaching every bulwark she erected around her heart. It was hopeless; she loved him more than ever. If he never really loved her in turn, if this—this desperate need for the pleasure of each other's bodies was all they ever shared, she would still be his, heart and soul. With a sob of anguish and joy, she gave in, throwing open the last locked door inside her heart. Her body tightened, strained toward him, and finally burned in climax.

Gerard felt her break, and gritted his teeth as he pumped furiously into her. Good *God*. He had never felt so hard, so frantic with a woman in all his life. She was his wife, his to take whenever he wanted her, and instead of languishing under that matrimonial respectability, his attraction only grew stronger. Even as she trembled beneath him and threw back her head with a passionate little cry that made his ballocks draw up, he kept thrusting, harder and faster. He was addicted to the feel of her coming around him, so wet and sweet and unbearably tight. He was addicted to the white-hot sparks of pleasure that shot through his veins as his own release boiled over within him. And most of all, he was addicted to the dreamy little smile she wore when his vision cleared of the haze of sexual satisfaction. That smile was for him, and when she wore it, she was the most entrancing sight he'd ever seen.

"Are you absolved?" she mumbled.

"Oh, surely not." He rested his head on her shoulder and cradled her close. He didn't have the strength to do more. A moment later her hands touched his shoulders, then her arms went around him, resting lightly on his back. God, this was as blissful as he could imagine being, with her body holding his like she'd never let him go.

"Why not?"

He sighed, rubbing his cheek against her skin. "It was too satisfying."

Her fingers combed through his hair, a delicate, tender touch that only amplified the contentment he felt. "That's wrong?"

"It must be. If everyone enjoyed penance that

much, there would be no check whatsoever on sin and vice."

She went still, then began to tremble. Gerard lifted his head in bemusement, only to realize she was shaking with suppressed laughter. "What?" he growled playfully.

"That makes no sense," she said, barely holding back her merriment.

"It makes perfect sense. Everyone sins because it is pleasurable. Penance atones for the sin, so it cannot be pleasurable." He paused. "In fact, it seems highly likely we have both just sinned egregiously."

She burst out laughing. "You're talking nonsense! We are married. Marriage exists as a remedy against sin. The curate most certainly did read that part."

"Did he, indeed?" Gerard lifted one shoulder and grinned. "It's obvious why I went into the army rather than the Church." And she only laughed harder.

His new wife was slowly turning him inside out. When she'd offered a marriage of convenience in that small, dark parlor at The Duck and Dog, Gerard had been strongly tempted by her fortune and mildly intrigued by the challenge of melting her frosty demeanor. He never imagined such a passionate woman lurked behind her cool, expressionless gaze. He wasn't even sure he would recognize that woman as his Kate. It was shocking what a flush of color and some animation did to her looks. She still wasn't quite beautiful, but now her face caught his attention and held it, as he wondered what each new expression would look like. Far from the quiet, guarded creature he had married, Kate had bloomed into a lovely woman who smiled and spoke without seeming to weigh each word first. And now she was laughing. Gerard was bewitched. Her eyes sparkled, her skin glowed, and she looked so happy he couldn't help smiling, too, even though she was laughing at him.

"Do you know, I don't think I've ever heard you laugh," he said on impulse.

She paused. "Oh. I never did laugh much."

"Why not?"

Her face stilled, not in that blank, withdrawn expression he hated so much, but in honest thought. "Nothing much made me laugh before," she finally said.

Gerard studied her. Her first husband deserved an early death for not giving her anything to laugh about. Had he given her something to cry about? "What did Howe do to you?" he murmured.

She blushed. "I always was a serious child."

That didn't answer his question but made him certain he wouldn't like the answer when he heard it. "All children laugh and play, even the serious ones. I've wondered for a while if . . ."

"What?" she asked warily when he paused again.

Gerard met her eyes. "Did he strike you?"

Her gaze skittered away. "Only a few times. He never really hurt me."

"Damn it," Gerard said through his teeth, trying not to curse at greater length. "I thought he must have. You would look so frightened sometimes . . ."

"I was never frightened of you," she said in a rush. "Only . . . uncertain."

"You have no reason to be frightened of me, Kate." He rolled onto his side, taking her with him so they were still face-to-face. "Why did you do it? Ask me to marry you?"

She smiled although a little uneasily. "Aren't you pleased I did?"

He gave her a leering grin. "Yes, but I've always wondered *why* . . ."

"I already told you—because of your great charm and heroic deeds—"

"Don't forget my handsome face," he added in mock affront.

Her face was scarlet, and she wouldn't meet his eyes. "And you looked so dashing in your red coat—"

He didn't feel like pressing her, not now. The question of why she wanted to marry him only made him remember how close he was to bringing her down into ruin with him. "And because I needed you."

The color faded from her cheeks. "I thought it would serve us both."

"It has. I did need you." He sighed and rubbed one hand over his face. He didn't want to admit his encroaching failure, but it would be cruel not to warn her. She would discover it sooner or later, the more they went out in Bath society. "But I have to confess, Kate, your gamble may not pay out well. Things are not looking . . . promising."

She was quiet for a moment. "Have you made no progress in finding the man you seek? Are you really about to lose your inheritance?"

He grimaced. *So she did hear the whispers last night.* "I have a description of the man who sent the notes that started this nightmare, and someone who claims he would know the man if he saw him again.

But I have no name, and the man himself seems to have vanished into thin air."

"That's progress," she said. "Though not enough. Is there another angle to pursue?"

He laughed, but it wasn't a happy sound. "Of course—there are probably half a dozen. This was only the most direct. Find the blackmailer, and I'd be able to determine what proof or incriminating material he possessed. Relieve him of that, and he would be shorn of his hold over us. He could say whatever he liked, and it wouldn't matter without the proof."

"Yes." She frowned. "Where could he have gotten his proof?"

"That's a harder question." He shook his head. "A number of places, from a number of people, I suppose." She listened so earnestly, with no judgment one way or the other. His brother Edward thought he was rash and a bit foolhardy, charging off to find a blackmailer who'd avoided their father's investigators. His brother Charlie no doubt just thought he was an idiot. His father, he thought, would approve, but only of his choice of action; he could almost hear Durham's impatient prodding to find something useful or make some key realization that would break the puzzle.

"Perhaps if you search those places, you'll discover who else might have it and how he got it."

"True. It won't alter the fact that someone has it and means to use it against us." He propped his head up on one hand. Kate gazed up at him, her eyes pure sapphire blue. Suddenly he found himself telling her—wanting to tell her. "You heard the rumors about my father? Sadly, they're true, in most respects.

When he was a young man, he made a rash, clandestine marriage with a young woman of high temper and low rank. The marriage was conducted by a reverend of questionable piety in a tavern near the Fleet, of all places. Too late they realized how foolish it was, but neither had the money for a divorce, and my father was ashamed of the mistake he'd made. They simply agreed to part ways, and that was that.

"Father claimed he tried to find her again when he inherited the dukedom. It came to him after his great-uncle died; he never expected to be a duke, or else he likely wouldn't have been allowed enough freedom to do such a damned foolish thing in the first place. But when he became one, he knew he must marry and have an heir, and he knew very well that first marriage would cause trouble. Despite his efforts—and knowing my father, they must have been thorough—he never found her. It had been twenty years. Finally he married my mother, and there was nary a murmur of any impediment. For decades he believed the first wife was dead, or so far removed from England she might as well be dead. Only a year ago did he learn otherwise, when a letter arrived saying simply 'I know about Dorothy Cope.'"

"His first wife?"

Gerard nodded. "I gather it set Father off on a frenzied search. So few people had known about the marriage at the time—only the minister who conducted it, his clerk, and of course my father and the woman herself. The only record would have been in the minister's register—my father burned whatever form of certificate he received, and there was no license. But this woman . . . God only knows what she's done and what she's said in the last sixty years. She could have told any number of people. She could still be living."

Kate was quiet for a moment. "So might the minister or his clerk."

"True," he granted, "but far less likely. The minister must have married hundreds of people. Would either remember one couple?"

"He doesn't have to remember, he has their names in a register. He might have come across it by chance and seized an opportunity."

"He'd be a very old man by now. If he wanted to blackmail my father, why wait?"

"Perhaps he just discovered it recently and realized what it might mean. Or his family might have uncovered it when he died."

He laced his fingers together and rolled onto his back, cushioning his head on his hands as he thought. "Possible. But it doesn't fit with the letters. The first arrived a year ago, with that one cryptic line. The second came three months later, and said Durham's secret would be exposed. The third asked for money, which was never collected, and the fourth merely restated the writer's intent to reveal Durham as a bigamist. If you suddenly discovered evidence of such a thing and decided to act upon it, would you patiently wait a year? Would you ask for money and make no effort to claim it?"

"Perhaps he was prevented."

"Then wouldn't you send another letter, making a new demand?" He shook his head. "It doesn't make sense."

For a moment they were both quiet. Kate's brow

puckered up in thought, very appealingly in Gerard's opinion. "If I were the clerk's granddaughter," she said slowly, "or the minister's, or any innocent person who came across this mysterious proof, I'm sure I wouldn't know the first thing about how to blackmail someone. Undoubtedly it would take me a while to work up the nerve to do it. Perhaps I would suffer pangs of remorse. I'm certain I wouldn't want everyone to know of my actions, which would mean taking care to conceal it. And how would I explain a large sum of money?"

"You could bury it in your garden and dig out a few pounds at a time."

"Even posting the letters would make me nervous," she added. "It must cost a good sum to send a letter from Bath to Sussex. I would be in a state of fright someone at the post office might ask why I was sending a letter to a duke."

"An excellent point." He grinned at her. "The clerk did remember the fellow who posted one letter. He'd never seen a letter to a duke before."

"I would be beside myself over that very worry," she said. "But once I'd put my mind to it, I wouldn't wait months, as you said. I would wish it to be finished as soon as possible. This person must have a very strong constitution, and a very strong desire to cause trouble. Every few months he's sent another letter to infuriate you all even more, as if he didn't wish you to think he'd gone away and forgotten. Like a cat letting a mouse run away, only to pounce on it again."

He looked at her in surprise. "That's true. Perhaps money isn't the villain's object at all. Perhaps he just wants to ruin my father—or rather, me and my brothers. No one ever questioned Durham's right to his title. He could have had ten wives and still held the dukedom. Even had he not already died, nothing the blackmailer did could displace him," he went on, slowly putting facts in order. "My mother died years ago, so is also beyond the reach of any harm. Charlie, Edward, and I are the ones who shall suffer—who *are* suffering. I can't think of anyone who would wish that on us, except Father's cousin Augustus, who stands next in line for the title if Charlie is denied it. And if Augustus is behind this plot, he's got no need at all of poking at us like caged bears. He can petition the Crown for the title and sweep it out from beneath us." He fell silent for a moment, trying to comprehend it. "So someone wishes to torment us at leisure. It would certainly explain the letters and their drawn-out timing. The demand for money that was never repeated. And so far, no public denunciation. All the blackmailer has done is turn my family upside down."

"How did the rumors begin if he hasn't denounced you?"

"My brother Edward told his fiancée."

Kate's face darkened, and for a moment she looked rather fierce. "His fiancée gossiped about your family troubles?"

"No," he said, surprisingly pleased by her outrage. "Her father sold the story to a gossip rag because he'd squandered his fortune at the gaming tables. He had staved off ruin on his daughter's expectations. If Edward were to be disinherited, he wouldn't be wealthy enough to save them."

"How appalling," she exclaimed.

"Edward's well rid of her," Gerard said frankly. "He thought he loved her, which is why he trusted her, but she obviously didn't return the feeling."

She stared at him. "Yes," she murmured after a pause. "If she didn't love him enough to keep his secret, he's well rid of her."

He pulled her into his arms, tucking her against his chest, and pressed a kiss to her shoulder. "And now you must keep it secret also. I don't want anyone to know what I'm searching for. If this fellow learns I'm in Bath looking for him, he'll be on guard."

"I won't say a word," she promised.

"Especially not to Lady Darby and Mrs. Woodforde."

She smiled in acknowledgment. "Especially not, although they are very dear ladies."

"Granted." He rested his cheek on her temple. He'd thought it was a kindness not to burden Kate with his worries, but it felt surprisingly good to talk it over with her. "You made excellent points about the minister and his clerk. I find it unlikely they would be behind this, but it's not impossible."

"If you're having difficulties finding the letter writer, it does no harm to look in different directions, just to be sure."

He sighed. "My father didn't even recall the clerk's name. And there may well be a hundred William Ogilvies in Somerset, to say nothing of all England."

"It's not that common a name. Surely a few inquiries wouldn't hurt."

"Not at all."

"Then I shall keep my ears alert for any mention of the name."

He smiled again at her loyal determination to help. It was rather endearing to think of her as his champion. "If you hear word of him, let me know at once."

"I will." She nodded firmly. "One way or another we'll find the wretch behind this."

We. Now it wasn't only for his sake; he had her reputation and happiness to protect as well. Gerard held her tight, and said a quick prayer he would be worthy of her trust and confidence. "One way or another."

Chapter 18

Much to Kate's delight, Cora Fitzwilliam sent an invitation to go walking. Feeling very pleased to have a friend her own age, she answered Cora's message in the affirmative, and that afternoon they set out.

Cora turned out to be a passionate walker. She suggested climbing Beechen Cliff, saying the view was beautiful, and Kate agreed. Together they crossed the river and climbed to the top of the cliff, which loomed just across the river to the south of Bath. It was a steeper climb than it looked from the safe confines of the town, and Kate, not much used to climbing hills, felt rather winded by the time they reached the top, and she paused to catch her breath. Showing no such signs of fatigue, Cora urged her on to a particular spot. "You can see all of Bath," she said, laughing. "Come! If I sit down here, I'll not get up for an hour, and the view is so much better from over there."

Kate was sure she could sit anywhere on the hillside and enjoy the view, as long as she was off her aching feet. But she let Cora tow her to the desired spot and was immediately glad. "How beautiful," she exclaimed. The town lay below, nestled into the curve of the River Avon, like a mosaic of white stone and dark slate roofs set into the surrounding green hills, spiraling out from the Abbey Church in the center. It seemed one could see for miles, and for a moment she felt almost dizzy at the endless stretch of landscape below her.

"I think so." Cora directed her servant to spread out the blanket on the grass and settled herself upon it. "I could sit here all day sometimes."

Kate made her way to the blanket and sat down, holding her breath for a moment as her ankles throbbed with relief. "I could certainly sit here for a while today."

Cora smiled. "It's not as bad going down. But I understand. The first time I came, I was afraid I'd never be able to make it back to town." She drew up her knees in a very unladylike posture and folded her arms around them, gazing over the view. "Now I walk here every week if the weather permits." She flashed a quick smile at Kate. "Though normally without such pleasant company."

"It's very peaceful." And solitary. It was the sort of retreat Kate liked, a quiet, lovely spot where she needn't feel dull or awkward. But she was quiet by nature. She wondered what brought vivacious Cora out here alone every week. "Thank you for inviting me to come with you."

"Nonsense! I'm so glad to have a friend who appreciates it. Most people think only of the other people in Bath—much like London, I understand. It grows tiring."

"Have you been long in Bath?"

Sorrow flickered over the other woman's face. "Since Danny was wounded last year. It would have been too hard on him to spend the winter isolated in the country."

"Yes," said Kate softly, thinking of the long years at Howe Manor in Sussex. Even she had found it dull and constraining. "It can be hard."

"But you must tell me of London, for I've never been," said Cora with renewed brightness.

Kate smiled ruefully. "This was only my second visit, and it was no happier than the first. I confess I haven't a good account of the city to give. I was still in mourning for my late husband when we went this year."

"Oh my dear," gasped Cora. "Forgive me—I'd no idea—"

"No, no! I didn't mean to . . ." She stopped, mortified. "I only meant I didn't get to enjoy many of London's delights."

"The fault is mine, for prying."

"How could you have known?" asked Kate simply. She avoided Cora's dismayed eyes. "In truth, don't think you caused me any pain. It wasn't a true mourning. I didn't love my first husband; we hardly knew each other. His death was merely like another of his long absences." She looked over the town below them. "I do believe I like Bath a great deal more than London anyway."

"You have taken it by storm." Cora took the hint, much to Kate's relief. "I vow, even Danny commented that he wished he could dance, when you and the captain arrived the other evening at the Assembly Rooms."

"I would have been very happy to dance with him." Kate hesitated. "Perhaps you would feel free to dance yourself, then."

Cora held up her hand in mock horror. "Come now—don't you take his side against me! I shan't dance just to please him, nor even you."

"Of course not! You must dance to please yourself."

"Precisely," Cora said, before Kate had completed the sentence. "It just doesn't please me to dance."

With a swift bolt of insight, Kate realized why Cora wouldn't dance, and why she came up to Beechen Cliff to be alone. "You loved your husband very much, didn't you?"

Cora's lips trembled, but her smile didn't dim. "Very much." She looked away, shading her eyes. "Marks! Bring the picnic, please." Her servant, lounging under a nearby stand of trees, nodded and got up to bring the basket. "Climbing the hill always makes me ravenously hungry," she confided to Kate. "I hope you are hungry as well, or I shall devour the whole luncheon."

Kate laughed, accepting the change of subject. She assured Cora she was also hungry, and they spread out the cold meats and strawberries the servant carried over. She liked Cora very much, and she was beginning to think the two of them weren't so dissimilar, despite their opposite natures. Cora thought she'd caused pain by asking a question that led, however inadvertently, to mention of the late Lord Howe. Kate, who had some acquaintance with burying feelings deep, saw now the subtle signs of anguish in her new friend. Gerard told her Cora was the widow of a naval man, nothing more. For a moment Kate allowed a little door in her mind to open, just enough to consider the possibility that her own husband might not come back from his next campaign, and all she would have of him would be the memories of their weeks in Bath and a condoling letter from his commanding officer. Just the thought made her chest tighten and her eyes blur. With a shiver she slammed that door shut.

"I have to visit Mrs. Goddard's shop," she said, grasping the first happy subject she could find. "I still have only the smallest wardrobe."

"Indeed?" Cora's eyes lit with pleasure and relief, as if she, too, were happy to shake off maudlin thoughts. "She's a wonderful dressmaker. Her advice is always perfectly attuned to my desires."

"I don't even know what my desires are," confessed Kate. "I was assured for so long that quiet colors like beige suited me, but I find—I find I prefer blue and green and other bright colors."

"Quiet colors!" exclaimed Cora. "No, of course not. The blue gown suited you beautifully the other night. Whoever said beige would flatter you?"

Kate bit her lip. "My mother."

"Oh." Cora put her hand over her mouth. "Well, not every mother has an eye for such things . . ."

"My mother does," Kate assured her. "She's far more beautiful than I."

Cora looked doubtful. "Beige?"

"The captain suggested I order a red dress."

"Hmm. Yes, a nice ruby red would look lovely," said Cora slowly, eyeing Kate with a thin line of concentration between her brows. "None of those bright, garish reds. Mrs. Goddard has a good selection of silks in, newly arrived. Oh!" Her face shone. "One of them is the most brilliant gold lustring. It would look splendid on you!"

"Gold?"

"Goodness, yes, with pearls on the bodice and perhaps scarlet trim—" She burst out laughing. "You've made me want to dash down the cliff right to her shop!"

"Really?" Kate smiled hesitantly. She had rarely ordered clothing on her own; her mother always managed to oversee the process. The idea of ordering clothing like Cora described sounded enormously appealing. Cora never looked less than lovely, even today, dressed for hill climbing. While Kate was pleased with the new clothing she had purchased already, it only made her eager to have more. "You are welcome to come and advise me—*most* welcome."

"I happily accept. A dressmaker's shop is my favorite spot on earth."

Kate glanced around the hillside. "After this one."

Cora grinned, and a look of true comradeship passed between them. "Yes. After this one."

Kate's belongings arrived from London a few days later. Unfortunately they arrived in the company of her mother and Lucien.

"There was no need to bring them yourself," she said, trying to conceal her dismay.

Mama was unwinding the veil from her hat and glancing around with delight and interest at the hall. "Why shouldn't we come? Bath is lovely, and I've never been. And my dear, dear daughter, so well married! And so suddenly! I was quite driven out of

London, darling, by the incessant questions about the captain. It was unendurable—really, my dear, if you didn't wish me to come to Bath, you should have kept your new husband in town long enough to satisfy everyone's curiosity." She gave Kate a vaguely admonishing glance. "It was a trying journey, you know, and my health hasn't been all it might be. And now you've not got even a kind word of welcome for your mother."

"You are very welcome to Bath, of course," Kate said after only a slight pause. She stepped forward to kiss her mother's offered cheek. "I just didn't expect you to come all the way out to Somerset and miss part of the Season in town. I know how you look forward to it all winter."

"For my only child, I shall bear the sacrifice." She smiled, her gaze wandering toward the stairs. "And where is your husband, dear? I am ever so anxious to know my son-in-law better."

"He's not at home now." She stepped back to allow Bragg and the footman to carry in her last trunk. As pleased as she was to have her things again, they came at rather a high cost. Lucien followed, slapping his gloves against his palm. He looked thinner, and there were shadows under his eyes. Kate avoided his gaze as she dipped a curtsey. "Welcome to Bath, Lucien."

"Thank you, Katherine my dear." His voice was as cool as ever. "I trust you are well." It didn't sound as though it would give him any pleasure.

All her wariness of Lucien rushed back. For a moment her muscles instinctively slid into the lax expressionless pose she had found such safety in during her years as a member of the Howe family. Everything inside her recoiled into the small, safe place inside her where she had learned to hide her emotions and thoughts, to make herself almost invisible.

Then she stopped herself. What was she doing? Marriage to Gerard had saved her from this. She was no longer subject to Lucien's disapproval, and she no longer had to hide behind a mask. She lifted her head and looked directly into his frosty blue eyes. "Yes, thank you, I am quite well," she said. Compared to what her life would have been with him, she was splendidly, brilliantly well. For a moment Gerard's lazy, seductive grin flashed across her mind, and she even smiled. "Very well indeed."

His mouth turned down. "I am glad to hear it."

"Do you plan to stay long in Bath?" she asked, when an awkward silence descended.

"Why, goodness, I don't know," exclaimed her mother. "I suppose we shall see how it suits us."

"A week," said Lucien at the same time.

Mama looked at him in unhappy surprise. "Oh no, Lucien dear. A week is far too short a time. I must see my daughter again and become acquainted with my new son-in-law. It is a mother's duty to see that her child is settled, you know—you would understand if you had children of your own. Really you must look for a bride. Perhaps a lady in Bath will accept you since none of the London gels took your fancy."

Lucien's eyes flashed with fury even though his face didn't change. "I cannot think of marriage at this time, madam. You may remember the reason why."

"Well, it was very hard of Katherine to disappoint you so, but you certainly would have done the same in her shoes. A Durham!" She sighed happily. "Where is he, Katherine dear?"

"He is out, Mama," Kate repeated.

"Oh." Her mother finally seemed to accept that she was telling the truth and quit peering around the hall. "Well, he will surely be home for dinner, and we shall see him then."

Kate gazed at her. This was always the way with Mama; when she wanted something, she kept at it until Kate wore down and gave it to her, no matter how reluctantly. She felt the old ingrained instinct to do it now, in fact. But she didn't want to dine with her mother fawning over Gerard and Lucien glowering at them all, and luckily they'd already promised to attend a dinner party with Cora and Lieutenant Carter. She kept her head up though her clasped fingers tensed around each other. "Yes, he will return home before dinner—"

"Lovely." Her mother turned a bright, almost proud smile on her. "What time shall we arrive, Katherine dear? I'm so accustomed to town hours, I've no idea how people live out in the country anymore."

"Unfortunately we are already engaged for dinner this evening and cannot dine with you," Kate finished evenly. "I hope you will be able to join us tomorrow evening."

The hall fell silent. Her mother's blue eyes rounded, and her lips parted. She managed to look hurt and irked at the same time. "Oh, Katherine . . . You won't change your plan even to see your own mother?"

"I'm very sorry, Mama. If you'd sent word you

were arriving, I would have been better prepared to entertain you. But our engagement is with dear friends, and neither the captain nor I will offend them by breaking it." She looked away from her mother's expression of tragic betrayal and glanced at Lucien, who was watching her with an unfamiliar interest. "If you haven't taken rooms yet, our man Bragg will be happy to help secure lodgings for you."

"We are at the White Hart Inn. We should go there and settle in, now that your things are delivered." He contemplated her speculatively for a moment. "When Captain de Lacey returns, please give him my regards. I should like to have a word with him at some time."

"Of course." Kate hid her surprise with a polite nod. "Thank you for bringing my things."

When her mother and Lucien left, Mama gazing at her with disapproval and disappointment, Kate sank down on the lid of a nearby trunk and drew in an unsteady breath. Part of her was amazed she'd actually defied her mother's wishes and held firm. Until that moment she hadn't realized how much her mother had controlled her life, but suddenly it became apparent that the last few weeks had been the first period of real independence in her life. Her mother had hovered over her when she was a child, constantly correcting and gently directing her in everything. Howe had imposed rules on her, although he left her much to her own devices so long as she obeyed them. Lucien was so intent on securing her money, he'd kept her a virtual prisoner. Only in Bath, away from her former life, did she feel bold enough— and even encouraged—to do as she wished. To visit the lending library whenever she liked. To buy a red dress. To lift her skirt in the dining room and make love to her husband on a chair.

She was still sitting there, smiling a little in memory of the last, when the door opened and the man in question walked in. Kate jumped to her feet, flushing at the indecency of her thoughts. "You're home early," she exclaimed.

"But welcome, I hope." He winked at her as he doffed his hat and tossed his gloves on the table, then frowned at the trunks still blocking the hall. "What the devil is this?"

"My trunks." She waved one hand helplessly. "All my things."

"Ah. Bragg!" His man popped out of the door at the rear of the hall. "Let's take these upstairs."

"They didn't arrive alone." Kate watched with slight shock as her husband stripped off his coat and hefted one end of the largest trunk himself as Bragg took the other end. "My mother and Lucien brought them to Bath personally."

Gerard shot her a sharp glance but said nothing. He and Bragg carried the trunk up the stairs and deposited it in her dressing room. Kate trailed along behind, watching with hidden admiration as her husband maneuvered the heavy trunk so easily.

"We'll get the other in a moment," he said to Bragg, waving his man out the door. When Birdie appeared in the open doorway with a dust cloth in her hand, Gerard held up a hand. "A moment, Mrs. Dennis." Then he closed the door and turned to Kate. "Is there a particular reason your mother and Lucien Howe felt compelled to journey all the way to Bath when a servant might have brought your trunks?"

She twisted her hands together. "I don't know. Lucien asked me to extend his best regards to you and indicated he would like a private word sometime."

"No doubt," he said dryly. "And your mother?"

Kate nibbled the inside of her lip. "She wishes to become better acquainted with you, she said."

He looked at her for a long moment. "I believe a little of your mother's company goes a long way."

She blushed. "I already invited them to dine tomorrow evening. I'm sorry."

"No, that's not what I meant." He came across the room and tipped up her chin until she looked at him. "I will see her as much as you wish to. Or as little."

"I cannot refuse to see my own mother."

"You don't have to. But if you wish to find yourself otherwise engaged most evenings . . ."

She bit her lip as his voice trailed off suggestively. It was tempting. She always felt dull and insignificant next to her beautiful, sparkling mother. How startling that Gerard should appear immune to Mama's charm. "We are already engaged several evenings this week."

"I certainly won't cancel an invitation from friends."

A smile crept over her face. "Nor would I."

"Well." He grinned. "We shall dine with them tomorrow night. Perhaps they'll become swept up in Bath society, and we shall be hoping for invitations from them."

She laughed, as he'd hoped she would. Gerard hoped his impressions of his mother-in-law and Lord Howe would improve on further acquaintance, but he doubted it. He sensed Mrs. Hollenbrook was drawn to titles and wealth, and that if he'd been Gerard de Lacey, son of a prosperous boot maker instead of the Duke of Durham, she wouldn't have nearly as much interest in getting to know him. He remembered what Tyrell, Kate's father's attorney, had said: Mrs. Hollenbrook was eager for her daughter to marry well. There was nothing exceptional in that, particularly when the daughter was an heiress, but she'd chosen a middle-aged viscount for her only child. Gerard could think of no less than four good, decent men in the army, all sons of dukes or earls, all in the prime of life, who would have waited attendance on any heiress with more than ten thousand pounds, were she ugly, quarrelsome, or elderly. Kate was none of those. If she'd been brought out properly, dressed becomingly, she would have had more than one suitor. Instead she ended up stashed quietly in the country while Howe went about his business. Even Lady Eccleston, society spy premiere, had heard nothing of Kate.

So why had Mrs. Hollenbrook been so keen on the Howe marriage? Was there something else between the families? Gerard didn't know, but knowing how lonely and neglected Kate had been during her first marriage made him loath to spend much time with his mother-in-law.

Nothing happened the next evening during dinner to change his mind. Mrs. Hollenbrook, for all her beauty, was the shallowest woman he'd ever met. To him, she was warm and solicitous; when he spoke to her, she gazed at him as if the sun shone at his command. Her demeanor toward Lord Howe was similar although with a touch of familiarity that put Gerard in mind of a mother artlessly embarrassing her grown son. But it was her effect on Kate that caught his attention more. When Kate spoke, her mother's reply often had some subtle shade of rebuke, and Gerard watched in silent dismay as his wife grew quieter as the evening went on. Finally he understood the ice maiden. If one's every word was judged lacking, why bother to speak?

When the ladies excused themselves after dinner, Gerard caught Kate's hand. "We won't be long," he breathed. He had no more desire to sit over port with Lucien Howe than he wanted to leave Kate to her mother's mercies.

She looked at him somberly, then the light was back in her eyes. "Good." She smiled and went out with her mother.

Relieved, Gerard waved to Bragg to pour the wine and bring out cigars. A quarter hour should be plenty of time, and they could rejoin the ladies.

"I hope it is not presumptuous of me, de Lacey, but I must speak to you on business." Howe faced him with grim resolve in his face.

"So soon after dinner?" He really didn't want to deal with "business" tonight.

Howe's lips thinned. "I came to Bath for nothing else."

"A letter would have sufficed." Gerard tossed back the rest of his wine. A quarter hour was too long after all. "Shall we join the ladies?"

A deep flush covered the other man's face. "The ladies can wait. You must see reason; that note is ruinous. I cannot pay four percent."

Gerard raised one eyebrow. "Your uncle expected

he could make the payments. Surely he knew his estate's income."

"Perhaps," said Howe in a stony voice. "Unfortunately he died a few months after signing it."

"Then where did the money go? Surely he didn't
spend all ten thousand pounds in a few months."

The viscount glared at him. "Very nearly, much to
my dismay."

Gerard snorted. "What terms do you want?"

"Leniency. I need time—a year—to reorder my finances. A rate of two percent would be more reasonable, especially between family."

"What, pray, is our familial relation?" he asked
sharply. "And I understand you don't have to repay
a farthing; there was a security, which you could
simply cede or sell to pay off the debt."

"That property has been in my family for decades," said Howe through his teeth. "Surely a gentleman would understand I cannot sell it."

"I expect you shall have to retrench, then. Make
economies. Reduce travel, and perhaps tailoring
bills." Howe, in his fine evening clothes, turned white
with fury at that, but Gerard didn't care. He remembered overspending his pocket money as a young
boy and having to ask his father for more, blithely
confident it would be given without scolding because
Durham was one of the richest estates in England.
But his father, who hadn't been born to wealth, made
him shovel out stalls in the stables for a week to impress upon him the value of economy and the dangers
of debt. He never forgot it. It irked him that Howe
had assumed he would secure Kate's fortune and so
had done nothing to address the debt until she mar-

ried someone else. It irked him that Howe's manner of negotiating was to blame his uncle and glare at Gerard with barely concealed contempt and hatred. He'd known men who scrambled desperately to save their properties, selling the silver to satisfy creditors. It didn't escape his notice that Howe's first line of attack was to ask for reduced terms. True, Howe had inherited the debt; but nothing in his conduct since made Gerard feel disposed to forgive it.

He rose. "Enough of business, sir. I hope you will join the ladies with me."

He went into the drawing room, Howe following in stiff silence. Both ladies looked up at his entrance with smiles, Mrs. Hollenbrook's one of dazzling delight, Kate's one of relief. He took the chair near her, feeling rather ready to be her knight again.

Conversation lagged. Kate suggested cards, but her mother sighed and said cards were for larger parties. Gerard was glad for it; he knew Mrs. Hollenbrook would want to partner him, and he didn't want to leave Kate to Howe.

"Perhaps some music," he suggested. No conversation was needed if there was music. From the corner of his eye he could see the clock on the mantel. Another hour, and the guests would go home if he had to tell Bragg to shove them out the door.

"Sadly I do not play anymore," said Mrs. Hollenbrook. "Katherine, dear, have you kept up your practicing? You were making such progress."

Kate looked self-conscious but got to her feet. "Very well, Mama." She went to the pianoforte in the corner and opened the cover.

Whatever her musical talent, it soon became clear

the pianoforte needed to be tuned. One note in particular was flat. When she struck it the second time with a dissonant twang, Gerard leaped to his feet and began singing. The song was a well-known hymn. He crossed the room to the pianoforte, and whenever that one bad note came up, he sang particularly loudly. Kate soon barely touched that key, leading to an odd break in the sound when his voice rose and the instrument fell almost silent. Dogs all over the Square would be howling if we keep this up, Gerard thought, and nothing could encourage their guests to depart faster. Howe already looked sick to his stomach, and even Mrs. Hollenbrook's mouth was pinched. Excellent. He reached out to turn the page of music and noticed Kate's shoulders were shaking, her lips trembling. She glanced up at him with eyes teary with laughter, and he grinned in relief.

If she could laugh about this, in front of her mother, all was well.

Chapter 19

~~~⎯⎯⎯⎯⎯⎯⎯⎯~~~

Mama expressed a wish to visit the Pump Room the next day. Kate hadn't gone yet, for a number of reasons, and so was curious to see the celebrated springs. Much to her mother's delight, the room was filled with Bath's most fashionable. Kate left her happily chatting with Lady Deane, also newly arrived in town, and went to fetch glasses of the mineral water.

"Dear Lady Gerard!" Mrs. Woodforde descended on her, towing her admiral behind her. "How fortunate to see you here!"

"How do you do?" Smiling, Kate dropped a curtsey. "It's a pleasure to see you. This is my first visit to the Pump Room."

"First! Goodness, we come every morning, for the admiral's health."

"We come for the society," said her husband. He was a lean, weathered man with sharp eyes who didn't look much in need of the healing waters.

"Nonsense," his wife protested. "We come for the waters. Now, Lady Gerard, have you signed the Visitor's Book? You simply must; everyone signs it. It is quite the register of Bath!"

"As I said," murmured Admiral Woodforde. "The society."

His wife just rolled her eyes and tucked Kate's arm firmly around her own. "We shall see who has arrived recently. My sister relies on me to report to her since Sir Philip disavows any need of the waters and of course Barbara herself would never dream of admitting weakness. Here we are." She turned the page, making no secret of her interest. "Lady Hurst has arrived! But you must meet her, my dear; she is a bit eccentric but wonderfully entertaining. Five husbands she's had—oh, the stories she can tell!" Mrs. Woodforde giggled, skimming down the next page. "Mr. Westley! Oh, a very foolish man. If ever he asks you to dance, you must refuse at once. I wouldn't receive him, either. Your ears won't recover for days."

"Katherine dear, have you forgotten me?" Her mother came up beside them. "I thought you were to fetch the water."

"Yes, Mama, I met my neighbor, Mrs. Woodforde, and stopped to greet her." Kate turned to Mrs. Woodforde, who was pretending not to listen. "Mrs. Woodforde, may I present my mother, Mrs. Hollenbrook. Mama, my neighbor. The Woodfordes live across Queen Square. Her sister, Lady Darby, has the house next to ours."

Eyeing each other with curiosity, the ladies curtsied. "How pleasant to make your acquaintance," said Mama with one of her beautiful, rather dreamy smiles.

"And yours," cried Mrs. Woodforde. "My sister and I envy you completely, ma'am, for having such a fine daughter. She has brightened Queen Square to no end."

"Really?" Her mother turned to Kate in surprise. "She was always such a quiet girl."

"Oh, you've no cause for complaint," Mrs. Woodforde said quickly. "Lady Gerard is a perfect lady! So fashionable, so amiable, and so charmingly doted on by her husband." She tittered, with a glance at Kate that made her blush. "He's a lucky man to have her."

"Oh. Yes," murmured Mama, looking a bit shocked. "It was quite a surprise when they married. He is one of the Durham family, you know. Katherine was raised in Sussex, near the ducal seat, but I never dreamed one of the sons would deign to look at her."

"Pish. He's a very clever fellow, that Captain de Lacey. Much like my husband the admiral—where did he go?" Mrs. Woodforde craned her neck, but her husband had strolled away. "Oh, he's off with Mr. Thorpe again, no doubt talking about cricket." She waved one hand with a smile. "But Captain de Lacey, I am sure, recognized a gem when he saw one. Especially today, when you look as pretty as a rose, my dear!" She winked at Kate, who smiled in return.

Mama regarded Kate's deep pink dress with a shadow of doubt. "You've taken such a turn, Katherine. You never wore pink before."

"I like it, Mama."

"Of course, dear," said her mother. "It's just a young lady's color, really."

At her slight emphasis on the word "young," Mrs. Woodforde's head came up and her eyes narrowed. She glanced at Kate, who tried to smile as if it meant nothing. Cora had assured her the pink was flattering, and she did like it. Her mother just wasn't accustomed to seeing her in it.

"I was talking with Lady Deane, Katherine, and she mentioned that the Countess of Swinton has just arrived in Bath. I believe, my dear, the Earl of Swinton is related very distantly to your husband. You must call on her." Mama beamed as if she'd just laid a great prize at Kate's feet.

"I've never heard him speak of Lady Swinton, but I will ask, Mama."

"A bit high in the instep, Lady Swinton," said Mrs. Woodforde to Kate but with her gaze on Mama.

"I'm sure she would be delighted to meet her new kinswoman." Mama smiled at Mrs. Woodforde. "Family is so important, you know."

"If the captain wishes to call on her, of course we shall," said Kate. "But I wouldn't wish to intrude on Lady Swinton otherwise."

"Oh, you must, Katherine," protested her mother. "She moves in the very best circles."

Kate wanted to walk away in mortification. Her mother was a terrible snob—oddly so, since she herself was only the daughter of a baron and the widow of a merchant. From Mrs. Woodforde's expression, she took Mama's meaning all too well. Suddenly Kate felt a flicker of anger. Mrs. Woodforde wasn't very fashionable, and her husband wasn't titled, but they were kind and warm, and had been friendly to her when she knew no one. She raised her chin. "I move in very nice circles as well, Mama. Mrs. Woodforde has become such a dear friend in only a few weeks. She and the admiral were so welcoming to me and Gerard." She used her husband's Christian name on purpose, unable to resist flaunting a little bit of intimacy.

Her neighbor smiled back at her, a touch proudly. "The best circles, I always say, are the ones filled with good company, regardless of their ranks."

"I quite agree." Kate grinned back at her.

"I merely wish you not to neglect your duty, Katherine," said her mother, opening her eyes wide. "Even if you do not care for rank, it wouldn't do to offend your husband's family."

Kate doubted Gerard would be very upset if they didn't call on Lady Swinton. He'd never once mentioned her name. He seemed to prefer the company of his army mates like Lieutenant Carter, and so did she.

"I daresay you'll meet Lady Swinton soon enough," said Mrs. Woodforde. "She's rather proud, but she attends the Assembly Rooms, particularly if there is a concert. The countess is very fond of opera."

"Oh," said Mama with a light laugh of chagrin. "I did not realize you were acquainted with Lady Swinton! Forgive me, Mrs. Woodforde."

"I'm acquainted with nearly everyone in Bath, and most of Somersetshire, too. I've lived here all my life and spent these last forty summers in Bath." She gave a firm nod. "One tends to meet everyone over time."

Most of Somersetshire? On impulse, Kate asked, "Have you ever met a gentleman by the name of William Ogilvie?"

Mrs. Woodforde's brow wrinkled. "Oh my. I don't think I ever met him, but years ago there was a scoundrel by that name in Bath. Not a very proper person, my dear; I believe he tried to sell shares in a trading company or some other obvious fraud. But that must have been . . . Goodness, decades ago, before you were born. Lady Darby might remember better. That's the only Ogilvie I can recall."

That sounded like it might be the same person. Kate smiled to hide the cautious excitement bubbling inside her. "Thank you. That is very helpful."

"Whatever could you want with such a person, Katherine?" exclaimed her mother.

"Perhaps nothing, Mama," she said calmly. But perhaps something vital. She resolved to find out more from Lady Darby.

The admiral returned to claim his wife then, and after polite introductions and farewells, Kate let her mother take her arm and lead her toward the pump. "I don't know what's come over you, Katherine," said her mother in quiet upset. "Asking about scoundrels? Refusing to call on family relations? You were once such a biddable child."

"Once." Kate took two glasses of the mineral water and handed one to her mother. "I feel more assertive, Mama."

"That is not an attractive quality in a woman," chided Mama. "I hardly know you anymore. What happened?"

Kate sipped the warm, strong-smelling water, and felt healthier at once. She set the glass down, ignoring her mother's reproving look. Once she would have dutifully finished the glass to please her mother; now she merely smiled. "I blame it on Bath."

Chapter 20

◦─◦◦◦─◦

Mama quickly tired of Kate's company. It had always been that way, but for the first time Kate felt simply relief and none of the previous sting. No doubt it was because she had Cora, and the Darbys and Woodfordes among other newly met acquaintances and friends, to occupy her time. Their table routinely hosted army fellows of Gerard's, along with their wives and sisters. They went out nearly every evening, to the Assembly Rooms or the theater or to parties. She walked with Cora during the mornings, so much so the hills no longer seemed steep. Even Birdie grew accustomed to them, and finally remarked to Kate that Bath was rather a pretty town, after all.

They still saw Mama and Lucien, of course. As usual, Mama was surrounded by gentlemen wherever she went. One gentleman, Lord Worley, seemed to be constantly at her elbow, and Kate even wondered if her mother might have set her cap for the handsome earl, only to learn there was already a Lady Worley. But Mama seemed happy, and Mama was a delight to know when she was happy. Lucien appeared to be applying himself to finding an heiress; he condescended to dance with a number of ladies even though Kate knew he viewed dancing as frivolous. She was able to meet him politely and even feel a bit of sympathy for him now that she wasn't subjected to his presence every day.

The only dark cloud was the Durham Dilemma, which had already reached into every drawing room in Bath. Kate heard snippets of it at every event they attended although she ignored each mention of it with cool civility. Those rumors didn't bother her much, as she had expected them. The gossip about her husband escorting another woman, however, was another story.

Mama inadvertently revealed it one morning over tea. "Lucien does wish you might persuade Captain de Lacey to speak with him," she said. "He tried again yesterday when he met the captain out riding with Lady Stanley, and the captain was very cold and refused him."

Kate paused. She didn't know Lady Stanley, but she knew of her. She was a very handsome, very bold widow with a nice fortune. She was also very energetic and renowned for her passion for riding—both horses and men. "The captain surely means what he says to Lucien."

"Lucien was afraid, my dear, that he interrupted something between the two of them. He said they were deep in warm conversation when he came upon them. He returned quite embarrassed about the matter." Mama sipped her tea. "Won't you have a word with Captain de Lacey?"

Kate's hands were cold around the teacup. She set it down. She'd been wrong the last time she saw him with a woman, that day in Milsom Street when he walked with Cora. Gerard hadn't mentioned Lady Stanley, though, and he told her all about Cora. "I will think about it, Mama," she murmured in response to her mother's question.

Mama smiled. "I knew you were still my sensible Katherine in spite of these new ways of yours. Lucien will be so grateful, my dear."

After Mama left, Kate returned to the sitting room. She told herself there was no evidence Gerard was seeing Lady Stanley. He still escorted her out every evening and slept in her bed every night. They talked more as well, and Kate felt they were happy together; she certainly was. If he was having an affair, he must be doing it very quietly. But . . . warm conversation? In spite of herself, a tear slipped down her face. Why did her mother have to mention Lady Stanley?

The door opened, and she leaped to her feet, scrubbing her cheeks dry. She met her husband in the hall as he took off his hat and gloves. "Did you have a pleasant ride?" she blurted out.

Gerard glanced at her in surprise. "Yes. A most excellent ride."

She nodded. Terrible images of him and Lady Stanley scrolled across her mind, no matter how hard she tried to stop them. "Did you ride with anyone?"

"Yes. Carter went out with me."

"Only Lieutenant Carter?"

His head came up. "Why do you ask that?"

The blood was pounding in her cheeks. She told herself she was a fool, and still she heard herself asking the question, bluntly and harshly. "You weren't riding with Lady Stanley?"

His face gave the reply. Kate turned and hurried up the stairs, filled with hurt and jealousy. Even if Lieutenant Carter rode with them, Gerard had been out with another woman, and he'd not told her.

He caught her in the dressing room as she searched in the wardrobe for her shawl. "Kate," he said in the firm, patient tone of someone addressing a lunatic, "don't be upset about this."

She shook her head, refusing to look at him. "Why should I be upset? Have you done something wrong?"

"I don't think so, no." Which wasn't an absolute denial.

"I'm sure you had a very good reason for riding out with another woman and not telling me about it." She gave up searching in the wardrobe and closed the door. Perhaps the shawl was still downstairs.

"Yes, I did," he snapped. "If you will listen, I will tell you."

In a better mood, she would have listened calmly. Unfortunately his tone of voice—short and a bit annoyed—sounded eerily like her first husband's tone when he brushed her aside. Suddenly she felt again like Katherine Howe, dull, insipid creature who was always the last to know what her husband was doing. She turned around to face Gerard, her hands clenched at her sides and her expression stony.

"I met Lady Stanley on the downs one morning a week ago. When she discovered we both like to range over the hills, she began coming out every morning."

Her hope that this would turn out as innocently as when she saw him walking with Cora on Milsom Street was squashed. Gerard had been riding with the woman for a *week*.

"Sometimes Carter comes out, too, sometimes not," he went on. "But I soon realized a very strong benefit of riding with her." He hesitated. "I didn't tell you because . . . well, because it's not particularly pleasant to tell. You remember we talked about my father's mystery."

"Yes," she said tonelessly. "Lady Stanley can help solve it?"

His mouth thinned. "Perhaps. And if she can, I'll not hesitate to use her to do so."

"You're prepared to have an affair with her so she'll help you . . . do what? Find the man blackmailing you?" Kate shook her head with sharp, angry jerks. "How will she do that?"

"Damn it, Kate, don't cut up at me," he growled. "I'm not having an affair with her. Merely . . . flirting a bit. Harmless innuendo. She hears everything in town, and I need to know who hates my family enough to want to ruin us. I'll be damned if I lose my good name because I wouldn't trade wit with a woman when nothing else has produced anything of use!"

Kate flushed. Whether he meant it or not, she felt the sting of that last phrase. After Mrs. Woodforde said she'd heard of a man named Ogilvie, Kate asked Lady Darby, who in turn asked her friend Mrs. Humphries, who had lived in Bath for over sixty years. She reported back that a man named Billy Ogilvie had indeed once caused a stir in Bath before being run out of town. She thought he'd been a speculator, or a radical, or something repugnant. After some thought, someone supplied the town of Allenton, a hamlet roughly a dozen or more miles away, as his possible origin. Gerard had cautioned her not to get her hopes up, but Kate sent off a letter anyway, just in case. So far there had been no reply, but she had tried. Apparently she should have thrown herself into society and embraced all the gossip instead. "I see."

He threw up his hands. "What's got into you about this?" His eyes narrowed. "Was your mother here?"

"How I heard about it is no importance," she said stiffly. "I hope Lady Stanley satisfies your every expectation."

"You're being irrational," he warned. "Kate, I'm not having an affair with her. I'm not *going* to have an affair with her. I came to Bath prepared to do a great deal worse in order to find this blackmailer. I didn't tell you because there's been nothing to tell— nothing's come of it yet, and nothing may. She's quite a dull woman, to be honest." He shook his head, looking greatly irked. "This is a pointless conversation."

Mortification mingled with anger rushed through her veins, obliterating any relief that he didn't want Lady Stanley. "I trust Lady Stanley knows she's being used."

His face darkened. "Sometimes one has to do whatever is necessary to get what one wants. Break a rule, bend a law, tell a lie—even by omission—because the end is too important to throw it away through propriety. No, I haven't told her; I let her think what she likes, but I have no intention of deviating from my plan. I'm looking for a blackmailer, Kate, not someone honest and decent who would be glad to meet me in Lady Stanley's drawing room for a civil conversation. Sometimes you have to fight underhanded to get what you need. Have you ever considered that?"

"Have I?" she exclaimed in fury. "I got you, didn't I?"

Gerard's eyebrows flew up. Kate's eyes widened as the echo of her words registered. She whirled away, wishing she could vanish into thin air.

For a long, terrible moment there was silence. "What do you mean by that?" he finally asked.

She flinched at his cautious but steely tone. "Nothing. I spoke in anger. I'm sorry."

"Don't lie to me, Kate."

She was shaking. Oh please God, what could she say to extricate herself from this moment? She lowered her head. "I'm not lying. I lost my temper and spoke without thinking. Please forgive me for being rude." Her mouth was dry, and the words came out in a whisper.

His footsteps seemed loud as he came closer. "You didn't mind being curt when you thought I was having an affair with Lady Stanley. When you speak without thinking, I find you often tell me more than when you pause to compose a suitable, bland reply." He traced a line down the nape of her neck, and her whole body tensed in response. "What did you mean, you fought for me?"

"I didn't say that," she tried, but he was still touching the bare skin of her back, stroking along her shoulder blades.

"That's what you meant."

She didn't want him to know. It was bad enough that he thought she'd asked him because he needed her money, and she needed his strength. It was bad enough that he viewed her as his odd, amusingly awkward wife. She could live with that. But for him to know she had asked him because she'd been infatuated with him for years . . . to know that she'd dreamed of him when he didn't even remember her face . . . that would be intolerable. Only pathetic lovelorn fools did that. Only if he had loved her back, even slightly, would Kate have admitted how much she cared for him.

Now she tried to pretend it was Howe asking her something. Howe had never been more than mildly interested in anything she thought, and that interest always passed if she refused to tell him. Gerard couldn't make her say it, she told herself; she was sure he wouldn't strike her. She simply had to keep her wits about her, and he would never discover it. She inhaled a calming breath and forced her shoulders to relax, despite the light touch of Gerard's finger still tingling along her spine. Slowly, deliberately, she turned to face him. "I meant nothing," she said in a placid voice. "Please don't pay any heed to it."

His eyes narrowed. "Do you know how I hate it when you do that?" he asked in a conversational tone.

She couldn't look him in the face for more than a moment. "There's nothing else to say. It was a foolish remark."

"I do so dislike . . ." He paused. "No, I absolutely *detest* it when you lie to me."

"It's not a lie," she protested, staring fixedly at his cravat pin. "I didn't mean anything by it."

He sighed. "Ah, Kate. We still don't understand each other yet, do we? I'm quite unable to let it go simply because you don't want to tell me. You didn't really think I would forget that you asked me to marry you, did you, or that I would never wonder why you chose me?"

"You know why."

"Yes; death, Lucien, or me. But I cannot decide why you chose me, of all the penniless, handsome men in London you might have approached."

She wet her lips. She didn't like lying to Gerard. It was hard to form the words, denying she cared anything at all for him when her heart jumped every time he smiled at her. Carefully she edged backward, hoping a few feet of distance would help. "Does it matter why I asked? You said yes, which must mean you were glad I asked."

He touched her chin, making her look at him. "It matters." He paused, studying her. "If you don't tell me, I shall have to seduce the answer from you."

Chapter 21

Her eyes popped open at that alarming threat. "It's really not worth all that! You—I—Truly, you are making much of nothing."

"Not worth pleasuring my wife? Why, madam, you do yourself a grave injustice."

"It's wrong to use seduction as punishment!"

"Punishment?" His smile was dangerous. "You won't feel punished, I promise."

Her breath came in anxious pants. She knew she wouldn't feel punished; that was the trouble. He knew just how to make her body feel alive, infused with fire. In fact, it was anticipation of all that which kept her feet stationary when she might have run for the door and escaped his questions.

His fingers traced a sizzling path down her throat to the swells of her breasts. She could feel her nipples rising, growing hard and sensitive inside her corset. Kate bit back a moan and made herself turn away; she was a fool to think she could brazen this out. Unfortunately she had left it too long. Gerard's arm snaked around her waist, pulling her against him so she could feel his arousal pressing hard against her back.

"You tell me you wish to be a good wife." His low whisper rumbled through her. His fingers traced the same path down her chest, and gooseflesh rippled over her skin. "Do you really?"

"Yes." Her voice was a thin squeak.

"Why did you try to lie to me? I can't abide it, Kate."

"It wasn't important," she gasped. His fingers were running along the inside edge of her bodice. He knew her breasts were exquisitely sensitive, and he was making the most of it.

"No?" His wandering touch paused. "I think it is—to me. I've wondered from the start why you proposed to me. Today you were jealous of my affections. Now you say, in a bit of reckless temper, you fought for me. How so?"

"I—I asked you." He slid one palm down her body, pausing to fondle her breast. Kate quaked as his thumb rolled firmly over an aching nipple. "Normally a woman waits and hopes a gentleman will propose to her . . ."

"Hmm, yes." He kissed her neck, a feathery touch of lips that sent sparks through her. "I like a bold woman." His hand drifted down her belly. "But you've never quite satisfied me on one point: why *me*?"

Her brain went blank as his fingers curved lightly but unmistakably into the furrow between her legs. Even through her dress and petticoats she could feel his touch, the soft stroke of his fingers finding that hidden point of pleasure with unerring accuracy.

"I wanted you," she whispered. Her hips moved helplessly, but she was caught. If she pressed backward, he was hard and promising against her bottom. If she moved forward, his fingers were there to drive her mad. She trembled from the effort of holding still.

He knew it, too. The heel of his hand bore her backward, and he flexed his hips. The pressure of his fingers between her legs and his erection at her back sent lust spilling through her. She wanted him, too much. She groped blindly for the table in front of her, not sure if she meant to balance herself or use it as an anchor point to pull away from him, but he forestalled both.

"Then you shall have me." With one step forward, he brought her right to the edge of the table. With one last biting kiss on her shoulder, he pushed her down until her hands hit the polished surface of the table. "Why lie about that? If you wanted me in your bed, you only had to ask."

"No, that's not what I . . ." Her voice died as he scooped up her skirt, flinging it over her back. Now his hand was on her bottom, squeezing and shaping her flesh even as he held her immobile for the increasingly persistent touch of his other hand, still stroking her through her skirts. In spite of herself she was growing wet. Pray God no one passing through Queen Square looked up at this window . . .

"Then what did you mean, Kate?" There was a *shush* of cloth; he was unbuttoning his falls. She closed her eyes. She could feel the moisture between her legs now, as her shift grew damp where he pressed it against her.

"Just . . . you," she said inanely. He slid his length, hot and thick, between her thighs, and her knees almost buckled. He was going to take her like this, from behind like an animal, bent over a table over-looking Queen Square, in the midst of an argument, and she was shaking with desire. She squirmed, not sure if she wanted to escape or spur him onward, and he responded by pressing the blunt head of his erection right against her—her—her quim. She blushed vividly; he had called it paradise.

"I can feel how much you do." He nudged forward, and Kate shuddered. "Why lie?"

"I didn't mean to . . ."

"But I mean to know why, just the same." He pressed into her, and she squeaked; it felt different this way, more primal. He forced his feet between hers and hiked her onto her toes as he pulled out. "Why did you want me?"

"Because . . ." He thrust, and her body clenched so hard she heard him suck in his breath.

"Why, Kate?" He began stroking into her, hard and deep but relentlessly slow. Tears ran down her face as she braced herself to take him, wanting him even as he scraped away at her restraint. "Tell me why . . ."

"Stop," she sobbed. "Stop asking!"

"Stop?" He paused midthrust, almost withdrawn. She moaned and tried to push her hips back into his. "You said stop," he said, holding her in place easily. "Was there something you wished to say?"

Kate pressed a fist against her mouth. Her heart was burning, her body screaming. If he had been unaffected, she might have been able to do it, but she heard the roughness in his voice and felt the tremors in his hand where he held her. He liked making love to her; perhaps that would be enough. She could

make him laugh. He was good to her, the matter with
Lady Stanley aside. She would give anything at all for
him to love her, but it would kill her if she laid her
heart at his feet and he looked at it in shock, horror,
amusement.

"Because you were desperate," she said recklessly.

"Was I?" He drove hard into her, and she bit her
lip to keep from moaning. "How kind of you to take
pity on me."

"And I didn't have time to wait," she added, gasping as he shoved aside the folds of her skirts and put
his hand between her legs.

"Yes, of course." He traced a shivery path through
the folds of her sex before settling directly on that
throbbing nub. "What else?"

"I thought you were likely to agree." She groped
for the far edge of the table, trying to steady herself.

"How calculating." He flicked his thumb, then
squeezed, very delicately, and she almost screamed.
"Why me?"

"Because . . ." She could feel her climax building,
sending shimmering waves of heat through her veins.
"Because . . ."

"Why?" He rocked back and forth, a tormenting
slow motion. "Why, Kate? Is it so terrible? Are you
carrying another man's child? Is there some other
threat to your fortune you neglected to reveal to
me? Did Charlie and Edward refuse you before you
asked me?"

"No . . . None of that . . ." She closed her eyes.

"Why, Kate?" He leaned over her, his breath
scalding on the nape of her neck. He bit her there, his
teeth scraping her skin. He was moving deep inside

her now—she could hear in his voice that he was just as close to oblivion as she was—

"Because I loved you," she whispered, as her climax came over her, hot and furious and debilitating. Gerard felt it; he growled against her shoulder and held her tightly against him before bucking so hard with his own release it seemed they would both fall to the floor.

The tide ebbed gradually. All she could hear was the pounding of her own heart and the ragged sound of his breathing. "I loved you," she whispered again, too drained to move, her breath making shadows of fog on the polished tabletop beneath her cheek. "For years . . . I loved you."

He didn't say anything or move for several minutes. Perhaps he hadn't heard. Vaguely she wondered if she should hope for that, or hope her great secret was finally revealed. "Kate," he said at last, sounding unutterably weary, "you can't love someone you don't know."

"I know." She closed her eyes. "It was silly and childish, but you were kind to me, once—years ago. I know you don't remember, but I do. It wasn't real love—calf-love, perhaps—but I never stopped. I never asked anyone else to marry me, nor would I have. If you had said no . . ." She flapped one hand helplessly. "I suppose Lucien might have persuaded me eventually."

He raised his head. "When was I kind to you?"

She sighed. A lone tear ran over the bridge of her nose and congealed under her cheek, cold and wet. "A long time ago. I was caught walking in the rain, and you took me up on your horse and rode me to my gate. I was soaked and miserable, yet you put your coat around me and made me laugh. It was before my father had made his fortune; young gentlemen had no interest in me. But you . . . you were wonderful."

The silence was terrible. After a moment he stepped away from her and let her skirts fall. She felt bereft, listening to him restore his clothing. She made no effort to rise, but Gerard lifted her with gentle hands and turned her to him. She tried to compose her countenance and keep her chin up, but the astonished, perplexed expression on his face was awful to behold. "When was this?"

She swallowed. "Ten . . . no, twelve years ago. It was nothing. I—I was silly to remember it."

"I took you up on my horse?" He was frowning now. "A dozen years ago—in '98 or so?" She nodded once. His frown deepened. "A girl in the rain, near Henfield . . ." he murmured. "I *do* remember—I think. I had taken Charlie's horse without permission and was trying to get home before he did. But she was so bedraggled . . . Was it really you, Kate?"

She just looked at him. Her eyes must be as red and puffy as they felt.

"And you asked me to marry you because of that?"

"You were the only man who ever put his arm around me," she said simply. "Willingly, anyway."

He stared at her, thunderstruck. "And you remembered it? That was enough for you to want to *marry* me?"

Her chin trembled, and she pressed her lips together to still it. She inhaled and straightened her shoulders. "As I said, my choices were few, and I hadn't much time."

"You might have made a bloody awful mistake!"

It was beginning to feel like she had. "I met Lord Howe three times before my father signed the marriage contract. No one cared whether we suited each other. My mother told me he was the best match I could hope for. At least I went into my second marriage"—she hesitated—"disposed to like you."

His expression changed. "Kate, I didn't mean it like that—merely that you approached a man you didn't know, hadn't spent any time with, had no mutual acquaintances to vouch for him. There are liars and cheats in every level of society, and many would be happy to lead you to the altar without any thought of you beyond your fortune."

"I know," she said softly. "It was a gamble."

Gerard stared at her in dumbstruck shock. At least she hoped that was all. Her first, deepest wish, that he would admit he loved her as well, had given way to a secondary wish for escape. She shouldn't have said anything. The longer he said nothing, the more certain she was that it had been a terrible error to tell him.

A loud knock sounded at the door. She started. Gerard blinked. "Not now!" he growled.

" 'Tis urgent, sir," called Bragg through the door. "About Reverend Ogilvie."

Gerard froze. He strode across the room and threw open the door with a snarl. "What?"

"His son is here," said Bragg, face scrupulously blank. "Or rather, son-in-law. In the drawing room."

For a long moment he was still. Kate could see the tendons in his neck above his neckcloth, which must have been pulled askew when he bent her over the

table and tossed up her skirts. "I'll be right down,"
he said quietly, and closed the door.

Slowly he turned to face her again. The room had
never seemed so large as it did right now, when a vast
ocean could have filled the distance between them. "I
should see him," he said at last.

She gave a tiny nod. There was no joy for her in
the chance that her letter would bring useful information. It might be the key he needed to unlock the
mysteries surrounding his family. That was surely
more important to him than her confession of feelings both rash and imprudent, to say nothing of un-
wanted. "Of course."

"Kate, I . . ." He cleared his throat, still looking
utterly nonplussed by her admission. "We shall talk
more later." He hesitated a moment, his face dark,
then left, closing the door behind him.

Kate stayed where she was. There was a faint ringing in her ears, and the floor seemed a very long way
down. She believed he cared for her, in some way.
Gerard was too honorable to mislead her so cruelly,
at least by intent. But just as clearly, he didn't love
her. If he had, he surely would have reacted with
delight, perhaps even declared his own love for her.
And she shouldn't be surprised. Hadn't he been just
as charming and solicitous of Cora as he'd been of
her? Didn't she already know herself to be quiet and
plain, not at all the sort of woman who appealed to
hearty, vigorous men? And now he'd all but told her
she'd made a mistake in marrying him.

Feeling very old and stupid, she made her way to
the chair, where her knees finally gave out. She didn't
know what to do. Part of her still clung to the hope

that it wasn't too late. Who knew what he might say later? But part of her wondered how long she could withstand it. He hadn't loved her before she told him, but she'd had no expectation of love from him. It was one thing to nurse a secret infatuation; a secret, after all, couldn't subject one to rejection and hurt.

But once the secret was told . . . Now it had the power to wound. Now Gerard knew just how much he owned her—not only her fortune, not only her body, but her very heart. Hearts should never be given, she realized too late. They should only be exchanged. But she had given hers and gotten nothing in return, and it felt like a gaping void inside her chest.

Birdie tapped at the door. "Madam?"

She wiped her eyes quickly, dashing away the tears that had gathered. "Come in, Birdie."

Her abigail rushed across the room. "Are you well? I heard raised voices. Oh, madam, if he hurt you—"

"No, Birdie. He didn't hurt me." He'd decimated her. Kate took a deep breath and squeezed Birdie's hand. "We had a slight disagreement." Another deep breath. She had cast off all her reserve and control and had to reassemble it one brick at a time. "I understand someone called to see Captain de Lacey?"

Birdie snorted. "Some ferrety little man. A thief, mark my words. But your eyes are red—let me bring some tea."

She shook her head. "No, I—I think I shall go for a walk. Some fresh air . . ."

"Of course. I'll get your shawl." Birdie whisked across the room to retrieve it from the wardrobe, where it had been all along. "Shall I bring an umbrella? There are some clouds."

Kate got to her feet, slowly, stiffly, like an old woman. "I'll go alone today, Birdie. Not far, just around the Square and perhaps to the Crescent. If it rains, I'll be home in a trice."

Birdie's face wrinkled in concern. "Are you certain, madam? You don't look well."

"I am perfectly well," she said desperately. If the man who had called about Reverend Ogilvie turned out to be nobody, Gerard might come back upstairs. No matter what he said, she needed a little time alone to clear her mind and settle her emotions. She had let her guard fall away and couldn't face him without at least some semblance of her old armor in place again. She tied on her bonnet with shaking fingers and let Birdie fold the shawl snugly around her shoulders.

"Don't go far," Birdie fussed as she hurried after Kate, down the stairs and through the hall. "Really, madam, I don't think you ought to go alone."

"I'll be fine." Her face heated as she passed the closed parlor door and caught the rumble of Gerard's voice. "I'll return in an hour or two."

"What should I tell the captain?" cried Birdie, as Kate flung open the door and rushed out.

She glanced back at her abigail, wringing her hands in the doorway. Her throat constricted. Birdie was acting out of true concern. "Nothing," she said, her voice breaking at the end. "Nothing but what I've told you." And she turned and fled.

Chapter 22

Gerard strode down the stairs. It was just his luck to have someone relevant to his search turn up in his own drawing room when something more shocking had happened. Kate loved him—and had for years. He couldn't comprehend how one polite gesture, years ago, in circumstances that would surely have moved any gentleman to do the same, could have made such an impression on her. He could have been anyone, for God's sake, and with no other confirmation of his worth or decency, Kate offered herself up to him more than a decade after he'd been kind—merely *kind*—to her.

For a moment he felt ashamed for ever believing her story that she was desperate to escape Lucien by marrying someone else, and that she chose him because his family scandal made him desperate as well. Of course Lucien Howe couldn't force a woman to marry him, especially not a widow of legal age with her own fortune. The Durham scandal had only just broken when she'd approached him. He should have known there was something more behind it . . . although he never would have guessed what. She loved him! Gerard had been determined to discover her true motives, but now he didn't know what to do with the knowledge. He had never expected to love his wife. He certainly had never expected her to love him.

But now he had to put it out of his mind, on the off chance the caller had something significant to say. That alone put him in a short temper. Who would have guessed Kate's blind query about the Fleet minister would yield anything? He flung open the drawing-room door. "Sir." He bowed. "I am Captain de Lacey. I understand you are a relation of Reverend Ogilvie."

The visitor was a stooped, spare man several decades older than he. The crown of his head shone bald and pale amid his thinning gray hair. He leaned heavily on a cane, but when he turned around, there was nothing frail or unsteady about his eyes. He put Gerard in mind of a giant fledgling, plucked and shriveled.

"Yes," murmured the other man. His shiny black gaze traveled up and down Gerard. "Excellent. I am Robert Nollworth." He gave a bow so stiff, Gerard expected his bones to creak. "I received a letter from your wife, I believe."

Receiving a letter was far different from having anything helpful to say. Gerard closed the door behind him and gestured to the sofa. "Indeed. Won't you be seated?"

Nollworth dipped his head. "That is very good of you, sir." He limped to the sofa and seated himself, keeping his cane before him and clasping his spidery fingers about the knob.

Gerard took the chair opposite, preparing himself for anything. "You believe your father-in-law is the man my wife wrote of?"

"It's a long journey to Bath from Allenton," Mr. Nollworth replied obliquely. "Almost twenty miles. I came yesterday, and I mean to return today."

"That was very good of you to come so far. I'm sure a letter in reply would have sufficed."

"No, not in this case." He tapped the side of his long, pointed nose. "Discretion, young man." Gerard raised his eyebrows in question, but Nollworth merely settled himself on the cushion. "Yes, I was acquainted with the man your wife wrote of."

"I am glad to hear it," said Gerard, hiding his surprise. "What can you tell me of him?"

The old man made a face. "Depends. What are you hoping to hear?"

Nollworth, he realized, was a cardplayer. He alone knew the value of the hand he held, and he meant to win with it. Precisely how much he meant to win was an open question, but Gerard had no doubt there was a figure fixed in the man's mind. Brilliant. This could take an eternity. He eased back in his own seat, keeping his face carefully blank. "I hope to hear the truth," he replied.

"Truth!" Nollworth's eyes glittered. "Very hard to pin that particular creature down sometimes, eh, young man?"

"Yes," said Gerard dryly.

"It bends and twists and looks one way in one light, and another way entirely from a different perspective. It's likely the most elusive thing in the world."

For a moment they took each other's measure in

silence. "How are you acquainted with Reverend Ogilvie?" he asked at last.

Nollworth cracked a humorless smile. "Through marriage. My wife is his daughter. His only child."

"Then you know where I can find him."

"Of course," said Nollworth, his smile growing. "He's not hard to find; been in the same place for these last ten years or more. You can find him in the churchyard, lying under a headstone that cost me a pretty penny."

Just as he'd hoped. Ogilvie was dead—not really surprising, given he would have been well over eighty if he still lived. The only better news would be that Dorothy Cope had been buried in the same church-yard for forty years. "I'm very sorry for your wife's loss," he said politely. "How kind of you to come personally to Bath to tell me."

Nollworth rocked back in his seat. "Yes, kind indeed. I imagine it comes as very welcome news to you."

"Neither welcome nor unwelcome," Gerard lied smoothly. "Merely . . . informative."

"Ah, *informative*," murmured Nollworth, linger-ing on the last word. "That's quite another matter."

So there was another card in his hand. "As my wife wrote you, I'm looking into a question of some family history. Reverend Ogilvie's name appeared, but only once. It was my hope, however faint, he might help sort out my questions. But the event was many years ago, though, and since the gentleman's gone to his heavenly reward . . ." Gerard lifted one hand in a gesture of acceptance. "It is a disappointment."

"Family history." Nollworth flashed his reptilian smile again. "Yes, I can imagine your disappointment." He scratched his chin. "I did wonder why someone might be looking for my dear papa-in-law. Caused a bit of a commotion, it did, when your letter arrived. You couldn't be a friend of his, or else you'd've known he was dead—and most likely be glad to leave him to the worms."

He inclined his head. "No, I was never acquainted with the man personally."

"That's right, you weren't." The visitor's hooded eyes burned with fiendish delight. Gerard could easily imagine him casting evil spells over a bubbling cauldron in the woods. "If you had been acquainted, you would know old Billy Ogilvie was the devil's own spit. You would know he was likely to help an old woman across the street only so he could pick her pocket. Anyone who knew him at all knew not to turn his back on Billy." Nollworth's lips stretched in a gruesome grin. "But then, you're a young fellow. Billy was before your time. He was much more of an age to know your father."

A carriage drove past the house, the rattle of its wheels loud in the silence that engulfed the room. "Yes," said Gerard evenly. "I expect he was."

"It was quite remarkable to get a letter from a duke's son. What on earth would such a person want with old Billy?" Nollworth's eyes weren't birdlike; they were a snake's eyes, cold and hungry. "I'm not a hasty man. I took my time to see if I wasn't being hoaxed. An hour reading the London papers was enough to make me think it was quite the opposite." He leaned forward, his skinny neck stretching out. "Old Billy held the key to this Durham Dilemma, didn't he?"

A muscle twitched in Gerard's jaw before he could stop it. "If he had, you may rest assured it would have been allowed to go to his grave with him. My father wasn't the sort to leave loose ends hanging."

Nollworth gave a thin, wheezy chuckle. "But he left this one, didn't he? One very long, very loose end. Dangling about, just waiting to snare his son by the neck."

"I'm not convinced of that." Gerard flicked his fingers. "But if he did, by some chance, my brothers and I are each prepared to snip that loose end cleanly off at the root." He smiled in warning. "We are, after all, Durham's own blood."

His visitor's lip curled. "A bit lax in your personal life, too, are you? I expect that don't matter much to a duke's son. Much is forgiven or overlooked in a son of nobility . . . unless he's just a bastard."

It wouldn't take much to wring Nollworth's thin, shriveled neck. Gerard's hands itched to try it, just to shake that gloating, superior look off his face. "You might do well to keep that in mind."

"Come now, young man, you don't want to lose your temper with me."

"Why not?" Gerard stretched out his legs and folded his arms, striving for a grasp on his temper that was growing more tenuous by the moment.

"Because I have something you might want very much." Nollworth made a show of picking delicately at a mole on the back of his left hand. "Old Billy died and cost me a plump purse to bury. My wife, sentimental woman, kept all his things. His watch, his damned drawings, all his books . . ."

"Sentimental, indeed."

"He kept ledgers, you know," Nollworth went on almost idly. "Notebooks and diaries and all sorts of records. They go back . . . Oh, decades, I expect. He did harbor dreams of being a regular curate, once upon a time. If only he'd had the good fortune to marry a rich lady, he might never have been sent to the Fleet. So damaging to a man's prospects, prison . . ."

Gerard let out his breath slowly, although his pulse leaped at the mention of ledgers and notebooks. Durham's confessional letter mentioned signing his name in the minister's register, in a tavern near the Fleet. If Nollworth had that register, or anything else affirming Durham's clandestine marriage, Gerard had to get it, no matter what Nollworth extorted from him. "What are you proposing?"

"I'm sure there's a fair value for something so important to your family history." Nollworth laughed his dry, dusty laugh. "To you, or to someone else. I only offer you first rights to it because I'm a family man myself."

He should be grateful for that pretense, Gerard supposed. "Very well. If you have anything of interest to me, we shall fix a price—as thanks for your discretion and consideration."

Nollworth reeked of triumph. "I knew we could reach an agreement. I leave within the hour. Don't be lazy."

"Send these books. Should they prove . . . informative, I shall be very, generously, grateful."

The old man's face darkened. "Oh, no, boy. I'm not traipsing back and forth to Bath, and I'm not letting the ledgers out of my sight until we make our bargain."

"You wish me to buy them sight unseen?" Gerard cocked an eyebrow. "Very well. Twenty pounds."

"Two hundred pounds!"

Gerard sniffed in disdain. "Impossible. They may well be useless to me."

Nollworth puckered up his face. "I'm sure there's others as might be interested. Who might become a duke if your sire proves a bigamist?"

Gerard counted to ten inside his head. "Fifty pounds."

Nollworth stabbed his cane into the floor. "No. You'll come with me, this very day, if you want anything to do with those books. I'm not a cheat, but I won't be cheated by you, either. Tell me now, sir: are you coming to see the books, or am I writing to a lord who might be a duke when I return home?"

They faced each other in silence. Nollworth obviously thought he held the winning hand. The hell of it was, he did. Gerard wanted—needed—to know what was in those books. If he could find some proof that his father's first marriage hadn't been fully legal, he could put an end to any danger from the blackmailer. If he found some proof the marriage *was* legal, all the more need to own it. The only way to know if Ogilvie's journals could help was to look at them. If they were useless, or Nollworth's father-in-law wasn't the William Ogilvie he sought, he could always walk away, but if not . . . Under no circumstances could Cousin Augustus be allowed to know about the registers, let alone possess them.

"I shall be ready in an hour," he said through thin lips.

Nollworth's oily smile broke out again. "I'll await

you down at the pub in Avon Street," he said graciously. He limped past Gerard into the hall, where he took his hat from Bragg and bowed politely. "Good day, sir."

Bragg watched him go down the steps before turning to Gerard. "Slippery otter, ain't he?"

"Poisonous as well." Gerard exhaled, his mind running over the preparations he had to make. "We leave in an hour. He may have something of interest. Send to Carter, and ask if he can come along on an errand out of town for a day or two. Get the horses saddled, and pack for two days." He paused. "Pack my pistols as well."

"Aye, Captain." Bragg hurried off.

Gerard flexed his fingers, cracking his knuckles. The urge to strike Nollworth had left his hands cramped from the tension of not forming fists. If not for the post clerk's description of the letter sender, Gerard would have suspected Nollworth himself was the blackmailer. The man certainly had the cold calculation and venality necessary. He was all but blackmailing Gerard now. If Nollworth had sent the earlier letters, he might have changed his strategy and decided to make one last bold demand.

But the earlier request for money had been for far more than Nollworth wanted, and no mention was made of it after the initial demand. Nollworth didn't seem the type to let a ransom demand languish and be ignored. If Nollworth was the blackmailer and possessed unqualified proof of Durham's marriage, he would have asked for more than two hundred pounds—and Gerard would have paid it.

So he had to go to Allenton and see what the man

had, and only an hour to prepare. He glanced at the stairs. What was the bloody rush? He had to see Kate, and talk to her, and try to explain—or rather, understand—but only an hour . . .

He took the stairs two at a time. "Kate!" He threw open the door, but the dressing room was empty. "Kate," he called again, heading for the bedroom. "Kate, where are you?"

"Madam has gone out." He whirled around to see Mrs. Dennis standing in the doorway, her face stony. "Is there something you wanted, sir?"

"Where did she go?"

"She wanted a walk." The abigail's glare made her feelings clear. "Alone."

Gerard shoved one hand through his hair. He strode to the window and peered out, but there was no sight of his wife. "When will she return?"

"In a bit."

"When, Mrs. Dennis?"

The woman jumped at his shout. "In an hour or two, she said."

He swore. Bragg slipped into the room, no doubt to pack. "Is my horse ready yet?"

"Not yet, sir," said the startled Bragg. Gerard swore again with greater feeling. Mrs. Dennis gasped, and Bragg leaped toward the door. "I'll do it myself, this very moment."

"No, I'll do it." He strode from the room and went down to the mews, where the boy was just leading his bay out to saddle. He waved the lad aside and saddled the horse himself with the efficiency of a cavalryman. A few minutes later he rode out into the street, looking in each direction for Kate. But she was nowhere to be seen, not down any street he passed riding through Bath, nor down any street he passed on the way home. He hoped she hadn't gone too far, but it was a nice day, excellent walking weather. She could be on top of Beechen Cliff for all he knew; she'd told him all about her walks there with Cora Fitzwilliam. He had to see her before he left. If nothing else, he had to tell her her letter had borne fruit. He tied the horse in front of the house in Queen Square as Carter trotted up.

"Bragg sent word you needed me," he called, touching his hat brim.

Gerard nodded, still glancing about for his wife. "It may turn out to be a blind end, but I would be very glad of your company."

Carter laughed. "Well, the army's left me well practiced at chasing down blind ends. I am at your disposal."

"Thank you, Carter." A flash of blue caught his eye. There—there she was, at the end of the street. He turned to go to her as Bragg came out to join them, leading his own horse and lugging bulging saddlebags for Gerard's horse over one shoulder.

"Captain, 'tis an hour," his man called.

Gerard just waved irately at him and continued on his way, eating up the distance with long strides. She saw him coming and her own steps slowed—a bad omen if ever he saw one. He muttered a curse, then almost stopped dead in his tracks as his mind blanked. What would he say to her? He felt stunned anew at her admission—she loved him! It was still soaking into his brain. The usual reply to such a declaration of course was a like one, but those words wouldn't come. What did that mean? Hard on the heels of that question followed shame that he had coerced the admission from her, and in such a manner. What sort of man used desire and passion against his wife? He didn't deserve her love even if she still felt any for him.

By the time they finally met, each was moving so slowly it seemed time had paused. Gerard stared at her pale, composed face and felt like a tongue-tied boy.

"Did your visitor provide any help?" she asked. Aside from the shadows in her eyes, there was no sign she was uneasy or upset. He wished she would show some emotion, any emotion. He would feel much better if she screamed at him, or even cried.

"Perhaps." Now he not only didn't know what to say, he was acutely conscious of the public nature of this conversation. Wasn't Lady Darby's house the one behind him? And another gossipy old lady no doubt lived in the one before him. God help either lady if she was listening at her window now. "He believes he can, that is."

Kate nodded calmly, as if they spoke of the weather. "I am glad to hear it." Her eyes flickered to something behind him. "Are you leaving?"

"Ah, yes." He cleared his throat. "Nollworth claims to have some ledgers that may prove illuminating. He won't just sell them to me but insists I come fetch them. They might be rubbish, of course. But hopefully they'll be valuable," he added quickly, realizing too late he was denigrating her efforts.

"I hope they will help." Her deep blue eyes were so steady and dark, the way they used to be just a few weeks ago. As if she'd pulled back from what happened around her and didn't want to discuss it any more than he did. Which surely meant he was making a dreadful hash of things.

"I have to go see if he has anything," he said, giving up any hope of a meaningful conversation or farewell. "I'll be back in two days."

"Of course. I understand."

He glanced over his shoulder. Behind him Bragg and Carter were waiting, pointedly facing away from him and Kate. In front of him she waited, contained and cool, for his response. A river of words—explanations, half-understood feelings, and other thoughts—rushed through his mind until they dammed themselves up inside his head. He needed more than an hour to think this through. He sighed. "I will see you then." He wanted to pull her close for a proper kiss, public street or not, but her pose wasn't welcoming; he couldn't do it. Instead he leaned down and brushed a light kiss on her cheek. She stood like a statue. He lifted his head and looked at her in growing despair.

"Good luck," was all she said, her expression unchanged.

He managed to nod before turning and striding back to his horse. Damn it. Damn Nollworth and his spectacularly bad timing. Damn Howe for bruising Kate's spirit so badly she wouldn't just have a blazing fit of temper and throw a pitcher at his head. Damn him for not once anticipating, even in the midst of the most glorious tupping imaginable, that his wife might fall even a little bit in love with him. "Let's be done with this," he muttered to Carter as he swung into the saddle and kicked the horse onward.

Chapter 23

Nollworth hadn't lied; he kept everything, not just of Ogilvie's. What he called his storeroom was really an old stable with sagging walls, filled almost to the rafters with old trunks and crates, broken furniture, rusty farm tools, and piles of other items that looked like pure rubbish. "His things'll be in there," said the old man, dragging aside a large piece of canvas covering some of the mess. "All of them."

"Where are the books?" Gerard coughed, waving aside the dust and straw bits stirred up.

"In there."

"Where? In the trunks?" Carter glanced at Gerard, who knew what he meant. It would take days to unpack them, let alone look through any books to determine if they were helpful at all. "All these trunks are filled with books?"

"Not all." Nollworth swabbed his face with a dirty handkerchief. "Some, though."

An angry screeching from outside sliced through the room. "Mr. Nollworth, what are you about? You, sirrah, are at your last prayers! I'll have an answer this time—you'll not be taking off for Bath for two days again and leaving the chores to me without so much as a by-your-leave—"

Nollworth could move with surprising speed when he wished. He was in the doorway in a flash. "Quiet, woman," he barked. "This is my business!"

"Those are my father's things!" the woman's voice raged, coming closer. "What are you plotting? If you think to sell them for scrap, I've a mind to—"

"Hush," ordered Nollworth. He flung wide the door, kicking up a fresh cloud of dust. "Hush, Mrs. Nollworth. We've guests." He flourished one arm toward Gerard and Carter. "See? Gentlemen, my wife, Mrs. Nollworth. My dear, this is Lord Captain de Lacey and Lieutenant Carter."

Mrs. Nollworth's mouth had dropped open at the sight of them. She was a stout, sturdy woman with a florid face and arms like a butcher's. She was clutching a large wooden ladle in a menacing manner but quickly hid it behind her back when she saw them. "Sirs," she said, dipping into an off-balance curtsey. "Er . . . Welcome to our home."

Carter's eyes drifted upward, over the rough shed. A chicken strutted through the open door and darted into the pile of cast-off furniture, clucking loudly. Gerard cleared his throat. "Thank you, madam. I hope we're not intruding."

She looked torn between the desire to maintain appearances and the urge to ask who the devil they were and why they were in her shed. "No," she said, looking to her husband for a moment. "Of course not."

"We'll leave you to it," said Nollworth quickly. "Come, Mrs. Nollworth."

"What—you're giving away Father's things?" protested his wife, resisting his efforts to push her out the door. "What's this about, Mr. Nollworth?"

"They just want to have a look," he said. "Come along with me, I'll explain . . ."

"Your father may have had some connection to my family many years ago," said Gerard. As much as he was enjoying the sight of Nollworth getting bullied, he had to look in those crates. "Your husband has agreed to allow me to look through his books."

"But you'll not be taking anything?" Mrs. Nollworth had her ladle up again and gave her husband a furious glance when he tried to urge her out the door.

Gerard gave her his most charming smile. "I wouldn't dream of doing so without your permission." So much for his hope of buying everything and carting it back to Bath to examine in more comfortable surroundings. "But if I should find something relevant to my family, I would very much like to take it back to show my brothers, who are just as curious as I. We would be suitably grateful, naturally."

Mrs. Nollworth's grip on her ladle eased. Her eyes went to her husband, who gave her a significant nod. "Well . . . I'm sure we can come to an agreement. If it's something of very dear interest to your family . . ." She put on a pious expression. "I'm sure my papa would wish to help you if he could."

"Thank you, madam."

Finally she allowed her husband to bundle her out the door. "Do call for help if you need it," she called back.

Gerard stepped to the doorway and gave her a parting smile as Nollworth dragged her toward the house. "We shall." He turned back to survey the mess once more. "Good God."

"My thoughts exactly." Carter carefully kicked a rusty pail out of the way. "You're certain what you need is in here?"

"If I was, I would have given him the two hundred pounds for the lot and had it carted back to Bath." Gerard set aside his hat and took off his jacket. "I understand if you cannot stay. Nollworth led me to believe it was a trunk or two full of books." He had explained their goal on the ride to Allenton.

Carter shook his head, following Gerard's lead and removing his coat and hat. "No, I've nothing to do in Bath. This is better than having Cora fret over me."

Kate. Gerard's eyes closed for a moment as the name Cora made him think of his wife. If only they'd been able to have a proper conversation before he left. If only he'd known what to say to her. If only . . . The best he could hope for now was that the right response would come to him as they worked, and he could patch things up with Kate when he returned to town.

"Let's start with that one." He kicked a nearby crate. "With any luck we'll find it in there and can be on our way by morning."

But it soon became clear that was not to be. The crate contained clothing and an odd collection of what appeared to be theatrical costumes. By the time they got to the bottom, without uncovering a single book of any kind, the air was thick with dust and the smell of mildewed wool. Gerard forced the door open all the way, and Carter opened the small, dirty window. The light was changing, shifting to long shadows, but Gerard had a feeling the whole structure would go up in flames if he lit the lantern hanging from a nail by the door.

Bragg returned from securing rooms at the nearby inn, and together they lifted down another crate. From the sheer weight of it, Gerard guessed it must have some books in it, but he was wrong; it was newspapers, sporting forms, betting slips, pamphlets, bills of every sort. Some was easy to discard, but there were letters interspersed with the rubbish, and he and Carter tried to make some sense of these before tossing them aside. He tried to sift through it as quickly as possible, but it was hopeless, given the waning light and the faded ink. He put down a stack and looked at his companions. Bragg had just finished repacking the first crate, and Carter was frowning over another letter, turning it on end to read the lines written crossways for economy. There was straw in his hair, and his shirtsleeves were almost black with grime. Gerard was sure he looked no better.

"Well, well, I see you're getting on well enough." Nollworth stood in the doorway, rubbing his hands.

Gerard got to his feet. "It would proceed a little faster if we could take things to a better place and examine them."

"Not a one," said Nollworth with a mean little smile. "My wife, you see, is very attached to her father's things. Won't give them up easily."

"So far I've not found anything worth taking," he muttered. "Carter?"

Carter caught his eye. "One man's private effects." He tossed the letter back into the open crate. "It should have been burned years ago."

Nollworth scowled. "Then you won't be back to-morrow, I expect."

"You persuaded us to come all this way. We'll be back tomorrow, and the day after, and the day after if we wish." He reached for his coat. "I shall not be pleased, Mr. Nollworth, if you've brought us on a fool's errand. If there are no ledgers or books in these trunks . . ." Gerard slapped his hat on this head. "You asked two hundred pounds for this dross. Some might call that extortion."

The old man glared viciously. "If you don't come back in the morn, I'll know what to do."

"We'll be back," Gerard said flatly. "Good eve, sir."

They retired to the inn and sat down to a late dinner. Carter was more animated than ever, and Gerard was glad of it. He listened almost absently as Carter talked of his recuperation and of his fears for his sister, who had lost her husband at the Battle of Basque Roads the previous year and, in Carter's belief, still felt his absence too keenly.

"I told her not to marry a sailing man," he said, gesturing to his wounded leg. "She could see how careless the army is of its men, and the Royal Navy is no better. But she would not be warned; a woman is utterly irrational when she fancies herself in love."

Gerard looked up, roused from his thoughts. "Irrational?"

Carter smiled ruefully. "Yes, I remember when Fitzwilliam began coming around, brash and clever. Cora thought the sun rose and set with his comings and goings, and anyone who said otherwise was a puling fool. My father tried to dissuade her, too, until my mother told him it was no use; Cora's heart was her own to give, and it wouldn't be given where her father directed."

Her own to give . . . "Was Fitzwilliam unworthy, then?"

Carter hesitated, sorrow flickering over his face. "No. He was worthy. It broke my sister's heart when his ship went down."

Gerard went to his room in a somber mood. He didn't want to break Kate's heart. Hell, he didn't think she was wise to trust him with such a fragile, precious thing. He thought of Cora Fitzwilliam, losing the husband she adored. He thought of his father's rough voice all those years ago, admitting he didn't want Gerard's mother to die. In his years in the army he'd seen hundreds of men die, and many of them left behind wives and children. Part of his desire for a simple marriage of convenience was rooted in that experience; he was only on leave from his regiment for a few months. There was a real chance a French marksman would pick him off in some battle, or a camp fever would catch him. Gerard hoped his bride would mourn him. But suffer a broken heart?

He got out a sheet of paper to write to Kate. He would express his gratitude for her affections. He would say he was honored to have won her heart. He would vow to be a good husband. He dipped the pen into the ink and poised the pen over the paper, and the words scattered. He watched morosely as the pen dripped once, twice on the paper before he shoved it back into the inkpot.

Tomorrow, then. Tomorrow he would send her a note. She would be curious to know how things were proceeding, and if he'd found anything helpful at Nollworth's. Yes, tomorrow, after a good night's sleep, he would find the right words. He slapped one hand down on the table, glad the decision was made, and his eye caught the paper. The ink had bled into two teardrop-shaped blots, rather like a heart split in two. Gerard swept up the paper and tossed it into the grate, where the fire seized it and consumed it at once. He watched the inky heart char and flake before finally disintegrating, and it made him feel like the lowest creature on earth.

Bloody, bloody hell.

Chapter 24

At first Kate was glad Gerard had gone. It gave her some privacy to settle her emotions and come to terms with the fact that he didn't love her. Hope still hovered around her heart, but wearily she wrestled it into quiet submission. Without his presence, she could view things more practically. When he wasn't there to seduce her or charm her, she was able to steady her heart and think. She would be herself again by the time he was home.

When he didn't return in two days, she reminded herself he hadn't known what he would find. Lieutenant Carter and Bragg had both gone with him, and surely one of them would send word if there was trouble, or if they needed anything. She told herself it must mean there was something to examine, something of value. Perhaps he was even now discovering the proof he sought that would establish once and for all his own legitimacy.

When he didn't return in four days, she began to wonder why he didn't send her a note, even a curt line to say he was delayed but all was well. Or even return home quickly to fetch fresh clothing. Allenton was less than twenty miles away, not an insurmountable distance to a man with a sound horse. Even Bragg would have been a welcome sight.

She went to visit Cora, hoping to hear if Lieutenant Carter might have written his sister. Much to her surprise and delight, the man himself was there when she arrived.

"How fortunate I should see you," he exclaimed.

"Yes," she said warmly. "I've been curious to know what you've discovered."

"Well, nothing yet, but de Lacey has hopes. Our fellow Ogilvie seems to have kept everything he ever picked up, and his daughter, Mrs. Nollworth, squirreled away every last piece of it. A fortunate turn for our purpose but dashed tedious to sort out. It may take another month to examine everything. The Nollworths are very particular, for all that they've stored every bill and worn-out hat as if they were treasures of antiquity."

"Then you believe it is the right man?"

Carter nodded. "It seems hard to credit there could be two such scoundrels of the same age named William Ogilvie, living in the same county. De Lacey is sure we'll find something of use."

"That would be wonderful," said Kate softly.

"Indeed." Carter grinned. "I daresay we'll find enough information to keep a scandal sheet in business if we keep looking. Ogilvie was a veritable Renaissance man of vice; illicit marriages are the least objectionable. I wrote Cora some of the more shocking episodes—why, there was one scheme with a Covent Garden pickpocket—"

"Danny!" Cora smiled at Kate even as she gave

her brother a look of warning. "I'm sure Kate has no wish to listen to you prattle on. I thought you had some errands to run as well."

Her brother flushed and gave Kate a contrite look. "Of course. De Lacey asked me to see to a few things for him. He'll have me flogged if I sit about gossiping. Forgive me, Lady Gerard. I'm back to Allenton soon; shall I give him your regards?"

"Yes, please," she said faintly. Apparently those "few things" Gerard had asked Lieutenant Carter to do didn't include calling on her or telling her how they were getting on. "Thank you, Lieutenant."

When the door closed behind him, she stirred her tea, staring into the depths of her cup. "Don't mind Danny," said Cora brightly after a moment. "He's become as chatty as an old woman since convalescing. I tried to encourage him to take up drawing, but he refused, which is a great pity. He used to be quite talented as a boy."

"He wrote to you." Kate raised her eyes.

Cora made a dismissive gesture. "He told me very little—nothing of import."

Gerard hadn't even done that much. "You could have told me," she murmured.

With a rustle of skirts her friend came to sit beside her on the small sofa. "Kate, you mustn't take it to heart. Danny told me they've been searching from early morning until it's too dark to see at night, in a filthy little storage room with that vile Nollworth pestering them every hour. You should take it as a mark of your good sense that they're so consumed; you had the thought to look for Reverend Ogilvie, and now look what you've uncovered . . ."

Kate set her teacup down. "I am pleased, and very hopeful."

Cora watched her with concerned eyes. "You look as though your heart is breaking," she said. "It grieves me to see it."

Kate said nothing.

"Does—does Captain de Lacey know you love him?" Cora asked gently. Kate glanced at her in alarm. "Don't worry," she rushed to add. "I would never breathe a word—but I do so want you to be happy, and it is the greatest joy to be happy with your own husband—"

Kate took a deep breath. "He knows." She exhaled slowly. "He hasn't been similarly afflicted."

"Oh, my dear." Cora wrapped her free hand around Kate's. "He cares for you a great deal. Everyone can see it. And he's so solicitous of your well-being."

She forced a shaky laugh. It was either that, or burst into tears. "That makes it worse, Cora. He's wonderful in every way, more than I could ever have asked for in a husband. And I think I would rather have a husband who never bought me jewels or held the umbrella for me, if only he loved me."

"He will," declared Cora firmly. "Who could not love you? It just takes time for a man to lose his heart, longer than it takes a woman."

"Perhaps." Kate straightened her spine. "But he plans to return to his regiment when he's settled this problem. I won't see him for a year or more if he goes on campaign. How likely is love to grow then?"

"My husband was at sea for most of our marriage. Our love *did* grow."

"Did he love you before he left?" Kate nodded

when Cora just bit her lip. "I don't blame him. He can't make himself love me, any more than I can make myself stop loving him. It would be so much easier if I could. We would enjoy a peaceful marriage of convenience and live our lives as amiable companions. Instead . . ." She brushed her hands over her skirt. "I was a fool to marry him. It would have been better to marry someone I cared little for, or not at all."

"Don't say that!" Cora's voice was suddenly fierce. "It was a risk, yes; but not a foolish one. He cares for you—how many loves grow from care and familiarity? At least you still have the chance of it." Her voice broke. "I had six months with my love, and now he's dead and gone forever."

A hot rush of shame burned Kate's face. How selfish she was, moping because her husband didn't love her. He did care for her. He was a better husband than most women hoped for. And Cora, who had once had what Kate longed for, had lost it irrevocably. "You're right," she said at once. "Forgive me; you are too kind to me, indulging my melancholy . . ."

"No." Cora swiped at her eyes and summoned a determined smile. "In your shoes I would feel the same. You deserve love. Don't give up on the captain yet."

Kate walked home in a pensive mood. Was she sorry she'd married Gerard? Not when he was near. No matter how much she tried to tamp it down, the hope of his feelings deepening still lingered, fanned a little brighter by Cora's words. But that didn't mean she knew what to do. Without the distraction of his presence, she could see how very different they were.

She was content to be quietly at home or with a few friends, while he had to be out doing something vigorous or dangerous. Once he rejoined his regiment, this would be her life: worrying about him, waiting for infrequent letters that might never come, fading back into her quiet, solitary ways.

Her mother called almost as soon as she reached home. Kate welcomed her in a subdued voice, which Mama's keen eye noted at once. "Darling, you look ill," was her pronouncement.

"I'm well, Mama. Will you take some tea?"

She let Kate fill her cup. "I don't think Bath agrees with you. Really, you looked feverish when I first arrived, and now your cheeks are as pale as frost."

"It has nothing to do with Bath." Kate stirred her tea, wishing she could add a drop of brandy to it. Her mother would take that as a sign of fatal illness, unfortunately.

"It must. This city doesn't suit me, either. Too close to the river, most likely. I've never been so unwell in my life. In fact, I came to tell you I'm returning to Cobham." Mama managed to look beautiful even as she claimed to be ill. "You should come with me."

She didn't want to go. Mama had purchased Cobham after Kate's father's death, as their family home was too small and dark for Mama's taste. At Cobham there would be nothing to do but endure her mother's self-absorbed flights of fancy and musings on all her own failings. "I cannot leave Bath, Mama. What would my husband say?"

"Has he returned?" Mama opened her eyes wide and looked around. "I thought he left town several days ago."

"He'll be home soon."

"Oh, my dear . . ." Mama put down her teacup and looked dismayed. "All men stray sooner or later," she said gently. "It's only a matter of time, and once he'd got your fortune . . . You know that, Katherine."

"He is away on business." Kate's face felt hot.

"Yes, they always say so. You mustn't blame yourself, dear."

"Mama," she said plaintively. "Please."

"Oh, Katherine." Her mother's eyes welled up. "I only wish to help you, but if you don't want my advice, I shall do my best to suffer for you in silence. Have some compassion. I've had the most dreadful headaches in this town. I do wish you would come with me to Cobham. It would do you a great deal of good to get away from this foul air. Your husband won't mind—he's not even here to miss you."

"Is Lucien leaving Bath as well?" She tried desperately to turn the conversation away from Gerard's absence.

"No, he refuses to go. He's grown so hard-hearted since you disappointed him." Mama sighed piteously. "It will be such an arduous journey alone. I thought my only daughter would take more pity on her mother."

"The captain is coming home soon," said Kate again. "Would you have me leave my husband?"

Mama's eyes opened wider. "But he's already left you. I'm sure he wouldn't mind if you came with me."

Kate felt it like a physical blow. "I'm sorry, Mama," she murmured. "No."

For two days she withstood her mother's fretting. For two days she waited in vain for any word from

Gerard. Anything at all would have been enough. But without his presence, she fell slowly back into her old habits regarding her mother. The longer her mother pressed her to leave Bath, the more she felt herself weakening. Too many years of giving in had taken their toll, and now Kate felt so battered by Gerard's departure and silence, she couldn't take her mother's constant faint pity. Mama thought Gerard must have found another woman by now, and as much as Kate didn't want to believe it—as much as she *didn't* believe it—it rubbed her heart raw to hear it suggested every day.

Finally she couldn't stand it anymore. If Gerard could go off without a word and not come back, so could she. She was going mad, waiting for a note he couldn't be bothered to send. Going to Cobham wasn't ideal, but it was the only avenue open to her. At least at Cobham she wouldn't lie awake at nights, straining her ears for the sound of his horse or the tread of his foot outside her door.

"Very well, Mama," she said at last. "I'll come with you."

"Oh, darling." Her mother gave her a misty smile. "I knew I could count on you. Cobham will be so good for you, too. Your nerves were always delicate. I vow, you look so pale; this shade of blue quite overwhelms you, Katherine."

She smiled resolutely. She was keeping her new dresses, whether Mama approved or not. "Only for a visit. I can't stay longer than a fortnight."

"What! Only a fortnight! But dearest, you shall hardly be settled back in before a fortnight is over. You must stay a month at least."

"A fortnight," Kate repeated. "Less if my husband sends for me."

"My poor child." Mama folded her gently into her arms. "Yes, of course, if he sends for you, you must go. But surely he won't tear you away from me again—Oh, but I must have you both at Cobham! Yes, if he comes, he must stay as well, now he is part of the family." She gave Kate a bright smile. "You'll feel better away from Bath. We'll leave in the morning."

She went to say good-bye to Cora while Birdie packed. When she said she was leaving Bath, Cora gasped. "But you will come back, won't you?" she cried.

"Of course," Kate assured her. "I just feel that some time away will restore my equilibrium."

Cora sighed in relief. "That is very reasonable. Do you want to leave a letter for Danny to carry to Captain de Lacey?"

"No." Kate gave a firm shake of her head. "I don't think I shall. We aren't much for writing letters, the captain and I."

Her friend's lips parted. "Oh," she said softly. "I see." She regarded Kate somberly for a moment. "Yes, perhaps you're right. What are letters to a man anyway?"

"Nothing much, I understand."

"And he would hardly keep you from going with your own mother."

"No man likes to thwart my mother's wishes."

"And he can always fetch you home if he misses you too desperately."

"He can," Kate agreed.

"Well." Cora nodded slowly. "All in all, I agree: you must make a visit to your mother." Then she heaved a sigh. "But I shall miss you!"

"And I you." Kate squeezed her friend's hands. "May I write to you?"

"I require it," declared Cora. "And I shall write you. I expect there will be something of great interest to report when Danny and the captain finally return to find you gone."

"Be that as it may, I am done sitting at home waiting." She squared her shoulders, trying to ignore the ache in her heart. "I have said all I had to say. If he wishes to make any response, he can find me at Cobham."

Chapter 25

Gerard was fast coming to wish he'd never heard of Reverend Ogilvie. He'd seen enough of Robert Nollworth to last six lifetimes, and breathed enough dust to fill all of Spain. Searching the dead reverend's trunks ended up meaning they must clear out Nollworth's wretched storeroom, since the Nollworths apparently kept every broken bucket and footstool they'd ever owned. One morning he and Carter got a section cleared, carting things into the stable yard so they could unearth more boxes and crates, only to have to drag everything back inside when it began to rain, and Mrs. Nollworth flew out of her house screaming that her belongings were being ruined. The chickens who roosted in the old stable were the pleasantest part of the whole ordeal, and Gerard could have happily killed and plucked a few of them just to have quiet.

In desperation he offered Nollworth a hundred pounds for the reverend's things, but now Nollworth felt even more sure of himself. He countered with five hundred pounds, which Gerard rashly rejected in a flash of temper.

But soon, by God, he sorely regretted it. Five hundred pounds would have been a small price to pay to get out of this circle of hell. Nollworth's storage stable was a filthy, ramshackle hovel. The town of Allenton was barely a village, with only one inn three miles away, close to the Bristol Road. The inn was almost as depressing and dirty as the storage shed, and Gerard set Bragg to cleaning everything, every day. When he returned home, he planned to burn every piece of clothing he'd brought with him, strongly suspecting it would have picked up vermin of all sorts. With a grim realization that he might have gotten in over his head, he finally wrote to his brother Edward. The explanation of why he needed help grew too tortured, so he settled for admitting he *did* need aid and imploring Edward to come at once. He told Bragg to send it off express and felt a bit of relief. Even just talking to his logical, rational brother would help.

But worst of all, he still didn't know what to say to Kate. Every night he pulled out fresh paper and ink and tried to write. He filled page after page with apologies and explanations, and every night he threw it all into the fire when he read what he'd written. But every day that he didn't send word to her built up the guilt he felt, as well as the pressure to write a decent letter the next day. Finally Gerard accepted that he couldn't put his thoughts on paper and would have to wait until he saw her in person, no matter how cowardly it felt.

Carter made a hurried trip to Bath for fresh supplies and unwittingly brought back a hair shirt for Gerard. "I saw your lady wife, by the way," he said as they began work on yet another crate the day after he returned. They had sifted through barely a quarter of the detritus, but this was one of the last five crates, presuming no more appeared from under the rubbish they were still clearing away. "She was curious to know what we'd uncovered."

His stomach knotted at the mention of his wife. Even as he felt like the lowest rogue alive, he missed her. Sleeping alone in the hard, flat bed at the inn, on a mattress so thin he could feel the ropes every time he shifted, he dreamed of waking to find her in his arms, her brass-bright hair tickling his chest, her soft skin warm against his. Behind closed eyelids, he could picture her sleepy smile when he turned her over and kissed her awake. He could hear her soft gasps of ecstasy as he made love to her. And worst of all, he couldn't forget the intoxicating peals of her laughter when they lay in bed and talked of nonsense. God. He was an idiot. He'd taken all that for granted, too caught up in his focus on finding the blackmailer to notice her devotion and wonder whence it sprang. A woman who said she would be content with a marriage of convenience didn't listen intently and sympathetically while he poured out the sordid story of his father's shameful past. Or allow him every sort of liberty with her body and follow his urging to take similar liberties with his. Or hold him so tenderly.

"How did she look?" His voice sounded distant.

Carter applied the iron bar to the lid of another crate. "She looked quite well."

Damn. She wasn't lying awake at night, as he was? She wasn't ready to rip out her hair in frustration from being separated, as he was? He should be glad she was well; instead, selfish bastard that he was, Gerard wished she'd evidenced some sign of longing. She hadn't sent a note to him back with Carter. He was almost glad of that, for his guilt at not writing to her would have been almost unbearable if she had.

In other words, he was content to sort Nollworth's rubbish, cowardly relieved that his wife, who loved him, hadn't written to him, thus proving herself far too good for the likes of him.

"Bloody hell," he said suddenly. "I'm sick of this." He grabbed the edge of the crate Carter had just pried open and heaved it up. Astonished, but realizing what he was about, Carter took hold of the other side and together they toppled the crate onto its side with a great smash. Straw flew everywhere, and a pair of chickens ran flapping and squawking out of the stable. On one knee, Gerard pawed through the things that tumbled out of the crate. "Find any books," he said to Carter. "We've wasted too much time looking through letters and other meaningless rot. A notebook or register is all I care for. Just leave the rest."

"As you say."

Abandoning any semblance of delicacy or care, they plowed into the rubbish in the stable, searching it as roughly as a pair of thieves. Crockery broke. Carter stepped on a hoe buried in the straw, and the handle flew up to smack him in the face. Gerard cracked his head on the sloping loft as he climbed over piles of ruined furniture to reach things stored high. A loose trunk latch scraped across his arm and ripped his sleeve almost off as he rooted through the straw that covered everything. But finally, at long last, he spied a small writing case hidden up in the eaves. The surface was stained with water, but when he hauled it down and broke the lock to open it, the contents were dry.

"Carter." Carefully Gerard lifted out one slim volume. It looked more like a betting notebook than a church register, but when he carried it to the light and opened to a random page, what he saw recorded within made him shout in triumph. "Carter!"

His friend clambered through the mess to his side. "Is that it?"

"Perhaps," muttered Gerard, paging gently through the book. The ink had faded to near invisibility, but by squinting, he could just make it out. "Married this tenth day of February, Henry Potts, bachelor, and Jane Ellis, spinster . . ." He closed the book. "I've had enough of picking through this rat's warren. I'm taking these and going back to Bath."

"Excellent news," said Carter fervently. He touched the swelling on his cheek where the hoe had struck him. "I was beginning to fear for our lives."

He retrieved the rest of the books from the case, eight in all, and carried them to the house with Carter at his heels. Nollworth met them at the door. "Eh, found something useful, have you?" he crowed, when he spied the books.

"Perhaps," said Gerard levelly. "Perhaps not. But my patience has run out, and this is your last chance to strike a bargain." He held up the notebooks. "Eighty pounds for these, and these alone."

Nollworth's brows descended. "One hundred fifty pounds!"

Gerard leaned closer and fixed a grim stare on the man. "Ninety pounds, and I won't burn down your miserable storeroom."

"What is this?" cried Mrs. Nollworth, hurrying up behind her husband. Her eyes lit on the books Gerard held. "Are those what you were seeking, sir?"

"I believe so, madam," said Gerard before Nollworth could speak. "I trust ninety pounds will compensate you for the loss of these."

Her mouth dropped open. "Ninety—! Why, that is very generous, sir—"

"Go back to your washing, woman," snarled her husband, his face red. "I'm dealing with these gentlemen."

"I will be glad to send back any books that have no meaning to my family," Gerard added, watching the wife's face. She at least had some trace of decency.

"Ninety pounds," she gasped again, fanning herself with one hand. "Why, yes, certainly you may borrow them for ninety pounds. I'm sure my good father would wish no less!"

"Martha, quiet your mouth!" Nollworth turned on Gerard, practically spitting in fury. "I'll have the money now, then."

"I'll write you a draft on my bank."

"Hard coin," snapped the older man with a baleful glare. "Now."

Gerard's jaw tightened. "I haven't got ninety pounds in coin in my pocket. I'll send my man back with it from Bath."

"You think me a fool? You'll not take so much as a page until I have the money in my hand. In fact," he went on, growing louder, "go on back to Bath. I can see you're not interested in these books. I'll just see if someone else might have a fancy for them!"

"Mr. Nollworth," exclaimed his wife, jamming her hands on her hips. "You're shaming us both! Ninety pounds!"

Carter cleared his throat. "I would be glad to ride to Bath and bring the funds."

Gerard tore his seething gaze off Nollworth. "You don't mind?"

His friend glanced at the Nollworths. "Not at all. It would be my pleasure. We've done twenty-mile rides many a time for Wellesley."

" 'Tis nearly forty miles to Bath and back."

Carter lowered his voice. "And a day well spent if it puts an end to this." He raised his eyes to Nollworth. "I'll leave at once."

Gerard exhaled. "Thank you." One more day, then he could return to Kate.

When he reached Queen Square two long days later, Gerard was hot, filthy, tired, and desperately eager to see Kate. He leaped up the step and let himself in, leaving Bragg to take the horses. He carried the notebooks in one hand. In the time it had taken Carter to ride to Bath and back to fetch the funds, Gerard had pored over the notebooks. Like many disreputable parsons, it appeared Ogilvie conducted his illicit weddings in several establishments, from taverns to the front parlor of a brothel. Each notebook had been assigned to one location, so the dates were all intermixed and sometimes not specified at all. The ink had faded to a pale yellow on the old paper, and in many cases the faint writing was illegible even under strong sunlight. An hour's reading was enough to make one's eyes burn and one's head ache fiercely. It would be quite a job to comb through them for one particular entry.

But the notebooks were his, thanks to Kate. She pursued the question of Ogilvie when he thought it hopeless. If Durham's clandestine marriage showed up in the pages of these books, it would be invaluable, either for proving the marriage illegal or for affording him the chance to destroy the only tangible proof of any connection between his father and Dorothy Cope. The London solicitor had said there were a few ways to affirm a marriage, whether it satisfied every legal requirement or not; a record of any sort was one. One way or another, there would be no record of any legal marriage when Gerard finished with the books. And he owed it entirely to his wife.

"Where is your mistress?" he demanded of the footman, Foley, who came running as he stood stripping off coat, hat, and gloves.

"M'lady left, sir, but His Grace has been waiting since yesterday."

"What?" Gerard stopped in shock. "His Grace?"

Foley nodded, looking a bit anxious. "Yes, my lord. The Duke of Durham."

Blast. His hands dropped. What was *he* doing here? "And milady is out?" he asked again, then sighed. "Where is His Grace?"

"In your study, sir."

Putting aside his disappointment that Kate wasn't at home, he strode to his study and pushed open the door. "What do you want?"

His eldest brother looked up from his book and

smiled sardonically. "A pleasure to see you also, Gerard."

Gerard ran his hands over his head and prayed for fortitude. Charlie sat in the chair behind his desk and was the picture of indolent elegance, from his languid posture to the elaborate tea tray sitting at his elbow. "Of course it's a pleasure to see you—a very unexpected one."

Charlie's lips twitched. "So I see." He closed his book and set it down. "Edward sends his regards."

"Where the devil is he? I specifically asked him to come."

"Yes, I know. I did warn him you would be cruelly disappointed by the substitution." His brother drew out a letter from his waistcoat pocket and made a show of unfolding it. " 'Edward, come to Bath with all haste. I require your help most urgently. I have the blackmailer's description, and may have discovered the minister's records, but cannot pursue both, as I must return home to my wife.' " Charlie glanced up with exaggerated surprise. "Wife? What wife?"

"*My* wife," growled Gerard, prowling restlessly around the room, listening for any sound indicating Kate's return. He dropped Ogilvie's notebooks on the corner of his desk. "The lady I married. You must have met her when you invaded my home. Why the bloody hell didn't Edward come?"

This seemed to amuse Charlie. "He refused to come, and you shan't be able to fault him when you hear the reason. I expect he's making love to his own wife at this moment. Your letter arrived on the day of his marriage, forming a rather unusual wedding gift."

"Edward, married?" Gerard was struck speechless all over again. "To whom—? Ah, the redheaded widow with the lovely bosom?"

"Indeed." Charlie inclined his head. "The fetching Lady Gordon apparently swept him off his feet. Or knocked him senseless. Perhaps both."

Gerard grinned a little, remembering the vibrant woman he'd met in London, the one Edward pointedly hadn't wanted him to meet. "She must have. Just a few weeks ago Edward claimed it was only some business about solicitors between them, and he couldn't wait to conclude it. He married her already? It took him almost a year to decide he would propose to Louisa Halston."

"Yes, I gather certain women are capable of inspiring a feverish urgency in men, like the sirens of old." Charlie reached for the teacup on the tray and raised it to his lips. "Perhaps you are familiar with this species, given you also gained a wife in that time— even earlier than Edward managed it. Did you marry her the moment you reached Bath, or the following morning?"

Gerard's shoulders slumped at the mention of his wife. He dropped into a chair and rubbed his face wearily. "I married her before I left London."

Charlie choked on his tea. "*What?*"

"I was sure Aunt Margaret would tell you if the gossip mill didn't. I married Viscount Howe's widow."

His brother's eyelids slid down until he was regarding Gerard almost lazily. "No, it never reached my ears. Love at first sight?" he asked in a silky tone.

Gerard closed his eyes. Not at first sight—not at

the hundredth sight. But whether it was the thousandth sight, or the ten thousandth, the persistent need to see Kate was driving him mad. He still didn't know what to say to her, but he believed, more and more strongly, that everything would fall into place when he saw her. It wasn't just that he had left things badly between them. He missed her. Only Charlie's unexpected arrival was staving off crushing disappointment that she wasn't at home now. The prospect of making her smile had made the long, hard ride back to Bath, undertaken at an impatient pace, seem both endless and a trifle. "Not quite," he said quietly to his brother's question. "But only because I was a damned fool."

"Ah. So tell me about her. Is she a beauty?"

Gerard lifted his head. "What do you mean? You haven't met her yet? Foley said you'd been waiting since yesterday."

"I have been. But your lady was not at home when I arrived yesterday, and the servant said both you and she had left Bath."

The blood drained from Gerard's face. He could feel it; he was actually light-headed for a moment. In three steps he was at the door. "Foley!" he shouted into the hall. "Foley!"

The footman came running. "Sir?"

"Where is Lady Gerard?" he demanded.

"Sh-she left, sir," he stammered. "A carriage came for her yesterday morning, and she and Mrs. Dennis went off in it. I don't know where, but they took some baggage."

Gerard reeled. She'd left him. Holy blessed God, he'd lost her before truly realizing he had her.

"She bade me tell you she left a note, sir," added the footman quickly. "I forgot a moment ago."

"Where is it?"

Foley opened his mouth, then closed it, looking uneasy.

"There was nothing on the desk," said Charlie, when Gerard swung a harsh glare on him. "It was quite bare."

With a muttered curse, Gerard pushed past his footman and went into the parlor. There was no letter on the mantel or either table. He bounded up the stairs to look in the dressing room, then the bedroom. Finally, there, a white rectangle caught his eye, lying on the writing desk by the window. He seized it with relief, hoping it meant she hadn't truly left, or she wanted him to follow, or something that could counter the sharp pain throbbing in his chest.

It did not.

At first he felt nothing but a stark, frozen numbness. It quickly wore off, burned away by fury. His hands shook as he folded the letter and forced it into his pocket, but his steps were steady as he went back down the stairs and through the hall past his brother.

"Where are you going?" exclaimed Charlie, as Gerard threw open the front door and strode out, hatless and coatless.

"To kill someone," he replied grimly.

Chapter 26

It was a brisk walk to the White Hart Inn. Charlie caught up to him as he turned up Barton Street. "What happened?" he demanded, breathing hard. "And must we run there like a pair of footmen?"

"You don't have to come at all."

"Edward would draw and quarter me if I let you commit murder." Charlie muttered a quick apology to a pair of gentlemen Gerard had roughly brushed past. "And who is the poor devil?"

"Lucien Howe."

He felt Charlie's keen glance. "London is whispering that he's on the verge of ruin."

"How thrilling it will be to tell them you witnessed his ultimate fall."

"I'd rather not, particularly not in a court where any judges might be listening. Why are you planning to kill Howe?"

Gerard just shook his head. He couldn't even say it out loud. Without pausing, he fished the note out of his pocket and handed it to his brother. Charlie inhaled sharply as he read, then returned it in silence. He didn't say another word of protest about Gerard's purpose.

They turned another corner, toward the crenellated towers atop the Abbey Church, which loomed over the buildings lining the street. The White Hart Inn stood opposite the church. Gerard headed directly for it, and a few minutes later was shown up to Lord Howe's room; it seemed he was expected. With Charlie still dogging his heels, he pressed a coin into the porter's hand and dismissed him, then knocked on the door.

Howe's face lit with satisfaction at the sight of him. "Ah, de Lacey." He gave a little bow. "I thought you might call on me."

"No doubt." Gerard tossed down the offensive letter. Unsealed, it flipped open so he could read it again: *If you wish to know where your wife is, call upon me at the White Hart.* "Where is she?"

"Katherine? Perfectly safe, I'm sure." Howe smiled, but only for a moment.

After a week struggling to sort out his feelings for Kate, and discovering that they ran deeper than he'd realized, Gerard was in no mood for Howe's prevarication or manipulation. He'd been fair—he'd asked politely first—and that was as far as he could restrain himself. He clipped Howe on the chin with a swift right, stepping into it for good effect. The viscount's head snapped up with a satisfying clack of teeth on teeth. "Where?" he repeated, fists still raised in threat. Howe stared at him in horror and staggered away, throwing up his hands protectively as Gerard lunged after him, catching him by the throat with one hand and the lapel with his other. With a thump he shoved Howe backward into the wall behind him, forcing the shorter man up onto his toes.

"Where is she?" he demanded again.

"Let me . . . down," wheezed Howe, clawing at Gerard's grip on his throat.

Gerard gave him a sharp shake, and Howe's head cracked against the wall. "Where's Kate? I'm not a patient man."

Howe's alarmed gaze darted past him. "Help!"

"I don't think he needs my help strangling you," said Charlie in a bored tone. "But if you don't answer his question, I'll gladly give it." Gerard gave Howe another thump against the wall for emphasis.

"Cobham!" squeaked Howe. He was an unhealthy shade of purple now. "She's only gone . . . to Cobham!"

Gerard loosened his grip on the man's throat. "Where the devil is Cobham?"

"Near Hungerford," he gasped. "A few miles off the Bath Road."

"Why?" growled Gerard.

"She went with her mother! Cobham is Mrs. Hollenbrook's home."

Gerard scowled but reluctantly released Howe, thrusting the man away from him. "You've got a dangerous disregard for your health, Howe, sending me a note like that." Then something struck him, and he frowned again. "Where's her note? My footman said she'd left one. And how the bloody hell did your letter come to be in its place?"

Massaging his throat, Howe backed warily away to the desk in the corner. He groped around for a moment, then held out a sealed letter. "The upstairs maid switched them for me," he said a little hoarsely, as Gerard snatched the letter from his hand. "Perhaps not the wisest move, but I did nothing to your wife. I merely seized the opportunity of her departure. I must speak to you—de Lacey, I am desperate."

"And exceptionally stupid," remarked Charlie. He hadn't batted an eye at Gerard's attack and was now watching in mild amusement, one elbow propped on the mantel.

Howe glanced at him in angry dismay. "I have little choice! If you call in that note, I'll be utterly ruined. I attempted to make my case decently, and you refused to discuss the matter. I beg you, for the sake of my tenants and dependents, grant me some leniency."

Gerard barely heard him. Kate's letter simply said she felt a separation would suit them both, and she was going with her mother for a visit at Cobham. She expressed her hope that he had found something useful in his trip to Allenton and concluded by wishing him a quick resolution to his family's trouble. She said nothing of when she would return.

"This debt was not of my making," Howe pleaded when Gerard made no answer. "I swear I shall honor it as any decent gentleman would, but I must have time. For God's sake, man, have some pity!"

But why would she go with her mother? Her mother was shallow and vain and had made Kate feel small and insignificant for most of her life. She was hardly the image of a loving and devoted mother. Surely even he was a better companion, great fool that he was. When Mrs. Hollenbrook first arrived in Bath, Kate seemed relieved when he said they didn't have to see her and Lucien Howe. And now she had left Gerard to go away with her mother?

He raised his head. Perhaps he'd gotten it all wrong. Perhaps her dislike had really been of Lucien. The man could have threatened her or made her miserable once Gerard was no longer in town to keep him at bay, and she left to escape him. Eyes narrowing, he jerked out a chair from the round table in the center of the room. "All right," he said. "Let us negotiate."

Howe's eyes skittered to Charlie, who merely drew out his pocket watch and made a show of checking it. The rashness of his actions seemed to have sunk in. "Thank you," he said warily, and took another chair.

They sat, each taking the other's measure. "I understand you pressured my wife to marry you at one time," Gerard said abruptly.

Howe flushed deep red. "It would have been a very prudent match."

"For you."

"Also for her," said the viscount stiffly. "She was a widow of advanced years. She was quiet and withdrawn, unlikely to attract suitors. Her only attraction was her fortune, which would have made her an object of prey to a host of villains." His glare said he included Gerard in their number. "I offered her a safe home, a respectable marriage, and a continuation of the life she led."

"How noble," said Gerard without sympathy. "You, naturally, had no interest in her fortune."

"Of course I did. My uncle left me no choice," Howe retorted. "You know very well why I wished to marry her—why I had to marry *her,* instead of a younger lady who might bear me children and better suit my temperament. It was not my most ardent desire, but I was prepared to make the best of it."

The best of it. Gerard had thought something like that, too, once upon a time. Before he'd become dependent on Kate's company. Entranced by her rare laugh. Thoroughly addicted to making her smile and cry out in pleasure. Before he realized that her absence opened a gaping hole inside him that had nothing to do with making the best of their hasty marriage.

Perhaps he was no better than Howe.

He raised his eyes to the other man's. "Did you ever hit her, as your uncle did?"

"Never!" Howe appeared genuinely appalled. "Never once! My uncle—?"

"If you were so desperate to beg my leniency, why did you follow her to Bath?" he interrupted. "Surely you could guess she wouldn't be eager for your company, and hounding a woman is no way to win favors with her husband."

For the first time the viscount looked vaguely uncomfortable. "It was not my idea. When her mother proposed the visit, though, I agreed because—because London had grown unwelcoming. Rumors of my ruin were everywhere."

"Yes, I know how that feels," said Gerard dryly. "You might also have reconsidered spreading that Durham Dilemma rubbish if you wished to renegotiate your debts."

Howe stiffened. "I confess I heard those rumors." He paused to master himself. "Not without some un-Christian enjoyment. But I did nothing to spread them. I believe gossip is a sin and an affront to God. I do not contribute to it."

Gerard remembered what his aunt and her friend

Lady Eccleston had called Howe: the young zealot. "The stories grew quite lurid immediately following your arrival, by some odd coincidence."

For a moment Howe said nothing. "I believe . . ." he began. "Mrs. Hollenbrook does not share my beliefs. I believe she felt no restraint in discussing the matter in public conversation."

Great God. His own mother-in-law was trying to ruin him? He exchanged a glance with Charlie, who raised his eyebrows. He turned back to Lord Howe. "You're blaming my wife's mother?"

Now the viscount's expression turned pitying. "You might as well learn her nature now. She wants but a cordial companion, and every rumor and whisper she's ever heard are readily shared. And she is, as you may have noticed, a very handsome woman; she rarely lacks for company. She depends upon it. Mrs. Hollenbrook becomes restive and cross without a man nearby to admire her, and the higher the man's rank and status, the better.

"From the moment you arrived as Katherine's husband, she spoke constantly of wishing to be on better terms with you, your family, your friends. Visiting Bath was the only way she could insert herself into your circles, although her hopes were mainly disappointed. In truth, I think her only gratification came from Lord Worley's company, and once he left, her interest in the city waned."

The name caught Gerard's attention. Worley again. It was undoubtedly mere coincidence, but it was a conspicuous one. He'd made a few subtle inquiries into the man but never learned much of interest. "Worley?"

Howe nodded. "Yes. The Earl of Worley. He's got property in Wiltshire. He and Mrs. Hollenbrook spent many evenings together."

Behind him Charlie made a slight noise. Gerard looked at his brother. There was an odd expression on Charlie's face, as if he'd just thought of something long forgotten. His brother said nothing, though, just turning away and walking to the window. Gerard focused his attention back on the man across the table from him, once again shoving aside the mention of Worley. "Is Mrs. Hollenbrook given to whims? She came to Bath barely a fortnight ago and now has gone home, not back to London."

"Whims," Howe repeated with a sour smile. "Whims and fancies and fits of temper that change course with the wind. I tell you, she was a principal reason I cared little for marrying Katherine. If the daughter should turn out to be like the mother, a man might run mad. She's thoroughly absorbed in herself—not from malice, I believe, but her desires are always paramount, and she wears away one's resistance. Even a man of discipline and resolve would find himself buckling under her entreaties. She weeps like a Madonna at the foot of the cross." He sighed heavily. "But now she is your mama-in-law, and not my concern. And if we could just strike a more equitable bargain—"

"Yes," murmured Gerard, his mind racing. "You may have six months' grace, and I shall drop the interest to two percent. I trust that will enable you to retrench."

Howe's expression broke with relief. "Blessed be! Thank you, sir."

Gerard shook his hand. "You will hear from my solicitor, confirming it."

He and Charlie left the inn in silence. Gerard shuffled things around in his mind, connecting parts and filling in gaps. He'd long thought her mother wasn't a good influence on Kate. Any woman who told Kate the hideous brown dress flattered her was either blind or cruel—and it was clear Mrs. Hollenbrook wasn't blind where fashion was concerned. Howe claimed it wasn't malicious, but Gerard wondered if, just perhaps, Mrs. Hollenbrook preferred Kate to remain a quiet, obedient creature so there was no possible chance of anyone's diverting attention from the mother to the daughter. It might not even be a deliberate choice, but he had known too many society beauties to think it was impossible.

In Kate's case, it was far from impossible that it might happen. Dressed in stylish, flattering gowns, buoyed with a bit of confidence, and encouraged by friends like Cora and even those two magpies, Lady Darby and Mrs. Woodforde, his Kate was arresting. She would never have the stunning looks and vivacious manners that often caught men's eyes and struck them dumb at first glance—like her mother—but she was something even more appealing at second glance: she was kind and warm and genuinely interested in others. Her wit was quiet but keen, and she never exercised it cruelly. Any man who spent half an hour in her company would quickly agree with Gerard that she was the proverbial hidden pearl, with a soft, quiet glow rather than the alluring sparkle of some women.

So why had she gone away with her mother? To

teach him a lesson? He almost hoped so; first, because he'd learned the lesson too well, and second because he was ready to repent until she forgave him. It would also mean she still loved him. He fervently hoped that was still true. If she'd gone away because she'd given up on him, it would be very bad.

His thoughts were interrupted when Charlie spoke. He stopped and turned, and heard another voice calling his name. A thin, balding fellow was chasing them, waving one arm and holding his hat with the other hand. "Captain de Lacey!"

"Yes?" As the man stumbled to a halt in front of them, breathing heavily, Gerard recognized him. "You're the postal clerk."

"Yes, sir," gasped the fellow, clutching one hand to his side. "William Brynfield, sir, of the Bath Post Office."

There was only one reason the postal clerk would be chasing him down the street. Gerard felt a flash of triumph. Beside him, Charlie cleared his throat expectantly. Damn it, he should have written more often to his brothers. But first he had to learn what the clerk knew. "Won't you come inside, Mr. Brynfield?" he said, giving Charlie a quick nod. "You look in need of a bit of rest."

"Thank you, sir. I could use a moment at that."

Gerard led the way into the house, torn between elation and frustration. Brynfield could be about to hand him the blackmailer, leaving his way open to ending the infuriating, nebulous threat over his name. But he burned to go after Kate that instant, blackmailer be damned. Impatiently he threw open the drawing-room door and waved the clerk to a seat.

"Yes, what is it?"

Mr. Brynfield perched on the edge of the sofa, breathing almost normally again. "I remembered what you said, my lord, about the letters you brought in, and the man who sent them. I've come to let you know—that is, I saw him again today."

His muscles tightened instinctively. "Today? In Bath?" Gerard demanded. "Just now?"

"This morning, sir. He came in to post another letter, and I recognized him at once." He puffed out his chest. "I've been watching for him ever since you came to see Mr. Watson, my lord," he said proudly. "I never forget a face, I don't, and I knew, if only I waited patiently enough, sooner or later he'd—"

"Yes, yes," interrupted Gerard. "Did you speak to him?"

"I did. He had two letters to post—both to London, sir—and I worked my brains to think how I could ask his name while he counted out the coins for postage. Finally I says, 'How good to see you again, Mr. Smythe. I'm delighted to see you've recovered enough to go out.' Well, he looked quite amazed, and said, 'You've mistake me, I'm not Mr. Smythe at all.'" The clerk was practically wiggling with excitement as he told his story. "I affected great astonishment, sir, and declared again that he must be Mr. Smythe, who has lived down the lane from my mother these last five years. 'I know your wife,' I told him. Well, he was not pleased by that. He said he had no wife, and I was mistaken. Again I pretended ignorance, and shook my head, muttering that he must have a fever of the brain to say such things, for didn't I know my own mother's neighbors? He was growing irate, my lord, and finally he exclaimed, 'My name, sirrah, is Hiram Scott, and you have taken leave of your senses if you think me someone else!'" Brynfield beamed at Gerard. "Unfortunately I had to remain at the counter, sir, and had no opportunity of following him. I would have come directly, but I've only just closed up the post office."

"I see," said Gerard slowly. "I left my card with Mr. Watson, that it might be given to this man."

Mr. Brynfield's expression shifted, becoming a shade coyer. "I know, my lord, but Mr. Watson wasn't in at the time, and I didn't have the card you left. I thought it best to find out as much as I could and report to you. After all, there's no telling whether the man would have called upon you had I handed him the card with your compliments."

And coming in person, the clerk could present his prize in triumph. Or perhaps he sensed that Gerard might prefer more subtle methods—which he did, no question. Now he had the man's name, and with no warning to the fellow that anyone would be looking for him. All in all, it was the best outcome possible.

"Quite right," he told the man. "Excellent work. I applaud your quick thinking. Er—would I be improper to express my gratitude more tangibly?"

The clerk's smile said it all. "I'm sure you could never be improper, my lord."

Gerard smiled back as he counted out some guineas. "I do try to avoid it. But a service must be rewarded."

"Thank 'ee very kindly, sir. I'm delighted to have been of use." The guineas disappeared into Brynfield's pocket in the blink of an eye. "And if I should see the gentleman in question again, I'll be pleased to let you know of it."

"By all means."

Gerard thought hard after William Brynfield had gone. Hiram Scott. The name meant nothing to him, but that counted for little. They only had to find him, then pry the truth from him. "Hiram Scott," he said absently. "What's his interest in Father's marriage?"

"I take it that's our fellow?" asked Charlie.

He glanced up, mildly surprised to see his brother still there. "Yes—apparently. I took the letters to the post office here, hoping someone might recall something about the sender. That clerk, Brynfield, marked one of the letters. He thought he'd know the man who sent it if he ever returned, and now . . ." He spread his hands wide.

Charlie came around the sofa and sat down, a thin line between his brows. "Who the devil is Hiram Scott?"

"I've no bloody idea."

"Why the hell would he be blackmailing Durham?"

"I've no bloody idea," repeated Gerard.

Charlie shot him a dark glance. "What bloody ideas *do* you have? I presume you have one or two after a month of searching."

He was quiet for a moment. Certain things had been coalescing in his mind ever since talking it over with Kate, and more and more he thought one question of hers pointed in the right direction. "I suspect we're being fooled—trifled with. I suspect he doesn't want money or anything at all from us. This fellow wants to ruin us, or perhaps only to drive us mad looking for something that probably doesn't exist."

Charlie's irritation dropped away. All expression vanished from his face, in fact. "Explain."

He took the chair opposite his brother. "Consider this. The letters arrived one at a time, more taunting than demanding or threatening. Durham sent out five investigators after the first one, but the second note makes no mention of their failure. Is it likely someone with such a keen interest in the matter wouldn't know, or suspect, Durham would take action? Not until the third note does the villain ask for anything, and he didn't even try to collect it. The last note never repeated the demand for money, only that the blackmailer could ruin Durham at any moment—but he never did. Not one whiff of this appeared anywhere before Durham died. Perhaps Louisa Halston beat him to it when Edward told her, but if you really wanted to press someone, wouldn't you threaten to tell a newspaper or a notorious gossip? It could be done anonymously, without danger to the instigator, and spread like wildfire until no one could tell where it began."

"But who is Hiram Scott that he would wish to torment Durham?"

He sighed. "Why would he wish to torment *us*? This did nothing to Father. The dukedom was his, and nothing could change that. It would embarrass, but not harm. We, on the other hand . . ."

Charlie's face looked like a stone mask. "But you don't know who Hiram Scott is. I don't know who Hiram Scott is. Why would he bedevil us?"

Gerard flipped one hand impatiently. "Perhaps he's Louisa Halston's secret lover and wished to disrupt Edward's engagement to her."

"Unlikely," replied Charlie. "She was promptly betrothed to the Marquis of Calverton."

"Perhaps he acted for Calverton."

"Then how the bloody hell did Calverton know about Dorothy Cope?" said Charlie crossly. "Whoever did this didn't blindly kick the hive; he knew something nobody's spoken of in sixty years. Where could he have gotten that information?"

"I don't know!" Gerard shoved his hands through his hair as his temper ran short. "He didn't learn it from the minister, though. I've just returned from unearthing his wedding registers, and if they've seen the light of day in ten years, I'll eat every page. The minister himself died a decade ago. You'll have to sort that out yourself."

"Then how—" Charlie stopped short. "Myself?"

Gerard nodded, jumping to his feet. "I'm going after Kate. You might be able to track down Scott since he was in Bath this morning. The notebooks are in my study; let me get them for you."

"Howe said she was well, merely visiting her mother. A day or two delay won't do any harm!" Charlie protested, following Gerard into the study.

"It will to me," he said simply. He picked up the eight notebooks and handed them to Charlie. "Somewhere in here may be proof of Father's clandestine wedding—or not. It's the best I could do. With this, and whatever you can find about Hiram Scott, you should have a good start on cleaving this Gordian knot."

"A name and some notebooks," said Charlie incredulously. "That's all?"

"It's more than Edward and I began with," Gerard

retorted. His brother's face was stony, but his eyes weren't. Curiosity conspired with his temper. "Why have you taken this so calmly, Charlie? Why do you act as though you don't give a bloody damn whether we all lose everything?"

Something flickered across Charlie's face, guilt or anxiety or even mere indignation, but he said nothing. Gerard threw up his hands and turned to go. He could leave for Cobham at first light if he sent Bragg out to get a fresh horse now.

"Do you truly think this whole thing has been aimed at us rather than at Durham?" asked Charlie slowly from behind him.

He shook his head. "I don't know. It seems as likely as anything else at the moment. Father said he burned the marriage certificate, so no one stumbled across that. These records have been hidden in a barn in Somerset for at least a decade, and likely longer. Augustus wouldn't blackmail Durham even if he stands to benefit the most; he'd have no need. The ransom was never claimed, nor even mentioned again. What else could be the purpose of this?"

Charlie looked down at the notebooks in his hand. "Do you have the blackmail letters? The originals?"

"Yes."

"May I have them?"

"Of course," said Gerard in surprise. He went to his desk and got them.

Charlie's face was drawn and troubled as he took them. For a moment he just looked at the letters, holding up one after the other. "Yes, it's my turn to take this on," he said quietly. He glanced up. "And you're right to retrieve your wife. Let me come with you."

"You don't have to," began Gerard.

"Please." Charlie gave a faint smile. "Allow me to meet my newest sister-in-law. I seem to be collecting them faster than I can make their acquaintance. Besides, my travel coach stands ready."

That was a good argument. "Very well." Gerard cleared his throat. "Thank you for coming to Bath, Charlie."

His brother tucked the blackmailer's letters into his pocket. All trace of indolence was gone from his demeanor. "I suppose I'm the only one left with time and freedom to solve this, as the last bachelor among us." He shot Gerard a measuring look. "Lady Howe was rumored to be a very wealthy woman. You married her because you feared we'd lose Durham and be left destitute, didn't you?"

Gerard thought back to his first meeting with Kate, when she'd been as somber and stiff as a schoolmistress making her proposal. Even then he'd been tantalized by the prospect of thawing her, though he'd never guessed how it would turn out. "Yes," he said softly. "I married her for money. But I'm going after her now for love."

Chapter 27

At Gerard's prodding, they left just after dawn the next morning. It was forty miles to Cobham. At first Gerard regretted leaving his horse behind, but as the miles rolled on he grew more appreciative of the coach. Charlie traveled in style, with Durham's best-sprung coach and four. It would also make the return journey more comfortable for Kate, assuming she returned to Bath with them—and Gerard meant to make sure of that. But even now that he knew where she was and that she was safe, he was having trouble keeping himself in check enough to sit still. Charlie finally told him to bugger himself before dropping his hat over his face and pretending to sleep. Gerard glared at him and resumed staring out the window, watching for the first sight of the house.

It was a very pretty estate, nestled in rolling green hills. Their approach had been noted, for the butler and two footmen were waiting in front of the house, standing at attention, when the coach rolled up the drive. Gerard leaped out as soon as the wheels stopped, hoping for a glimpse of Kate, but the only lady to greet them when they were shown into the drawing room was her mother.

"Captain." With a fond smile Mrs. Hollenbrook floated across the carpet and extended her hand. "What a delight to see you again!"

"The pleasure is all mine." He took her hand and bowed briefly. "You must forgive me for presuming upon family, but I've brought my brother. May I present the Duke of Durham?"

Like the beam from a lantern, her attention swung fully from Gerard to Charlie. "Your Grace!" Mrs. Hollenbrook gazed at Charlie as if he were the Prince Regent himself before sinking into a curtsey so deep, her knee must have touched the floor.

"Er . . . Yes." Charlie's eyebrows were halfway up his forehead, a sight Gerard had never seen before. Who would have guessed the clinging, simpering Mrs. Hollenbrook could reduce his eternally bored and insouciant brother to this?

"Welcome to my humble home." Their hostess rose gracefully, beaming at him. "I never dreamed of such an honor, sir. May I serve you tea? Or coffee? Anything you would like at all, I'm sure we can provide."

Charlie cast Gerard a glance. "Thank you, madam. That is most . . . hospitable."

As she turned toward the bell, Gerard seized his brother's arm. "I have to find Kate," he whispered.

"I'm coming with you," Charlie said, with a wary glance at Mrs. Hollenbrook.

"No!" He shook off Charlie's restraining hand. "I need to speak to Kate without her mother about, and all you have to do to distract her is sit there and be a duke."

"I knew I shouldn't have left London," muttered Charlie after a pause.

"Think of it as the first of many duties you'll have to endure for Durham." He then added, "Thank you."

"Go." His brother had assumed a rather grim but regal expression. "Try to be charming, Gerard. I shan't endure any duty forever."

Gerard grinned and slipped out of the room as Charlie stepped forward, asking some question of Mrs. Hollenbrook to cover his brother's escape. How fortunate Charlie had come along after all.

He found her in the garden. It had been terraced on the side of a hill and rose through four levels. She was on the third level, a wide straw hat on her head and a basket over one arm. She appeared to be cutting flowers, and added one to the basket as he shaded his eyes and looked up at her. The breeze caught her light green skirts, swirling them around her legs. The wide brim of her hat hid most of her face, but he could see the soft curve of her mouth as she bent down and chose another flower. It was a mundane task, but just watching the way she moved acted as a balm on him; a riot of thoughts and feelings, shrieking furies with spurs and daggers that had prodded him mercilessly for days, suddenly fell into calm order. He'd been right, that all would become clear when he saw her again. It hit him then that she was beautiful—not her face, but *her,* that ineffable something within her that made her Kate. He'd been too blind to see it, just as he'd been so focused on finding the blackmailer, he never wondered about the man's true purpose. He'd been fooling himself about his marriage from the start, but no longer.

After a moment she turned his way. He just caught sight of her face before she noticed him, and her expression blanked.

"Kate!" He bounded up the steps. "Wait—"

"Wait for what?" She regarded him levelly.

Gerard stopped. There was a dispassionate assurance in her eyes that hadn't been there before. He hated the uncertain, skittish look in her face, but this new calm unsettled him. It gave the impression she had made up her mind, and he would not be able to change it. "Wait for me," he said. "I want to speak to you." He wanted to snatch her into his arms and hold her close, to breathe deeply of the orange-water perfume she wore, to finally appreciate the treasure he had unwittingly gained when he married her. Who would have guessed, when she made her blunt and pragmatic proposal, the bride was of infinitely more value than the fortune?

"What a surprise to see you here," she said.

"Is it?" He cocked his head. "You left Bath without a word of farewell, and you're surprised to see me?"

A lovely flush rose in her cheeks, but her voice never wavered. "I trust you got my note."

"Nearly not," Gerard replied. "Lucien Howe took it."

"Lucien?" A small frown pinched her brow. "How did he get it?"

"He paid the upstairs maid to steal it for him."

"Well." She looked down at the basket on her arm and shuffled the flowers in it. "Birdie never trusted her."

"In its place he left what looked like a ransom note." Gerard cleared his throat. "He should recover in good time."

She darted a measuring look at him from under her lashes. "You struck Lucien?"

"Just once. I thought he was behind your absence." He paused. "And then when I read your note, I thought you'd left me."

Her chin went up a fraction. "I did."

For some reason he liked that spark of defiance. He never could resist any challenge she threw at him. "Ah. Then all that talk of love . . . ?"

"I didn't lie." The pulse in her throat was throbbing noticeably. "Nor, I think, did you."

"No, Kate, I never lied to you. I told you at the beginning I wanted to take you to bed."

Scarlet rushed up her face. "Not because you loved me."

"No," he agreed. "I didn't know you enough to love you." He gave her a meaningful glance. "But I did want to bed you."

"Men can bed any woman," she said stiffly. "It means nothing."

He paused. "Nothing," he repeated thoughtfully. "It rarely means nothing. And sometimes, in very particular circumstances, it means a great deal."

Then he stopped and just stood there, looking at her with those blue, blue eyes, so tall and dark and painfully attractive. Kate had hoped a few days away from him would steady her nerves and quiet her longings, but it didn't seem to have worked that way. Her silly, stupid heart leaped into her throat when she looked down to see him standing at the foot of the terrace, and now it was beating so hard her chest hurt. He had come after her—but why? She was more defenseless than ever against the pathetic yearnings of her heart and body.

"How fascinating," she said, hoping he didn't see how her fingers were clenched into her palms. "One would never guess from the behavior of certain gentlemen."

"Devil take them. We're speaking only of one gentleman." He laid one hand on his chest, still watching her closely.

She forced her eyebrows up. "Indeed. What did it mean, then, when you said you wished to bed me?"

"It meant I wished to be a good husband, and someday, a good father. It meant you intrigued me, with your prickly, bold manner, and I've never been able to ignore a challenge."

"A challenge!" She turned away, but he caught hold of her hand and refused to let her go.

"A maddening, delicious challenge," he repeated. She could hear the amusement lurking under his tone and tugged against his restraining hand, furious that he was laughing at her. "What sort of woman would follow me across London in the middle of the night and propose marriage? She's impressed by my heroism, and of course by my noble father—even though that same father caused the distress that made her think I would be desperate for a wealthy wife—but she doesn't expect ours to be a real marriage. Still, should I refuse her offer, she lists marriage to Lucien Howe and death as her only alternatives. Curious, don't you think?"

"Very curious!" she snapped. "A clever man would have sensed a trap and fled for his life!"

He chuckled, again preventing her from storming away. "Sadly for you, my darling, I'm not that clever. You laid your trap too well. But once I was caught, I did what any prisoner would do."

"Plot an escape?"

He stepped up right behind her, so close she could feel the heat of him at her back. Kate bit the inside of her cheek to control the desire that flared helplessly inside her. "I decided to explore my cage," he murmured, pulling off her hat and tossing it aside. "To test my warden." He laid his cheek against her temple and drew his fingertips up her arm until she shivered. "To see if I might thaw my bride's icy demeanor and discover her real reason for wedding me."

Kate held very, very still.

"And she melted like caramel," he went on in his dark whisper. "Hot and sweet enough to make me crave more, no matter how much I tasted. I gorged myself on her, not stopping to wonder why she had resisted such a decadent pleasure at the beginning."

"I thought I wouldn't please you," she said, her voice strained. "I hoped we could become . . . affectionate companions first . . . before you grew disappointed with me . . ."

"Damn Howe. Your mother should be whipped for marrying you to him."

She shivered. "I told myself it would be all right if you didn't love me, so long as you *liked* me—I wanted to please you—"

"Damn your mother." He sighed. "Surely you recognized just how much you pleased me."

Every inch of her body blushed. "Well—yes—you did appear satisfied—"

"Appear?" He raised his head. "I *appeared* satisfied? Oh, darling, no wonder you left me. What a terrible husband I've been if you remain uncertain on that score."

"And I hoped that might lead to other, finer feelings," she finished in desperation.

For a moment he was quiet. Kate wished she could see his face, and then was glad she couldn't. "No," he said at last. "It didn't, although I don't wish to minimize the exceedingly fine feelings it did arouse. If that had been your only charm, though, it wouldn't have led to any deeper feelings. No, I believe it was the first morning we lay in bed and laughed together that I fell in love with you."

She flinched. "You didn't."

"Hush." He squeezed her. "You claimed to fall in love while riding through the rain twelve years ago. At least I was in a warm, comfortable bed with a beautiful woman when I lost my heart."

Kate wrenched out of his arm. "Don't say that—there's no need to be cruel."

"How dare you insult my taste," he said, as she began to walk away. Her flowers had scattered from the basket and lay wilting on the path, but she stepped on them blindly. "You're not walking out on me a second time," he warned her. She picked up her skirts and ran, and a moment later she heard his footsteps pounding after her.

She jumped off the step at the end of the path and took off down the hill, across the lawn toward the maze. Her mother kept saying she would raze the unfashionable curiosity, but it couldn't be seen from the house, so it still stood. Kate ran into the entrance and whisked around the first turn, vaguely remembering a shortcut to the center of the maze. She needed just a little space, a few minutes alone. Her heart had twisted so hard when Gerard called her beautiful, she'd almost fainted. How could he say that, when she knew very well it wasn't true—when he had admitted it himself on their wedding day? He was offended that she had left him and was just trying to charm her back before people started to talk. But that he would lie to her about it . . . She couldn't bear it.

He crashed into the maze just as she made the second turn. "Kate," he called. "I wasn't being cruel." He slowed to a walk down the entrance path. Kate crept quietly along her own path, wishing she could believe him.

"Kate," he called again, quieter this time, "I was an idiot, but I'm not a liar." She could hear his steps, then a flash of blue caught her eye through the branches of the hedge. He was on the path parallel to hers. She froze in her tracks and waited even though he would have to go all the way to the end and make the second left before he could get to her. "I've never told a woman I loved her," he said. "It took me too damned long to admit it, and now I have to bare my heart to a shrub. Can you even hear me?" Perversely Kate held her tongue. What would he do?

After a moment he sighed. "Very well," he muttered, and his voice boomed out, so loudly she jumped. "Katherine de Lacey, before God as my witness, I love you more than any man should ever love a woman." A clutch of birds burst out of the hedges and flew away in a chorus of squawks. "I love the way your eyes snap when you're irked at me. I love the way your nose wrinkles when you laugh at some nonsense I say. I love the way you ask old ladies for help finding a blackmailer. I love the way you look with your skirt up around your—Ah!"

Kate shrieked as his hand thrust through the hedge and seized her wrist. She pulled, fighting down the hysterical laughter that threatened to burst forth as Gerard peered at her through the leaves and branches, a perplexed but determined expression on his face. "There you are," he said.

"And there *you* are," she retorted, motioning to the hedge that divided them. "What did you plan to do next?"

He glanced up, and from side to side, as if measuring the hedge. Then to her astonishment, he wedged his shoulder into the tangle of branches, and pushed and shoved his way right through, never once letting go of her.

"You knocked a hole in the maze!" Kate gawked at the ragged, broken gap in the hedge.

"It will grow back." He brushed some leaves from his hair and fixed his gaze on her. "I didn't dare loose my grip on you again. I presume you know the way through this?"

"I—well, I think so—"

"Which way to the center?" Keeping a firm grip on her hand, he started off.

"The other way," she said, hurrying behind him. Without a word he turned on his heel and strode through the maze, pulling her along so rapidly she could barely give directions. When they reached the small clearing in the center, he released her. Kate retreated a few steps, her eyes warily on him.

"You make it dashed hard for a fellow to apologize." He pulled off his coat and threw it aside.

She lifted her chin, trying not to notice the hunger in his eyes as he unbuttoned his waistcoat. "Why must you apologize?"

"Not for thinking you beautiful." Off came the waistcoat. "If I'm the only man in the world who realizes your true beauty, so much the better." He started toward her like a predatory beast. "No, I must apologize for not being worthy of your love. But I do intend to atone for it as best I can."

She dragged her gaze from his gleaming white shirtsleeves. "This isn't the kind of love I spoke of."

That stopped him. His expression sobered. "Do you not believe me capable of any other kind?"

"It's not that," she said softly. "But I cannot help but wonder . . . if you are here now, saying this, only because I left and piqued your manly pride."

"Pride," he repeated. "You may ask Carter how much pride I displayed, digging through Nollworth's wretched stable in search of Ogilvie's notebooks with all the poise of a baited bear because of the way we parted. You may ask the innkeeper how many reams of paper I burned, trying to find the right words to tell you how much I missed you. You might ask Lucien Howe to show you the bruises I put on his neck when I thought he had something to do with your disappearance, and it was *not* because my pride was piqued." He spread his hands. "Pride is for the trivial things in life that make one feel important. I didn't realize how fully you owned my heart until I returned to Bath and discovered you'd left, taking it with you. I would have realized it then even if you'd never said a word."

She just looked at him, yearning to believe but wary.

Gerard tilted his head, studying her. "You misled me, you know. When you made your proposal, you led me to believe you were a quiet, dull mouse, uninterested in sharing my bed or my life. I was your means to avoid Lucien, you said, and you only asked me because I was in similarly desperate straits."

Kate flushed in mortification. "I *was* like that—"

He shook his head slowly. "No. Your mother thought you should be, and she molded you into that creature. Howe was happy not to think about you at all and left you as you were. But you yourself . . . You want more. You like colors"—he glanced pointedly at the stylish green dress she wore—"and you look lovely in them. You like dancing at balls and visiting with Cora; even Lady Darby and Mrs. Woodforde bring you happiness. And you like being wicked and wanton in bed with me, driving me mad with wanting you."

"Well—yes," she whispered, sure her face would catch fire any second. "I do like those things, but I never suspected I would . . ."

"Just as I never expected, that night at The Duck and Dog, how much I would fall in love with you," he said gently. "If I'd come today because of pride, I could have sent a servant out to fetch you like a piece of lost baggage. Instead I wrecked your mother's maze so you wouldn't put me off a moment longer. Because I do love you, and I've been in misery since I went to Allenton."

Her heart strained toward him. She swallowed hard, winding the sash of her dress around her shaking fingers. "You already know I love you."

"Do you still?"

Wordlessly she nodded. There was too much cautious hope in his voice for her to contemplate denying it.

His face eased. "May I apologize now?"

She nodded again.

With slow, deliberate steps he walked up to her. He smoothed back a loose strand of hair before cupping his fingers reverently around her face, tipping up her chin. Kate gave a little sob of relief when his lips finally touched hers. She clung to his wrists, kissing him back with all the love in her heart. He made a low sound deep in his throat, deepening the kiss until the ground seemed to buckle beneath her feet.

"I'm sorry I left you even for a day," he rasped. His body pressed in on hers. "God, how I've missed you, Kate . . ."

His arousal was hard and heavy against her belly. She reached down to glide her palm over the length. "So I see."

His laugh was wild and short. "It's been like that since I saw you in the garden. Am I forgiven?"

"Yes." She wound her arms around his neck, stretching up on her toes to draw his head back down to hers, his lips to hers. His hand slid around her neck, then down her back to the small of her waist, where he anchored her to him with one firm tug.

"I'm going to make love to you," he breathed. "So you'll never doubt that I love you."

Kate blinked, dizzy with lust and kisses and the heady thrill of his love. "We're outdoors."

"God won't be offended," he said, dragging up her skirt and petticoat with one hand. "We're married. I've been assured it's not a sin to ravish my own wife, fortunately for my eternal soul."

"Yes, but—" He untied her garter and pushed her stocking down, sliding his palm up and down her thigh before cupping her bottom. "My mother might come looking for us," Kate said unsteadily.

"She's well occupied." Gerard nipped the tender skin at the side of her neck with his teeth. "Charlie knows his duty."

"Charlie?" She swayed on her feet, unable to protest as he urged her down, onto his discarded coat.

"Hmm," he murmured against her throat, his lips whispering over her skin. "My brother. He came to help, and he's doing a brilliant job."

One by one he undid the buttons that held her bodice closed so he could spread it wide open. He pressed kisses down her bosom, uttering a few mild oaths as he tried to push her corset out of the way.

She smiled and ran her hands over his shoulders. "It's tied in back."

"Curse it." He abandoned the corset and raked up her skirts. His head dropped, and she felt his hands between her legs, guiding his length into her. He rubbed the head of it against her, and her belly spasmed in anticipation. His gaze lifted to meet hers. "Mine," he whispered, thrusting hard. "Mine." He hooked his elbow under her knee and pressed it back to her shoulder. "All mine." He stroked hard and deep, right to the very center of her. Kate's eyes rolled back as her body shuddered under his possession. With each stroke he seemed to penetrate deeper. "Take me," he demanded as he moved. "Love me. All of me."

"Everything," she gasped. With a squirm and a stretch, she got her other leg up and to the side, spreading herself wide open for his possession. Gerard bared his teeth in triumph; a bead of sweat ran down his brow. He paused only to lean down to kiss her quickly, then redoubled his efforts. Tears leaked from her eyes. Kate felt as though her blood had caught fire. When she felt the pressure rising in her, she instinctively caught her breath, holding it until the wave crested and broke, and she screamed in ecstasy. Every muscle in her body seemed drawn tight. Gerard fell to his elbows, clasping her shoulders, then thrust once more. His hips bucked, his back heaved, and she felt the hot pulse of his climax inside her.

Kate dragged her arms over his shoulders. His breath was rapid and hot against her shoulder, and his weight pressed her flat. She opened her eyes and gazed up at the pure blue summer sky, and smiled. "I have you," she whispered, brushing the damp hair away from his temple. "Now you're mine. Forever."

His lips touched her jaw. "Forever."

Chapter 28

They walked back to the house some time later, when Gerard finally said Charlie would never forgive him otherwise. He put his jacket over her shoulders and took her hand in his, possessively threading his fingers between hers. Kate looked down at their interlocked fingers and felt something lurch inside her. Her fingers were small and pale between his, but somehow they fit together perfectly. Still trying to shake all the leaves and twigs out of his hair, Gerard caught sight of her face and stopped. "What's wrong?"

She smiled and lowered her gaze. "Nothing."

He caught hold of her chin, rubbing his thumb across her lower lip. "Nothing at all?"

"No." Not when he was near, touching her, looking at her with those sharp blue eyes that would forever remind her of the sky on this day. "Except . . ." Her lips trembled as she took him in. "Except everyone will know . . ."

He grinned. The sleeve of his jacket was snagged and dirty from his trip through the hedge. A small leaf was still caught in the rumpled waves of his hair.

But it was the stains on the knees of his trousers that looked most incriminating to her eyes, thick dark smudges with traces of green, as if the wearer had ground them into the field vigorously and repeatedly.

"Everyone will know what?" he asked, when she just shook her head in mute agony, trying not to burst out laughing. "That I was overcome with passion for my wife and seduced her under the approving gaze of God? Or that I had to destroy the landscaping to swear my love to her?"

"I don't mind if everyone knows of the second," she said with a blush. "Although I suspect some will guess at the first."

He just laughed. As they strolled back to the house, hand in hand, he told her about the notebooks, the postal clerk, and Charlie's arrival. Kate exclaimed with excitement that he'd found something and had a trail to follow, but grew quiet as the implications of that became clear. By the time they reached the graveled path that led past the garden back into the morning room, much of the joy bubbling inside her had fallen flat.

"Will you have to leave Bath again, to search for this Mr. Scott?" she finally blurted out.

He took his time answering. "I don't think he'll be in Bath, no."

Oh dear. She thought of Lieutenant Carter, champing at the bit to return to his regiment, and how at ease Gerard was in his own scarlet coat. She had closed her mind to the inevitable question of what would happen when Gerard went back to the army, but now it loomed larger in her mind. And if he would be off searching for the blackmailer until then . . . She sighed quietly, trying not to be selfish and keep him from his search. It just seemed very hard to say good-bye to him so soon, especially at this blissful moment.

"I don't know where Mr. Scott might be," he went on. "I expect Charlie will have a devil of a time finding him, though."

She darted a cautious glance at him. "Your brother will be staying to help in the hunt, then?"

"He's not staying with us," said Gerard. "But he *is* going to find our man. On the very, very long trip to Cobham, it struck me rather forcefully that I'm not at liberty to run around the country chasing villains, as I once was."

Kate kept her eyes trained on the ground, knowing if she looked at him again, she'd lose her composure. "I would never stop you from your pursuit."

"And that's why I can't go." He turned her around to face him. "My brothers thought I was mad to come on this unicorn hunt. Charlie thought it was a waste of time, and Edward feared I'd do something rash, like shoot the man and get myself arrested for murder. I'm sure they expected nothing good would come of it, and so far, little has—except you." He paused, his fingers sliding lightly down her throat, her breast, her belly. "And perhaps someone else."

Her mouth dropped open as she grasped his meaning. "No . . ."

"We've been married over a month now," he reminded her. "If you're not with child yet, you very likely will be soon, given how persistently I think wicked thoughts about you."

"I was married ten years to Lord Howe without

once conceiving," she said numbly. "It is too much to hope for . . ."

"Perhaps I'm more virile than Howe." He gave her a naughty smirk.

Kate blushed. "Far, far more. But . . ." Her protest faded as she tried to think when her last bleeding had been. At least a week before they married, she thought, but she couldn't be certain. "It is surely too soon to know."

"But not too soon to prepare." He grinned. "I told you I wished to have children."

Her hand crept over her belly, wonderingly, protectively. "As did I," she confessed softly. "But it seemed I never would."

"My father left me a small estate in Cornwall. If all goes well with Durham, and nothing comes of this damned dilemma, I want to take you there. If you don't like it, we'll return to London, or Bath, or find another house suitable for a family." He folded his arms around her, resting his cheek on her temple. "But I'm not leaving you, either way."

"Your commission," she protested.

"I've given eight years to His Majesty. That ought to be enough. I never intended to stay in my whole life."

But he hadn't meant to sell out yet. Kate bit her lip in worry. "Your brothers," she said. "Your inheritance."

"Now that, I do intend to keep. I'll help Charlie as I can, but he admitted it himself: he's the only one without a wife now, and utterly free to pursue it. He's also the eldest, the heir. It's his battle even more than mine or Edward's."

As if summoned, the door opened, and a tall, dark-haired man who looked vaguely like Gerard stepped out, Kate's mother at his side. "I see you found her," he said, his dark eyes fixed on Kate.

Gerard laughed, squeezing her tight for a moment before releasing her. "I did indeed. Darling, may I present my brother Charles, the Duke of Durham. Charlie, my bride, Kate."

"Curtsey, Katherine," murmured her mother.

Kate flushed. She sank down, but to her astonishment the duke stepped forward and took her hand. "There's no need for such formality. I am pleased beyond all measure to make your acquaintance at last, my dear." He raised her hand to his lips and pressed a light kiss to her knuckles. "Welcome to our family."

"Thank you, Your Grace."

His dark eyes gleamed, and his smile was sheer sin. "Call me Durham. We are brother and sister now."

"His Grace indicated you would be staying only a short while," said Mama in her mildly reproachful way. "Do assure him you mean to stay a month, Katherine." Without waiting for a reply, she turned her best smile back on the duke. "Cobham is very pleasant this time of year. We would be honored to have you rusticate with us, sir."

"No doubt." The duke's sharp eyes flickered down to Gerard's dirty knees, and Kate blushed again as his wicked smile widened. "Alas, I have pressing concerns elsewhere. I must leave on the morrow."

Disappointment mingled with frustration on Mama's face for a moment. "As you say, Your Grace." She glanced at Kate. "Katherine dear, you must help me plan dinner for our guests. And good heavens, what have you done to your hair?"

Charlie tipped his head, and Gerard fell in step beside him, strolling away from the women. He looked over his shoulder twice at Kate before his brother spoke.

"Well done, little brother."

He grinned. "I know."

Charlie stopped and turned to study Kate as well. She was nodding patiently at whatever her mother was saying in obvious supplication; but she saw them watching her and gave a small smile. Her face shone, and Gerard thought she'd never looked more beautiful. His heart gave an answering thump as he smiled back at her. Yes, he liked being in love. It was even better than being married.

"I do believe you were right," murmured Charlie thoughtfully. "Not a beauty . . . until she looks at you."

"She's uncommonly lovely," he replied, although secretly he thought it might be true. Something about her face did change when she looked his way, something bright and breathless that made her glow. He was fortunate that was his view, and not the besotted expression his own face wore when he looked her way.

"What did you want to discuss?"

Charlie blew out his breath and gazed away, across the neatly scythed lawn. "I had hoped you would come with me in pursuit of this scoundrel, but I sense that isn't likely."

Gerard quit watching his wife from the corner of his eye. "No. I have to settle Kate in a proper home, fit for a family."

"Good God, already?" exclaimed Charlie.

"Perhaps. I've taken quite a liking to marriage."

He sighed. "That's clear, from the state of your trousers; Bragg will never get the grass stains out." He gave Gerard a sly look. "You always were fond of fresh air and exercise."

Gerard laughed. "I've given you all I know, Charlie. Hiram Scott passes through Bath every so often, it seems, from the post dates of the letters. If he lives near Bath, he must be a recluse—I've looked everywhere in the town and never heard the name. And it's conceivable the postal clerk made a mistake. Whatever you find in Ogilvie's journals may prove helpful, or useless, but at least someone else—namely cousin Augustus—hasn't got them. If we're correct that Scott is tormenting us, you should be amply prepared to turn the tables on him."

They had discussed all this on the journey to Cobham. Charlie was quiet for a moment. "Lord Worley's name was mentioned."

"Yes. He spoke to me one night. Seems to take a bit of delight in our humiliation, but he's hardly alone in that. It caught my attention, but I saw no other connection, even if he spent every waking moment with Mrs. Hollenbrook."

Gerard expected some insight, but Charlie just nodded. "Well. Shall you remain here, or may I take you as far as Bath tomorrow?"

"Once you leave, the sun may stop shining here," said Gerard wryly. "Kate and I would be very glad of your carriage back to Bath."

"Ah, yes. I believe nothing so splendid as my arrival has ever before occurred in this part of the country."

Charlie's mouth twitched in amusement. "Be sure to settle yourself in a house without a dower property."

"Rest assured, it won't be large enough for *all* our family."

Kate was coming toward them. Gerard drew her to him, slipping his arm around her waist. God, it felt good to have her at his side again. "My mother humbly invites you to dine with us this evening, Your Grace," she said to Charlie. "She hopes you will stay the night as well, as the inns nearby aren't half-decent enough for such an illustrious person."

"By God, you have to leave tomorrow," declared Gerard. "Your head will be swelled to enormous proportions if you stay."

Charlie laughed. "I fear you are right. I most gratefully accept your mother's invitation, my dear. But you must remember to call me Durham, or even Charlie."

She blushed but smiled. "It is an honor merely not to curtsey when we meet, sir."

Still amused, Charlie turned back to Gerard. "So it is. If I haven't congratulated you yet, Gerard, allow me to say you are a fortunate man."

He looked at Kate, whose eyes shone back at him, brimming with love. "Exceptionally so," he said. "More than I ever expected."

essa Neville had never met the Earl of Gresham, but she hated him just the same.

She was not normally given to hating people. It was a waste of time and a rather indulgent emotion, in her opinion, and Lord knew there was enough indulgence and emotion in her family already. Had she encountered Lord Gresham under different circumstances, chances were she would have thought little of the gentleman, if she even noticed him at all. Earls, especially of his status and notoriety, were far out of her normal circles, and she was quite happy that way.

Awareness of him, however, was forced upon her, and not in the best way. She supposed there might be good reasons one could be forcibly aware of someone, but generally it was a bad reason. And at this particular moment, in this particular way, Lord Gresham managed to leave her annoyed, impatient, and disgusted with him and herself.

His first offense was not really a personal failing. By simple bad luck, she arrived at the York Hotel, Bath's finest, only a few minutes before the Gresham entourage. To be fair, her mood was already on edge by then. Eugenie Bates, her elderly companion, had been in such a state of nerves over the journey that she hadn't been ready to leave on time, and so had made them later than Tessa wished. It was a very warm day, making travel even more uncomfortable than usual as the heat and brilliant sun seemed to wilt everything but Eugenie's ability to worry aloud. By the time they reached Bath in the late afternoon, Tessa was already tired, hungry, and heartily wishing she had defied her sister and left Eugenie at home. She'd told herself all would be better once they reached the hotel and she could change out of her wool traveling dress, have a refreshing cool drink, and stretch her legs. She'd all but leaped down from the hired travel chaise, so anxious was she to settle Eugenie into the hotel, not knowing there was another trial to come.

But no sooner had she walked through the doors and given her name than there came the rattle of harness and a clatter of wheels in the street, and almost immediately a hue and a cry rose. The hotelier, who had come forward to welcome her, excused himself in a rush and hurried out to see the commotion. The arrival's title reached her ears in a whisper both delighted and alarmed: the Earl of Gresham!

When Eugenie, straggling in Tessa's wake, heard the name, she gasped. "Oh, my dear! I did not know this hotel catered to such an elegant crowd!"

"It is a hotel, Eugenie," replied Tessa, watching the staff rush past her without a second glance. "It caters to whomever can pay the bill."

"Lady Woodall will be so disappointed she missed such a sight!" Eugenie's fatigue had vanished. She watched in open fascination as servants bustled back and forth, bringing in luggage and carrying it up the stairs.

"I am sure my sister will be nearly as delighted when she reads your account of his arrival." Tessa thought her sister would have stationed herself in the hall to look fetching, hoping to secure an introduction. Louise was anticipating her life in London with almost feverish eagerness, and being acquainted with an earl would have made her faint with joy. At least Eugenie was too shy to thrust herself forward that way.

"Oh, my dear, we must wait and catch a glimpse of the gentleman!" Mrs. Bates caught sight of Tessa's wry smile and blushed. She was such a pink and white creature, Eugenie Bates. Tessa had been making her blush since she was a schoolgirl of ten, when Eugenie, a poor but beloved distant cousin of her mother's, had come to live with them. All it took now was a certain look, because Eugenie had a vast experience of what Tessa's looks might mean. "So I might relate it to Lady Woodall," she protested. "Not to be rude, of course."

"Naturally," agreed Tessa. "It wouldn't be rude at all, as we were standing here first, and because we simply have no choice but to wait until the hotel staff remember we exist."

"Oh, I'm sure they haven't forgotten us! Mr. Lucas will surely return at any moment. Are you tired, dear Tessa? Should we sit down in the lounge over there?" Mrs. Bates's desire to maintain her post was clear, but she dutifully gestured to the small sofa on the other side of the room.

Tessa, who *was* tired and *did* want to sit down,

patted her hand. "I'm perfectly fine. And here comes the earl now." She was glad of that last part. Eugenie could have her glimpse of the noble personage, the hotel staff could grovel at his feet, and the sooner that was done, the sooner Tessa would have her own peaceful room. She obligingly stepped back to allow her companion an unimpeded view of his progress.

"Good heavens, an earl!" Eugenie hurried forward, her face alight. "I encountered a marquess once, but it was quite by accident—I expect he thought I was a woman of low morals, for he was very forward! For my own part, I was so amazed he spoke to me, I'm sure I gave no very good account of myself, either. And of course I was acquainted with your dear papa, and now your brother, but otherwise I've never seen anyone of such rank!"

"Not true. You once saw one of the royal princesses in Wells taking the waters."

Eugenie waved it off. "That was from afar, dear! This is very near, only a few feet apart. I shall be able to see every detail of his person, and whether he has a kind face, and what sort of gloves he wears. Lady Woodall will be so anxious to know what is fashionable for gentlemen in London, so she might order accordingly for young Lord Woodall . . ."

Tessa stopped listening whenever issues of fashion arose, especially anything to do with Louise's idea of fashion. It wasn't that she didn't care about her own appearance, or didn't wish to look smart. She just had no patience for endless dithering over the merits of ivory gloves versus fawn gloves, or whether a blue gown should have white ribbons or blond lace or perhaps seed pearls for embellishment. She had been born with an unfortunately firm and decisive personality, much to the dismay of her frivolous sister. In the time it took Tessa to change her dress and arrange her hair, Louise could scarcely choose a handkerchief. Eugenie fell much too easily under Louise's spell, although she did improve when away from her. And since Tessa had been persuaded that she had little choice but to bring Eugenie with her on this trip, she could only pray the lingering influence of her sister faded quickly.

Her mind drifted as Eugenie breathlessly narrated the earl's infuriatingly slow progress into the hotel. She had a great deal to accomplish this week, and she did hope for a few days of seeing the sights before leaving. Tessa might be immune to the lure of a milliner's shop, but she loved to spend a pleasant hour in a bookshop, and the coffee houses of Bath occupied a special place in her heart. Eugenie was looking forward to visiting her sister and seeing the famous Pump Room, with strict instructions from Louise to take note of what all the ladies wore. If Tessa could have left her companion behind in Bath, she would have done so, to the greater happiness of both of them. Eugenie would have enjoyed herself a great deal more than out in a small town in the coalfields, but Louise had insisted Tessa couldn't possibly go alone. And once Louise set her mind on something, it was best just to admit defeat. Pyrrhus himself would have conceded the battle was not worth fighting.

"My dear!" Eugenie's voice went up a register in excitement. "My dear, he is coming!"

So much the better, thought Tessa, since no one would serve them until he came through; but she obligingly stepped forward to see what sort of man could upend the entire York Hotel.

Mr. Lucas, the hotel proprietor, ushered the earl through the door himself. Lord Gresham was moderately tall and wore clothing of unmistakable elegance and quality. He turned on the doorstep to speak to someone still outside, and she studied his profile. A high forehead, square jaw, straight nose. His dark hair curled against his collar, just a bit longer than fashionable. From the tips of his polished boots to the crown of his fashionable beaver hat, he exuded wealth and privilege.

"Such a handsome gentleman!" breathed Eugenie beside her, clinging to Tessa's arm as if she would faint. "I've never seen the like!"

"I would like him a great deal better if he hadn't been responsible for everyone deserting us to carry up *his* luggage," she replied.

"And his carriage is so elegant! Everything a gentleman should be, I'm sure," went on Eugenie, either ignoring or not hearing Tessa's comment. "How fortunate we should be in Bath at the same time, at the very same hotel! I do believe Lady Woodall mentioned his name recently—oh, she shall be in transports that we have seen him! What was it she was saying about him?" Her brow knitted anxiously. "I'm sure it was some *bon mot* that would amuse you, my dear . . ."

Tessa suppressed a sigh. She didn't listen to Louise's gossip, and Eugenie didn't remember it. What a pair they made. She shifted her weight; her shoes were beginning to pinch her feet.

Lord Gresham smiled, then laughed at whatever

was said outside, and finally walked into the hotel. He moved like a man who knew others would pause to watch him walk by. It was the bold, unhurried stride of someone with the world in his pocket and had a whiff of predatory grace, as if he understood just how arresting his appearance was and meant to use it to his best advantage. Because Eugenie was right: he was a blindingly attractive man.

Tessa had learned the hard way to be wary of very attractive men. They often thought it counted for too much, and in her experience, a handsome man was not a man to be trusted. And this man, who not only had the face of a minor deity but an earldom and, from the looks of his clothing, a substantial income, was nearly everything she had come to mistrust and dislike. That was all without considering how he had inconvenienced her, however unknowingly. Together, it pushed her strained temper to the breaking point. She arched her brows critically and murmured to Eugenie, "He looks indolent to me."

Here the earl committed his second grievous offense. He was several feet away from her, with Mr. Lucas hovering beside him and a servant—probably his valet—trailing close behind, and yet when she spoke the peevish words in a hushed whisper, Lord Gresham paused. When his head came up and he turned to look directly at her with startling dark eyes, Tessa knew, with a wincing certainty, that he had heard her.

Eugenie sucked in her breath with a long, whistling wheeze. She sank into a deep curtsey, dragging Tessa down with her. Chagrined at being so careless, Tessa ducked her head and obediently curtseyed. She fervently wished she had arrived half an hour earlier, so she and Eugenie could have been comfortably ensconced in their rooms before he appeared. Now she would have to be very certain she never ran into the earl again; if he remembered her face, or heaven forbid, learned her name and connected her to Louise, her sister would quite possibly murder her.

For a moment the earl just looked at her, his gaze somehow piercing, even though she still thought he looked like a languid, lazy sort. Then, incredibly, one corner of his mouth twitched and a sinful smile slowly spread over his face, as if he knew every disdainful thought she'd had about him, and was amused—or even challenged—by them. Tessa could hear Eugenie gasping for air beside her, and she could feel the heat of the blood rushing to her cheeks, but she couldn't look away. Still smiling in that enigmatic, wicked way, Lord Gresham bowed his head to her, and then finally—*finally*—walked away.

"Oh, my," moaned Eugenie. Her fingers still dug into Tessa's arm, and it took some effort to pry her off and lead her to a chair in the corner. "Oh, my . . ."

"I'm sorry," said Tessa, abashed. "I never dreamed he would overhear; I was wrong to say it out loud. But Eugenie, he won't remember. Or if he does, it will be some amusing story he tells his friends about the shrewish lady at the York Hotel."

"What if we see him again?" whispered Eugenie in anguish. "He might remember, Tessa, he might! And your sister, so hopeful about her new life in London! He's quite an established member of the haut ton; he could ruin her!"

"I will hide my face if he approaches," she promised. "You know I would never deliberately upset Louise—and you shouldn't either. Telling her about this will only send her into a spell and cause her to worry needlessly." It would also unleash a flurry of letters to Tessa, full of despair and blame. She prayed Eugenie wouldn't set her sister off. "And really, I am very sorry. It was badly done of me, and I won't make the same mistake again." She did so hate it when her temper got away from her, and this time it could leave Eugenie on the verge of a fainting fit for the duration of their stay in Bath. Seen in that light, the coming week seemed endless, and she applied herself to reassuring her companion.

Once the earl's retinue had proceeded up the stairs, someone finally remembered them and came to conduct them to their rooms. Tessa helped Eugenie up the stairs, still patting her hand as the porter led them to a lovely suite and carried in their luggage. When she finally coaxed Eugenie to lie down with a cool cloth on her forehead, her first instinct was to leave. She could slip out of the room and soothe her cross mood with a short walk before dinner. If she happened across a new novel or delicious confection on Milsom Street, so much the better. Eugenie would be immensely cheered by a small gift, and a novel would keep her occupied for several days. Tessa hadn't wanted anyone other than Mary, her maid, to come with her, and already she was chafing at Eugenie's presence.

She pulled the door of the bedroom gently closed and quietly crossed the sitting room. "I'm going out for a walk," she told Mary softly, throwing her shawl around her shoulders and picking up her reticule.

"See to Mrs. Bates; she'll likely have a headache." Eugenie was very prone to having headaches when she heard Tessa had done something she disapproved of. Mary might as well be forewarned to have her favored remedy, a good bottle of sherry, at hand.

Some instinct made her pause at the door. Instead of just leaving, she opened it a few inches and took a quick look out. The first person she saw was Mr. Lucas, the hotelier. The second person was the Earl of Gresham. He had shed his long overcoat and hat by now, displaying a figure that didn't look the slightest bit soft or lazy. His dark hair fell in tempting waves to his collar, and somehow up close he didn't look like a languid fop at all. Tessa froze, hoping to remain invisible by virtue of holding very, very still. Mindful of her recent promise to Eugenie, she all but held her breath as the men came nearer, just a few feet away from her door. Her prayers seemed to be answered as they passed without looking her way, but only for a moment. When she cautiously inched the door open a bit more and peered around it to see that they were gone, she beheld a door only a few feet down the corridor—almost opposite her own—standing open, with Mr. Lucas ushering the odiously keen-eared earl through it.

Tessa closed the door without a sound. Well. This was a dilemma. How could she leave her rooms if he might be passing in the corridor at any moment? She could ask for a new suite, perhaps, in another part of the hotel, but that would be a terrible bother. On the other hand, having to sneak in and out of her own hotel room was the height of inconvenience. What was she to do now?

She shook her head at her own dithering. "Mary, did you bring a veil?" she asked her maid, who was bustling about the room unpacking the valises.

"Yes, ma'am." Mary produced the veil, draping it over her bonnet, and Tessa picked up her parasol as well. She would not be held prisoner in her own room, but neither did she want to break her promise to Eugenie so soon. Not that he was bound to recognize her, even if he did see her. Eugenie was worried over nothing. She was well beneath the notice of any earl, particularly a vain, arrogant one. On her guard this time, she let herself out of the room and safely escaped the hotel.

Charles de Lacey, Earl of Gresham, was having a hard time ridding himself of Mr. Lucas, the smooth and somewhat oily hotel proprietor. He had no objection to being personally greeted nor to being shown to his rooms, and then to a larger, better suite when the first was unacceptable. But then he wanted the man to leave, and instead Mr. Lucas stayed, blathering on about his hotel's service. Mostly, Charlie was tired and longed to prop up his stiff leg, nearly healed by now though still ungainly, but Mr. Lucas was undeniably annoying as well.

"Yes, that will be all," he said at last, resorting to a lofty, bored voice. "Thank you, Mr. Lucas." He motioned to Barnes, his valet, who obediently whisked the obsequious hotelier out the door.

"Fetch something to eat, Barnes."

"Yes, Your Grace." Without being asked, Barnes offered the cane he had just removed from the trunk. With a grimace, Charlie took it, inhaling deeply as he shifted his weight off the injured limb. He was trying to wean himself off the cane, but by evening it was still welcome, much to his disgust. He hobbled about the room before settling himself in the chair by the window overlooking George Street.

When Barnes had arranged a tray of sandwiches and a bottle of claret on a nearby table, Charlie dismissed him and leaned back in his chair, foot propped on a stool. He had made it to Bath. What now? His brother Gerard was in some sort of trouble, and Edward, shockingly, had refused to come to his aid. It wasn't even the most serious problem Edward had handed him recently, but this one Charlie felt he might be able to address. The other problem, the one that conjured a red haze of fury every time he thought of it, reposed in the leather dispatch case on the writing desk across the room. Inside were all the documents and correspondence left by his father, the investigators, and the solicitors relating to that damned Durham Dilemma, as the wags in London had dubbed the disaster. Charlie didn't want to look at it. He'd forced himself to bring it along to Bath, but just thinking about it left him angry at his father, irked at his brother, and deeply, privately, alarmed that his entire life now hung by a thread.

He let his head drop back against the chair and closed his eyes. How ironic that the first time anyone expected great things of him, the stakes were so high. He hoped Gerard's problem would be easier to address than the question of how to prove himself Durham's legitimate heir. Right now he didn't want to think of anything beyond his dinner and the glass of wine in his hand. If the lady from downstairs could see him now, she would surely think him the most indolent, useless fellow on earth.

A smile touched his lips, picturing her defiant expression when she realized he'd heard her disdainful remark. She was sorry he'd overheard, but not sorry at all for saying it. What a prudish bit of skirt. No doubt she had a collection of prayer books and doted on her brood of small dogs. Charlie was accustomed to people making up their minds about him before they ever met him, but for some reason she amused him. It was always so unfortunate when a woman with a mouth like hers turned out to be a judgmental harridan. In fact, if she looked less cross, he might have even said she was attractive, but it was hard to call any woman a beauty when she was looking down her nose at him. He wondered if she'd formed her opinion of him from the London gossip sheets or if his infamy had preceded him to Bath.

He raised his glass in a silent toast to her. For tonight at least he would be indolent and damned happily. And he hoped the thought rankled her deeply.

Next month, don't miss these exciting new love stories only from Avon Books

A Week to be Wicked by Tessa Dare
When a confirmed spinster and notorious rogue find themselves on a road to Scotland, time is not on their side. Who would have known that in one week such an unlikely pair could find a world of trouble, and maybe . . . just maybe . . . everlasting love?

The Art of Duke Hunting by Sophia Nash
On a ship in a storm-swept sea, a duke with no desire to wed and a countess who swears she'll never give her heart away find desperate passion. But they must forget their moment of folly, for if the *ton* were to learn their secret, all their fondest dreams could be ruined.

Confessions from an Arranged Marriage by Miranda Neville
It happened the usual way. He had no plans for marriage, she abhorred his wastrel ways...but a moment of mistaken identity, an illicit embrace, and the gossiping tongues changed everything. Will their marriage be one of convenience . . . or so much more?

Perilous Pleasures by Jenny Brown
Lord Ramsay has long awaited his revenge. But when the daughter of his sworn enemy is delivered into his hands, he isn't prepared for the vulnerable, courageous woman he finds. As passion burns as bright as a star—Ramsay and the bewitching Zoe will be bound together in a desperate struggle that can only be vanquished by love.

At Avon Books, we know your passion for romance—once you finish one of our novels, you find yourself wanting more.

May we tempt you with . . .

- **Excerpts** from our upcoming releases.

- Entertaining **extras**, including authors' personal photo albums and book lists.

- Behind-the-scenes **scoop** on your favorite characters and series.

- **Sweepstakes** for the chance to win free books, romantic getaways, and other fun prizes.

- Writing **tips** from our authors and editors.

- **Blog** with our authors and find out why they love to write romance.

- **Exclusive content** that's not contained within the pages of our novels.

Join us at
www.avonbooks.com

AVON

An Imprint of HarperCollins*Publishers*
www.avonromance.com

978-0-06-209264-9

978-0-06-208478-1

978-0-06-211535-5

978-0-06-204515-7

978-0-06-207998-5

978-0-06-178209-1